W9-CEI-849

F
ABR

Abraham, Daniel.

A betrayal in
winter.

$24.95

DATE			

A BETRAYAL IN WINTER

Tor Books by Daniel Abraham

>+<

The Long Price Quartet
A Shadow in Summer
A Betrayal in Winter
*An Autumn War

*Denotes forthcoming book

A BETRAYAL IN WINTER

> + <

Book Two
of the
Long Price Quartet

> + <

Daniel
Abraham

TOR®

A Tom Doherty Associates Book
New York

A Betrayal in Winter: Book Two of the Long Price Quartet

Copyright © 2007 by Daniel Abraham

Edited by James Frenkel

Maps by Jackie Aher

A Tor Book
Published by Tom Doherty Associates, LLC
175 Fifth Avenue
New York, NY 10010

www.tor.com

Tor® is a registered trademark of Tom Doherty Associates, LLC.

Library of Congress Cataloging-in-Publication Data

Abraham, Daniel.
    A betrayal in winter / Daniel Abraham.—1st ed.
        p. cm. — (Long price quartet ; bk. 2)
    "A Tom Doherty Associates book."
    ISBN-13: 978-0-7653-1341-6
    ISBN-10: 0-7653-1341-3
        I. Title.

    PS3601.B677B48 2007
    813'.6—dc22

                                    2007060366

First Edition: August 2007

Printed in the United States of America

0   9   8   7   6   5   4   3   2   1

To Kat and Scarlet

ACKNOWLEDGMENTS

This book and this series would not be as good if I hadn't had the help of Walter Jon Williams, Melinda Snodgrass, Yvonne Coates, Sally Gwylan, Emily Mah-Tippets, S. M. Stirling, Terry England, Ian Tregellis, Sage Walker, and the other members of the New Mexico Critical Mass Workshop.

I also owe debts of gratitude to Shawna McCarthy and Danny Baror for their enthusiasm and faith in the project, to James Frenkel for his unstinting support and uncanny ability to take a decent manuscript and make it better, and to Tom Doherty and the staff at Tor for their kindness and support of a new author.

And I am especially indebted to Paul Park, who told me to write what I fear.

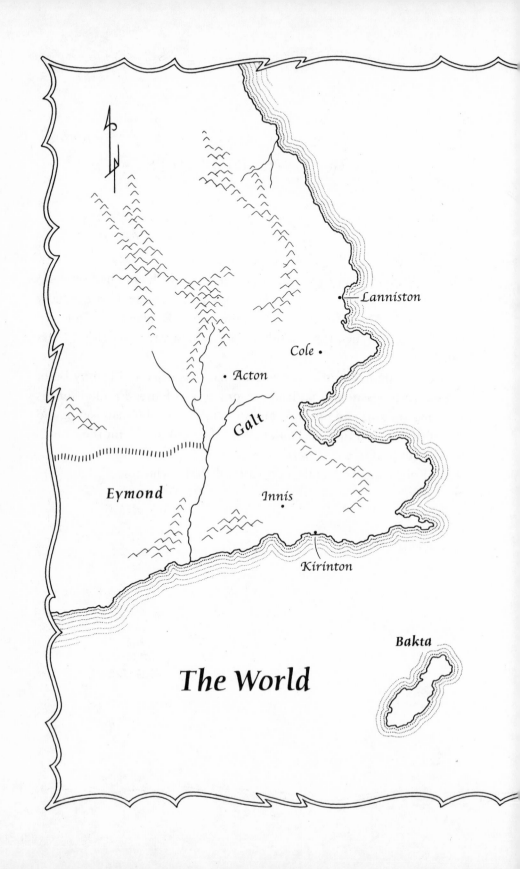

Lanniston

Cole

Acton

Galt

Eymond

Innis

Kirinton

Bakta

The World

Machi •

Cetani •

Amnat-
tan

The Village of the
Dai-Kvo

Tan-
Sadar
•

Utani •   Yalakeht •

• Udun

Pathai
•

Saraykeht
•

Chaburi-tan

Nantani   Lachi
•   •
Shosheyn-tan

The Cities
of the Khaiem

A BETRAYAL IN WINTER

PROLOG

>+< "There's a problem at the mines," his wife said. "One of your treadmill pumps."

Biitrah Machi, the eldest son of the Khai Machi and a man of forty-five summers, groaned and opened his eyes. The sun, new-risen, set the paper-thin stone of the bedchamber windows glowing. Hiami sat beside him.

"I've had the boy set out a good thick robe and your seal boots," she said, carrying on her thought, "and sent him for tea and bread."

Biitrah sat up, pulling the blankets off and rising naked with a grunt. A hundred things came to his half-sleeping mind. *It's a pump—the engineers can fix it* or *Bread and tea? Am I a prisoner?* or *Take that robe off, love—let's have the mines care for themselves for a morning.* But he said what he always did, what he knew she expected of him.

"No time. I'll eat once I'm there."

"Take care," she said. "I don't want to hear that one of your brothers has finally killed you."

"When the time comes, I don't think they'll come after me with a treadmill pump."

Still, he made a point to kiss her before he walked to his dressing chamber, allowed the servants to array him in a robe of gray and violet, stepped into the sealskin boots, and went out to meet the bearer of the bad tidings.

"It's the Daikani mine, most high," the man said, taking a pose of apology formal enough for a temple. "It failed in the night. They say the lower passages are already half a man high with water."

Biitrah cursed, but took a pose of thanks all the same. Together, they walked through the wide main hall of the Second Palace. The caves shouldn't have been filling so quickly, even with a failed pump. Something else had gone wrong. He tried to picture the shape of the Daikani mines, but the excavations in the mountains and plains around Machi were numbered in the dozens, and the details blurred. Perhaps four ventilation shafts. Perhaps six. He would have to go and see.

His private guard stood ready, bent in poses of obeisance, as he came out into the street. Ten men in ceremonial mail that for all its glitter would turn a knife. Ceremonial swords and daggers honed sharp enough to shave with. Each of his two brothers had a similar company, with a similar purpose. And the time would come, he supposed, that it would descend to that. But not today. Not yet. He had a pump to fix.

He stepped into the waiting chair, and four porters came out. As they lifted him to their shoulders, he called out to the messenger.

"Follow close," he said, his hands flowing into a pose of command with the ease of long practice. "I want to hear everything you know before we get there."

They moved quickly through the grounds of the palaces—the famed towers rising above them like forest trees above rabbits—and into the black-cobbled streets of Machi. Servants and slaves took abject poses as Biitrah passed. The few members of the utkhaiem awake and in the city streets took less extreme stances, each appropriate to the difference in rank between themselves and the man who might one day renounce his name and become the Khai Machi.

Biitrah hardly noticed. His mind turned instead upon his passion—the machinery of mining: water pumps and ore graves and hauling winches. He guessed that they would reach the low town at the mouth of the mine before the fast sun of early spring had moved the width of two hands.

They took the south road, the mountains behind them. They crossed the sinuous stone bridge over the Tidat, the water below them still smelling of its mother glacier. The plain spread before them, farmsteads and low towns and meadows green with new wheat. Trees were already pushing forth new growth. It wouldn't be many weeks before the lush spring took root, grabbing at the daylight that the winter stole away. The messenger told him what he could, but it was little enough, and before they had reached the halfway point, a wind rose whuffling in Biitrah's ears and making conversation impossible. The closer they came, the better he recalled these particular mines. They weren't the first that House Daikani had leased from the Khai—those had been the ones with six ventilation shafts. These had four. And slowly—more slowly than it once had—his mind recalled the details, spreading the problem before him like something written on slate or carved from stone.

By the time they reached the first outbuildings of the low town, his fingers had grown numb, his nose had started to run from the cold, he had four different guesses as to what might have gone wrong, and ten questions in mind whose answers would determine whether he was correct. He went directly to the mouth of the mine, forgetting to stop for even bread and tea.

HIAMI SAT BY THE BRAZIER, KNOTTING A SCARF FROM SILK THREAD AND LIS-tening to a slave boy sing old tunes of the Empire. Almost-forgotten emperors loved and fought, lost, won, and died in the high, rich voice. Poets and their slave spirits, the andat, waged their private battles sometimes with deep sincerity and beauty, sometimes with bedroom humor and bawdy rhymes—but all of them ancient. She couldn't stand to hear anything written after the great war that had destroyed those faraway palaces and broken those song-recalled lands. The new songs were all about the battles of the Khaiem—three brothers who held claim to the name of Khai. Two would die, one would forget his name and doom his own sons to another cycle of blood. Whether they were laments for the fallen or celebrations of the victors, she hated them. They weren't songs that comforted her, and she didn't knot scarves un-less she needed comfort.

A servant came in, a young girl in austere robes almost the pale of mourning, and took a ritual pose announcing a guest of status equal to Hiami's.

"Idaan," the servant girl said, "Daughter to the Khai Machi."

"I know my husband's sister," Hiami snapped, not pausing in her handwork. "You needn't tell me the sky is blue."

The servant girl flushed, her hands fluttering toward three different poses at once and achieving none of them. Hiami regretted her words and put down the knotting, taking a gentle pose of command.

"Bring her here. And something comfortable for her to sit on."

The servant took a pose of acknowledgment, grateful, it seemed, to know what response to make, and scampered off. And then Idaan was there.

Hardly twenty, she could have been one of Hiami's own daughters. Not a beauty, but it took a practiced eye to know that. Her hair, pitch dark, was pleated with strands of silver and gold. Her eyes were touched with paints, her skin made finer and paler than it really was by powder. Her robes, blue silk embroidered with gold, flattered her hips and the swell of her breasts. To a man or a younger woman, Idaan might have seemed the loveliest woman in the city. Hiami knew the difference between talent and skill, but of the pair, she had greater respect for skill, so the effect was much the same.

They each took poses of greeting, subtly different to mark Idaan's blood relation to the Khai and Hiami's greater age and her potential to become someday the first wife of the Khai Machi. The servant girl trotted in with a good chair, placed it silently, and retreated. Hiami halted her with a gesture and motioned to the singing slave. The servant girl took a pose of obedience and led him off with her.

Hiami smiled and gestured toward the seat. Idaan took a pose of thanks much less formal than her greeting had been and sat.

"Is my brother here?" she asked.

"No. There was a problem at one of the mines. I imagine he'll be there for the day."

Idaan frowned, but stopped short of showing any real disapproval. All she said was, "It must seem odd for one of the Khaiem to be slogging through tunnels like a common miner."

"Men have their enthusiasms," Hiami said, smiling slightly. Then she sobered. "Is there news of your father?"

Idaan took a pose that was both an affirmation and a denial.

"Nothing new, I suppose," the dark-haired girl said. "The physicians are watching him. He kept his soup down again last night. That makes almost ten days in a row. And his color is better."

"But?"

"But he's still dying," Idaan said. Her tone was plain and calm as if she'd been talking about a horse or a stranger. Hiami put down her thread, the half-finished scarf in a puddle by her ankles. The knot she felt in the back of her throat was dread. The old man was dying, and the thought carried its implications with it—the time was growing short. Biitrah, Danat, and Kaiin Machi—the three eldest sons of the Khai— had lived their lives in something as close to peace as the sons of the Khaiem ever could. Otah, the Khai's sixth son, had created a small storm all those years ago by refusing to take the brand and renounce his claim to his father's chair, but he had never appeared. It was assumed that he had forged his path elsewhere or died unknown. Certainly he had never caused trouble here. And now every time their father missed his bowl of soup, every night his sleep was troubled and restless, the hour drew nearer when the peace would have to break.

"How are his wives?" Hiami asked.

"Well enough," Idaan said. "Or some of them are. The two new ones from Nantani and Pathai are relieved, I think. They're younger than I am, you know."

"Yes. They'll be pleased to go back to their families. It's harder for the older women, you know. Decades they've spent here. Going back to cities they hardly remember . . ."

Hiami felt her composure slip and clenched her hands in her lap. Idaan's gaze was on her. Hiami forced a simple pose of apology.

"No. *I'm* sorry," Idaan said, divining, Hiami supposed, all the fear in her heart from her gesture. Hiami's lovely, absent-minded, warm, silly husband and lover might well die. All his string and carved wood models and designs might fall to disuse, as abandoned by his slaughter as she would be. If only he might somehow win. If only he might kill his own brothers and let their wives pay this price, instead of her.

"It's all right, dear," Hiami said. "I can have him send a messenger to you when he returns if you like. It may not be until morning. If he thinks the problem is interesting, he might be even longer."

"And then he'll want to sleep," Idaan said, half smiling, "and I might not see or hear from him for days. And by then I'll have found some other way to solve my problems, or else have given up entirely."

Hiami had to chuckle. The girl was right, and somehow that little shared intimacy made the darkness more bearable.

"Perhaps I can be of some use, then," Hiami said. "What brings you here, sister?"

To Hiami's surprise, Idaan blushed, the real color seeming slightly false under her powder.

"I've . . . I wanted Biitrah to speak to our father. About Adrah. Adrah Vaunyogi. He and I . . ."

"Ah," Hiami said. "I see. Have you missed a month?"

It took a moment for the girl to understand. Her blush deepened.

"No. It's not that. It's just that I think he may be the one. He's from a good family," Idaan said quickly, as if she were already defending him. "They have interests in a trading house and a strong bloodline and . . ."

Hiami took a pose that silenced the girl. Idaan looked down at her hands, but then she smiled. The horrified, joyous smile of new love discovered. Hiami remembered how once it had felt, and her heart broke again.

"I will talk to him when he comes back, no matter how dearly he wants his sleep," Hiami said.

"Thank you, Sister," Idaan said. "I should . . . I should go."

"So soon?"

"I promised Adrah I'd tell him as soon as I spoke to my brother. He's waiting in one of the tower gardens, and . . ."

Idaan took a pose that asked forgiveness, as if a girl needed to be forgiven for wanting to be with a lover and not a woman her mother's age knotting silk to fight the darkness in her heart. Hiami took a pose that accepted the apology and released her. Idaan grinned and turned to go. Just as the blue and gold of her robe was about to vanish through the doorway, Hiami surprised herself by calling out.

"Does he make you laugh?"

Idaan turned, her expression questioning. Hiami's mind flooded again with thoughts of Biitrah and of love and the prices it demanded.

"Your man. Adrah? If he doesn't make you laugh, Idaan, you mustn't marry him."

Idaan smiled and took a pose of thanks appropriate for a pupil to her master, and then was gone. Hiami swallowed until she was sure the fear was under control again, picked up her knotwork and called for the slave to return.

THE SUN WAS GONE, THE MOON A SLIVER NO WIDER THAN A NAIL CLIPPING. Only the stars answered the miners' lanterns as Biitrah rose from the earth into darkness. His robes were wet and clung to his legs, the gray and violet turned to a uniform black. The night air was bitingly cold. The mine dogs yipped anxiously and paced in their kennels, their breath pluming like his own. The chief engineer of House Daikani's mines took a pose of profound thanks, and Biitrah replied graciously, though his fingers were numb and awkward as sausages.

"If it does that again, call for me," he said.

"Yes, most high," the engineer said. "As you command."

Biitrah's guard walked him to the chair, and his bearers lifted him. It was only now, with the work behind him and the puzzles all solved, that he felt the exhaustion. The thought of being carried back to the palaces in the cold and mud of springtime was only slightly less odious than the option of walking under his own power. He gestured to the chief armsman of his guard.

"We'll stay in the low town tonight. The usual wayhouse."

The armsman took a pose of acknowledgment and strode forward, leading his men and his bearers and himself into the unlit streets. Biitrah pulled his arms inside his robes and hugged bare flesh to flesh. The first shivers were beginning. He half regretted now that he hadn't disrobed before wading down to the lowest levels of the mine.

Ore was rich down in the plain—enough silver to keep Machi's coffers full even had there been no other mines here and in the mountains to the north and west—but the vein led down deeper than a well. In its first generation, when Machi had been the most distant corner of the Empire, the poet sent there had controlled the andat Raising-Water, and the stories said that the mines had flowed up like fountains under that power. It wasn't until after the great war that the poet Manat Doru had first captured Stone-Made-Soft and Machi had come into its own as the center for the most productive mines in the world and the home of the metal trades—ironmongers, silversmiths, Westland alchemists, needlemakers. But Raising-Water had been lost, and no one had yet discovered how to recapture it. And so, the pumps.

He again turned his mind back on the trouble. The treadmill pumps were of his own design. Four men working together could raise their own weight in water sixty feet in the time the moon—always a more reliable measure than the seasonally fickle northern sun—traveled the width of a man's finger. But the design wasn't perfect yet. It was clear from his day's work that the pump, which finally failed the night before, had been working at less than its peak for weeks. That was why the water level had been higher than one night's failure could account for. There were several possible solutions to that.

Biitrah forgot the cold, forgot his weariness, forgot indeed where he was and was being borne. His mind fell into the problem, and he was lost in it. The wayhouse, when it appeared as if by magic before them, was a welcome sight: thick stone walls with one red lacquered door at the ground level, a wide wooden snow door on the second story, and smoke rising from all its chimneys. Even from the street, he could smell seasoned meat and spiced wine. The keeper stood on the front steps with a pose of welcome so formal it bent the old, moon-faced man nearly double. Biitrah's bearers lowered his chair. At the last moment, Biitrah remembered to shove his arms back into their sleeves so that he could take a pose accepting the wayhouse keeper's welcome.

"I had not expected you, most high," the man said. "We would have prepared something more appropriate. The best that I have—"

"Will do," Biitrah said. "Certainly the best you have will do."

The keeper took a pose of thanks, standing aside to let them through the doorway as he did. Biitrah paused at the threshold, taking a formal pose of thanks. The old man seemed surprised. His round face and slack skin made Biitrah think of a pale grape just beginning to dry. He could be my father's age, he thought, and felt in his breast the bloom of a strange, almost melancholy, fondness for the man.

"I don't think we've met," Biitrah said. "What's your name, neighbor?"

"Oshai," the moon-faced man said. "We haven't met, but everyone knows of the Khai Machi's kindly eldest son. It is a pleasure to have you in this house, most high."

The house had an inner garden. Biitrah changed into a set of plain, thick woolen robes that the wayhouse kept for such occasions and joined his men there. The keeper himself brought them black-sauced noodles, river fish cooked with dried figs, and carafe after stone carafe of rice wine infused with plum. His guard, at first dour, relaxed as the night went on, singing together and telling stories. For a time, they seemed to forget who this long-faced man with his graying beard and thinning hair was and might someday be. Biitrah even sang with them at the end, intoxicated as much by the heat of the coal fire, the weariness of the day, and the simple pleasure of the night, as by the wine.

At last he rose up and went to his bed, four of his men following him. They would sleep on straw outside his door. He would sleep in the best bed the wayhouse offered. It was the way of things. A night candle burned at his bedside, the wax scented with honey. The flame was hardly down to the quarter mark. It was early. When he'd been a boy of twenty, he'd seen candles like this burn their last before he slept, the light of dawn blocked by goose-down pillows around his head. Now he couldn't well imagine staying awake to the half mark. He shuttered the candlebox, leaving only a square of light high on the ceiling from the smoke hole.

Sleep should have come easily to him as tired, well fed, half drunk as he was, but it didn't. The bed was wide and soft and comfortable. He could already hear his men snoring on their straw outside his door. But his mind would not be still.

They should have killed each other when they were young and didn't understand what a precious thing life is. That was the mistake. He and his brothers had forborne instead, and the years had drifted by. Danat had married, then Kaiin. He, the oldest of them, had met Hiami and followed his brothers' example last. He had two daughters, grown and now themselves married. And so here he and his brothers were. None of them had seen fewer than forty summers. None of them hated the other two. None of them wanted what would come next. And still, it would come. Better that the slaughter had happened when they were boys, stupid the way boys are. Better that their deaths had come before they carried the weight of so much life behind them. He was too old to become a killer.

Sleep came somewhere in these dark reflections, and he dreamed of things more pleasant and less coherent. A dove with black-tipped wings flying through the galleries of the Second Palace; Hiami sewing a child's dress with red thread and a gold needle too soft to keep its point; the moon trapped in a well and he himself called to design the pump that would raise it. When he woke, troubled by some need his sleep-sodden mind couldn't quite place, it was still dark. He needed to drink water or to pass it, but no, it was neither of these. He reached to un-shutter the candlebox, but his hands were too awkward.

"There now, most high," a voice said. "Bat it around like that, and you'll have the whole place in flames."

Pale hands righted the box and pulled open the shutters, the candle-light revealing the moon-faced keeper. He wore a dark robe under a gray woolen traveler's cloak. His face, which had seemed so congenial before, filled Biitrah with a sick dread. The smile, he saw, never reached the eyes.

"What's happened?" he demanded, or tried to. The words came out slurred and awkward. Still, the man Oshai seemed to catch the sense of them.

"I've come to be sure you've died," he said with a pose that offered this as a service. "Your men drank more than you. Those that are breathing are beyond recall, but you . . . Well, most high, if you see morning the whole exercise will have been something of a waste."

Biitrah's breath suddenly hard as a runner's, he threw off the blankets, but when he tried to stand, his knees were limp. He stumbled toward the assassin, but there was no strength in the charge. Oshai, if that was his name, put a palm to Biitrah's forehead and pushed gently back. Biitrah fell to the floor, but he hardly felt it. It was like violence being done to some other man, far away from where he was.

"It must be hard," Oshai said, squatting beside him, "to live your whole life known only as another man's son. To die having never made a mark of your own on the world. It seems unfair somehow."

Who, Biitrah tried to say. *Which of my brothers would stoop to poison?*

"Still, men die all the time," Oshai went on. "One more or less won't keep the sun from rising. And how are you feeling, most high? Can you get up? No? That's as well, then. I was half-worried I might have to pour more of this down you. Undiluted, it tastes less of plums."

The assassin rose and walked to the bed. There was a hitch in his step, as if his hip ached. *He is old as my father*, but Biitrah's mind was too dim to see any humor in the repeated thought. Oshai sat on the bed and pulled the blankets over his lap.

"No hurry, most high. I can wait quite comfortably here. Die at your leisure."

Biitrah, trying to gather his strength for one last movement, one last attack, closed his eyes but then found he lacked the will even to open them again. The wooden floor beneath him seemed utterly comfortable; his limbs were heavy and slack. There were worse poisons than this. He could at least thank his brothers for that.

It was only Hiami he would miss. And the treadmill pumps. It would have been good to finish his design work on them. He would have liked to have finished more of his work. His last thought that held any real coherence was that he wished he'd gotten to live just a little while more.

He did not know it when his killer snuffed the candle.

HIAMI HAD THE SEAT OF HONOR AT THE FUNERAL, ON THE DAIS WITH THE Khai Machi. The temple was full, bodies pressed together on their cushions as the priest intoned the rites of the dead and struck his silver chimes. The high walls and distant wooden ceiling held the heat poorly; braziers had been set in among the mourners. Hiami wore pale mourning robes and looked at her hands. It was not her first funeral. She had been present for her father's death, before her marriage into the highest family of Machi. She had only been a girl then. And through the years, when a member of the utkhaiem had passed on, she had sometimes sat and heard these same words spoken over some other body, listened to the roar of some other pyre.

This was the first time it had seemed meaningless. Her grief was real and profound, and this flock of gawkers and gossips had no relation to it. The Khai Machi's hand touched her own, and she glanced up into his eyes. His hair, what was left of it, had gone white years before. He smiled gently and took a pose that expressed his sympathy. He was graceful as an actor—his poses inhumanly smooth and precise.

Biitrah would have been a terrible Khai Machi, she thought. He would never have put in enough practice to hold himself that well.

And the tears she had suffered through the last days remembered her. Her once-father's hand trembled as if uneased by the presence of genuine feeling. He leaned back into his black lacquer seat and motioned for a servant to bring him a bowl of tea. At the front of the temple, the priest chanted on.

When the last word was sung, the last chime struck, bearers came and lifted her husband's body. The slow procession began, moving through the streets to the pealing of hand bells and the wailing of flutes. In the central square, the pyre was ready—great logs of pine stinking of oil and within them a bed of hard, hot-burning coal from the mines. Biitrah was lifted onto it and a shroud of tight metal links placed over him to hide the sight when his skin peeled from his noble bones. It was her place now to step forward and begin the conflagration. She moved slowly. All eyes were on her, and she knew what they were thinking. Poor woman, to have been left alone. Shallow sympathies that would have been extended as readily to the wives of the Khai Machi's other sons, had their men been under the metal blanket. And in those voices she heard also the excitement, dread, and anticipation that these bloody paroxysms carried. When the empty, insincere words of comfort were said, in the same breath they would move on to speculations. Both of Biitrah's brothers had vanished. Danat, it was said, had gone to the mountains where he had a secret force at the ready, or to Lachi in the south to gather allies, or to ruined Saraykeht to hire mercenaries, or to the Dai-kvo to seek the aid of the poets and the andat. Or he was in the temple, gathering his strength, or he was cowering in the basement of a low town comfort house, too afraid to come to the streets. And every story they told of him, they also told of Kaiin.

It had begun. At long last, after years of waiting, one of the men who might one day be Khai Machi had made his move. The city waited for the drama to unfold. This pyre was only the opening for them, the first notes of some new song that would make this seem to be about something honorable, comprehensible, and right.

Hiami took a pose of thanks and accepted a lit torch from the firekeeper. She stepped to the oil-soaked wood. A dove fluttered past her, landed briefly on her husband's chest, and then flew away again. She felt herself smile to see it go. She touched the flame to the small kindling and stepped back as the fire took. She waited there as long as tradition required and then went back to the Second Palace. Let the others watch the ashes. Their song might be starting, but hers here had ended.

Her servant girl was waiting for her at the entrance of the palace's great hall. She held a pose of welcome that suggested there was some news waiting for her. Hiami was tempted to ignore the nuance, to walk through to her chambers and her fire and bed and the knotwork scarf that was now nearly finished. But there were tear-streaks on the girl's cheeks, and who was Hiami, after all, to treat a suffering child unkindly? She stopped and took a pose that accepted the welcome before shifting to one of query.

"Idaan Machi," the servant girl said. "She is waiting for you in the summer garden."

Hiami shifted to a pose of thanks, straightened her sleeves, and walked quietly down the palace halls. The sliding stone doors to the garden were open, a breeze too cold to be comfortable moving through the hall. And there, by an empty fountain surrounded by bare-limbed cherry trees, sat her once-sister. If her formal robes were not the pale of mourning, her countenance contradicted them: reddened eyes, paint and powder washed away. She was a plain enough woman without them, and Hiami felt sorry for her. It was one thing to expect the violence. It was another to see it done.

She stepped forward, her hands in a pose of greeting. Idaan started to her feet as if she'd been caught doing something illicit, but then she took an answering pose. Hiami sat on the fountain's stone lip, and Idaan lowered herself, sitting on the ground at her feet as a child might.

"Your things are packed," Idaan said.

"Yes. I'll leave tomorrow. It's weeks to Tan-Sadar. It won't be so hard, I think. One of my daughters is married there, and my brother is a decent man. They'll treat me well while I make arrangements for my own apartments."

"It isn't fair," Idaan said. "They shouldn't force you out like this. You belong here."

"It's tradition," Hiami said with a pose of surrender. "Fairness has nothing to do with it. My husband is dead. I will return to my father's house, whoever's actually sitting in his chair these days."

"If you were a merchant, no one would require anything like that of you. You could go where you pleased, and do what you wanted."

"True, but I'm not, am I? I was born to the utkhaiem. You were born to a Khai."

"And women," Idaan said. Hiami was surprised by the venom in the word. "We were born women, so we'll never even have the freedoms our brothers do."

Hiami laughed. She couldn't help herself, it was all so ridiculous. She took her once-sister's hand and leaned forward until their foreheads almost touched. Idaan's tear-red eyes shifted to meet her gaze.

"I don't think the men in our families consider themselves unconstrained by history," she said, and Idaan's expression twisted with chagrin.

"I wasn't thinking," she said. "I didn't mean that . . . Gods . . . I'm sorry, Hiami-kya. I'm so sorry. I'm so sorry . . ."

Hiami opened her arms, and the girl fell into them, weeping. Hiami rocked her slowly, cooing into her ear and stroking her hair as if she were comforting a babe. And as she did, she looked around the gardens. This would be the last time she saw them. Thin tendrils of green were rising from the soil. The trees were bare, but their bark had an undertone of green. Soon it would be warm enough to turn on the fountains.

She felt her sorrow settle deep, an almost physical sensation. She understood the tears of the young that were even now soaking her robes at the shoulder. She would come to understand the tears of age in time. They would be keeping her company. There was no need to hurry.

At length, Idaan's sobs grew shallower and less frequent. The girl pulled back, smiling sheepishly and wiping her eyes with the back of her hand.

"I hadn't thought it would be this bad," Idaan said softly. "I knew it would be hard, but this is . . . How did they do it?"

"Who, dear?"

"All of them. All through the generations. How did they bring themselves to kill each other?"

"I think," Hiami said, her words seeming to come from the new sorrow within her and not from the self she had known, "that in order to become one of the Khaiem, you have to stop being able to love. So perhaps Biitrah's tragedy isn't the worst that could have happened."

Idaan hadn't followed the thought. She took a pose of query.

"Winning this game may be worse than losing it, at least for the sort of man he was. He loved the world too much. Seeing that love taken from him would have been bad. Seeing him carry the deaths of his brothers with him . . . and he wouldn't have been able to go slogging through the mines. He would have hated that. He would have been a very poor Khai Machi."

"I don't think I love the world that way," Idaan said.

"You don't, Idaan-kya," Hiami said. "And just now I don't either. But I will try to. I will try to love things the way he did."

They sat a while longer, speaking of things less treacherous. In the end, they parted as if it were just another absence before them, as if there would be another meeting on another day. A more appropriate farewell would have ended with them both in tears again.

The leave-taking ceremony before the Khai was more formal, but the emptiness of it kept it from unbalancing her composure. He sent her back to her family with gifts and letters of gratitude, and assured her that she would always have a place in his heart so long as it beat. Only when he enjoined her not to think ill of her fallen husband for his weakness did her sorrow threaten to shift to rage, but she held it down. They were only words, spoken at all such events. They were no more about Biitrah than the protestations of loyalty she now recited were about this hollow-hearted man in his black lacquer seat.

After the ceremony, she went around the palaces, conducting more personal farewells with the people whom she'd come to know and care for in Machi, and just as dark fell, she even slipped out into the streets of the city to press a few lengths of silver or small jewelry into the hands of a select few friends who were not of the utkhaiem. There were tears and insincere promises to follow her or to one day bring her back. Hiami accepted all these little sorrows with perfect grace. Little sorrows were, after all, only little.

She lay sleepless that last night in the bed that had seen all her nights since she had first come to the north, that had borne the doubled weight of her and her husband, witnessed the birth of their children and her present mourning, and she tried to think kindly of the bed, the palace, the city and its people. She set her teeth against her tears and tried to love the world. In the morning, she would take a flatboat down the Tidat, slaves and servants to carry her things, and leave behind forever the bed of the Second Palace where people did everything but die gently and old in their sleep.

1

>+< Maati took a pose that requested clarification. In another context, it would have risked annoying the messenger, but this time the servant of the Dai-kvo seemed to be expecting a certain level of disbelief. Without hesitation, he repeated his words.

"The Dai-kvo requests Maati Vaupathai come immediately to his private chambers."

It was widely understood in the shining village of the Dai-kvo that Maati Vaupathai was, if not a failure, certainly an embarrassment. Over the years he had spent in the writing rooms and lecture halls, walking the broad, clean streets, and huddled with others around the kilns of the firekeepers, Maati had grown used to the fact that he would never be entirely accepted by those who surrounded him; it had been eight years since the Dai-kvo had deigned to speak to him directly. Maati closed the brown leather book he had been studying and slipped it into his sleeve. He took a pose that accepted the message and announced his readiness. The white-robed messenger turned smartly and led the way.

The village that was home to the Dai-kvo and the poets was always beautiful. Now in the middle spring, flowers and ivies scented the air and threatened to overflow the well-tended gardens and planters, but no stray grass rose between the paving stones. The gentle choir of wind chimes filled the air. The high, thin waterfall that fell beside the palaces shone silver, and the towers and garrets—carved from the mountain face itself—were unstained even by the birds that roosted in the eaves. Men spent lifetimes, Maati knew, keeping the village immaculate and as impressive as a Khai on his seat. The village and palaces seemed as grand as the great bowl of sky above them. His years living among the men of the village—only men, no women were permitted—had never entirely robbed Maati of his awe at the place. He struggled now to hold himself tall, to appear as calm and self-possessed as a man summoned to the Dai-kvo regularly. As he passed through the archways that led to the palace, he saw several messengers and more than a few of the brown-robed poets pause to look at him.

He was not the only one who found his presence there strange.

The servant led him through the private gardens to the modest apartments of the most powerful man in the world. Maati recalled the last time he had been there—the insults and recriminations, the Dai-kvo's scorching sarcasm, and his own certainty and pride crumbling around him like sugar castles left out in the rain. Maati shook himself. There was no reason for the Dai-kvo to have called him back to repeat the indignities of the past.

There are always the indignities of the future, the soft voice that had become Maati's muse said from a corner of his mind. Never assume you can survive the future because you've survived the past. Everyone thinks that, and they've all been wrong eventually.

The servant stopped before the elm-and-oak-inlaid door that led, Maati remembered, to a meeting chamber. He scratched it twice to announce them, then opened the door and motioned Maati in. Maati breathed deeply as a man preparing to dive from a cliff into shallow water and entered.

The Dai-kvo was sitting at his table. He had not had hair since Maati had met him twenty-three summers before when the Dai-kvo had only been Tahi-kvo, the crueler of the two teachers set to sift through the discarded sons of the Khaiem and utkhaiem for likely candidates to send on to the village. His brows had gone pure white since he'd become the Dai-kvo, and the lines around his mouth had deepened. His black eyes were just as alive.

The other two men in the room were strangers to Maati. The thinner one sat at the table across from the Dai-kvo, his robes deep blue and gold, his hair pulled back to show graying temples and a thin white-flecked beard. The thicker—with both fat and muscle, Maati thought—stood at window, one foot up on the thick ledge, looking into the gardens, and Maati could see where his clean-shaven jaw sagged at the jowl. His robes were the light brown color of sand, his boots hard leather and travel worn. He turned to look at Maati as the door closed, and there was something familiar about him—about both these new

men—that he could not describe. He fell into the old pose, the first one
he had learned at the school.

"I am honored by your presence, most high Dai-kvo."

The Dai-kvo grunted and gestured to him for the benefit of the two
strangers.

"This is the one," the Dai-kvo said. The men shifted to look at him,
graceful and sure of themselves as merchants considering a pig. Maati
imagined what they saw him for—a man of thirty summers, his forehead
already pushing back his hairline, the smallest of pot bellies. A soft man
in a poet's robes, ill-considered and little spoken of. He felt himself start
to blush, clenched his teeth, and forced himself to show neither his
anger nor his shame as he took a pose of greeting to the two men.

"Forgive me," he said. "I don't believe we have met before, or if we
have, I apologize that I don't recall it."

"We haven't met," the thicker one said.

"He isn't much to look at," the thin one said, pointedly speaking to
the Dai-kvo. The thicker scowled and sketched the briefest of apologetic poses. It was a thread thrown to a drowning man, but Maati found
himself appreciating even the empty form of courtesy.

"Sit down, Maati-cha," the Dai-kvo said, gesturing to a chair. "Have
a bowl of tea. There's something we have to discuss. Tell me what
you've heard of events in the winter cities."

Maati sat and spoke while the Dai-kvo poured the tea.

"I only know what I hear at the teahouses and around the kilns, most
high. There's trouble with the glassblowers in Cetani; something about
the Khai Cetani raising taxes on exporting fishing bulbs. But I haven't
heard anyone taking it very seriously. Amnat-Tan is holding a summer
fair, hoping, they say, to take trade from Yalakeht. And the Khai
Machi . . ."

Maati stopped. He realized now why the two strangers seemed familiar; who they reminded him of. The Dai-kvo pushed a fine ceramic
bowl across the smooth-sanded grain of the table. Maati fell into a pose
of thanks without being aware of it, but did not take the bowl.

"The Khai Machi is dying," the Dai-kvo said. "His belly's gone rotten. It's a sad thing. Not a good end. And his eldest son is murdered.
Poisoned. What do the teahouses and kilns say of that?"

"That it was poor form," Maati said. "That no one has seen the

Khaiem resort to poison since Udun, thirteen summers ago. But neither of the brothers has appeared to accuse the other, so no one . . . Gods! You two are . . ."

"You see?" the Dai-kvo said to the thin man, smiling as he spoke. "No, not much to look at, but a decent stew between his ears. Yes, Maati-cha. The man scraping my windowsill with his boots there is Danat Machi. This is his eldest surviving brother, Kaiin. And they have come here to speak with me instead of waging war against each other because neither of them killed their elder brother Biitrah."

"So they . . . you think it was Otah-kvo?"

"The Dai-kvo says you know my younger brother," the thickset man—Danat—said, taking his own seat at the only unoccupied side of the table. "Tell me what you know of Otah."

"I haven't seen him in years, Danat-cha," Maati said. "He was in Saraykeht when . . . when the old poet there died. He was working as a laborer. But I haven't seen him since."

"Do you think he was satisfied by that life?" the thin one—Kaiin—asked. "A laborer at the docks of Saraykeht hardly seems like the fate a son of the Khaiem would embrace. Especially one who refused the brand."

Maati picked up the bowl of tea, sipping it too quickly as he tried to gain himself a moment to think. The tea scalded his tongue.

"I never heard Otah speak of any ambitions for his father's chair," Maati said.

"And is there any reason to think he would have spoken of it to you?" Kaiin said, the faintest sneer in his voice. Maati felt the blush creeping into his cheeks again, but it was the Dai-kvo who answered.

"There is. Otah Machi and Maati here were close for a time. They fell out eventually over a woman, I believe. Still, I hold that if Otah had been bent on taking part in the struggle for Machi at that time, he would have taken Maati into his confidence. But that is hardly our concern. As Maati here points out, it was years ago. Otah may have become ambitious. Or resentful. There's no way for us to know that—"

"But he refused the brand—" Danat began, and the Dai-kvo cut him off with a gesture.

"There were other reasons for that," the Dai-kvo said sharply. "They aren't your concern."

Danat Machi took a pose of apology and the Dai-kvo waved it away.

Maati sipped his tea again. This time it didn't burn. To his right, Kaiin Machi took a pose of query, looking directly at Maati for what seemed the first time.

"Would you know him again if you saw him?"

"Yes," Maati said. "I would."

"You sound certain of it."

"I am, Kaiin-cha."

The thin man smiled. All around the table a sense of satisfaction seemed to come from his answer. Maati found it unnerving. The Dai-kvo poured himself more tea, the liquid clicking into his bowl like a stream over stones.

"There is a very good library in Machi," the Dai-kvo said. "One of the finest in the fourteen cities. I understand there are records there from the time of the Empire. One of the high lords was thinking to go there, perhaps, to ride out the war, and sent his books ahead. I'm sure there are treasures hidden among those shelves that would be of use in binding the andat."

"Really?" Maati asked.

"No, not really," the Dai-kvo said. "I expect it's a mess of poorly documented scraps overseen by a librarian who spends his copper on wine and whores, but I don't care. For our purposes, there are secrets hidden in those records important enough to send a low-ranking poet like yourself to sift though. I have a letter to the Khai Machi that will explain why you are truly there. He will explain your presence to the utkhaiem and Cehmai Tyan, the poet who holds Stone-Made-Soft. Let them think you've come on my errand. What you will be doing instead is discovering whether Otah killed Biitrah Machi. If so, who is backing him. If not, who did, and why."

"Most high—" Maati began.

"Wait for me in the gardens," the Dai-kvo said. "I have a few more things to discuss with the sons of Machi."

The gardens, like the apartments, were small, well kept, beautiful, and simple. A fountain murmured among carefully shaped, deeply fragrant pine trees. Maati sat, looking out. From the side of mountain, the world spread out before him like a map. He waited, his head buzzing, his heart in turmoil. Before long he heard the steady grinding sound of footsteps on gravel, and he turned to see the Dai-kvo making his way down the path toward him. Maati stood. He had not known the Dai-kvo had started walking with a cane. A servant followed at a distance, carrying a chair, and did not approach until the Dai-kvo signaled. Once the chair was in place, looking out over the same span that Maati had been considering, the servant retreated.

"Interesting, isn't it?" the Dai-kvo said.

Maati, unsure whether he meant the view or the business with the sons of Machi, didn't reply. The Dai-kvo looked at him, something part smile, part something less congenial on his lips. He drew forth two packets—letters sealed in wax and sewn shut. Maati took them and tucked them in his sleeve.

"Gods. I'm getting old. You see that tree?" the Dai-kvo asked, pointing at one of the shaped pines with his cane.

"Yes, most high."

"There's a family of robins that lives in it. They wake me up every morning. I always mean to have someone break the nest, but I've never quite given the order."

"You are merciful, most high."

The old man looked up at him, squinting. His lips were pressed thin, and the lines in his face were black as charcoal. Maati stood waiting. At length, the Dai-kvo turned away again with a sigh.

"Will you be able to do it?" he asked.

"I will do as the Dai-kvo commands," Maati said.

"Yes, I know you'll go there. But will you be able to tell me that he's there? You know if he is behind this, they'll kill him before they go on to each other. Are you able to bear that responsibility? Tell me now if you aren't, and I'll find some other way. You don't have to fail again."

"I won't fail again, most high."

"Good. That's good," the Dai-kvo said and went silent. Maati waited so long for the pose that would dismiss him that he wondered whether the Dai-kvo had forgotten he was there, or had chosen to ignore him as an insult. But the old man spoke, his voice low.

"How old is your son, Maati-cha?"

"Twelve, most high. But I haven't seen him in some years."

"You're angry with me for that." Maati began to take a pose of denial, but checked himself and lowered his arms. This wasn't the time for court politics. The Dai-kvo saw this and smiled. "You're getting wiser, my boy. You were a fool when you were young. In itself, that's not such a bad thing. Many men are. But you embraced your mistakes. You defended them against all correction. That was the wrong path, and don't think I'm unaware of how you've paid for it."

"As you say, most high."

"I told you there was no place in a poet's life for a family. A lover here or there, certainly. Most men are too weak to deny themselves that much. But a wife? A child? No. There isn't room for both what they require and what we do. And I told you that. You remember? I told you that, and you . . ."

The Dai-kvo shook his head, frowning in remembered frustration. It was a moment, Maati knew, when he could apologize. He could repent his pride and say that the Dai-kvo had indeed known better all along. He remained silent.

"I was right," the Dai-kvo said for him. "And now you've done half a job as a poet and half a job as a man. Your studies are weak, and the woman took your whelp and left. You've failed both, just as I knew you would. I'm not condemning you for that, Maati. No man could have taken on what you did and succeeded. But this opportunity in Machi is what will wipe clean the slate. Do this well and it will be what you're remembered for."

"Certainly I will do my best."

"Fail at it, and there won't be a third chance. Few enough men have two."

Maati took a pose appropriate to a student receiving a lecture. Considering him, the Dai-kvo responded with one that closed the lesson, then raised his hand.

"Don't destroy this chance in order to spite me, Maati. Failing in this will do me no harm, and it will destroy you. You're angry because I told you the truth, and because what I said would happen, did. Consider while you go north, whether that's really such a good reason to hate me."

THE OPEN WINDOW LET IN A COOL BREEZE THAT SMELLED OF PINE AND RAIN. Otah Machi, the sixth son of the Khai Machi, lay on the bed, listening to the sounds of water—rain pattering on the flagstones of the wayhouse's courtyard and the tiles of its roof, the constant hushing of the river against its banks. A fire danced and spat in the grate, but his bare skin was still stippled with cold. The night candle had gone out, and he hadn't bothered to relight it. Morning would come when it came.

The door slid open and then shut. He didn't turn to look.

"You're brooding, Itani," Kiyan said, calling him by the false name he'd chosen for himself, the only one he'd ever told her. Her voice was low and rich and careful as a singer's. He shifted now, turning to his side. She knelt by the grate—her skin smooth and brown, her robes the formal cut of a woman of business, one strand of her hair fallen free. Her face was thin—she reminded him of a fox sometimes, when a smile just touched her mouth. She placed a fresh log on the fire as she spoke. "I half expected you'd be asleep already."

He sighed and sketched a pose of contrition with one hand.

"Don't apologize to me," she said. "I'm as happy having you in my rooms here as in the teahouse, but Old Mani wanted more news out of you. Or maybe just to get you drunk enough to sing dirty songs with him. He's missed you, you know."

"It's a hard thing, being so loved."

"Don't laugh at it. It's not a love to carry you through ages, but it's more than some people ever manage. You'll grow into one of those pinched old men who want free wine because they pity themselves."

"I'm sorry. I don't mean to make light of Old Mani. It's just . . ."

He sighed. Kiyan closed the window and relit the night candle.

"It's just that you're brooding," she said. "And you're naked and not under the blankets, so you're feeling that you've done something wrong and deserve to suffer."

"Ah," Otah said. "Is that why I do this?"

"Yes," she said, untying her robes. "It is. You can't hide it from me, Itani. You might as well come out with it."

Otah held the thought in his mind. *I'm not who I've told you I am. Itani Noygu is the name I picked for myself when I was a child. My father is dying, and brothers I can hardly recall have started killing each other, and I find it makes me sad.* He wondered what Kiyan would say to that. She prided herself on knowing him—on knowing people and how their minds worked. And yet he didn't think this was something she'd already have guessed.

Naked, she lay beside him, pulling thick blankets up over them both.

"Did you find another woman in Chaburi-Tan?" she asked, half-teasing. But only half. "Some young dancing girl who stole your heart, or some other bit of your flesh, and now you're stewing over how to tell me you're leaving me?"

"I'm a courier," Otah said. "I have a woman in every city I visit. You know that."

"You don't," she said. "Some couriers do, but you don't."

"No?"

"No. It took me half a year of doing everything short of stripping bare for you to notice me. You don't stay in other cities long enough for a woman to chip through your reserve. And you don't have to push away the blankets. You may want to be cold, but I don't."

"Well. Maybe I'm just feeling old."

"A ripe thirty-three? Well, when you decide to stop running across the world, I'd always be pleased to hire you on. We could stand another pair of hands around the place. You could throw out the drunks and track down the cheats that try to slip away without paying."

"You don't pay enough," Otah said. "I talk to Old Mani. I know what your wages are."

"Perhaps you'd get extra for keeping me warm at nights."

"Shouldn't you offer that to Old Mani first? He's been here longer than I have."

Kiyan slapped his chest smartly, and then nestled into him. He found himself curling toward her, the warmth of her body drawing him like a familiar scent. Her fingers traced the tattoo on his breast—the ink had faded over time, blurring lines that had once been sharp and clear.

"Jokes aside," she said, and he could hear a weariness in her voice, "I would take you on, if you wanted to stay. You could live here, with me. Help me manage the house."

He caressed her hair, feeling the individual strands as they flowed across his fingertips. There was a scattering of white among the black that made her look older than she was. Otah knew that they had been there since she was a girl, as if she'd been born old.

"That sounds like you're suggesting marriage," he said.

"Perhaps. You wouldn't have to, but . . . it would be one way to arrange things. That isn't a threat, you know. I don't need a husband. Only if it would make you feel better, we could . . ."

He kissed her gently. It had been weeks, and he was surprised to find how much he'd missed the touch of her lips. Weeks of travel weariness slipped away, the deep unease loosened its hold on his chest, and he took comfort in her. He fell asleep with her arm over his body, her breath already soft and deep with sleep.

In the morning, he woke before she did, slipped out of the bed, and dressed quietly. The sun was not up, but the eastern sky had lightened and the morning birds were singing madly as he took himself across an ancient stone bridge into Udun.

A river city, Udun was laced with as many canals as roadways. Bridges humped up high enough for barges to pass beneath them, and the green water of the Qiit lapped at old stone steps that descended into the river mud. Otah stopped at a stall on the broad central plaza and traded two lengths of copper for a thick wedge of honey bread and a bowl of black, smoky tea. Around him, the city slowly came awake—the streets and canals filling with traders and merchants, beggars singing at the corners or in small rafts tied at the water's edge, laborers hauling wagons along the wide flagstoned streets, and birds bright as shafts of sunlight—blue and red and yellow, green as grass, and pink as dawn. Udun was a city of birds, and their chatter and shriek and song filled the air as he ate.

The compound of House Siyanti was in the better part of the city, just downstream from the palaces, where the water was not yet fouled by the wastes of thirty thousand men and women and children. The red brick buildings rose up three stories high, and a private canal was filled with barges in the red and silver of the house. The stylized emblem of the sun and stars had been worked into the brick archway that led to the central courtyard, and Otah passed beneath it with a feeling like coming home.

Amiit Foss, the overseer for the house couriers, was in his offices, ordering around three apprentices with sharp words and insults, but no blows. Otah stepped in and took a pose of greeting.

"Ah! The missing Itani. Did you know the word for half-wit in the tongue of the Empire was *itani-nah?*"

"All respect, Amiit-cha, but no it wasn't."

The overseer grinned. One of the apprentices—a girl of perhaps thirteen summers—whispered something angrily, and the boy next to her giggled.

"Fine," the overseer said. "You two. I need the ciphers rechecked on last week's letters."

"But I wasn't the one . . . ," the girl protested. The overseer took a pose that commanded her silence, and the pair, glowering at each other, stalked away.

"I get them when they're just growing old enough to flirt," Amiit said, sighing. "Come back to the meeting rooms. The journey took longer than I'd expected."

"There were some delays," Otah said as he followed the older man back. "Chaburi-Tan isn't as tightly run as it was last time I was out there."

"No?"

"There are refugees from the Westlands."

"There are always refugees from the Westlands."

"Not this many," Otah said. "There are rumors that the Khai Chaburi-Tan is going to restrict the number of Westlanders allowed on the island."

Amiit paused, his hands on the carved wood door of the meeting rooms. Otah could almost see the implications of this thought working themselves out behind the overseer's eyes. A moment later, Amiit looked up, raised his eyebrows in appreciation, and pushed the doors open.

Half the day was spent in the raw silk chairs of the meeting rooms while Amiit took Otah's report and accepted the letters—sewn shut and written in cipher—that Otah had carried with him.

It had taken Otah some time to understand all that being a courier implied. When he had first arrived in Udun six years before, hungry, lost and half-haunted by the memories he carried with him, he had still believed that he would simply be carrying letters and small packages from one place to another, perhaps waiting for a response, and then taking those to where they were expected. It would have been as right to say that a farmer throws some seeds in the earth and returns a few months later to see what's grown. He had been lucky. His ability to win friends easily had served him, and he had been instructed in what the couriers called the gentleman's trade: how to gather information that might be of use to the house, how to read the activity of a street corner or market, and how to know from that the mood of a city. How to break ciphers and re-sew letters. How to appear to drink more wine than you actually did, and question travelers on the road without seeming to.

He understood now that the gentleman's trade was one that asked a lifetime to truly master, and though he was still a journeyman, he had found a kind of joy in it. Amiit knew what his talents were, and chose assignments for him in which he could do well. And in return for the trust of the house and the esteem of his fellows, Otah did the best work he could, brokering information, speculation, gossip, and intrigue. He had traveled through the summer cities in the south, west to the plains and the cities that traded directly with the Westlands, up the eastern coasts where his knowledge of obscure east island tongues had served him well. By design or happy coincidence, he had never gone farther north than Yalakeht. He had not been called on to see the winter cities.

Until now.

"There's trouble in the north," Amiit said as he tucked the last of the opened letters into his sleeve.

"I'd heard," Otah said. "The succession's started in Machi."

"Amnat-Tan, Machi, Cetani. All of them have something brewing. You may need to get some heavier robes."

"I didn't think House Siyanti had much trade there," Otah said, trying to keep the unease out of his voice.

"We don't. That doesn't mean we never will. And take your time. There's something I'm waiting for from the west. I won't be sending you out for a month at least, so you can have some time to spend you money. Unless . . ."

The overseer's eyes narrowed. His hands took a pose of query.

"I just dislike the cold," Otah said, making a joke to cover his unease. "I grew up in Saraykeht. It seemed like water never froze there."

"It's a hard life," Amiit said. "I can try to give the commissions to other men, if you'd prefer."

And have them wonder why it was that I wouldn't go, Otah thought. He took a pose of thanks that also implied rejection.

"I'll take what there is," he said. "And heavy wool robes besides."

"It really isn't so bad up there in summer," Amiit said. "It's the winters that break your stones."

"Then by all means, send someone else in the winter."

They exchanged a few final pleasantries, and Otah left the name of Kiyan's wayhouse as the place to send for him, if he was needed. He spent the afternoon in a teahouse at the edge of the warehouse district, talking with old acquaintances and trading news. He kept an ear out for word from Machi, but there was nothing fresh. The eldest son had been poisoned, and his remaining brothers had gone to ground. No one knew where they were nor which had begun the traditional struggle. There were only a few murmurs of the near-forgotten sixth son, but every time he heard his old name, it was like hearing a distant, threatening noise.

He returned to the wayhouse as darkness began to thicken the treetops and the streets fell into twilight, brooding. It wasn't safe, of course, to take a commission in Machi, but neither could he safely refuse one. Not without a reason. He knew when gossip and speculation had grown hot enough to melt like sugar and stick. There would be a dozen reports of Otah Machi from all over the cities, and likely beyond as well. If even a suggestion was made that he was not who he presented himself to be, he ran the risk of being exposed, dragged into the constant, empty, vicious drama of succession. He would sacrifice quite a lot to keep that from happening. Going north, doing his work, and returning was what he would have done, had he been the man he claimed to be. And so perhaps it was the wiser strategy.

And also he wondered what sort of man his father was. What sort of man his brother had been. Whether his mother had wept when she sent her boy away to the school where the excess sons of the high families became poets or fell forever from grace.

As he entered the courtyard, his dark reverie was interrupted by laughter and music from the main hall, and the scent of roast pork and baked yams mixed with the pine resin. When he stepped in, Old Mani slapped an earthenware bowl of wine into his hands and steered him to a bench by the fire. There were a good number of travelers—merchants from the great cities, farmers from the low towns, travelers each with a story and a past and a tale to tell, if only they were asked the right questions in the right ways.

It was later, the warm air busy with conversation, that Otah caught sight of Kiyan across the wide hall. She had on a working woman's robes, her hair tied back, but the expression on her face and the angle of her body spoke of a deep contentment and satisfaction. She knew her place was here, and she was proud of it.

Otah found himself suddenly stilled by a longing for her unlike the simple lust that he was accustomed to. He imagined himself feeling the same satisfaction that he saw in her. The same sense of having a place in the world. She turned to him as if he had spoken and tilted her head—not an actual formal pose, but nonetheless a question.

He smiled in reply. This that she offered was, he suspected, a life worth living.

———

CEHMAI TYAN'S DREAMS, WHENEVER THE TIME CAME TO RENEW HIS LIFE'S struggle, took the same form. A normal dream—meaningless, strange, and trivial—would shift. Something small would happen that carried a weight of fear and dread out of all proportion. This time, he dreamt he was walking in a street fair, trying to find a stall with food he liked, when a young girl appeared at his side. As he saw her, his sleeping mind had already started to rebel. She held out her hand, the palm painted the green of summer grass, and he woke himself trying to scream.

Gasping as if he had run a race, he rose, pulled on the simple brown robes of a poet, and walked to the main room of the house. The worked stone walls seemed to glow with the morning light. The chill spring air fought with the warmth from the low fire in the grate. The thick rugs felt softer than grass against Cehmai's bare feet. And the andat was waiting at the game table, the pieces already in place before it—black basalt and white marble. The line of white was already marred, one stone disk shifted forward into the field. Cehmai sat and met his opponent's pale eyes. There was a pressure in his mind that felt the way a windstorm sounded.

"Again?" the poet asked.

Stone-Made-Soft nodded its broad head. Cehmai Tyan considered the board, recalled the binding—the translation that had brought the thing across from him out of formlessness—and pushed a black stone into the empty field of the board. The game began again.

The binding of Stone-Made-Soft had not been Cehmai's work. It had been done generations earlier, by the poet Manat Doru. The game of stones had figured deeply in the symbolism of the binding—the fluid lines of play and the solidity of the stone markers. The competition between a spirit seeking its freedom and the poet holding it in place. Cehmai ran his fingertip along his edge of the board where Manat Doru's had once touched it. He considered the advancing line of white stones and crafted his answering line of black, touching stones that long-dead men had held when they had played the same game against the thing that sat across from him now. And with every victory, the binding was renewed, the andat held more firmly in the world. It was an excellent strategy, in part because the binding had also made Stone-Made-Soft a terrible player.

The windstorm quieted, and Cehmai stretched and yawned. Stone-Made-Soft glowered down on its failing line.

"You're going to lose," Cehmai said.

"I know," the andat replied. Its voice was a deep rumble, like a distant rockslide—another evocation of flowing stone. "Being doomed doesn't take away from the dignity of the effort, though."

"Well said."

The andat shrugged and smiled. "One can afford to be philosophical when losing means outliving one's opponent. This particular game? You picked it. But there are others we play that I'm not quite so crippled at."

"I didn't pick this game. I haven't seen twenty summers, and you've seen more than two hundred. I wasn't even a dirty thought in my grandfather's head when you started playing this."

The andat's thick hands took a formal position of disagreement.

"We have always been playing the same game, you and I. If you were someone else at the start, it's your problem."

They never started speaking until the game's end was a forgone conclusion. That Stone-Made-Soft was willing to speak was as much a sign that this particular battle was drawing to its end as the silence in Cehmai's mind. But the last piece had not yet been pushed when a pounding came on the door.

"I know you're in there! Wake up!"

Cehmai sighed at the familiar voice and rose. The andat brooded over the board, searching, the poet knew, for some way to win a lost game. He clapped a hand on the andat's shoulder as he passed by it toward the door.

"I won't have it," the stout, red-cheeked man said when the opened door revealed him. He wore brilliant blue robes shot with rich yellow and a copper torc of office. Not for the first time, Cehmai thought Baarath would have been better placed in life as the overseer of a merchant house or farm than within the utkhaiem. "You poets think that because you have the andat, you have everything. Well, I've come to tell you it isn't so."

Cehmai took a pose of welcome and stepped back, allowing the man in.

"I've been expecting you, Baarath. I don't suppose you've brought any food with you?"

"You have servants for that," Baarath said, striding into the wide room, taking in the shelves of books and scrolls and maps with his customary moment of lust. The andat looked up at him with its queer, slow smile, and then turned back to the board.

"I don't like having strange people wandering though my library," Baarath said.

"Well, let's hope our friend from the Dai-kvo won't be strange."

"You are an annoying, contrary man. He's going to come in here and root through the place. Some of those volumes are very old, you know. They won't stand mishandling."

"Perhaps you should make copies of them."

"I am making copies. But it's not a fast process, you know. It takes a great deal of time and patience. You can't just grab some half-trained scribes off the street corners and set them to copying the great books of the Empire."

"You also can't do the whole job by yourself, Baarath. No matter how much you want to."

The librarian scowled at him, but there was a playfulness in the man's eyes. The andat shifted a white marker forward and the noise in Cehmai's head murmured. It had been a good move.

"You hold an abstract thought in human form and make it play tricks, and you tell me what's not possible? Please. I've come to offer a trade. If you'll—"

"Wait," Cehmai said.

"If you'll just—"

"Baarath, you can be quiet or you can leave. I have to finish this."

Stone-Made-Soft sighed as Cehmai took his seat again. The white stone had opened a line that had until now been closed. It wasn't one he'd seen the andat play before, and Cehmai scowled. The game was still over, there was no way for the andat to clear his files and pour the white markers to their target squares before Cehmai's dark stones had reached their goal. But it would be harder now than it had been before the librarian came. Cehmai played through the next five moves in his mind, his fingertips twitching. Then, decisively, he pushed the black marker forward that would block the andat's fastest course.

"Nice move," the librarian said.

"What did you want with me? Could you just say it so I can refuse and get about my day?"

"I was going to say that I will give this little poet-let of the Dai-kvo's full access if you'll let me include your collection here. It really makes more sense to have all the books and scrolls cataloged together."

Cehmai took a pose of thanks.

"No," he said. "Now go away. I have to do this."

"Be reasonable! If I choose—"

"First, you will give Maati Vaupathai full access because the Dai-kvo and the Khai Machi tell you to. You have nothing to bargain with. Second, I'm not the one who gave the orders, nor was I consulted on them. If you want barley, you don't negotiate with a silversmith, do you? So don't come here asking concessions for something that I'm not involved with."

A flash of genuine hurt crossed Baarath's face. Stone-Made-Soft touched a white marker, then pulled back its hand and sank into thought again. Baarath took a pose of apology, his stance icy with its formality.

"Don't," Cehmai said. "I'm sorry. I don't mean to be a farmer's wife about the thing, but you've come at a difficult time."

"Of course. This children's game upon which all our fates depend. No, no. Stay. I'll see myself out."

"We can talk later," Cehmai said to the librarian's back.

The door closed and left Cehmai and his captive, or his ward, or his other self, alone together.

"He isn't a very good man," Stone-Made-Soft rumbled.

"No, he's not," Cehmai agreed. "But friendship falls where it falls. And may the gods keep us from a world where only the people who deserve love get it."

"Well said," the andat replied, and pushed forward the white stone Cehmai knew it would.

The game ended quickly after that. Cehmai ate a breakfast of roast lamb and boiled eggs while Stone-Made-Soft put away the game pieces and then sat, warming its huge hands by the fire. There was a long day before them, and after the morning's struggle, Cehmai was dreading it. They were promised to go to the potter's works before midday. A load of granite had come from the quarries and required his services before it could be shaped into the bowls and vases for which Machi was famed. After midday, he was needed for a meeting with the engineers to consider the plans for House Pirnat's silver mine. The Khai Machi's engineers were concerned, he knew, that using the andat to soften the stone around a newfound seam of ore would weaken the structure of the mine. House Pirnat's overseer thought it worth the risk. It would be like sitting in a child's garden during a mud fight, but it had to be done. Just thinking of it made him tired.

"You could tell them I'd nearly won," the andat said. "Say you were too shaken to appear."

"Yes, because my life would be so much better if they were all afraid of turning into a second Saraykeht."

"I'm only saying that you have options," the andat replied, smiling into the fire.

The poet's house was set apart from the palaces of the Khai and the compounds of the utkhaiem. It was a broad, low building with thick stone walls nestled behind a small and artificial wood of sculpted oaks. The snows of winter had been reduced to gray-white mounds and frozen pools in the deep shadows where sunlight would not touch them. Cehmai and the andat strode west, toward the palaces and the Great Tower, tallest of all the inhuman buildings of Machi. It was a relief to walk along streets in sunlight rather than the deep network of tunnels to which the city resorted when the drifts were too high to allow even the snow doors to open. Brief days, and cold profound enough to crack stone, were the hallmarks of the Machi winter. The terrible urge to be out in the gardens and streets marked her spring. The men and women Cehmai passed were all dressed in warm robes, but their faces were bare and their heads uncovered. The pair paused by a firekeeper at his kiln. A singing slave stood near enough to warm her hands at the fire as she filled the air with traditional songs. The palaces of the Khai loomed before them—huge and gray with roofs pitched sharp as axe blades—and the city and the daylight stood at their backs, tempting as sugar ghosts on Candles Night.

"It isn't too late," the andat murmured. "Manat Doru used to do it all the time. He'd send a note to the Khai claiming that the weight of holding me was too heavy, and that he required his rest. We would go down to a little teahouse by the river that had sweetcakes that they cooked in oil and covered with sugar so fine it hung in the air if you blew on it."

"You're lying to me," Cehmai said.

"No," the andat said. "No, it's truth. It made the Khai quite angry sometimes, but what was he to do?"

The singing slave smiled and took a pose of greeting to them that Cehmai returned.

"We could stop by the spring gardens that Idaan frequents. If she were free she might be persuaded to join us," the andat said.

"And why would the daughter of the Khai tempt me more than sweetcakes?"

"She's well-read and quick in her mind," the andat said, as if the question had been genuine. "You find her pleasant to look at, I know. And her demeanor is often just slightly inappropriate. If memory serves, that might outweigh even sweetcakes."

Cehmai shifted his weight from foot to foot, then, with a commanding gesture, stopped a servant boy. The boy, seeing who he was, fell into a pose of greeting so formal it approached obeisance.

"I need you to carry a message for me. To the Master of Tides."

"Yes, Cehmai-cha," the boy said.

"Tell him I have had a bout with the andat this morning, and find myself too fatigued to conduct business. And tell him that I will reach him on the morrow if I feel well enough."

The poet fished through his sleeves, pulled out his money pouch and took out a length of silver. The boy's eyes widened, and his small hand reached out toward it. Cehmai drew it back, and the boy's dark eyes fixed on his.

"If he asks," Cehmai said, "you tell him I looked quite ill."

The boy nodded vigorously, and Cehmai pressed the silver length into his palm. Whatever errand the boy had been on was forgotten. He vanished into the austere gloom of the palaces.

"You're corrupting me," Cehmai said as he turned away.

"Constant struggle is the price of power," the andat said, its voice utterly devoid of humor. "It must be a terrible burden for you. Now let's see if we can find the girl and those sweetcakes."

2

>+< "They tell me you knew my son," the Khai Machi said. The grayness of his skin and yellow in his long, bound hair were signs of something more than the ravages of age. The Dai-kvo was of the same generation, but Maati saw none of his vigor and strength here. The sick man took a pose of command. "Tell me of him."

Maati stared down at the woven reed mat on which he knelt and fought to push away the weariness of his travels. It had been days since he had bathed, his robes were not fresh, and his mind was uneasy. But he was here, called to this meeting or possibly this confrontation, even before his bags had been unpacked. He could feel the attention of the servants of the Khai—there were perhaps a dozen in the room. Some slaves, others attendants from among the highest ranks of the utkhaiem. The audience might be called private, but it was too well attended for Maati's comfort. The choice was not his. He took the bowl of heated wine he had been given, sipped it, and spoke.

"Otah-kvo and I met at the school, most high. He already wore the black robes awarded to those who had passed the first test when I met him. I . . . I was the occasion of his passing the second."

The Khai Machi nodded. It was an almost inhumanly graceful movement, like a bird or some finely wrought mechanism. Maati took it as a sign that he should continue.

"He came to me after that. He . . . he taught me things about the school and about myself. He was, I think, the best teacher I have known. I doubt I would have been chosen to study with the Dai-kvo if it hadn't been for him. But then he refused the chance to become a poet."

"And the brand," the Khai said. "He refused the brand. Perhaps he had ambitions even then."

He was a boy, and angry, Maati thought. He had beaten Tahi-kvo and Milah-kvo on his own terms. He'd refused their honors. Of course he didn't accept disgrace.

The utkhaiem high enough to express an opinion nodded among themselves as if a decision made in heat by a boy not yet twelve might explain a murder two decades later. Maati let it pass.

"I met him again in Saraykeht," Maati said. "I had gone there to study under Heshai-kvo and the andat Removing-the-Part-That-Continues. Otah-kvo was living under an assumed name at the time, working as a laborer on the docks."

"And you recognized him?"

"I did," Maati said.

"And yet you did not denounce him?" The old man's voice wasn't angry. Maati had expected anger. Outrage, perhaps. What he heard instead was gentler and more penetrating. When he looked up, the red-rimmed eyes were very much like Otah-kvo's. Even if he had not known before, those eyes would have told him that this man was Otah's father. He wondered briefly what his own father's eyes had looked like and whether his resembled them, then forced his mind back to the matter at hand.

"I did not, most high. I regarded him as my teacher, and . . . and I wished to understand the choices he had made. We became friends for a time. Before the death of the poet took me from the city."

"And do you call him your teacher still? You call him Otah-kvo. That is a title for a teacher, is it not?"

Maati blushed. He hadn't realized until then that he was doing it.

"An old habit, most high. I was sixteen when I last saw Otah-cha. I'm thirty now. It has been almost half my life since I have spoken with him. I think of him as a person I once knew who told me some things I found of use at the time," Maati said, and sensing that the falsehood of those words might be clear, he continued with some that were more nearly true. "My loyalty is to the Dai-kvo."

"That is good," the Khai Machi said. "Tell me, then. How will you conduct this examination of my city?"

"I am here to study the library of Machi," Maati said. "I will spend my mornings there, most high. After midday and in the evenings I will move through the city. I think . . . I think that if Otah-kvo is here it will not be difficult to find him."

The gray, thin lips smiled. Maati thought there was condescension in them. Perhaps even pity. He felt a blush rise in his cheeks, but kept his face still. He knew how he must appear to the Khai's weary eyes, but he would not flinch and confirm the man's worst suspicions. He swallowed once to loosen his throat.

"You have great faith in yourself," the Khai Machi said. "You come to my city for the first time. You know nothing of its streets and tunnels, little of its history, and you say that finding my missing son will be easy for you."

"Rather, most high, I will make it easy for him to find me."

It might have been his imagination—he knew from experience that he was prone to see his own fears and hopes in other people instead of what was truly there—but Maati thought there might have been a flicker of approval on the old man's face.

"You will report to me," the Khai said. "When you find him, you will come to me before anyone else, and I will send word to the Dai-kvo."

"As you command, most high," Maati lied. He had said that his loyalty lay with the Dai-kvo, but there was no advantage he could see to explaining all that meant here and now.

The meeting continued for a short time. The Khai seemed as exhausted by it as Maati himself was. Afterward, a servant girl led him to his apartments within the palaces. Night was already falling as he closed the door, truly alone for the first time in weeks. The journey from his home in the Dai-kvo's village wasn't the half-season's trek he would have had from Saraykeht, but it was enough, and Maati didn't enjoy the constant companionship of strangers on the road.

A fire had been lit in the grate, and warm tea and cakes of honeyed almonds waited for him at a lacquered table. He lowered himself into the chair, rested his feet, and closed his eyes. Being here, in this place, had a sense of unreality to it. To have been entrusted with anything of importance was a surprise after his loss of status. The thought stung, but he forced himself to turn in toward it. He had lost a great deal of the Dai-kvo's trust between his failure in Saraykeht and his refusal to disavow Liat, the girl who had once loved Otah-kvo but left both him and the fallen city to be with Maati, when it became clear she was bearing his child. If there had been time between the two, perhaps it might have been different. One scandal on the heels of the other, though, had been too much. Or so he told himself. It was what he wanted to believe.

A scratch at the door roused him from his bitter reminiscences. He straightened his robes and ran a hand through his hair before he spoke.

"Come in."

The door slid open and a young man of perhaps twenty summers wearing the brown robes of a poet stepped in and took a pose of greeting. Maati returned it as he considered Cehmai Tyan, poet of Machi. The broad shoulders, the open face. Here, Maati thought, is what I should have been. A talented boy poet who studied under a master while young enough to have his mind molded to the right shape. And when the time came, he had taken that burden on himself for the sake of his city. As I should have done.

"I only just heard you'd arrived," Cehmai Tyan said. "I left orders at the main road, but apparently they don't think as much of me as they pretend."

There was a light humor in his voice and manner. As if this were a game, as if he were a person whom anyone in Machi—or in the world—could truly treat with less than total respect. He held the power to soften stone—it was the concept, the essential idea, that Manat Doru had translated into a human form all those generations ago. This wide-faced, handsome boy could collapse every bridge, level every mountain. The great towers of Machi could turn to a river of stone, fast-flowing and dense as quicksilver, which would lay the city to ruin at his order. And he made light of being ignored as if he were junior clerk in some harbormaster's house. Maati couldn't tell if it was an affectation or if the poet was really so utterly naïve.

"The Khai left orders as well," Maati said.

"Ah, well. Nothing to be done about that, then. I trust everything is acceptable with your apartments?"

"I . . . I really don't know. I haven't really looked around yet. Too busy sitting on something that doesn't move, I suppose. I close my eyes, and I feel like I'm still jouncing around on the back of a cart."

The young poet laughed, a warm sound that seemed full of self-confidence and summer light. Maati felt himself smiling thinly and mentally reproved himself for being ungracious. Cehmai dropped onto a cushion beside the fire, legs crossed under him.

"I wanted to speak with you before we started working in the morning," Cehmai said. "The man who guards the library is . . . he's a good man, but he's protective of the place. I think he looks on it as his trust to the ages."

"Like a poet," Maati said.

Cehmai grinned. "I suppose so. Only he'd have made a terrible poet. He's puffed himself three times larger than anyone else just by having the keys to a building full of papers in languages only half a dozen people in the city can read. If he'd ever been given something important to do, he'd have popped like a tick. Anyway, I thought it might ease things if I came along with you for the first few days. Once Baarath is used to you, I expect he'll be fine. It's that first negotiation that's tricky."

Maati took a pose that offered gratitude, but was also a refusal.

"There's no call to take you from your duties," he said. "I expect the order of the Khai will suffice."

"I wouldn't only be doing it as a favor to you, Maati-kvo," Cehmai said. The honorific took Maati by surprise, but the young poet didn't seem to notice his reaction. "Baarath is a friend of mine, and sometimes you have to protect your friends from themselves. You know?"

Maati took a pose that was an agreement and looked into the flames. Sometimes men could be their own worst enemies. That was truth. He remembered the last time he had seen Otah-kvo. It had been the night Maati had admitted what Liat had become to him and what he himself was to her. His old friend's eyes had gone hard as glass. Heshai-kvo, the poet of Saraykeht, had died just after that, and Maati and Liat had left the city together without seeing Otah-kvo again.

The betrayal in those dark eyes haunted him. He wondered how much the anger had festered in his old teacher over the years. It might have grown to hatred by now, and Maati had come to hunt him down. The fire danced over the coal, flames turning the black to gray, the stone to powder. He realized that the boy poet had been speaking, and that the words had escaped him entirely. Maati took a pose of apology.

"My mind wandered. You were saying?"

"I offered to come by at first light," Cehmai said. "I can show you where the good teahouses are, and there's a streetcart that sells the best hot eggs and rice in the city. Then, perhaps, we can brave the library?"

"That sounds fine. Thank you. But now I think I'd best unpack my things and get some rest. You'll excuse me."

Cehmai bounced up in a pose of apology, realizing for the first time that his presence might not be totally welcome, and Maati waved it away. They made the ritual farewells, and when the door closed, Maati sighed and rose. He had few things: thick robes he had bought for the journey north, a few books including the small leatherbound volume of his dead master's that he had taken from Saraykeht, a packet of letters from Liat, the most recent of them years old now. The accumulated memories of a lifetime in two bags small enough to carry on his back if needed. It seemed thin. It seemed not enough.

He finished the tea and almond cakes, then went to the window, slid the paper-thin stone shutter aside, and looked out into the darkness. Sunset still breathed indigo into the western skyline. The city glittered with torches and lanterns, and to the south the glow of the forges of the smith's quarter looked like a brush fire. The towers rose black against the stars, windows lit high above him where some business took place in the dark, thin air. Maati sighed, the night cold in his face and lungs. All these unknown streets, these towers, and the lacework of tunnels that ran beneath the city: midwinter roads, he'd heard them called. And somewhere in the labyrinth, his old friend and teacher lurked, planning murder.

Maati let his imagination play a scene: Otah-kvo appearing before him in the darkness, blade in hand. In Maati's imagination, his eyes were hard, his voice hoarse with anger. And there he faltered. He might call for help and see Otah captured. He might fight him and end the thing in blood. He might accept the knife as his due. For a dream with so vivid a beginning, Maati could not envision the end.

He closed the shutter and went to throw another black stone onto the fire. His indulgence had turned the room chilly, and he sat on the cushion near the fire as the air warmed again. His legs didn't fold as easily as Cehmai's had, but if he shifted now and again, his feet didn't go numb. He found himself thinking fondly of Cehmai—the boy was easy to befriend. Otah-kvo had been like that, too.

Maati stretched and wondered again whether, if all this had been a song, he would have sung the hero's part or the villain's.

NO ONE HAD EVER SEEN IDAAN'S REBELLIONS AS HUNGER. THAT HAD BEEN their fault. If her friends or her brothers transgressed against the etiquette of the court, consequences came upon them, shame or censure.

But Idaan was the favored daughter. She might steal a rival girl's gown or arrive late to the temple and interrupt the priest. She could evade her chaperones or steal wine from the kitchens or dance with inappropriate men. She was Idaan Machi, and she could do as she saw fit, because she didn't matter. She was a woman. And if she'd never screamed at her father in the middle of his court that she was as much his child as Biitrah or Danat or Kaiin, it was because she feared in her bones that he would only agree, make some airy comment to dismiss the matter, and leave her more desperate than before.

Perhaps if once someone had taken her to task, had treated her as if her actions had the same weight as other people's, things would have ended differently.

Or perhaps folly is folly because you can't see where it moves from ambition into evil. Arguments that seem solid and powerful prove hollow once it's too late to turn back. Arguments like *Why should it be right for them but wrong for me?*

She haunted the Second Palace now, breathing in the emptiness that her eldest brother had left. The vaulted arches of stone and wood echoed her soft footsteps, and the sunlight that filtered though the stone shutters thickened the air to a golden twilight. Here was the bedchamber, bare even of the mattress he and his wife had slept upon. There, the workshop where he had labored on his enthusiasms, keeping engineers by his side sometimes late into the night or on into morning. The tables were empty now. Dust lay thick on them, ignored even by the servants until the time came for some new child of the Khaiem to take residence . . . to live in this opulence and keep his ear pricked for the sound of his brother's hunting dogs.

She heard Adrah coming long before he stepped into the room. She recognized his gait by the sound of it, and didn't call. He was clever, she thought bitterly; if he wanted to find her, he could puzzle it out. Adrah Vaunyogi, bright-eyed and broad-shouldered, father of her children if all went well. Whatever *well* meant anymore.

"There you are," Adrah said. She could see his anger in the way he held his body.

"What have I done this time?" she demanded, her tone carrying a sarcasm that dismissed his concerns even before he spoke them. "Did your patrons want me to wear red on a day I chose yellow?"

The mention of his backers, even as obliquely as that, made him stiffen and peer around, looking for slaves or servants who might over-hear. Idaan laughed—a cruel, short sound.

"You look like a kitten with a bell on its tail," she said. "There's no one here but us. You needn't worry that someone will roll the rock off our little conspiracy. We're as safe here as anywhere."

Adrah strode over and crouched beside her all the same. He smelled of crushed violets and sage, and it struck Idaan that it had not been so long ago that the scent would have warmed her heart and brought a flush to her cheeks. His face was long and pretty—almost too pretty to be a man's. She had kissed those lips a thousand times, but now it seemed like the act of another woman—some entirely different Idaan Machi whose body and memory she had inherited when the first girl died. She smiled and raised her hands in a pose of formal query.

"Are you mad?" Adrah demanded. "Don't speak about them. Not ever. If we're found out . . ."

"Yes. You're right. I'm sorry," Idaan said. "I wasn't thinking."

"There are rumors you spent a day with Cehmai and the andat. You were seen."

"The rumors are true, and I meant to be seen. I can't see how my having a close relationship to the poet would hurt the cause, and in fact I think it will help, don't you? When the time comes that half the houses of the utkhaiem are vying for my father's chair, an upstart house like yours would do well to boast a friendship with Cehmai."

"I think being married to a daughter of the Khai will be quite enough, thank you," Adrah said, "and your brothers aren't dead yet, in case you'd forgotten."

"No. I remember."

"I don't want you acting strangely. Things are too delicate just now for you to start attracting attention. You are my lover, and if you are off half the time drinking rice wine with the poet, people won't be saying that I have strong friendship with him. They'll be saying that he's cuck-olding me, and that Vaunyogi is the wrong house to draw a new Khai from."

"So you don't want me seeing him, or you just want more discretion when I do?" Idaan asked.

That stopped him. His eyes, deep brown with flecks of red and green, peered into hers. A sudden memory, powerful as illness, swept over her of a winter night when they had met in the tunnels. He had gazed at her then by firelight, had been no further from her than he was now. She wondered how these could be those same eyes. Her hand rose as if by itself and stroked his cheek. He folded his hands around hers.

"I'm sorry," she said, ashamed of the catch in her voice. "I don't want to quarrel with you."

"What are you doing, little one?" he asked. "Don't you see how dangerous this is that we're doing? Everything rests on it."

"I know. I remember the stories. It's strange, don't you think, that my brothers can slaughter each other and all the people do is applaud, but if I take a hand, it's a crime worse than anything."

"You're a woman," he said, as if that explained everything.

"And you," she said calmly, almost lovingly, "are a schemer and an agent of the Galts. So perhaps we deserve each other."

She felt him stiffen and then force the tension away. His smile was crooked. She felt something warm in her breast—painful and sad and warm as the first sip of rum on a midwinter night. She wondered if it might be hatred, and if it were, whether it was for herself or this man before her.

"It's going to be fine," he said.

"I know," she said. "I knew it would be hard. It's the *ways* it's hard that surprise me. I don't know how I should act or who I should be. I don't know where the normal grief that anyone would feel stops or turns into something else." She shook her head. "This seemed simpler when we were only talking about it."

"I know, love. It will be simple again, I promise you. It's only this in the middle that feels complicated."

"I don't know how they do it," she said. "I don't know how they kill one another. I dream about him, you know. I dream that I am walking through the gardens or the palaces and I see him in among a crowd of people." Tears came to her eyes unbidden, flowing warm and thick down her cheeks, but her voice, when she continued, was steady and calm as a woman predicting the weather. "He's always happy in the dreams. He's always forgiven me."

"I'm sorry," he said. "I know you loved him."

Idaan nodded, but didn't speak.

"Be strong, love. It will be over soon. It will all be finished very soon."

She wiped the tears away with the back of her hand, her knuckles darkened where her paints were running, and pulled him close. He seemed to hold back for a moment, then folded against her, his arms around her trembling shoulders. He was warm and the smell of sage and violet was mixed now with his skin—the particular musk of his body that she had treasured once above all other scents. He murmured small comforts into her ears and stroked her hair as she wept.

"Is it too late?" she asked. "Can we stop it, Adrah? Can we take it all back?"

He kissed her eyes, his lips soft as a girl's. His voice was calm and implacable and hard as stone. When she heard it, she knew he had been thinking himself down the same pathways and had come to the same place.

"No, love. It's too late. It was too late as soon as your brother died. We have started, and there's no ending it now except to win through or die."

They stayed still in each others' embrace. If all went well, she would die an old woman in this man's arms, or he would die in hers. While their sons killed one another. And there had been a time not half a year ago she'd thought the prize worth winning.

"I should go," she murmured. "I have to attend to my father. There's some dignitary just come to the city that I'm to smile at."

"Have you heard of the others? Kaiin and Danat?"

"Nothing," Idaan said. "They've vanished. Gone to ground."

"And the other one? Otah?"

Idaan pulled back, straightening the sleeves of her robes as she spoke.

"Otah's a story that the utkhaiem tell to make the song more interesting. He's likely not even alive any longer. Or if he is, he's wise enough to have no part of this."

"Are you certain of that?"

"Of course not," she said. "But what else can I give you?"

They spoke little after that. Adrah walked with her through the gardens of the Second Palace and then out to the street. Idaan made her way to her rooms and sent for the slave boy who repainted her face. The sun hadn't moved the width of two hands together before she strode again though the high palaces, her face cool and perfect as a player's mask. The formal poses of respect and deference greeted and steadied her. She was Idaan Machi, daughter of the Khai and wife, though none knew it yet, of the man who would take his place. She forced confidence into her spine, and the men and women around her reacted as if it were real. Which, she supposed, meant that it was. And that the sorrow and darkness they could not see were false.

When she entered the council chambers, her father greeted her with a silent pose of welcome. He looked ill, his skin gray and his mouth pinched by the pain in his belly. The delicate lanterns of worked iron and silver made the wood-sheathed walls glow, and the cushions that lined the floor were thick and soft as pillows. The men who sat on them—yes, men, all of them—made their obeisances to her, but her father motioned her closer. She walked to his side and knelt.

"There is someone I wish you to meet," her father said, gesturing to an awkward man in the brown robes of a poet. "The Dai-kvo has sent him. Maati Vaupathai has come to study in our library."

Fear flushed her mouth with the taste of metal, but she simpered and took a pose of welcome as if the words had meant nothing. Her mind raced, ticking through ways that the Dai-kvo could have discovered her, or Adrah, or the Galts. The poet replied to her gesture with a formal pose of gratitude, and she took the opportunity to look at him more closely. The body was soft as a scholar's, the lines of his face round as dough, but there was a darkness to his eyes that had nothing to do with color or light. She felt certain he was someone worth fearing.

"The library?" she said. "That's dull. Surely there are more interesting things in the city than room after room of old scrolls."

"Scholars have strange enthusiasms," the poet said. "But it's true, I've never been to any of the winter cities before. I'm hoping that not all my time will be taken in study."

There had to be a reason that the Dai-kvo and the Galts wanted the same thing. There had to be a reason that they each wanted to plumb the depths of the library of Machi.

"And how have you found the city, Maati-cha?" she asked. "When you haven't been studying."

"It is as beautiful as I had been told," the poet said.

"He has been here only a few days," her father said. "Had he come earlier, I would have had your brothers here to guide him, but perhaps you might introduce him to your friends."

"I would be honored," Idaan said, her mind considering the thousand ways that this might be a trap. "Perhaps tomorrow evening you would join me for tea in the winter gardens. I have no doubt there are many people who would be pleased to join us."

"Not too many, I hope," he said. He had an odd voice, she thought. As if he was amused at something. As if he knew how badly he had shaken her. Her fear shifted slightly, and she raised her chin. "I already find myself forgetting names I should remember," the poet continued. "It's most embarrassing."

"I will be pleased to remind you of my own, should it be required," she said. Her father's movement was almost too slight to see, but she caught it and cast her gaze down. Perhaps she had gone too far. But when the poet spoke, he seemed to have taken no offense.

"I expect I will remember yours, Idaan-cha. It would be very rude not to. I look forward to meeting your friends and seeing your city. Perhaps even more than closeting myself in your library."

He had to know. He *had* to. Except that she was not being led away under guard. She was not being taken to the quiet chambers and questioned. If he did not know, he must only suspect.

Let him suspect, then. She would get word to Adrah and the Galts. They would know better than she what to do with this Maati Vaupathai. If he was a threat, he would be added to the list. Biitrah, Danat, Kaiin, Otah, Maati. The men she would have to kill or have killed. She smiled at him gently, and he nodded to her. One more name could make little difference now, and he, at least, was no one she loved.

"WHEN ARE THEY SENDING YOU?" KIYAN ASKED AS SHE POURED OUT THE bucket. Gray water flowed over the bricks that paved the small garden at the back of the wayhouse. Otah took the longhandled brush and swept the water off to the sides, leaving the walkway deep red and glistening in the sunlight. He felt Kiyan's gaze on him, felt the question in the air. The gardens smelled of fresh turned earth. Spices for the kitchen grew here. In a few weeks, the place would be thick with growing things: basil and mint and thyme. He imagined scrubbing these bricks week after week over the span of years until they wore smooth or he died, and felt an irrational surge of fondness for the walkway. He smiled to himself.

"Itani?"

"I don't know. That is, I know they want me to go to Machi in two weeks time. Amiit Foss is sending half the couriers he has up there, it seems."

"Of course he is. It's where everything's happening."

"But I haven't decided to go."

The silence bore down on him now, and he turned. Kiyan stood in the doorway—in her doorway. Her crossed arms, her narrowed eyes, and the single frown-line drawn vertically between her brows, made Otah smile. He leaned on his brush.

"We need to talk, sweet," he said. "There are some things . . . we have some business, I think, to attend to."

Kiyan answered by taking the brush from him, leaning it against the wall, and marching to a meeting room at the back of the house. It was small but formal, with a thick wooden door and a window that looked out on the corner of the interior courtyard. The sort of place she might give to a diplomat or a courier for an extra length of copper. The sort of place it would be difficult to be overheard. That was as it should be.

Kiyan sat carefully, her face as blank as that of a man playing tiles. Otah sat across from her, careful not to touch her hand. She was holding herself back, he knew. She was restraining herself from hoping until she knew, so that if what he said did not match what she longed to hear, the disappointment would not be so heavy. For a moment, his mind flickered back to a bathhouse in Saraykeht and another woman's eyes. He had had this conversation once before, and he doubted he would ever have it again.

"I don't want to go to the north," Otah said. "For more reasons than one."

"Why not?" Kiyan asked.

"Sweet, there are some things I haven't told you. Things about my family. About myself. . . ."

And so he began, slowly, carefully, to tell the story. He was the son of the Khai Machi, but his sixth son. One of those cast out by his family and sent to the school where the sons of the Khaiem and utkhaiem struggled in hope of one day being selected to be poets and wield the power of the andat. He had been chosen once, and had walked away. Itani Noygu was the name he had chosen for himself, the man he had made of himself. But he was also Otah Machi.

He was careful to tell the story well. He more than half expected her to laugh at him. Or to accuse him of a self-aggrandizing madness. Or to sweep him into her arms and say that she'd known, she'd always known he was something more than a courier. Kiyan defeated all the stories he had spun in his dreams of this moment. She merely listened, arms crossed, eyes turned toward the window. The vertical line between her brows deepened slightly, and that was all. She did not move or ask questions until he had nearly reached the end. All that was left was to tell her he'd chosen to take her offer to work with her here at the wayhouse, but she knew that already and lifted her hands before he could say the words.

"Itani . . . lover, if this isn't true . . . if this is a joke, please tell me. Now."

"It isn't a joke," he said.

She took a deep breath, letting it out slowly. When she spoke, she seemed calm in a way that he knew meant rage beyond expression. At the first tone of it, his heart went tight.

"You have to leave. Now. Tonight. You have to leave and never come back."

"Kiyan-kya . . ."

"No. No *kya*. No *sweet*. No *my love*. None of that. You have to leave my house and you can't ever come back or tell anyone who you are or who I am or that we knew each other once. Do you understand that?"

"I understand that you're angry with me," Otah said, leaning toward her. "You have a right to be. But you don't know how carefully I have had to guard this."

Kiyan tilted her head, like a fox that's heard a strange noise, then laughed once.

"You think I'm upset you didn't tell me? You think I'm upset because you had a secret and you didn't spill it the first time we shared a bed? Itani, this may surprise you, but I have secrets a thousand times less important than that, and I've kept them a hundred times better."

"But you want me to leave?

"Of course I want you to leave. Are you dim? Do you know what happened to the men who guarded your eldest brother? They're dead. Do you recall what happened when the Khai Yalakeht's sons turned on each other six years back? There were a dozen corpses before that was through, and only two of them were related to the Khai. Now look around you. How do you expect me to protect my house? How can I protect Old Mani? And think before you speak, because if you tell me that you'll be strong and manly and protect me, I swear by all the gods I'll turn you in myself."

"No one will find out," Otah said.

She closed her eyes. A tear broke free, tracing a bright line down her cheek. When he leaned close, reaching out to wipe it away, she slapped his hand before it touched her.

"I would almost be willing to take that chance, if it were only me. Not quite, but nearly. It isn't, though. It's everyone and everything I've worked for."

"Kiyan-kya, together we could . . ."

"Do nothing. Together we could do nothing, because you are leaving now. And odd as it sounds, I *do* understand. Why you concealed what you did, why you told me now. And I hope ghosts haunt you and chew out your eyes at night. I hope all the gods there are damn you for making me love you and then doing this to me. Now get out. If you're here in half a hand's time, I will call for the guard."

Outside the window, a flutter of wings and then the fluting melody of a songbird. The constant distant sound of the river. The scent of pine.

"Do you believe me?" she asked. "That I'll call the guard on you if you stay?"

"I do," he said.

"Then go."

"I love you."

"I know you do, 'Tani-kya. Go."

House Siyanti had quarters in the city for its people—small rooms hardly large enough for a cot and a brazier, but the blankets were thick and soft, and the kitchens sold meals at half the price a cart on the street would. When the rain came that night, Otah lay in the glow of the coals and listened to patter of water against leaves mix with the voices from the covered courtyard. Someone was playing a nomad's harp, and the music was lively and sorrowful at the same time. Sometimes voices would rise up together in song or laughter. He turned Kiyan's words over in his mind and noticed how empty they made him feel.

He'd been a fool to tell her, a fool to say anything. If he had only kept his secrets secret, he could have made a life for himself based on lies, and if the brothers he only knew as shadows and moments from a half-recalled childhood had ever discovered him, Kiyan and Old Mani and anyone else unfortunate enough to know him might have been killed without even knowing why.

Kiyan had not been wrong.

A gentle murmur of thunder came and went. Otah rose from his cot and walked out. Amiit Foss kept late hours, and Otah found him sitting at a fire grate, poking the crackling flames with a length of iron while he joked over his shoulder with the five men and four women who lounged on cushions and low chairs. He smiled when he saw Otah and called for a bowl of wine for him. The gathering looked so calm and felt so relaxed that only someone in the gentleman's trade would have recognized it for the business meeting that it was.

"Itani-cha is one of the couriers I mean to send north, if I can pry him away from his love of sloth and comfort," Amiit said with a smile. The others greeted him and made him welcome. Otah sat by the fire and listened. There would be nothing said here that he was not permitted to know. Amiit's introduction had established with the subtlety of a master Otah's rank and the level of trust to be afforded him, and no one in the room was so thick as to misunderstand him.

The news from the north was confusing. The two surviving sons of Machi had vanished. Neither had appeared in the other cities of the Khaiem, going to courts and looking for support as tradition would have them do. Nor had the streets of Machi erupted in bloodshed as their bases of power within the city vied for advantage. The best estimates were that the old Khai wouldn't see another winter, and even some of the houses of the utkhaiem seemed to be preparing to offer up their sons as the new Khai should the succession fail to deliver a single living heir. Something very quiet was happening, and House Siyanti—like everyone else in the world—was aching with curiosity. Otah could hear it in their voices, could see it in the way they held their wine. Even when the conversation shifted to the glassblowers of Cetani and the collapse of the planned summer fair in Amnat-Tan, all minds were drawn toward Machi. He sipped his wine.

Going north was dangerous. He knew that, and still it didn't escape him that the Khai Machi dying by inches was his father, that these men were the brothers he knew only as vague memories. And because of these men, he had lost everything again. If he was going to be haunted his whole life by the city, perhaps he should at least see it. The only thing he risked was his life.

At length, the conversation turned to less weighty matters and—without a word or shift in voice or manner—the meeting was ended. Otah spoke as much as any, laughed as much, and sang as loudly when the pipe players joined them. But when he stretched and turned to leave, Amiit Foss was at his side. Otah and the overseer left together, as if they had only happened to rise at the same time, and Otah knew that no one in the drunken, boisterous room they left had failed to notice it.

"So, it sounds as if all the interesting things in the world were happening in Machi," Otah said as they strode back through the hallways of the house compound. "You are still hoping to send me there?"

"I've been hoping," Amiit Foss agreed. "But I have other plans if you have some of your own."

"I don't," Otah said, and Amiit paused. In the dim lantern light, Otah let the old man search his face. Something passed over Amiit, the ghost of some old sorrow, and then he took a pose of condolence.

"I thought you had come to quit the house," Amiit said.

"I'd meant to," Otah said, surprised at himself for admitting it.

Amiit gestured Otah to follow him, and together they retired to Amiit's apartments. The rooms were large and warm, hung with tapestries and lit by a dozen candles. Otah sat on a low seat by a table, and Amiit took a box from his shelf. Inside were two small porcelain bowls and a white stoppered bottle that matched them. When Amiit poured, the scent of rice wine filled the room.

"We drink to the gods," Amiit said, raising his bowl. "May they never drink to us."

Otah drank the wine at a gulp. It was excellent, and he felt his throat grow warmer. He looked at the empty bowl in his fingers and nodded. Amiit grinned.

"It was a gift from an old friend," Amiit said. "I love to drink it, but I hate to drink alone."

"I'm pleased to be of service," Otah said as Amiit filled the bowl again.

"So things with the woman didn't work out?"

"No," Otah said.

"I'm sorry."

"It was entirely my fault."

"If it's true, you're a wise man to know it, and if not, you're a good man for saying it. Either way."

"I think it would be . . . that is, if there are any letters to be carried, I think travel might be the best thing just now. I don't really care to stay in Udun."

Amiit sighed and nodded.

"Tomorrow," he said. "Come to my offices in the morning. We'll arrange something."

Afterwards, they finished the rice wine and talked of nothing important—of old stories and old travels, the women they had known and loved or else hated. Or both. Otah said nothing of Kiyan or the north, and Amiit didn't press him. When Otah rose to leave, he was surprised to find how drunk he had become. He navigated his way to his room and lay on the couch, mustering the resolve to pull off his robes. Morning found him still dressed. He changed robes and went down to the bathhouse, forcing his mind back over his conversations of the night before. He was fairly certain he had said nothing to implicate himself or make Amiit suspect the nature of his falling out with Kiyan. He wondered what the old man would have made of the truth, had he known it.

The packet of letters waited for him, each sewn and sealed, in a leather bag on Amiit Foss' desk. Most were for trading houses in Machi, though there were four that were to go to members of the utkhaiem. Otah turned the packet in his hands. Behind him, one of the apprentices said something softly and another giggled.

"You have time to reconsider," Amiit said. "You could go back to her on your knees. If the letters wait another day, there's little lost. And she might relent."

Otah tucked the letters into their pouch and slipped it into his sleeve.

"An old lover of mine once told me that everything I'd ever won, I won by leaving," Otah said.

"The island girl?"

"Did I mention her last night?"

"At length," Amiit said, chuckling. "That particular quotation came up twice, as I recall. There might have been a third time too. I couldn't really say."

"I'm sorry to hear that. I hope I didn't tell you all my secrets," Otah said, making a joke of his sudden unease. He didn't recall saying anything about Maj, and it occurred to him exactly how dangerous that night had been.

"If you had, I'd make it a point to forget them," Amiit said. "Nothing a drunk man says on the day his woman leaves him should be held against him. It's poor form. And this is, after all, a gentleman's trade, ne?"

Otah took a pose of agreement.

"I'll report what I find when I get back," he said, unnecessarily. "Assuming I haven't frozen to death on the roads."

"Be careful up there, Itani. Things are uncertain when there's the scent of a new Khai in the wind. It's interesting, and it's important, but it's not always safe."

Otah shifted to a pose of thanks, to which his supervisor replied in kind, his face so pleasantly unreadable that Otah genuinely didn't know how deep the warning ran.

3

When Maati considered the mines—something he had rarely had occasion to do—he had pictured great holes going deep into the earth. He had not imagined the branchings and contortions of passages where miners struggled to follow veins of ore, the stench of dust and damp, the yelps and howls of the dogs that pulled the flat-bottomed sledges filled with gravel, or the darkness. He held his lantern low, as did the others around him. There was no call to raise it. Nothing more would be seen, and the prospect of breaking it against the stone overhead was unpleasant.

"There can be places where the air goes bad, too," Cehmai said as they turned another twisting corner. "They take birds with them because they die first."

"What happens then?" Maati asked. "If the birds die?"

"It depends on how valuable the ore is," the young poet said. "Abandon the mine, or try to blow out the bad air. Or use slaves. There are men whose indentures allow that."

Two servants followed at a distance, their own torches glowing. Maati had the sense that they would all, himself included, have been better pleased to spend the day in the palaces. All but the andat. Stone-Made-Soft alone among them seemed untroubled by the weight over them and the gloom that pressed in when the lanterns flickered. The wide, calm face seemed almost stupid to Maati, the andat's occasional pronouncements simplistic compared with the thousand-layered comments of Seedless, the only andat he'd known intimately. He knew better than to be taken in. The form of the andat might be different, the mental bindings that held it might place different strictures upon it, but the hunger at its center was as desperate. It was an andat, and it would long to return to its natural state. They might seem as different as a marble from a thorn, but at heart they were all the same.

And Maati knew he was walking through a tunnel not so tall he could stand to his full height with a thousand tons of stone above him. This placid-faced ghost could bring it down on him as if they'd been crawling through a hole in the ocean.

"So, you see," Cehmai was saying, "the Daikani engineers find where they want to extend the mine out. Or down, or up. We have to leave that to them. Then I will come through and walk through the survey with them, so that we all understand what they're asking."

"And how much do you soften it?"

"It varies," Cehmai said. "It depends on the kind of rock. Some of them you can almost reduce to putty if you're truly clear where you want it to be. Then other times, you only want it to be easier to dig through. Most often, that's when they're concerned about collapses."

"I see," Maati said. "And the pumps? How do those figure in?"

"That was actually an entirely different agreement. The Khai's eldest son was interested in the problem. The mines here are some of the lowest that are still in use. The northern mines are almost all in the mountains, and so they aren't as likely to strike water."

"So the Daikani pay more for being here?"

"No, not really. The pumps he designed usually work quite well."

"But the payment for them?"

Cehmai grinned. His teeth and skin were yellowed by the lantern light.

"It was a different agreement," Cehmai said again. "The Daikani let him experiment with his designs and he let them use them."

"But if they worked well . . ."

"Other mines would pay the Khai for the use of the pumps if they wished for help building them. Usually, though, the mines will help each other on things like that. There's a certain . . . what to call it . . . brotherhood? The miners take care of each other, whatever house they work for."

"Might we see the pumps?"

"If you'd like," he said. "They're back in the deeper parts of the mine. If you don't mind walking down farther. . . ."

Maati forced a grin and did not look at the wide face of the andat turning toward him.

"Not at all," he said. "Let's go down."

The pumps, when he found them at last, were ingenious. A series of treadmills turned huge corkscrews that lifted the water up to pools where another corkscrew waited to lift it higher again. They did not keep the deepest tunnels dry—the walls there seemed to weep as Maati waded through warm, knee-high water—but they kept it clear enough to work. Machi had, Cehmai assured him, the deepest tunnels in the world. Maati did not ask if they were the safest.

They found the mine's overseer here in the depths. Voices seemed to carry better in the watery tunnels than up above, but Maati could not make out the words clearly until they were almost upon him. A small, thick-set man with a darkness to him that made Maati think of grime worked so deeply into skin that it would never come clean, he took a pose of welcome as they approached.

"We've an honored guest come to the city," Cehmai said.

"We've had many honored guests in the *city*," the overseer said, with a grin. "Damn few in the bottom of the hole, though. There's no palaces down here."

"But Machi's fortunes rest on its mines," Maati said. "So in a sense these are the deepest cellars of the palaces. The ones where the best treasures are hidden."

The overseer grinned.

"I like this one," he said to Cehmai. "He's got a quick head on him."

"I heard about the pumps the Khai's eldest son had designed," Maati said. "I was wondering if you could tell me of them?"

The grin widened, and the overseer launched into an expansive and delighted discussion of water and mines and the difficulty of removing the one from the other. Maati listened, struggling to follow the vocabulary and grammar particular to the trade.

"He had a gift for them," the overseer said, at last. His voice was melancholy. "We'll keep at them, these pumps, and they'll get better, but not like they would have with Biitrah-cha on them."

"He was here, I understand, on the day he was killed," Maati said. He saw the young poet's head shift, turning to consider him, and he ignored it as he had the andat's.

"That's truth. And I wish he'd stayed. His brothers aren't bad men, but they aren't miners. And . . . well, he'll be missed."

"I had thought it odd, though," Maati said. "Whichever brother killed him, they had to know where he would be—that he would be called out here, and that the work would take so much of the day that he wouldn't return to the city itself."

"I suppose that's so," the overseer said.

"Then someone knew your pumps would fail," Maati said.

The lamplight flickered off the surface of the water, casting shadows up the overseer's face as this sank in. Cehmai coughed. Maati said nothing, did not move, waited. If any man here had been involved with it, the overseer was most likely. But Maati saw no rage or wariness in his expression, only the slow blooming of implication that might be expected in a man who had not thought the murder through. So perhaps he could be used after all.

"You're saying someone sabotaged my pumps to get him out here," the overseer said at last.

Maati wished deeply that Cehmai and his andat were not present—this was a thing better done alone. But the moment had arrived, and there was nothing to be done but go forward. The servants at least were far enough away not to overhear if he spoke softly. Maati dug in his sleeve and came out with a letter and a small leather pouch, heavy with silver lengths. He pressed them both into the surprised overseer's hands.

"If you should discover who did, I would very much like to speak with them before the officers of the utkhaiem or the head of your House. That letter will tell you how to find me."

The overseer tucked away the pouch and letter, taking a pose of thanks which Maati waved away. Cehmai and the andat were silent as stones.

"And how long is it you've been working these mines?" Maati asked, forcing a lightness to his tone he did not feel. Soon the overseer was regaling them with stories of his years underground, and they were walking together toward the surface again. By the time Maati stepped out from the long, sloping throat of the mine and into daylight, his feet were numb. A litter waited for them, twelve strong men prepared to carry the three of them back to the palaces. Maati stopped for a moment to wring the water from the hem of his robes and to appreciate having nothing but the wide sky above him.

"Why was it the Dai-kvo sent you?" Cehmai asked as they climbed into the wooden litter. His voice was almost innocent, but even the an-dat was looking at Maati oddly.

"There are suggestions that the library may have some old refer-ences that the Dai-kvo lacks. Things that touch on the grammars of the first poets."

"Ah," Cehmai said. The litter lurched and rose, swaying slightly as the servants bore them away back to the palaces. "And nothing more than that?"

"Of course not," Maati said. "What more could there be?"

He knew that he was convincing no one. And that was likely a fine thing. Maati had spent his first days in Machi learning the city, the courts, the teahouses. The Khai's daughter had introduced him to the gatherings of the younger generation of the utkhaiem as the poet Cehmai had to the elder. Maati had spent each night walking a differ-ent quarter of the city, wrapped in thick wool robes with close hoods against the vicious cold of the spring air. He had learned the intrigues of the court: which houses were vying for marriages to which cities, who was likely to be extorting favors for whom over what sorts of indiscre-tion, all the petty wars of a family of a thousand children.

He had used the opportunities to spread the name of Itani Noygu—saying only that he was an old friend Maati had heard might be in the city, whom he would very much like to see. There was no way to say that it was the name Otah Machi had invented for himself in Saraykeht, and even if there had been, Maati would likely not have done so. He had come to realize exactly how little he knew what he ought to do.

He had been sent because he knew Otah, knew how his old friend's mind worked, would recognize him should they meet. They were ad-vantages, Maati supposed, but it was hard to weigh them against his in-experience. There was little enough to learn of making discreet inquiries when your life was spent in the small tasks of the Dai-kvo's village. An overseer of a trading house would have been better suited to the task. A negotiator, or a courier. Liat would have been better, the woman he had once loved, who had once loved him. Liat, mother of the boy Nayiit, whom Maati had held as a babe and loved more than water or air. Liat, who had been Otah's lover as well.

For the thousandth time, Maati put that thought aside.

When they reached the palaces, Maati again thanked Cehmai for

taking the time from his work to accompany him, and Cehmai—still
with the half-certain stance of a dog hearing an unfamiliar sound—
assured him that he'd been pleased to do so. Maati watched the slight
young man and his thick-framed andat walk away across the flagstones
of the courtyard. Their hems were black and sodden, ruining the drape
of the robes. Much like his own, he knew.

Thankfully, his own apartments were warm. He stripped off his
robes, leaving them in a lump for the servants to remove to a launderer,
and replaced them with the thickest he had—lamb's wool and heavy
leather with a thin cotton lining. It was the sort that natives of Machi
wore in deep winter, but Maati pulled it close about him, vowing to use
it whenever he went out, whatever the others might think of him. His
boots thrown into a corner, he stretched his pale, numb feet almost into
the fire grate and shuddered. He would have to go to the wayhouse
where Biitrah Machi had died. The owners there had spoken to the officers of the utkhaiem, of course. They had told their tale of the moon-
faced man who had come with letters of introduction, worked in their
kitchens, and been ready to take over for a night when the overseers all
came down ill. Still, he could not be sure there was nothing more to
know unless he made his visit. Some other day, when he could feel his
toes.

The summons came to him when the sun—red and angry—was just
preparing to slide behind the mountains to the west. Maati pulled on
thick, warm boots of soft leather, added his brown poet's robes over the
warmer ones, and let himself be led to the Khai Machi's private chambers. He passed through several rooms on his way—a hall of worked
marble the color of honey with a fountain running through it like a
creek, a meeting chamber large enough to hold two dozen at a single
table, then a smaller corridor that led to chambers of a more human size.
Ahead of him, a woman passed from one side of the corridor to the other
leaving the impression of night-black hair, warm brown skin, and robes
the yellow of sunrise. One of the wives, Maati knew, of a man who had
several.

At last, the servant slid open a door of carved rosewood, and Maati
stepped into a room hardly larger than his own bedroom. The old man
sat on a couch, his feet toward the fire that burned in the grate. His
robes were lush, the silks seeming to take up the firelight and dance
with it. They seemed more alive than his flesh. Slowly, the Khai raised

a clay pipe to his mouth and puffed on it thoughtfully. The smoke smelled rich and sweet as a cane field on fire.

Maati took a pose of greeting as formal as high court. The Khai Machi raised an ancient eyebrow and only smiled. With the stem of the pipe, he pointed to the couch opposite him and nodded to Maati that he should sit.

"They make me smoke this," the Khai said. "Whenever my belly troubles me, they say. I tell them they might as well make it air, burn it by the bushel in all the firekeeper's kilns, but they only laugh as if it were wit, and I play along."

"Yes, most high."

There was a long pause as the Khai contemplated the flames. Maati waited, uncertain. He noticed the catch in the Khai Machi's breath, as if it pained him. He had not noticed it before.

"Your search for my outlaw son," the Khai said. "It is going well?"

"It is early yet, most high. I have made myself visible. I have let it be known that I am looking into the death of your son."

"You still expect Otah to come to you?"

"Yes."

"And if he does not?"

"Then it will take more time, most high. But I will find him."

The old man nodded, then exhaled a plume of pale smoke. He took a pose of gratitude, his wasted hands holding the position with the grace of a lifetime's practice.

"His mother was a good woman. I miss her. Iyrah, her name was. She gave me Idaan too. She was glad to have a child of her own that she could keep."

Maati thought he saw the old man's eyes glisten for a moment, lost as he was in old memories of which Maati could only guess the substance. Then the Khai sighed.

"Idaan," the Khai said. "She's treated you gently?"

"She's been nothing but kind," Maati said, "and very generous with her time."

The Khai shook his head, smiling more to himself than his audience.

"That's good. She was always unpredictable. Age has calmed her, I think. There was a time she would study outrages the way most girls study face paints and sandals. Always sneaking puppies into court or stealing dresses she fancied from her little friends. She relied on me to keep her safe, however far she flew," he said, smiling fondly. "A mischievous girl, my daughter, but good-hearted. I'm proud of her."

Then he sobered.

"I am proud of all my children. It's why I am not of one mind on this," the Khai said. "You would think that I should be, but I am not. With every day that the search continues, the truce holds, and Kaiin and Danat still live. I've known since I was old enough to know anything that if I took this chair, my sons would kill each other. It wasn't so hard before I knew them, when they were only the idea of sons. But then they were Biitrah and Kaiin and Danat. And I don't want any of them to die."

"But tradition, most high. If they did not—"

"I know why they must," the Khai said. "I was only wishing. It's something dying men do, I'm told. Sit with their regrets. It's likely that which kills us as much as the sickness. I sometimes wish that this had all happened years ago. That they had slaughtered each other in their childhood. Then I might have at least one of them by me now. I had not wanted to die alone."

"You are not alone, most high. The whole court . . ."

Maati broke off. The Khai Machi took a pose accepting correction, but the amusement in his eyes and the angle of his shoulders made a sarcasm of it. Maati nodded, accepting the old man's point.

"I can't say which of them I would have wanted to live, though," the Khai said, puffing thoughtfully on his pipe. "I love them all. Very dearly. I cannot tell you how deeply I miss Biitrah."

"Had you known him, you would have loved Otah as well."

"You think so? Certainly you knew him better than I. I can't think he would have thought well of me," the Khai said. Then, "Did you go back? After you took your robes? Did you go to see you parents?"

"My father was very old when I went to the school," Maati said. "He died before I completed my training. We did not know each other."

"So you have never had a family."

"I have, most high," Maati said, fighting to keep the tightness in his chest from changing the tone of his voice. "A lover and a son. I had a family once."

"But no longer. They died?"

"They live. Only not with me."

The Khai considered him, bloodshot eyes blinking slowly. With his thin, wrinkled skin, he reminded Maati of a very old turtle or else a very young bird. The Khai's gaze softened, his brows tilting in understanding and sorrow.

"It is never easy for fathers," the Khai said. "Perhaps if the world had needed less from us."

Maati waited a long moment until he trusted his voice.

"Perhaps, most high."

The Khai exhaled a breath of gray, his gaze trapped by the smoke.

"It isn't the world I knew when I was young," the old man said. "Everything changed when Saraykeht fell."

"The Khai Saraykeht has a poet," Maati said. "He has the power of the andat."

"It took the Dai-kvo eight years and six failed bindings," the Khai said. "And every time word came of another failure, I could see it in the faces of the court. The utkhaiem may put on proud faces, but I've seen the fear that swims under that ice. And you were there. You said so in the audience when I greeted you."

"Yes, most high."

"But you didn't say everything you knew," the Khai said. "Did you?"

The yellowed eyes fixed on Maati. The intelligence in them was unnerving. Maati felt himself squirming, and wondering what had happened to the melancholy dying man he'd been speaking with only moments before.

"I . . . that is . . ."

"There were rumors that the poet's death was more than an angry east island girl's revenge. The Galts were mentioned."

"And Eddensea," Maati said. "And Eymond. There was no end of accusation, most high. Some even believed what they charged. When the cotton trade collapsed, a great number of people lost a great amount of money. And prestige."

"They lost more than that," the Khai said, leaning forward and stabbing at the air with the stem of his pipe. "The money, the trade. The standing among the cities. They don't signify. Saraykeht was the death of *certainty*. They lost the conviction that the Khaiem would hold the world at bay, that war would never come to Saraykeht. And we lost it here too."

"If you say so, most high."

"The priests say that something touched by chaos is never made whole," the Khai said, sinking back into his cushions. "Do you know what they mean by that, Maati-cha?"

"I have some idea," Maati said, but the Khai went on.

"It means that something unthinkable can only happen once. Because after that, it's not unthinkable any longer. We've *seen* what happens when a city is touched by chaos. And now it's in the back of every head in every court in all the cities of the Khaiem."

Maati frowned and leaned forward.

"You think Cehmai-cha is in some danger?"

"What?" the Khai said, then waved the thought away, stirring the smoky air. "No. Not that. I think my city is at risk. I think Otah . . . my upstart son . . ."

He's forgiven you, a voice murmured in the back of Maati's mind. The voice of Seedless, the andat of Saraykeht. They were the words the andat had spoken to Maati in the instant before Heshai's death had freed it.

It had been speaking of Otah.

"I've called you here for a reason, Maati-cha," the Khai said, and Maati pulled his attention back to the present. "I didn't care to speak of it around those who would use it to fuel gossip. Your inquiry into Biitrah's death. You must move more quickly."

"Even with the truce?"

"Yes, even at the price of my sons returning to their tradition. If I die without a successor chosen—especially if Danat and Kaiin are still gone to ground—there will be chaos. The families of the utkhaiem start thinking that perhaps they would sit more comfortably in my chair, and schemes begin. Your task isn't only to find Otah. Your task is to protect my city."

"I understand, most high."

"You do not, Maati-cha. The spring roses are starting to bloom, and I will not see high summer. Neither of us has the luxury of time."

THE GATHERING WAS ALL THAT CEHMAI HAD HOPED FOR, AND LESS. SPRING breezes washed the pavilion with the scent of fresh flowers. Kilns set along the edges roared behind the music of reed organ, flute, and drum. Overhead, the stars shone like gems strewn on dark velvet. The long months of winter had given musicians time to compose and practice new songs, and the youth of the high families week after weary week to tire of the cold and dark and the terrible constriction that deep winter brought to those with no business to conduct on the snow.

Cehmai laughed and clapped time with the music and danced. Women and girls caught his eye, and he, theirs. The heat of youth did where heavier robes would otherwise have been called for, and the draw of body to body filled the air with something stronger than the perfume of flowers. Even the impending death of the Khai lent an air of license. Momentous things were happening, the world's order was changing, and they were young enough to find the thought romantic.

And yet he could not enjoy it.

A young man in an eagle's mask pressed a bowl of hot wine into his hand, and spun away into the dance. Cehmai grinned, sipped at it, and faded back to the edge of the pavilion. In the shadows behind the kilns, Stone-Made-Soft stood motionless. Cehmai sat beside it, put the bowl on the grass, and watched the revelry. Two young men had doffed their robes entirely and were sprinting around the wide grounds in nothing but their masks and long scarves trailing from their necks. The andat shifted like the first shudder of a landslide, then was still again. When it spoke, its voice was so soft that they would not be heard by the others.

"It wouldn't be the first time the Dai-kvo had lied."

"Or the first time I'd wondered why," Cehmai said. "It's his to decide what to say and to whom."

"And yours?"

"And mine to satisfy my curiosity. You heard what he said to the overseer in the mines. If he truly didn't want me to know, he would have lied better. Maati-kvo is looking into more than the library, and that's certain."

The andat sighed. Stone-Made-Soft had no more need of breath than did a mountainside. The exhalation could only be a comment. Cehmai felt the subject of their conversation changing even before the andat spoke.

"She's come."

And there, dressed black as rooks and pale as mourning, Idaan Machi moved among the dancers. Her mask hid only part of her face and not her identity. Wrapped as he was by the darkness, she did not see him. Cehmai felt a lightening in his breast as he watched her move through the crowd, greeting friends and looking, he thought, for something or perhaps someone among them. She was not beautiful—well painted, but any number of the girls and women were more nearly perfect. She was not the most graceful, or the best spoken, or any of the hundred things that Cehmai thought of when he tried to explain to himself why this girl should fascinate him. The closest he could come was that she was interesting, and none of the others were.

"It won't end well," the andat murmured.

"It hasn't begun," Cehmai said. "How can something end when it hasn't even started?"

Stone-Made-Soft sighed again, and Cehmai rose, tugging at his robes to smooth their lines. The music had paused and someone in the crowd laughed long and high.

"Come back when you've finished and we'll carry on our conversation," the andat said.

Cehmai ignored the patience in its voice and strode forward, back into the light. The reed organ struck a chord just as he reached Idaan's side. He brushed her arm, and she turned—first annoyed and then surprised and then, he thought, pleased.

"Idaan-cha," he said, the exaggerated formality acting as its opposite without taking him quite into the intimacy that the *kya* suffix would have suggested. "I'd almost thought you wouldn't be joining us."

"I almost wasn't," she said. "I hadn't thought you'd be here."

The organ set a beat, and the drums picked it up; the dance was beginning again. Cehmai held out a hand and, after a pause that took a thousand years and lasted perhaps a breath, Idaan took it. The music began in earnest, and Cehmai spun her, took her under his arm, and was turned by her. It was a wild tune, rich and fast with a rhythm like a racing heart. Around him the others were grinning, though not at him. Idaan laughed, and he laughed with her. The paving stones beneath them seemed to echo back the song, and the sky above them received it.

As they turned to face each other, he could see the flush in Idaan's cheek, and felt the same blood in his own, and then the music whirled them off again.

In the center of the frenzy, someone took Cehmai's elbow from behind, and something round and hard was pressed into his hands. A man's voice whispered urgently in his ear.

"Hold this."

Cehmai faltered, confused, and the moment was gone. He was suddenly standing alone in a throng of people, holding an empty bowl—a thread of wine wetting the rim—while Adrah Vaunyogi took Idaan Machi through the steps and turns of the dance. The pair shifted away from him, left him behind. Cehmai felt the flush in his cheek brighten. He turned and walked through the shifting bodies, handing the bowl to a servant as he left.

"He *is* her lover," the andat said. "Everyone knows it."

"I don't," Cehmai said.

"I just told you."

"You tell me things all the time; it doesn't mean I agree to them."

"This thing you have in mind," Stone-Made-Soft said. "You shouldn't do it."

Cehmai looked up into the calm gray eyes set in the wide, placid face. He felt his own head lift in defiance, even as he knew the words were truth. It was stupid and mean and petty. Adrah Vaunyogi wasn't even entirely in the wrong. There was a perspective by which the little humiliation Cehmai had been dealt was a small price for flirting so openly with another man's love.

And yet.

The andat nodded slowly and turned to consider the dancers. It was easy enough to pick out Idaan and Adrah. They were too far for Cehmai to be sure, but he liked to think she was frowning. It hardly mattered. Cehmai focused on Adrah's movements—his feet, shifting in time with the drums while Idaan danced to the flutes. He doubled his attention, feeling it through his own body and also the constant storm at the back of his mind. In that instant he was both of them—a single being with two bodies and a permanent struggle at the heart. And then, at just the moment when Adrah's foot came back to catch his weight, Cehmai reached out. The paving stone gave way, the smooth stone suddenly soft as mud, and Adrah stumbled backward and fell, landing on his rear, legs splayed. Cehmai waited a moment for the stone to flow back nearer to smooth, then let his consciousness return to its usual state. The storm that was Stone-Made-Soft was louder, more present in his mind, like the proud flesh where a thorn has scratched skin. And like a scratch, Cehmai knew it would subside.

"We should go," Cehmai said, "before I'm tempted to do something childish."

The andat didn't answer, and Cehmai led the way through the night-dark gardens. The music floated in the distance and then faded. Far from the kilns and dancing, the night was cold—not freezing, but near it. But the stars were brighter, and the moon glowed: a rim of silver that made the starless thumbprint darker by contrast. They passed by the temple and the counting house, the bathhouse and base of the great tower. The andat turned down a side path then, and paused when Cehmai did not follow.

Stone-Made-Soft took a pose of query.

"Is this not where you were going?" it asked.

Cehmai considered, and then smiled.

"I suppose it is," he said, and followed the captive spirit down the curving pathway and up the wide, shallow steps that led to the library. The great stone doors were barred from within, but Cehmai followed the thin gravel path at the side of the building, keeping close to the wall. The windows of Baarath's apartments glowed with more than a night candle's light. Even with the night half gone, he was awake. The door slave was an ancient man, and Cehmai had to shake him by the shoulder before he woke, retreated into the apartments, and returned to lead them in.

The apartments smelled of old wine, and the sandalwood resin that Baarath burned in his brazier. The tables and couches were covered with books and scrolls, and no cushion had escaped from some ink stain. Baarath, dressed in deep red robes thick as tapestry, rose from his desk and took a pose of welcome. His copper torc of office was lying discarded on the floor at his feet.

"Cehmai-cha, to what do I owe this honor?"

Cehmai frowned. "Are you angry with me?" he asked.

"Of course not, great poet. How could a poor man of books dare to feel angry with a personage like yourself?"

"Gods," Cehmai said as he shifted a pile of papers from a wide chair. "I don't know, Baarath-kya. Do tell me."

"Kya? Oh, you are too familiar with me, great poet. I would not suggest so deep a friendship as that with a man so humble as myself."

"You're right," Cehmai said, sitting. "I was trying to flatter you. Did it work?"

"You should have brought wine," the stout man said, taking his own seat. The false graciousness was gone, and a sour impatience in its place. "And come at an hour when living men could talk business. Isn't it late for you to be wandering around like a dazed rabbit?"

"There was a gathering at the rose pavilion. I was just going back to my apartments and I noticed the lights burning."

Baarath made a sound between a snort and a cough. Stone-Made-Soft gazed placidly at the marble walls, thoughtful as a lumberman judging the best way to fell a tree. Cehmai frowned at him, and the andat replied with a gesture more eloquent than any pose. *Don't blame me. He's your friend, not mine.*

"I wanted to ask how things were proceeding with Maati Vaupathai," Cehmai said.

"About time someone took an interest in that annoying, feckless idiot. I've met cows with more sense than he has."

"Not proceeding well, then?"

"Who can tell? *Weeks*, it's been. He's only here about half the morning, and then he's off dining with the dregs of the court, taking meetings with trading houses, and loafing about in the low towns. If I were the Dai-kvo, I'd pull that man back home and set him to plowing fields. I've eaten hens that were better scholars."

"Cows and hens. He'll be a whole farmyard soon," Cehmai said, but his mind was elsewhere. "What does he study when he is here?"

"Nothing in particular. He picks up whatever strikes him and spends a day with it, and then comes back the next for something totally unrelated. I haven't told him about the Khai's private archives, and he hasn't bothered to ask. I was sure, you know, when he first came, that he was after something in the private archives. But now it's like the library itself might as well not exist."

"Perhaps there is some pattern in what he's looking at. A common thread that places them all together."

"You mean maybe poor old Baarath is too simple to see the picture when it's being painted for him? I doubt it. I know this place better than any man alive. I've even made my own shelving system. I have read more of these books and seen more of their relationships than anyone. When I tell you he's wandering about like tree fluff on a breezy day, it's because he *is*."

Cehmai tried to feel surprise, and failed. The library was only an excuse. The Dai-kvo had sent Maati Vaupathai to examine the death of Biitrah Machi. That was clear. Why he would choose to do so, was not. It wasn't the poets' business to take sides in the succession, only to work with—and sometimes cool the ambitions of—whichever son survived. The Khaiem administered the city, accepted the glory and tribute, passed judgment. The poets kept the cities from ever going to war one against the other, and fueled the industries that brought wealth from the Westlands and Galt, Bakta, and the east islands. But something had happened, or was happening, that had captured the Dai-kvo's interest.

And Maati Vaupathai was an odd poet. He held no post, trained under no one. He was old to attempt a new binding. By many standards, he was already a failure. The only thing Cehmai knew of him that stood out at all was that Maati had been in Saraykeht when that city's poet was murdered and the andat set free. He thought of the man's eyes, the darkness that they held, and a sense of unease troubled him.

"I don't know what the point of that sort of grammar would be," Baarath said. "Dalani Toygu's was better for one thing, and half the length."

Cehmai realized that the Baarath had been talking this whole time, that the subject had changed, and in fact they were in the middle of a debate on a matter he couldn't identify. All this without the need that he speak.

"I suppose you're right," Cehmai said. "I hadn't seen it from that angle."

Stone-Made-Soft's calm, constant near-smile widened slightly.

"You should have, though. That's my point. Grammars and translations and the subtleties of thought are your trade. That I know more about it than you and that Maati person is a bad sign for the world. Note this, Cehmai-kya, write down that I said it. It's that kind of ignorance that will destroy the Khaiem."

"I'll write down that you said it," Cehmai said. "In fact, I'll go back to my apartments right now and do that. And afterwards, I'll crawl into bed, I think."

"So soon?"

"The night candle's past its center mark," Cehmai said.

"Fine. Go. When I was your age, I would stay up nights in a row for the sake of a good conversation like this, but I suppose the generations weaken, don't they?"

Cehmai took a pose of farewell, and Baarath returned it.

"Come by tomorrow, though," Baarath said as they left. "There's some old imperial poetry I've translated that might interest you."

Outside, the night had grown colder, and few lanterns lit the paths and streets. Cehmai pulled his arms in from their sleeves and held his fingers against his sides for warmth. His breath plumed blue-white in the faint moonlight, and even the distant scent of pine resin made the air seem colder.

"He doesn't think much of our guest," Cehmai said. "I would have thought he'd be pleased that Maati took little interest in the books, after all the noise he made."

When Stone-Made-Soft spoke, its breath did not fog. "He's like a girl bent on protecting her virginity until she finds no one wants it."

Cehmai laughed.

"That is entirely too apt," he said, and the andat took a pose accepting the compliment.

"You're going to do something," it said.

"I'm going to pay attention," Cehmai said. "If something needs doing, I'll try to be on hand."

They turned down the cobbled path that led to the poet's house. The sculpted oaks that lined it rustled in the faint breeze, rubbing new leaves together like a thousand tiny hands. Cehmai wished that he'd thought to bring a candle from Baarath's. He imagined Maati Vaupathai standing in the shadows with his appraising gaze and mysterious agenda.

"You're frightened of him," the andat said, but Cehmai didn't answer.

There *was* someone there among the trees—a shape shifting in the darkness. He stopped and slid his arms back into their sleeves. The andat stopped as well. They weren't far from the house—Cehmai could see the glow of the lantern left out before his doorway. The story of a poet slaughtered in a distant city raced in his mind until the figure came out between him and his doorway, silhouetted in the dim light. Cehmai's heart didn't slow, but it did change contents.

She still wore the half-mask she'd had at the gathering. Her black and white robes shifted, the cloth so rich and soft, and he could hear it even over the murmur of the trees. He stepped toward her, taking a pose of welcome.

"Idaan," he said. "Is there something . . . I didn't expect to find you here. I mean . . . I'm doing this rather badly, aren't I?"

"Start again," she said.

"Idaan."

"Cehmai."

She took a step toward him. He could see the flush in her cheek and smell the faint, nutty traces of distilled wine on her breath. When she spoke, her words were sharp and precise.

"I saw what you did to Adrah," she said. "He left a heel mark in the stone."

"Have I given offense?" he asked.

"Not to me. He didn't see it, and I didn't say."

In the back of his mind, or in some quarter of his flesh, Cehmai felt Stone-Made-Soft receding as if in answer to his own wish. They were alone on the dark path.

"It's difficult for you, isn't it?" she said. "Being a part of the court and yet not. Being among the most honored men in the city, and yet not of Machi."

"I bear it. You've been drinking."

"I have. But I know who I am and where I am. I know what I'm doing."

"What are you doing, Idaan-kya?"

"Poets can't take wives, can they?"

"We don't, no. There's not often room in our lives for a family."

"And lovers?"

Cehmai felt his breath coming faster and willed it to slow. An echo of amusement in the back of his mind was not his own thought. He ignored it.

"Poets take lovers," he said.

She stepped nearer again, not touching, not speaking. There was no chill to the air now. There was no darkness. Cehmai's senses were as fresh and bright and clear as midday, his mind as focused as the first day he'd controlled the andat. Idaan took his hand and slowly, deliberately, drew it through the folds of her robes until it cupped her breast.

"You . . . you have a lover, Idaan-kya. Adrah . . ."

"Do you want me to sleep here tonight?"

"Yes, Idaan. I do."

"And I want that too."

He struggled to think, but his skin felt as though he was basking in some hidden sun. There seemed to be some sound in his ears that he couldn't place that drove away everything but his fingertips and the cold-stippled flesh beneath them.

"I don't understand why you're doing this," he said.

Her lips parted, and she moved half an inch back. His hand pressed against her skin, his eyes were locked on hers. Fear sang through him that she would take another step back, that his fingers would only remember this moment, that this chance would pass. She saw it in his face, she must have, because she smiled, calm and knowing and sure of herself, like something from a dream.

"Do you care?" she asked.

"No," he said, half-surprised at the answer. "No, I truly don't."

THE CARAVAN LEFT THE LOW TOWN BEFORE DAWN, CARTWHEELS RATTLING on the old stone paving, oxen snorting white in the cold, and the voices of carters and merchants light with the anticipation of journey's end. The weeks of travel were past. By midday, they would cross the bridge over the Tidat and enter Machi. The companionship of the road—already somewhat strained by differences in political opinions and some unfortunate words spoken by one of the carters early in the journey—would break apart, and each of them would be about his own business again. Otah walked with his hands in his sleeves and his heart divided between dread and anticipation. Itani Noygu was going to Machi on the business of his house—the satchel of letters at his side proved that. There was nothing he carried with him that would suggest anything else. He had come away from this city as a child so long ago he had only shreds of memory left of it. A scent of musk, a stone corridor, bathing in a copper tub when he was small enough to be lifted with a single hand, a view from the top of one of the towers. Other things as fragmentary, as fleeting. He could not say which memories were real and which only parts of dreams.

It was enough, he supposed, to be here now, walking in the darkness. He would go and see it with a man's eyes. He would see this place that had sent him forth and, despite all his struggles, still had the power to poison the life he'd built for himself. Itani Noygu had made his way as an indentured laborer at the seafronts of Saraykeht, as a translator and fisherman and midwife's assistant in the east islands, as a sailor on a merchant ship, and as a courier in House Siyanti and all through the cities. He could write and speak in three tongues, play the flute badly, tell jokes well, cook his own meals over a half-dead fire, and comport himself well in any company from the ranks of the utkhaiem to the denizens of the crudest dockhouse. This from a twelve-year-old boy who had named himself, been his own father and mother, formed a life out of little more than the will to do so. Itani Noygu was by any sane standard a success.

It was Otah Machi who had lost Kiyan's love.

The sky in the east lightened to indigo and then royal blue, and Otah could see the road out farther ahead. Between one breath and the next, the oxen came clearer. And the plains before them opened like a vast scroll. Far to the north, mountains towered, looking flat as a painting and blued by the distance. Smoke rose from low towns and mines on the plain, the greener pathway of trees marked the river, and on the horizon, small as fingers, rose the dark towers of Machi, unnatural in the landscape.

Otah stopped as sunlight lit the distant peaks like a fire. The brilliance crept down and then the distant towers blazed suddenly, and a moment later, the plain flooded with light. Otah caught his breath.

This is where I started, he thought. I come from here.

He had to trot to catch back up with the caravan, but the questioning looks were all answered with a grin and a gesture. The enthusiastic courier still naïve enough to be amazed by a sunrise. There was nothing more to it than that.

House Siyanti kept no quarters in Machi, but the gentleman's trade had its provisions for this. Other Houses would extend courtesy even to rivals so long as it was understood that the intrigues and prying were kept to decorous levels. If a courier were to act against a rival House or carried information that would too deeply tempt his hosts, it was better form to pay for a room elsewhere. Nothing Otah carried was so specific or so valuable, and once the caravan had made its trek across the plain and passed over the wide, sinuous bridge into Machi, Otah made his way to the compound of House Nan.

The structure itself was a gray block three stories high that faced a wide square and shared walls with the buildings on either side. Otah stopped by a street cart and bought a bowl of hot noodles in a smoky black sauce for two lengths of copper and watched the people passing by with a kind of doubled impression. He saw them as the subjects of his training: people clumped at the firekeepers' kilns and streetcarts meant a lively culture of gossip, women walking alone meant little fear of violence, and so on in the manner that was his profession. He also saw them as the inhabitants of his childhood. A statue of the first Khai Machi stood in the square, his noble expression undermined by the pigeon streaks. An old, rag-wrapped beggar sat on the street, a black lacquer box before her, and chanted songs. The forges were only a few streets away, and Otah could smell the sharp smoke; could even, he thought, hear the faint sound of metal on metal. He sucked down the last of the noodles and handed back the bowl to a man easily twice his age.

"You're new to the north," the man said, not unkindly.

"Does it show?" Otah asked.

"Thick robes. It's spring, and this is warm. If you'd been here over winter, your blood would be able to stand a little cold."

Otah laughed, but made note. If he were to fit in well, it would mean suffering the cold. He would have to sit with that. He did want to understand the place, to see it, if only for a time, through the eyes of a native, but he didn't want to swim in ice water just because that was the local custom.

The door servant at the gray House Nan left him waiting in the street for a while, then returned to usher him to his quarters—a small, windowless room with four stacked cots that suggested he would be sharing the small iron brazier in the center of the room with seven other men, though he was the only one present just then. He thanked the servant, learned the protocols for entering and leaving the house, got directions to the nearest bathhouse, and after placing the oiled leather pouch that held his letters safely with the steward, went back out to wash off the journey.

The bathhouse smelled of iron pipes and sandalwood, but the air was warm and thick. A launderer had set up shop at the front, and Otah gave over his robes to be scrubbed and kiln-dried with the understanding that it doomed him to be in the baths for at least the time it took the sun to move the width of two hands. He walked naked to the public baths and eased himself into the warm water with a sigh.

"Hai!" a voice called, and Otah opened his eyes. Two older men and a young woman sat on the same submerged bench on which he rested. One of the older men spoke.

"You've just come in with the 'van?"

"Indeed," Otah said. "Though I hope you could tell by looking more than smell."

"Where from?"

"Udun, most recently."

The trio moved closer. The woman introduced them all—overseers for a metalworkers group. Silversmiths, mostly. Otah was gracious and ordered tea for them all and set about learning what they knew and thought, felt and feared and hoped for, and all of it with smiles and charm and just slightly less wit displayed than their own. It was his craft, and they knew it as well as he did, and would exchange their thoughts and speculations for his gossip. It was the way of traders and merchants the world over.

It was not long before the young woman mentioned the name of Otah Machi.

4

>+< "If it *is* the upstart behind it all, it's a poor thing for Machi," the older man said. "None of the trading houses would know him or trust him. None of the families of the utkhaiem would have ties to him. Even if he's simply never found, the new Khai will always be watching over his shoulder. It isn't good to have an uncertain line in the Khai's chair. The best thing that could happen for the city would be to find him and put a knife through his belly. Him, and any children he's got meantime."

Otah smiled because it was what a courier of House Siyanti would do. The younger man sniffed and sipped his bowl of tea. The woman shrugged, the motion setting small waves across the water.

"It might do us well to have someone new running the city," she said. "It's clear enough that nothing will change with either of the two choices we have now. Biitrah. He at least was interested in mechanism. The Galts have been doing more and more with their little devices, and we'd be fools to ignore what they've managed."

"Children's toys," the older man said, waving the thought away.

"Toys that have made them the greatest threat Eddensea and the Westlands have seen," the younger man said. "Their armies can move faster than anyone else's. There isn't a warden who hasn't felt the bite of them. If they haven't been invaded, they've had to offer tribute to the Lords Convocate, and that's just as bad."

"The ward being sacked might disagree," Otah said, trying for a joke to lighten the mood.

"The problem with the Galts," the woman said, "is they can't hold what they take. Every year it's another raid, another sack, another fleet carrying slaves and plunder back to Galt. But they never keep the land.

They'd have much more money if they stayed and ruled the Westlands. Or Eymond. Or Eddensea."

"Then we'd have only them to trade with," the younger man said. "That'd be ugly."

"The Galts don't have the andat," the older man said, and his tone carried the rest: they don't have the andat, so they are not worth considering.

"But if they did," Otah said, hoping to keep the subject away from himself and his family. "Or if we did not—"

"If the sky dives into the sea, we'll be fishing for birds," the older man said. "It's this Otah Machi who's uneasing things. I have it on good authority that Danat and Kaiin have actually called a truce between them until they can rout out the traitor."

"Traitor?" Otah asked. "I hadn't heard that of him."

"There are stories," the younger man said. "Nothing anyone has proved. Six years ago, the Khai fell ill, and for a few days, they thought he might die. Some people suspected poison."

"And hasn't he turned to poison again? Look at Biitrah's death," the younger man said. "And I tell you the Khai Machi hasn't been himself since then, not truly. Even if Otah were to claim the chair, it'd be better to punish him for his crimes and raise up one of the high families."

"It could have been bad fish," the woman said. "There was a lot of bad fish that year."

"No one believes that," the older man said.

"Which of the others would be best for the city now that Biitrah is gone?" Otah asked.

The older man named Kaiin, and the younger man and woman Danat, in the same moment, the syllables grinding against each other in the warm, damp air, and they immediately fell to debate. Kaiin was a master negotiator; Danat was better thought of by the utkhaiem. Kaiin was prone to fits of temper, Danat to weeks of sloth. Each man, to hear it, was a paragon of virtue and little better than a street thug. Otah listened, interjected comments, asked questions crafted to keep the conversation alive and on its course. His mind was hardly there.

When at last he made his excuses, the three debaters hardly paused in their wrangle. Otah dried himself by a brazier and collected his robes—laundered now, smelling of cedar oil and warm from the kiln. The streets were fuller than when he had gone into the bathhouse. The sun would fall early, disappearing behind the peaks to the west long before the sky grew dark, but it still hovered two hands above the mountainous horizon.

Otah walked without knowing where he was walking to. The black cobbles and tall houses seemed familiar and exotic at the same time. The towers rose into the sky, glowing in the sunlight. At the intersection of three large streets, Otah found a courtyard with a great stone archway inlaid with wood and metal sigils of chaos and order. Harsh forge smoke from the east mixed with the greasy scent of a cart seller's roasting duck and, for a moment, Otah was possessed by the memory of being a child no more than four summers old. The smoke scent wove with the taste of honeybread nearly too hot to eat, the clear open view of the valley and mountains from the top of the towers, and a woman's skin—mother or sister or servant. There was no way to know.

It was a ghost memory, strong and certain as stone, but without a place in his life. Something had happened, once, that tied all these senses together, but it was gone and he would never have it. He was upstart and traitor. Poisoner and villain. None of it was true, but it made for an interesting story to tell in the teahouses and meeting rooms—a variation on the theme of fratricide that the Khaiem replayed in every generation. A deep fatigue pressed into him. He had been an innocent to think that he might be forgotten, that Otah Machi might escape the venomous speculation of the traders and merchants, high families and low townsmen. There was no use for truth when spectacle was at issue. And there was nothing in the city that could matter less than the half-recalled memories of a courier's abandoned childhood. The life he'd built mattered less than ashes to these people. His death would be a relief to them.

He returned to House Nan just as the stars began to glimmer in the deep northern sky. There was fresh bread and pepper-baked lamb, distilled rice wine and cold water. The other men who were to share his room joined him at the table, and they laughed and joked, traded information and gossip from across the world. Otah slid back comfortably into Itani Noygu, and his smiles came more easily as the night wore on, though a cold core remained in his breast. It was only just before he went to crawl into his cot that he found the steward, recovered his pouch of letters, and prepared himself.

All the letters were, of course, still sewn shut, but Otah checked the knots. None had been undone so far as he could tell. It would have been a breach of the gentleman's trade to open letters held in trust, and it would have been foolishness to trust to honor. Had House Nan been willing to break trust, that would have been interesting to know as well. He laid them out on his cot, considering.

Letters to the merchant houses and lower families among the utkhaiem were the most common. He didn't carry a letter for the Khai himself—he would have balked at so high a risk—but his work would take him to the palaces. And there were audiences, no doubt, to which he could get an invitation. If he chose, he could go to the Master of Tides and claim business with members of the court. It wouldn't even require stretching the truth very far. He sat in silence, feeling as if there were two men within him.

One wanted nothing more than to embrace the fear and flee to some distant island and be pleased to live wondering whether his brothers would still be searching him out. The other was consumed by an anger that drove him forward, deeper into the city of his birth and the family that had first discarded him and then fashioned a murderer from his memory.

Fear and anger. He waited for the calm third voice of wisdom, but it didn't come. He was left with no better plan than to act as Itani Noygu would have, had he been nothing other than he appeared. When at last he repacked his charges and lay on his cot, he expected that sleep would not come, but it did, and he woke in the morning forgetful of where he was and surprised to find that Kiyan was not in the bed beside him.

The palaces of the Khai were deep within the city, and the gardens around them made it seem more like a walk into some glorious low town than movement into the center of a great city. Trees arched over the walkways, branches bright with new leaves. Birds fluttered past him, reminding him of Udun and the wayhouse he had almost made his home. The greatest tower loomed overhead, dark stone rising up like twenty palaces, one above the other. Otah stopped in a courtyard before the lesser palace of the Master of Tides and squinted up at the great tower, wondering whether he had ever been to the top of it. Wondering whether being here, now, was valor, cowardice, foolishness, or wisdom; the product of anger or fear or the childish drive to show that he could defy them all if he chose.

He gave his name to the servants at the door and was led to an antechamber larger than his apartments back in Udun. A slave girl plucked a lap harp, filling the high air with a sweet, slow tune. He smiled at her and took a pose of appreciation. She returned his smile and nodded, but her fingers never left the strings. The servant, when he came, wore robes of deep red shot with yellow and a silver armband. He took a pose of greeting so brief it almost hadn't happened.

"Itani Noygu. You're Itani Noygu, then? Ah, good. I am Piyun See, the Master of Tides' assistant. He's too busy to see you himself. So House Siyanti has taken an interest in Machi, then?" he said. Otah smiled, though he meant it less this time.

"I couldn't say. I only go where they send me, Piyun-cha."

The assistant took a pose of agreement.

"I had hoped to know the court's schedule in the next week," Otah said. "I have business—"

"With the poet. Yes, I know. He left your name with us. He said we should keep a watch out for you. You're wise to come to us first. You wouldn't imagine the people who simply drift through on the breeze as if the poets weren't members of the court."

Otah smiled, his mouth tasting of fear, his heart suddenly racing. The poet of Machi—Cehmai Tyan, his name was—had no reason to know Itani Noygu or expect him. This was a mistake or a trap. If it was a trap, it was sloppy, and if a mistake, dangerous. The lie came to his lips as gracefully as a rehearsed speech.

"I'm honored to have been mentioned. I hadn't expected that he would remember me. But I'm afraid the business I've come on may not be what he had foreseen."

"I wouldn't know," the assistant said as he shifted. "Visiting dignitaries might confide in the Master of Tides, but I'm like you. I follow orders. Now. Let me see. I can send a runner to the library, and if he's there . . ."

"Perhaps it would be best if I went to the poet's house," Otah said. "He can find me there when he isn't—"

"Oh, we haven't put him there. Gods! He has his own rooms."

"His own rooms?"

"Yes. We have a poet of our own, you know. We aren't going to put Cehmai-cha on a cot in the granary every time the Dai-kvo sends us a guest. Maati-cha has apartments near the library."

The air seemed to leave the room. A dull roar filled Otah's ears, and he had to put a hand to the wall to keep from swaying. Maati-cha. The name came like an unforeseen blow.

Maati Vaupathai. Maati whom Otah had known briefly at the school, and to whom he had taught the secrets he had learned before he turned his back on the poets and all they offered. Maati whom he had found again in Saraykeht, who had become his friend and who knew that Itani Noygu was the son of the Khai Machi.

The last night they had seen one another—thirteen, fourteen summers ago—Maati had stolen his lover and Otah had killed Maati's master. He was here now, in Machi. And he was looking for Otah. He felt like a deer surprised by the hunter at its side.

The servant girl fumbled with her strings, the notes of the tune coming out a jangle, and Otah shifted his gaze to her as if she'd shouted. For a moment, their eyes met and he saw discomfort in her as she hurried back to her song. She might have seen something in his face, might have realized who was standing before her. Otah balled his fists at his sides, pressing them into his thighs to keep from shaking. The assistant had been speaking. Otah didn't know what he'd said.

"Forgive me, but before we do anything, would you be so kind . . . ," Otah feigned an embarrassed simper. "I'm afraid I had one bowl of tea too many this morning, and waters that run in, run out. . . ."

"Of course. I'll have a slave take you to—"

"No need," Otah said as he stepped to the door. No one shouted. No one stopped him. "I'll be back with you in a moment."

He walked out of the hall, forcing himself not to run though he could feel his heartbeat in his neck, and his ribs seemed too small for his breath. He waited for the warning yell to come—armsmen with drawn blades or the short, simple pain of an arrow in his breast. Generations of his uncles had spilled their blood, spat their last breaths perhaps here, under these arches. He was not immune. Itani Noygu would not protect him. He controlled himself as best he could, and when he reached the gardens, boughs shielding him from the eyes of the palaces, he bolted.

IDAAN SAT AT THE OPEN SKY DOORS, HER LEGS HANGING OUT OVER THE VOID, and let her gaze wander the moonlit valley. The glimmers of the low towns to the south. The Daikani mine where her brother had gone to die. The Poinyat mines to the west and southeast. And below the soles of her bare feet, Machi itself: the smoke rising from the forges, the torches and lanterns glimmering in the streets and windows smaller and dimmer than fireflies. The winches and pulleys hung in the darkness above her, long lengths of iron chain in guides and hooks set in the stone, ready to be freed should there be call to haul something up to the high reaches of the tower or lower something down. Chains that clanked and rattled, uneasy in the night breeze.

She leaned forward, forcing herself to feel the vertigo twist her stomach and tighten her throat. Savoring it. Scoot forward a few inches, no more effort really than standing from a chair, and then the sound of wind would fill her ears. She waited as long as she could stand and then drew back, gasping and nauseated and trembling. But she did not pull her legs back in. That would have been weakness.

It was an irony that the symbols of Machi's greatness were so little used. In the winter, there was no heating them—all the traffic of the city went in the streets, or over the snows, or through the networks of tunnels. And even in summer, the endless spiraling stairways and the need to haul up any wine or food or musical instruments made the gardens and halls nearer the ground more inviting. The towers were symbols of power, existing to show that they could exist and little enough more. A boast in stone and iron used for storage and exotic parties to impress visitors from the other courts of the Khaiem. And still, they made Idaan think that perhaps she could imagine what it would be to fly. In her way she loved them, and she loved very few things these days.

It was odd, perhaps that she had two lovers and still felt alone. Adrah had been with her for longer, it felt, than she had been herself. And so it had surprised her that she was so ready to betray him in another man's bed. Perhaps she'd thought that by being a new man's lover, she would strip off that old skin and become innocent again.

Or perhaps it was only that Cehmai had a sweet face and wanted her. She was young, she thought, to have given up flirtation and courtship. She'd been angry with Adrah for embarrassing Cehmai at the dance. She'd promised herself never to be owned by a man. And also, killing Biitrah had left a hunger in her—a need that nothing yet had sated.

She liked Cehmai. She longed for him. She needed him in a way she couldn't quite fathom, except to say that she hated herself less when she was with him.

"Idaan!" a voice whispered from the darkness behind her. "Come away from there! You'll be seen!"

"Only if you're fool enough to bring a torch," she said, but she pulled her feet back in from the abyss and hauled the great bronze-bound oaken sky doors shut. For a moment, there was nothing—black darker than closing her eyes—and then the scrape of a lantern's hood and the flame of a single candle. Crates and boxes threw deep shadows on the stone walls and carved cabinets. Adrah looked pale, even in the dim light. Idaan found herself amused and annoyed—pulled between wanting to comfort him and the desire to point out that it wasn't his family they were killing. She wondered if he knew yet that she had taken the poet to bed and whether he would care. And whether she did. He smiled nervously and glanced around at the shadows.

"He hasn't come," Idaan said.

"He will. Don't worry," Adrah said, and then a moment later: "My father has drafted a letter. Proposing our union. He's sending it to the Khai tomorrow."

"Good," Idaan said. "We'll want that in place before everyone finishes dying."

"Don't."

"If we can't speak of it to each other, Adrah-kya, when will we ever? It isn't as if I can go to our friends or the priest." Idaan took a pose of query to some imagined confidant. "Adrah's going to take me as his wife, but it's important that we do it now, so that when I've finished slaughtering my brothers, he can use me to press his suit to become the new Khai without it seeming so clearly that I'm being traded at market. And don't you love this new robe? It's Westlands silk."

She laughed bitterly. Adrah did not step back, quite, but he did pull away.

"What is it, Idaan-kya?" he said, and Idaan was surprised by the pain in his voice. It sounded genuine. "Have I done something to make you angry with me?"

For a moment, she saw herself through his eyes—cutting, ironic, cruel. It wasn't who she had been with him. Once, before they had made this bargain with Chaos, she had had the luxury of being soft and warm. She had always been angry, only not with him. How lost he must feel.

Idaan leaned close and kissed him. For one terrible moment, she meant it—the softness of his lips against hers stirring something within her that cried out to hold and be held, to weep and wail and take comfort. Her flesh also remembered the poet, the strange taste of another man's skin, the illusion of hope and of safety that she'd felt in her betrayal of the man who was destined to share her life.

"I'm not angry, sweet. Only tired. I'm very tired."

"This will pass, Idaan-kya. Remember that this part only lasts a while."

"And is what follows it better?"

He didn't answer.

The candle had hardly burned past another mark when the moon-faced assassin appeared, moving like darkness itself in his back cotton robe. He put down his lantern and took a pose of welcome before dusting a crate with his sleeve and sitting. His expression was pleasant as a fruit seller in a summer market. It only made Idaan like him less.

"So," Oshai said. "You called, I've come. What seems to be the problem?"

She had intended to begin with Maati Vaupathai, but the pretense of passive stupidity in Oshai's eyes annoyed her. Idaan raised her chin and her brows, considering him as she would a garden slave. Adrah looked back and forth between the two. The motion reminded her of a child watching his parents fighting. When she spoke, she had to try not to spit.

"I would know where our plans stand," she said. "My father's ill, and I hear more from Adrah and the palace slaves than from you."

"My apologies, great lady," Oshai said without a hint of irony. "It's only that meetings with you are a risk, and written reports are insupportable. Our mutual friends . . ."

"The Galtic High Council," Idaan said, but Oshai continued as if she had not spoken.

". . . have placed agents and letters of intent with six houses. Contracts for iron, silver, steel, copper, and gold. The negotiations are under way, and I expect we will be able to draw them out for most of the summer, should we need to. When all three of your brothers die, you will have been wed to Adrah, and between the powerful position of his house, his connection with you, and the influence of six of the great houses whose contracts will suddenly ride on his promotion to Khai, you should be sleeping in your mother's bed by Candles Night."

"My mother never had a bed of her own. She was only a woman, remember. Traded to the Khai for convenience, like a gift."

"It's only an expression, great lady. And remember, you'll be sharing Adrah here with other wives in your turn."

"I won't take others," Adrah said. "It was part of our agreement."

"Of course you won't," Oshai said with a nod and an insincere smile. "My mistake."

Idaan felt herself flush, but kept her voice level and calm when she spoke.

"And my brothers? Danat and Kaiin?"

"They are being somewhat inconvenient, it's true. They've gone to ground. Frightened, I'm told, by your ghost brother Otah. We may have to wait until your father actually dies before they screw up the courage to stand against each other. But when they do, I will be ready. You know all this, Idaan-cha. It can't be the only reason you've asked me here?" The round, pale face seemed to harden without moving. "There had best be something more pressing than seeing whether I'll declaim when told."

"Maati Vaupathai," Idaan said. "The Dai-kvo's sent him to study in the library."

"Hardly a secret," Oshai said, but Idaan thought she read a moment's unease in his eyes.

"And it doesn't concern your owners that this new poet has come for the same prize they want? What's in those old scrolls that makes this worth the risk for you, anyway?"

"I don't know, great lady," the assassin said. "I'm trusted with work of this delicate nature because I don't particularly care about the points that aren't mine to know."

"And the Galts? Are they worried about this Maati Vaupathai poking through the library before them?"

"It's . . . of interest," Oshai said, grudgingly.

"It was the one thing you insisted on," Idaan said, stepping toward the man. "When you came to Adrah and his father, you agreed to help us in return for access to that library. And now your price may be going away."

Will your support go, too? The unasked question hung in the chill air. If the Galts could not have what they wanted from Adrah and Idaan and the books of Machi, would the support for this mad, murderous scheme remain? Idaan felt her heart tripping over faster, half hoping that the answer might be no.

"It is the business of a poet to concern himself with ancient texts," Oshai said. "If a poet were to come to Machi and not avail himself of its library, that would be odd. This coincidence of timing is of interest. But it's not yet a cause for alarm."

"He's looking into the death of Biitrah. He's been down to the mines. He's asking questions."

"About what?" Oshai said. The smile was gone.

She told him all she knew, from the appearance of the poet to his interest in the court and high families, the low towns and the mines. She recounted the parties at which he had asked to be introduced, and to whom. The name he kept mentioning—*Itani Noygu*. The way in which his interest in the ascension of the next Khai Machi seemed to be more than academic. She ended with the tale she'd heard of his visit to the Daikani mines and to the wayhouse where her brother had died at Oshai's hands. When she was finished, neither man spoke. Adrah looked stricken. Oshai, merely thoughtful. At length, the assassin took a pose of gratitude.

"You were right to call me, Idaan-cha," he said. "I doubt the poet knows precisely what he's looking for, but that he's looking at all is bad enough."

"What do we do?" Adrah said. The desperation in his voice made Oshai look up like a hunting dog hearing a bird.

"*You* do nothing, most high," Oshai said. "Neither you nor the great lady does anything. I will take care of this."

"You'll kill him," Idaan said.

"If it seems the best course, I may. . . ."

Idaan took a pose appropriate to correcting a servant. Oshai's words faded.

"I was not asking, Oshai-cha. You'll kill him."

The assassin's eyes narrowed for a moment, but then something like amusement flickered at the corners of his mouth and the glimmer of candlelight in his eyes grew warmer. He seemed to weigh something in his mind, and then took a pose of acquiescence. Idaan lowered her hands.

"Will there be anything else, most high?" Oshai asked without taking his gaze from her.

"No," Adrah said. "That will be all."

"Wait half a hand after I've gone," Oshai said. "I can explain myself, and the two of you together borders on the self-evident. All three would be difficult."

And with that, he vanished. Idaan looked at the sky doors. She was tempted to open them again, just for a moment. To see the land and sky laid out before her.

"It's odd, you know," she said. "If I had been born a man, they would have sent me away to the school. I would have become a poet or taken the brand. But instead, they kept me here, and I became what they're afraid of. Kaiin and Danat are hiding from the brother who has broken the traditions and come back to kill them for the chair. And here I am. I *am* Otah Machi. Only they can't see it."

"I love you, Idaan-kya."

She smiled because there was nothing else to do. He had heard the words, but understood nothing. It would have meant as much to talk to a dog. She took his hand in hers, laced her fingers with his.

"I love you too, Adrah-kya. And I will be happy once we've done all this and taken the chair. You'll be the Khai Machi, and I will be your wife. We'll rule the city together, just as we always planned, and everything will be right again. It's been half a hand by now. We should go."

They parted in one of the night gardens, he to the east and his family compound, and she to the south, to her own apartments, and past them and west to tree-lined path that led to the poet's house. If the shutters were closed, if no light shone but the night candle, she told herself she wouldn't go in. But the lanterns were lit brightly, and the shutters open. She paced quietly through the grounds, peering in through windows, until she caught the sound of voices. Cehmai's soft and reasonable, and then another. A man's, loud and full of a rich self-importance. Baarath, the librarian. Idaan found a tree with low branches and deep shadows and sat, waiting with as much patience as she could muster, and silently willing the man away. The full moon was halfway across the sky before the two came to the door, silhouetted. Baarath swayed like a drunkard, but Cehmai, though he laughed as loud and sang as poorly, didn't waver. She watched as Baarath took a sloppy pose of farewell and stumbled off along the path. Cehmai watched him go, then looked back into the house, shaking his head.

Idaan rose and stepped out of the shadows.

She saw Cehmai catch sight of her, and she waited. He might have another guest—he might wave her away, and she would have to go back through the night to her own apartments, her own bed. The thought filled her with black dread until the poet put one hand out to her, and with the other motioned toward the light within his house.

Stone-Made-Soft brooded over a game of stones, its massive head cupped in a hand twice the size of her own. The white stones, she noticed, had lost badly. The andat looked up slowly and, its curiosity satisfied, it turned back to the ended game. The scent of mulled wine filled the air. Cehmai closed the door behind her, and then set about fastening the shutters.

"I didn't expect to see you," the poet said.

"Do you want me to leave?"

There were a hundred things he could have said. Graceful ways to say yes, or graceless ways to deny it. He only turned to her with the slightest smile and went back to his task. Idaan sat on a low couch and steeled herself. She couldn't say why she was driven to do this, only that the impulse was much like draping her legs out the sky doors, and that it was what she had chosen to do.

"Daaya Vaunyogi is approaching the Khai tomorrow. He is going to petition that Adrah and I be married."

Cehmai paused, sighed, turned to her. His expression was melancholy, but not sorrowful. He was like an old man, she thought, amused by the world and his own role in it. There was a strength in him, and an acceptance.

"I understand," he said.

"Do you?"

"No."

"He is of a good house, their bloodlines—"

"And he's well off and likely to oversee his family's house when his father passes. And he's a good enough man, for what he is. It isn't that I can't imagine why he would choose to marry you, or you him. But, given the context, there are other questions."

"I love him," Idaan said. "We have planned to do this for . . . we have been lovers for almost two years."

Cehmai sat beside a brazier, and looked at her with the patience of a man studying a puzzle. The coals had burned down to a fine white ash.

"And you've come to be sure I never speak of what happened the other night. To tell me that it can never happen again."

The sense of vertigo returned, her feet held over the abyss.

"No," she said.

"You've come to stay the night?"

"If you'll have me, yes."

The poet looked down, his hands laced together before him. A cricket sang, and then another. The air seemed thin.

"Idaan-kya, I think it might be better if—"

"Then lend me a couch and a blanket. If you . . . let me stay here as a friend might. We are friends, at least? Only don't make me go back to my rooms. I don't want to be there. I don't want to be with people and I can't stand being alone. And I . . . I like it here."

She took a pose of supplication. Cehmai rose and for a moment she was sure he would refuse. She almost hoped he would. Scoot forward, no more effort than sitting up, and then the sound of wind. But Cehmai took a pose that accepted her. She swallowed, the tightness in her throat lessening.

"I'll be back. The shutters . . . it might be awkward if someone were to happen by and see you here."

"Thank you, Cehmai-kya."

He leaned forward and kissed her mouth, neither passionate nor chaste, then sighed again and went to the back of the house. She heard the rattle of wood as he closed the windows against the night. Idaan looked at her hands, watching them tremble as she might watch a waterfall or a rare bird. An effect of nature, outside herself. The andat shifted and turned to look at her. She felt her brows rise, daring the thing to speak. Its voice was the low rumble of a landslide.

"I have seen generations pass, girl. I've seen young men die of age. I don't know what you are doing, but I know this. It will end in chaos. For him, and for you."

Stone-Made-Soft went silent again, stiller than any real man, not even the pulse of breath in it. She glared into the wide, placid face and took a pose of challenge.

"It that a threat?" she asked.

The andat shook its head once—left, and then right, and then still as if it had never moved in all the time since the world was young. When it spoke again, Idaan was almost startled at the sound.

"It's a blessing," it said.

"What did he look like?" Maati asked.

Piyun See, chief assistant to the Master of Tides, frowned and glanced out the window. The man sensed that he had done something wrong, even if he could not say what it had been. It made him reluctant. Maati sipped tea from a white stone bowl and let the silence stretch.

"A courier. He wore decent robes. He stood half a head taller than you, and had a good face. Long as a northman's."

"Well, that will help me," Maati said. He couldn't keep his impatience entirely to himself.

Piyun took a pose of apology formal enough to be utterly insincere.

"He had two eyes and two feet and one nose, Maati-cha. I thought he was *your* acquaintance. Shouldn't you know better than I what he looks like?"

"If it is the man."

"He didn't seem pleased to hear you'd been asking after him. He made an excuse and lit out almost as soon as he heard of you. It isn't as if I knew that he wasn't to be told of you. I didn't have orders to hold back your name."

"Did you have orders to volunteer me to him?" Maati asked.

"No, but . . ."

Maati waved the objection away.

"House Siyanti. You're sure of that?"

"Of course I am."

"How do I reach their compound?"

"They don't have one. House Siyanti doesn't trade in the winter cities. He would be staying at a wayhouse. Or sometimes the houses here will let couriers take rooms."

"So other than the fact that he came, you can tell me nothing," Maati said.

This time the pose of apology was more sincere. Frustration clamped Maati's jaw until his teeth hurt, but he forced himself into a pose that thanked the assistant and ended the interview. Piyun See left the small meeting room silently, closing the door behind him.

Otah was here, then. He had come back to Machi, using the same name he had had in Saraykeht. And that meant . . . Maati pressed his fingertips to his eyes. That meant nothing certain. That he was here suggested that Biitrah's death was his work, but as yet it was only a suggestion. He doubted that the Dai-kvo or the Khai Machi would see it that way. His presence was as much as proof to them, and there was no way to keep it secret. Piyun See was no doubt spreading the gossip across the palaces even now—the visiting poet and his mysterious courier. He had to find Otah himself, and he had to do it now.

He straightened his robes and stalked out to the gardens, and then the path that would lead him to the heart of the city. He would begin with the teahouses nearest the forges. It was the sort of place couriers might go to drink and gossip. There might be someone there who would know of House Siyanti and its partners. He could discover whether Itani Noygu had truly been working for Siyanti. That would bring him one step nearer, at least. And there was nothing more he could think of to do now.

The streets were busy with children playing street games with rope and sticks, with beggars and slaves and water carts and firekeepers' kilns, with farmers' carts loaded high with spring produce or lambs and pigs on their way to the fresh butcher. Voices jabbered and shouted and sang, the smells of forge smoke and grilling meat and livestock pressed like a fever. The city seemed busy as an anthill, and Maati's mind churned as he navigated his way through it all. Otah had come to the winter cities. Was he killing his brothers? Had he chosen to become the Khai Machi?

And if he had, would Maati have the strength to stop him?

He told himself that he could. He was so focused and among so many distractions that he almost didn't notice his follower. Only when he found what looked like a promising alley—hardly more than a shoulder-wide crack between two long, tall buildings—did he escape the crowds long enough to notice. The sound of the street faded in the dim twilight that the band of sky above him allowed. A rat, surprised by him, scuttled through an iron grating and away. The thin alley branched, and Maati paused, looked down the two new paths, and then glanced back. The path behind him was blocked. A dark cloak, a raised hood, and shoulders so broad they touched both walls. Maati hesitated, and the man behind him didn't move. Maati felt the skin at the back of his neck tighten. He picked one turning of the alleyway and walked down it briskly until the dark figure reached the intersection as well and turned after him. Then Maati ran. The alley spilled out into another street, this less populous. The smoke of the forges made the air acrid and hazy.

Maati raced toward them. There would be men there—smiths and tradesmen, but also firekeepers and armsmen.

When he reached the mouth where the street spilled out onto a major throughway, he looked back. The street behind him was empty. His steps slowed, and he stopped, scanning the doorways, the rooftops. There was nothing. His pursuer—if that was what he had been—had vanished. Maati waited there until he'd caught his breath, then let himself laugh. No one was coming. No one had followed. It was easy to see how a man could be eaten by his fears. He turned to the metalworkers' quarter.

The streets widened here, with shops and stalls facing out, filled with the tools of the metal trades as much as their products. The forges and smith's houses were marked by the greened copper roofs, the pillars of smoke, the sounds of yelling voices and hammers striking anvils. The businesses around them—sellers of hammers and tongs, suppliers of ore and wax blocks and slaked lime—all did their work loudly and expansively, waving hands in mock fury and shouting even when there was no call to. Maati made his way to a teahouse near the center of the district where sellers and workers mixed. He asked after House Siyanti, where their couriers might be found, what was known of them. The brown poet's robes granted him an unearned respect, but also wariness. It was three hands before he found an answer—the overseer of a consortium of silversmiths had had word from House Siyanti. The courier had said the signed contracts could be delivered to House Nan, but only after they'd been sewn and sealed. Maati gave the man two lengths of silver and his thanks and had started away before he realized he would also need better directions. An older man in a red and yellow robe with a face round and pale as the moon overheard his questions and offered to guide him there.

"You're Maati Vaupathai," the moon-faced man said as they walked. "I've heard about you."

"Nothing scandalous, I hope," Maati said.

"Speculations," the man said. "The Khaiem run on gossip and wine more than gold or silver. My name is Oshai. It's a pleasure to meet a poet."

They turned south, leaving the smoke and cacophony behind them. As they stepped into a smaller, quieter street, Maati looked back, half expecting to see the looming figure in the dark robes. There was nothing.

"Rumor has it you've come to look at the library," Oshai said.

"That's truth. The Dai-kvo sent me to do research for him."

"Pity you've come at such a delicate time. Succession. It's never an easy thing."

"It doesn't affect me," Maati said. "Court politics rarely reach the scrolls on the back shelves."

"I hear the Khai has books that date back to the Empire. Before the war."

"He does. Some of them are older than the copies the Dai-kvo has. Though, in all, the Dai-kvo's libraries are larger."

"He's wise to look as far afield as he can, though," Oshai said. "You never know what you might find. Was there something in particular he expected our Khai to have?"

"It's complex," Maati said. "No offense, it's just . . ."

Oshai smiled and waved the words away. There was something odd about his face—a weariness or an emptiness around his eyes.

"I'm sure there are many things that poets know that I can't comprehend," the guide said. "Here, there's a faster way down through here."

Oshai moved forward, taking Maati by the elbow and leading him down a narrow street. The houses around them were poorer than those near the palaces or even the metalworkers' quarter. Shutters showed the splinters of many seasons. The doors on the street level and the second-floor snow doors both tended to have cheap leather hinges rather than worked metal. Few people were on the street, and few windows open. Oshai seemed perfectly at ease despite his heightened pace so Maati pushed his uncertainty away.

"I've never been in the library myself," Oshai said. "I've heard impressive things of it. The power of all those minds, and all that time. It isn't something that normal men can easily conceive."

"I suppose not," Maati said, trotting to keep up. "Forgive me, Oshai-cha, but are we near House Nan?"

"We won't be going much further," his guide said. "Just around this next turning."

But when they made the turn, Maati found not a trading house's compound, but a small courtyard covered in flagstone, a dry cistern at its center. The few windows that opened onto the yard were shuttered or empty. Maati stepped forward, confused.

"Is this . . . ," he began, and Oshai punched him hard in the belly.

Maati stepped back, surprised by the attack, and astounded at the man's strength. Then he saw the blade in the guide's hand, and the blood on it. Maati tried to back away, but his feet caught the hem of his robe. Oshai's face was a grimace of delight and hatred. He seemed to jump forward, then stumbled and fell.

When his hands—out before him to catch his fall—touched the ground, the flagstone splashed. Oshai's hands vanished to the wrist. For a moment that seemed to last for days, Maati and his attacker both stared at the ground. Oshai began to struggle, pulling with his shoulders to no effect. Maati could hear the fear in the muttered curses. The pain in his belly was lessening, and a warmth taking its place. He tried to gather himself, but the effort was such that he didn't notice the dark-robed figures until they were almost upon him. The larger one had thrown back its hood and the wide, calm face of the andat considered him. The other form—smaller, and more agitated—knelt and spoke in Cehmai's voice.

"Maati-kvo! You're hurt."

"Be careful!" Maati said. "He's got a knife."

Cehmai glanced at the assassin struggling in the stone and shook his head. The poet looked very young, and yet familiar in a way that Maati hadn't noticed before. Intelligent, sure of himself. Maati was struck by an irrational envy of the boy, and then noticed the blood on his own hand. He looked down, and saw the wetness blackening his robes. There was so much of it.

"Can you walk?" Cehmai said, and Maati realized it wasn't the first time the question had been asked. He nodded.

"Only help me up," he said.

The younger poet took one arm and the andat the other and gently lifted him. The warmth in Maati's belly was developing a profound ache in its center. He pushed it aside, walked two steps, then three, and the world seemed to narrow. He found himself on the ground again, the poet leaning over him.

"I'm going for help," Cehmai said. "Don't move. Don't try to move. And don't die while I'm gone."

Maati tried to raise his hands in a pose of agreement, but the poet was already gone, pelting down the street, shouting at the top of his lungs. Maati rolled his head to one side to see the assassin struggling in vain and allowed himself a smile. A thought rolled through his mind, elusive and dim, and he shook himself, willing a lucidity he didn't possess. It was important. Whatever it was bore the weight of terrible significance. If he could only bring himself to think it. It had something to do with Otah-kvo and all the thousand times Maati had imagined their meeting. The andat sat beside him, watching him with the impassive distance of a statue, and Maati didn't know that he intended to speak to it until he heard his own words.

"It isn't Otah-kvo," he said. The andat shifted to consider the captive trapped by stone, then turned back.

"No," it agreed. "Too old."

"No," Maati said, struggling. "I don't mean that. I mean he wouldn't do this. Not to me. Not without speaking to me. It isn't him."

The andat frowned and shook its massive head.

"I don't understand."

"If I die," Maati said, forcing himself to speak above a whisper, "you have to tell Cehmai. It isn't Otah-kvo that did this. There's someone else."

5

>+<   The chamber was laid out like a temple or a theater. On the long, sloping floor, representatives of all the high families sat on low stools or cushions. Beyond them sat the emissaries of the trading houses, the people of the city, and past them rank after rank of servants and slaves. The air was rich with the smells of incense and living bodies. Idaan looked out over the throng, though she knew proper form called for her gaze to remain downcast. Across the dais from her, Adrah knelt, his posture mirroring hers, except that his head was held high. He was, after all, a man. His robes were deep red and woven gold, his hair swept back and tied with bands of gold and iron like a child of the Empire. He had never looked more handsome. Her lover. Her husband. She considered him as she might a fine piece of metalwork or a well-rendered drawing. As a likeness of himself.

His father sat beside him on a bench, dressed in jewels and rich cloth. Daaya Vaunyogi was beaming with pride, but Idaan could see the unease in the way he held himself. The others would see only the patriarch of one high family marrying his son into the blood of the Khaiem—it was reason enough for excitement. Of all the people there, only Idaan would also see a traitor against his city, forced to sit before the man whose sons he conspired to slaughter and act as if his pet assassin was not locked in a room with armsmen barring the way, his intended victim alive. Idaan forced herself not to smirk at his weakness.

Her father spoke. His voice was thick and phlegmy, and his hands trembled so badly that he took no formal poses.

"I have accepted a petition from House Vaunyogi. They propose that the son of their flesh, Adrah, and the daughter of my blood, Idaan, be joined."

He waited while the appointed whisperers repeated the words, the hall filled, it seemed, with the sound of a breeze. Idaan let her eyes close for a long moment, and opened them again when he continued.

"This proposal pleases me," her father said. "And I lay it before the city. If there is cause that this petition be refused, I would know of it now."

The whisperers dutifully passed this new statement through the hall as well. There was a cough from nearby, as if in preparation to speak. Idaan looked over. There in the first rank of cushions sat Cehmai and his andat. Both of them were smiling pleasantly, but Cehmai's eyes were on hers, his hands in a pose of offering. It was the same pose he might have used to ask if she wanted some of the wine he was drinking or a lap blanket on a cold night. Here, now, it was a deeper thing. *Would you like me to stop this?* Idaan could not reply. No one was looking at Cehmai, and half the eyes in the chamber were on her. She looked down instead, as a proper girl would. She saw the movement in the corner of her eye when the poet lowered his hands.

"Very well," her father said. "Adrah Vaunyogi, come here before me."

Idaan did not look up as Adrah stood and walked with slow, practiced steps until he stood before the Khai's chair. He knelt again, with his head bowed, his hands in a pose of gratitude and submission. The Khai, despite the grayness in his skin and the hollows in his cheeks, held himself perfectly, and when he did move, the weakness did not undo the grace of a lifetime's study. He put a hand on the boy's head.

"Most high, I place myself before you as a man before his elder," Adrah said, his voice carrying the ritual phrases through the hall. Even with his back turned, the whisperers had little need to speak. "I place myself before you and ask your permission. I would take Idaan, your blood issue, to be my wife. If it does not please you, please only say so, and accept my apology."

"I am not displeased," her father said.

"Will you grant me this, most high?"

Idaan waited to hear her father accept, to hear the ritual complete itself. The silence stretched, profound and horrible. Idaan felt her heart begin to race, fear rising up in her blood. Something had happened; Oshai had broken. Idaan looked up, prepared to see armsmen descending upon them. But instead, she saw her father bent close to Adrah—so close their foreheads almost touched. There were tears on the sunken cheeks. The formal reserve and dignity was gone. The Khai was gone.

All that remained was a desperately ill man in robes too gaudy for a sick house.

"Will you make her happy? I would have one of my children be happy."

Adrah's mouth opened and shut like a fish pulled from the river. Idaan closed her eyes, but she could not stop her ears.

"I . . . most high, I will do . . . Yes. I will."

Idaan felt her own tears forcing their way into her eyes like traitors. She bit her lip until she tasted blood.

"Let it be known," her father said, "that I have authorized this match. Let the blood of the Khai Machi enter again into House Vaun-yogi. And let all who honor the Khaiem respect this transfer and join in our celebration. The ceremony shall be held in thirty-four days, on the opening of summer."

The whisperers began, but the hush of their voices was quickly drowned out by cheering and applause. Idaan raised her head and smiled as if the smears on her cheeks were from joy. Every man and woman in the chamber had risen. She turned to them and took a pose of thanks, and then to Adrah and his father, and then, finally, to her own. He was still weeping—a show of weakness that the gossips and back-biters of the court would be chewing over for days. But his smile was so genuine, so hopeful, that Idaan could do nothing but love him and taste ashes.

"Thank you, most high," she said. He bowed his head, as if honoring her.

The Khai Machi left the dais first, attended by servants who lifted him into his litter and others who bore him away. Then Idaan herself re-treated. The others would escape according to the status of their families and their standing within them. It would be a hand and a half before the chamber was completely empty. Idaan strode along white marble corridors to a retiring room, sent away her servants, locked the door and sobbed until her heart was empty again. Then she washed her face in cool water from her basin, arrayed her kohl and blush, whitener and lip rouge before a mirror and carefully made a mask of her skin.

There would be talk, of course. Even without her father's unseemly display of humanity—and she hated them all for the laughter and amusement *that* would occasion—there would be enough to pick apart. The strength of Adrah's voice would be commented on. The way in which he carried himself. Even his unease when the ritual slipped from its form might speak well of him in people's memory. It was a small thing, of course. In the minds of the witnesses, it had been clear that she would be the daughter of a Khai only very briefly and merely sister to the Khai was a lower status. House Vaunyogi was buying something whose value would soon drop. It must be a love match, they would say, and pretend to be touched. She wondered if it wouldn't be better—cleaner—to simply burn the city and everyone in it, herself included. Let a hot iron clean and seal it like searing a wound. It was a passing fantasy, but it gave her comfort.

A knock came, and she arranged her robes before unlocking the door. Adrah stood, his house servants behind him. He had not changed out of his ritual robes.

"Idaan-kya," he said, "I was hoping you might come have a bowl of tea with my father."

"I have gifts to present to your honored father," Idaan said, gesturing to a cube of cloth and bright paper the size of a boar. It was already lashed to a carrying pole. "It is too much for me. Might I have the aid of your servants?"

Two servants had already moved forward to lift the burden.

Adrah took a pose of command, and she answered with one of acquiescence, following him as he turned and left. They walked side by side through the gardens, not touching. Idaan could feel the gazes of the people they passed, and kept her expression demure. By the time they reached the palaces of the Vaunyogi, her cheeks ached with it. Idaan and Adrah walked with their entourage through a hall of worked rosewood and mother-of-pearl, and to the summer garden where Daaya Vaunyogi sat beneath a stunted maple tree and sipped tea from a stone bowl. His face was weathered but kindly. Seeing him in this place was like stepping into a woodcut from the Old Empire—the honored sage in contemplation. The gift package was placed on the table before him as if it were a meal.

Adrah's father put down his bowl and took a pose that dismissed the servants.

"The garden is closed," he said. "We have much to discuss, my children and I."

As soon as the doors were shut and the three were alone, his face fell. He sank back to his seat like a man struck by fever. Adrah began to pace. Idaan ignored them both and poured herself tea. It was over-brewed and bitter.

"You haven't heard from them, then, Daaya-cha?"

"The Galts?" the man said. "The messengers I send come back empty handed. When I went to speak to their ambassador, they turned me away. Things have gone wrong. The risk is too great. They won't back us now."

"Did they say that?" Idaan asked.

Daaya took a pose that asked clarification. Idaan leaned forward, holding back the snarl she felt twisting at her lip.

"Did they *say* they wouldn't back us, or is it only that you fear they won't?"

"Oshai," Daaya said. "He knows everything. He's been my intermediary from the beginning. If he tells what he knows—"

"If he does, he'll be killed," Idaan said. "That he injured a poet is bad enough, but he murdered a son of the Khaiem without being a brother to him. He knows what would happen. His best hope is that someone intercedes for him. If he speaks what he knows, he dies badly."

"We have to free him," Adrah said. "We have to get him out. We have to show the Galts that we can protect them."

"We will," Idaan said. She drank down her tea. "The three of us. And I know how we'll do it."

Adrah and his father looked at her as if she'd just spat out a serpent. She took a pose of query.

"Shall we wait for the Galts to take action instead? They've already begun to distance themselves. Shall we take some members of your house into our confidence? Hire some armsmen to do it for us? Assume that our secrets will be safer the more people know?"

"But . . . ," Adrah said.

"If we falter, we fail," Idaan said. "I know the way to the cages. He's kept underground now; if they move him to the towers, it gets harder. I asked that we meet in a place with a private exit. This garden. There is a way out of it?"

Daaya took an acknowledging pose, but his face was pale as bread dough.

"I thought there would be others you wished to consult," he said.

"There's nothing to consult over," Idaan said and pulled open the gifts she had brought to her new marriage. Three dark cloaks with deep hoods, three blades in dark leather sheaths, two unstrung hunter's bows with dark-shafted arrows, two torches, a pot of smoke pitch and a bag to carry it. And beneath it, a wall stand of silver with the sigils of order and chaos worked in marble and bloodstone. Idaan passed the blades and cloaks to the men.

"The servants will only know of the wall stand. These others we can give to Oshai to dispose of once we have him," Idaan said. "The smoke pitch we can use to frighten the armsmen at the cages. The bows and blades are for those that don't flee."

"Idaan-kya," Adrah said, "this is madness, we can't . . ."

She slapped him before she knew she meant to. He pressed a palm to his cheek, and his eyes glistened. But there was anger in him too. That was good.

"We do the thing now, while there are servants to swear it was not us. We do it quickly, and we live. We falter and wail like old women, and we die. Pick one."

Daaya Vaunyogi broke the silence by taking a cloak and pulling it on. His son looked to him, then to her, then, trembling began to do the same.

"You should have been born a man," her soon-to-be father said. There was disgust in his voice.

The tunnels beneath the palaces were little traveled in spring. The long winter months trapped in the warrens that laced the earth below Machi made even the slaves yearn for daylight. Idaan knew them all. Long winter months stealing unchaperoned up these corridors to play on the river ice and snow-shrouded city streets had taught her how to move through them unseen. They passed the alcove where she and Janat Saya had kissed once, when they were both too young to think it more than something that they should wish to do. She led them through the thin servant's passage she'd learned of when she was steal-ing fresh applecakes from the kitchens. Memories made the shadows seem like old friends from better times, when her mischief had been innocent.

They made their way from tunnel to tunnel, passing through wide chambers unnoticed and passages so narrow they had to stoop and go singly. The weight of stone above them made the journey seem like traveling through a mine.

They knew they were nearing the occupied parts of the tunnels as much by the smell of shit from the cages and acrid smoke as by the torchlight that danced at the corridor's mouth. Thick timber beams framed the hall. Idaan paused. This was only a side gallery—little used, rarely trafficked. But it would do, she thought.

"What now?" Adrah asked. "We light the pitch? Simulate a fire?"

Idaan took the pot from its bag and weighed it in her hands.

"We simulate nothing, Adrah-kya," she said. She tossed the pot at the base of a thick timber support and tossed her lit torch onto the blackness. It sputtered for a moment, then caught. Idaan unslung the bow from her shoulder and draped a fold of the cloak over it. "Be ready."

She waited as the flames caught. If she waited too long, they might not be able to pass the fire. If she was too quick, the armsmen might be able to put out the blaze. A deep calm seemed to descend upon her, and she felt herself smile. Now would be a fine moment, she thought, and screamed, raising the alarm. Adrah and Daaya followed her as she stumbled through the darkness and into the cages. In the time it took for her to take two breaths of the thickening air, they found themselves in the place she'd hoped: a wide gallery in torchlight, the air already becoming dense with smoke, and iron cages set into the stone where prisoners waited on the justice of the Khai. Two armsmen in leather and bronze armor scuttled to the three of them, their eyes round with fear.

"There's a fire in the gallery!" Daaya shrilled. "Get water! Get the watch!"

The prisoners were coming to the front of the cages now. Their cries of fear added to the confusion. Idaan pretended to cough as she considered the problem. There were two more armsmen at the far end of the cages, but they were coming closer. Of the first two who had approached, one had raced off toward the fire, the other down a well-lit tunnel, she presumed towards aid. And then midway down the row of cages on the left, she caught a glimpse of the Galts' creature. There was real fear in his eyes.

Adrah panicked as the second pair came close. With a shriek, he drew his blade, hewing at the armsmen like a child playing at war. Idaan cursed, but Daaya was moving faster, drawing his bow and sinking a dark shaft into the man's belly as Idaan shot at his chest and missed. But Adrah was lucky—a wild stroke caught the armsman's chin and seemed to cleave his jaw apart. Idaan raced to the cages, to Oshai. The moon-faced assassin registered a moment's surprise when he saw her face within the hood, and then Oshai closed his eyes and spat.

Adrah and Daaya rushed to her side.

"Do not speak," Oshai said. "Nothing. Every man here would sell you for his freedom, and there are people who would buy. Do you understand?"

Idaan nodded and pointed toward the thick lock that barred the door. Oshai shook his head.

"The Khai's Master of Blades keeps the keys," Oshai said. "The cages can't be opened without him. If you meant me to leave with you, you didn't think this through very well."

Adrah whispered a curse, but Oshai's eyes were on Idaan. He smiled thinly, his eyes dead as a fish's. He saw it when she understood, and he nodded, stepped back from the bars, and opened his arms like a man overwhelmed by the beauty of a sunrise. Idaan's first arrow took him in the throat. There were two others after that, but she thought they likely didn't matter. The first shouts of the watch echoed. The smoke was thickening. Idaan walked away, down the route she had meant to take when the prisoners were free. She'd meant to free them all, adding to the chaos. She'd been a fool.

"What have you done?" Daaya Vaunyogi demanded once they were safely away in the labyrinth. "What have you done?"

Idaan didn't bother answering.

Back in the garden, they sank the blades and the cloaks in a fountain to lie submerged until Adrah could sneak back in under cover of night and get rid of them. Even with the dark hoods gone, they all reeked of smoke. She hadn't foreseen that either. Neither of the men met her eyes. And yet, Oshai was beyond telling stories to the utkhaiem. So perhaps things hadn't ended so badly.

She gave her farewells to Daaya Vaunyogi. Adrah walked with her back through the evening-dimmed streets to her rooms. That the city seemed unchanged struck her as odd. She couldn't say what she had expected—what the day's events should have done to the stones, the air—but that it should all be the same seemed wrong. She paused by a beggar, listening to his song, and dropped a length of silver into the lacquered box at his feet.

At the entrance to her rooms, she sent her servants away. She did not wish to be attended. They would assume she smelled of sex, and best that she let them. Adrah peered at her, earnest as a puppy, she thought. She could see the distress in his eyes.

"You had to," he said, and she wondered if he meant to comfort her or convince himself. She took a pose of agreement. He stepped forward, his arms curving to embrace her.

"Don't touch me," she said, and he stepped back, paused, lowered his arms. Idaan saw something die behind his eyes, and felt something wither in her own breast. So this is what we are, she thought.

"Things were good once," he said, as if willing her to say *and they will be again*. The most she could give him was a nod. They had been good once. She had wanted and admired and loved him once. And even now, a part of her might love him. She wasn't sure.

The pain in his expression was unbearable. Idaan leaned forward, kissed him briefly on the lips, and went inside to wash the day off her skin. She heard his footsteps as he walked away.

Her body felt wrung out and empty. There were dried apples and sugared almonds waiting for her, but the thought of food was foreign. Gifts had arrived throughout the day—celebrations of her being sold off. She ignored them. It was only after she had bathed, washing her hair three times before it smelled more of flowers than smoke, that she found the note.

It rested on her bed, a square of paper folded in quarters. She sat naked beside it, reached out a hand, hesitated, and then plucked it open. It was brief, written in an unsteady hand.

Daughter, it said. *I had hoped that you might be able to spend some part of this happy day with me. Instead, I will leave this. Know that you have my blessings and such love as a weary old man can give. You have always delighted me, and I hope for your happiness in this match.*

When her tears and sobbing had exhausted her, Idaan carefully gathered the scraps of the note together and placed them together under her pillow. Then she bowed and prayed to all the gods and with all her heart that her father should die, and die quickly. That he should die without discovering what she was.

MAATI WAS LOST FOR A TIME IN PAIN, THEN DISCOMFORT, AND THEN PAIN again. He didn't suffer dreams so much as a pressing sense of urgency without goal or form, though for a time he had the powerful impression that he was on a boat, rocked by waves. His mind fell apart and re-formed itself at the will of his body.

He came to himself in the night, aware that he had been half awake for some time; that there had been conversations in which he had participated, though he couldn't say with whom or on what matters. The room was not his own, but there was no mistaking that it belonged to the Khai's palace. No fire burned in the grate, but the stone walls were warm with stored sunlight. The windows were shuttered with shaped stone, the only light coming from the night candle that had burned almost to its quarter mark. Maati pulled back the thin blankets and considered the puckered gray flesh of his wound and the dark silk that laced it closed. He pressed his belly gently with his fingertips until he thought he knew how delicate he had become. When he stood, tottering to the night pot, he found he had underestimated, but that the pain was not so excruciating that he could not empty his bladder. After, he pulled himself back into bed, exhausted. He intended only to close his eyes for a moment and gather his strength, but when he opened them, it was morning.

He had nearly resolved to walk from his bed to the small writing table near the window when a slave entered and announced that the poet Cehmai and the andat Stone-Made-Soft would see him if he wished. Maati nodded and sat up carefully.

The poet arrived with a wide plate of rice and river fish in a sauce that smelled of plums and pepper. The andat carried a jug of water so cold it made the stone sweat. Maati's stomach came to life with a growl at the sight.

"You're looking better, Maati-kvo." the young poet said, putting the plate on the bed. The andat pulled two chairs close to the bed and sat in one, its face calm and empty.

"I looked worse than this?" Maati asked. "I wouldn't have thought that possible. How long has it been?"

"Four days. The injury brought on a fever. But when they poured onion soup down you, the wound didn't smell of it, so they decided you might live after all."

Maati lifted a spoon of fish and rice to his mouth. It tasted divine.

"I think I have you to thank for that," Maati said. "My recollection isn't all it could be, but . . ."

"I was following you," Cehmai said, taking a pose of contrition. "I was curious about your investigations."

"Yes. I suppose I should have been more subtle."

"The assassin was killed yesterday."

Maati took another bite of fish.

"Executed?"

"Disposed of," the andat said and smiled.

Cehmai told the story. The fire in the tunnels, the deaths of the guards. The other prisoners said that there had been three men in black cloaks, that they had rushed in, killed the assassin, and vanished. Two others had choked to death on the smoke before the watchmen put the fire out.

"The story among the utkhaiem is that you discovered Otah Machi. The Master of Tides' assistant said that you'd been angry with him for being indiscreet about your questions concerning a courier from Udun. Then the attack on you, and the fire. They say the Khai Machi sent for you to hunt his missing son, Otah."

"Part true," Maati said. "I was sent to look for Otah. I knew him once, when we were younger. But I haven't found him, and the knife man was . . . something else. It wasn't Otah."

"You said that," the andat rumbled. "When we found you, you said it was someone else."

"Otah-kvo wouldn't have done it. Not that way. He might have met me himself, but sending someone else to do it? No. He wasn't behind that," Maati said, and then the consequence of that fell into place. "And so I think he must not have been the one who killed Biitrah."

Cehmai and his andat exchanged a glance and the young poet drew a bowl of water for Maati. The water was as good as the food, but Maati could see the unease in the way Cehmai looked at him. If he had ached less or been farther from exhaustion, he might have been subtle.

"What is it?" Maati asked.

Cehmai drew himself up, then sighed.

"You call him Otah-kvo."

"He was my teacher. At the school, he was in the black robes when I was new arrived. He . . . helped me."

"And you saw him again. When you were older."

"Did I?" Maati asked.

Cehmai took a pose that asked forgiveness. "The Dai-kvo would hardly have trusted a memory that old. You were both children at the school. We were all children there. You knew him when you were both men, yes?"

"Yes," Maati said. "He was in Saraykeht when . . . when Heshai-kvo died."

"And you call him Otah-kvo," Cehmai said. "He was a friend of yours, Maati-kvo. Someone you admired. He's never stopped being your teacher."

"Perhaps. But he's stopped being my friend. That was my doing, but it's done."

"I'm sorry, Maati-kvo, but are you certain Otah-kvo is innocent because he's innocent, or only because you're certain? It would be hard to accept that an old friend might wish you ill . . ."

Maati smiled and sipped the water.

"Otah Machi may well wish me dead. I would understand it if he did. And he's in the city, or was four days ago. But he didn't send the assassin."

"You think he isn't hoping for the Khai's chair?"

"I don't know. But I suppose that's something worth finding out. Along with who it was that killed his brother and started this whole thing rolling."

He took another mouthful of rice and fish, but his mind was elsewhere.

"Will you let me help you?"

Maati looked up, half surprised. The young poet's face was serious, his hands in a pose of formal supplication. It was as if they were back in the school and Cehmai was a boy asking a boon of the teachers. The andat had its hands folded in its lap, but it seemed mildly amused. Before Maati could think of a reply, Cehmai went on.

"You aren't well yet, Maati-kvo. You're the center of all the court gossip now, and anything you do will be examined from eight different views before you've finished doing it. I know the city. I know the court. I can ask questions without arousing suspicion. The Dai-kvo didn't choose to take me into his confidence, but now that I know what's happening—"

"It's too much of a risk," Maati said. "The Dai-kvo sent me because I know Otah-kvo, but he also sent me because my loss would mean nothing. You hold the andat—"

"It's fine with me," Stone-Made-Soft said. "Really, don't let me stop you."

"If I ask questions *without* you, I run the same risks, and without the benefits of shared information," Cehmai said. "And expecting me not to wonder would be unrealistic."

"The Khai Machi would expel me from his city if he thought I was endangering his poet," Maati said. "And then I wouldn't be of use to anyone."

Cehmai's dark eyes were both deadly serious and also, Maati thought, amused. "This wouldn't be the first thing I've kept from him," the young poet said. "Please, Maati-kvo. I want to help."

Maati closed his eyes. Having someone to talk with, even if it was only a way to explore what he thought himself, wouldn't be so bad a thing. The Dai-kvo hadn't expressly forbidden that Cehmai know, and even if he had, the secret investigation had already sent Otah-kvo to flight, so any further subterfuge seemed pointless. And the fact was, he likely couldn't find the answers alone.

"You have saved my life once already."

"I thought it would be unfair to point that out," Cehmai said.

Maati laughed, then stopped when the pain in his belly bloomed. He lay back, blowing air until he could think again. The pillows felt better than they should have. He'd done so little, and he was already tired. He glanced mistrustfully at the andat, then took a pose of acceptance.

"Come back tonight, when I've rested," Maati said. "We'll plan our strategy. I have to get my strength back, but there isn't much time."

"May I ask one other thing, Maati-kvo?"

Maati nodded, but his belly seemed to have grown more sensitive for the moment and he tried not to move more than that. It seemed laughing wasn't a wise thing for him just now.

"Who are Liat and Nayiit?"

"My lover. Our son," Maati said. "I called out for them, did I? When I had the fever?"

Cehmai nodded.

"I do that often," Maati said. "Only not usually aloud."

6

>+<   There were four great roads that connected the cities of the Khaiem, one named for each of the cardinal directions. The North Road that linked Cetani, Machi, and Amnat-Tan was not the worst, in part because there was no traffic in the winter, when the snows let men make a road wherever desire took them. Also the stones were damaged more by the cycle of thaw and frost that troubled the north only in spring and autumn. In high summer, it rarely froze, and for a third of the year it did not thaw. The West Road—far from the sea and not so far south as to keep the winters warm—required the most repair.

"They'll have crews of indentured slaves and laborers out in shifts," the old man in the cart beside Otah said, raising a finger as if his oratory was on par with the High Emperor's, back when there had been an empire. "They start at one end, reset the stones until they reach the other, and begin again. It never ends."

Otah glanced across the cart at the young woman nursing her babe and rolled his eyes. She smiled and shrugged so slightly that their orator didn't notice the movement. The cart lurched down into and up from another wide hole where the stones had shattered and not yet been replaced.

"I have walked them all," the old man said, "though they've worn me more than I've worn them. Oh yes, much more than I've worn them."

He cackled, as he always seemed to when he made this observation. The little caravan—four carts hauled by old horses—was still six days from Cetani. Otah wondered whether his own legs were rested enough that he could start walking again.

He had bought an old laborer's robe of blue-gray wool from a rag shop, chopped his hair to change its shape, and let his thin beard start to grow in. Once his whiskers had been long enough to braid, but the east islanders he'd lived with had laughed at him and pretended to mistake him for a woman. After Cetani, it would take another twenty days to reach the docks outside Amnat-tan. And then, if he could find a fishing boat that would take him on, he would be among those men again, singing songs in a tongue he hadn't tried out in years, explaining again, either with the truth or outrageous stories, why his marriage mark was only half done.

He would die there—on the islands or on the sea—under whatever new name he chose for himself. Itani Noygu was gone. He had died in Machi. Another life was behind him, and the prospect of beginning again, alone in a foreign land, tired him more than the walking.

"Now, southern wood's too soft to really build with. The winters are too warm to really harden them. Up here there's trees that would blunt a dozen axes before they fell," the old man said.

"You know everything, don't you grandfather?" Otah said. If his annoyance was in his voice, the old man noticed nothing, because he cackled again.

"It's because I've been everywhere and done everything," the old man said. "I even helped hunt down the Khai Amnat-Tan's older brother when they had their last succession. There were a dozen of us, and it was the dead of winter. Your piss would freeze before it touched ground. Oh, eh . . ."

The old man took a pose of apology to the young woman and her babe, and Otah swung himself out of the cart. It wasn't a story he cared to hear. The road wound through a valley, high pine forest on either side, the air sharp and fragrant with the resin. It was beautiful, and he pictured it thick with snow, the image coming so clear that he wondered whether he might once have seen it that way. When the clatter of hooves came from the west, he forced himself again to relax his shoulders and look as curious and excited as the others. Twice before, couriers on fast horses had passed the 'van, laden with news, Otah knew, of the search for him.

It had taken an effort of will not to run as fast as he could after he had been discovered, but the search was for a false courier either plotting murder or fleeing like a rabbit. No one would pay attention to a plodding laborer off to stay with his sister's family in a low town outside Cetani. And yet, as the horses approached, tension grew in his breast.

He prepared himself for the shock if one of the riders had a familiar face.

There were three this time—utkhaiem to judge by their robes and the quality of their mounts—and none of them men he knew. They didn't slow for the 'van, but the armsmen of the 'van, the drivers, the dozen hangers-on like himself all shouted at them for news. One of them turned in his saddle and yelled something, but Otah couldn't make it out and the rider didn't repeat it. Ten days on the road. Six more to Cetani. The only challenge was not to be where they were looking for him.

They reached a wayhouse with the sun still three and a half hands above the treetops. The building was of northern design: stone walls thick as the span of a man's arm and stables and goat pen on the ground floor where the heat of the animals would rise and help warm the place in the winter. While the merchants and armsmen argued over whether to stop now or go farther and sleep in the open, Otah ran his eyes over the windows and walked around to the back, looking for all the signs Kiyan had taught him to know whether the keeper was working with robbers or keeping an unsafe kitchen. The house met all of her best marks. It seemed safe.

By the time he'd returned to the carts, his companions had decided to stay. After Otah had helped stable the horses, they shifted the carts into a locked courtyard. The caravan's leader haggled with the keeper about the rooms and came to an agreement that Otah privately thought gave the keep the better half. Otah made his way up two flights of stairs to the room he was to share with five armsmen, two drivers, and the old man. He curled himself up in a corner on the floor. It was too small a room, and one of the drivers snored badly. A little sleep when things were quiet would only make the next day easier.

He woke in darkness to the sound of music—a drum throbbed and a flute sighed. A man's voice and a woman's moved in rough harmony. He wiped his eyes with the sleeve of his robe and went down to the main room. The members of his 'van were all there and half a dozen other men besides. The air smelled of hot wine and roast lamb, pine trees and smoke. Otah sat at a rough, worn table beside one of the drivers and watched.

The singer was the keep himself; a pot-bellied man with a nose that had been broken and badly set. He drew the deep beat from a skin and earthenware drum as he sang. His wife was shapely as a potato with an ugly face and a missing eye tooth, but their voices were well suited and their affection for each other forgave them much. Otah found himself tapping his fingertips against the table to match the drumbeats.

His mind went back to Kiyan, and the nights of music and stories and gossip he had spent in her wayhouse, far away to the south. He wondered what she was doing tonight, what music filled the warm air and competed with the murmur of the river.

When the last note had faded to silence, the crowd applauded, yelped, and howled their appreciation. Otah made his way to the singer—he was shorter than Otah had thought—and took his hand. The keeper beamed and blushed when Otah told him how good the music had been.

"We've had a few years practice, and there's only so much to do when the days are short," the keep said. "The winter choirs in Machi make us sound like street beggars."

Otah smiled, regret pulling at him that he would never hear those songs, and a moment later he heard his name being spoken.

"Itani Noygu's what he was calling himself," one of the merchants said. "Played a courier for House Siyanti."

"I think I met him," a man said whom Otah had never met. "I knew there was something odd about the man."

"And the poet . . . the one that had his belly opened for him? He's picking the other Siyanti men apart like they were baked fish. The upstart has to wish that job had been done right the first time."

"Sounds as if I've missed something," Otah said, putting on his most charming smile. "What's this about a poet's belly?"

The merchant frowned at the interruption until Otah motioned to the keep's wife and bought bowls of hot wine for the table. After that, the gossip flowed more freely.

Maati Vaupathai had been attacked, and the common wisdom held that Otah had arranged it. The most likely version was that the upstart had been passing as a courier, but others said that he had made his way into the palaces dressed as a servant or a meat seller. There was no question, though, that the Khai had sent out runners to all the winter cities asking for the couriers and overseers of House Siyanti to attend him at court. Amiit Foss, the man who'd been the upstart's overseer in Udun, was being summoned in particular. It wasn't clear yet whether

Siyanti had knowingly backed the Otah Machi, but if they had, it would mean the end of their expansion into the north. Even if they hadn't, the house would suffer.

"And they're sure he was the one who had the poet killed?" Otah asked, using all the skill the gentleman's trade had taught him to hide his deepening despair and disgust.

"It seems they were in Saraykeht together, this poet and the upstart. That was just before Saraykeht fell."

The implications of that hung over the room. Perhaps Otah Machi had somehow been involved with the death of Heshai, the poet of Saraykeht. Who knew what depravity the sixth son of the Khai Machi might sink to? It was a ghost story for them; a tale to pass a night on the road; a sport to follow.

Otah remembered the old, frog-mouthed poet, remembered his kindness and his weakness and his strength. He remembered the regret and the respect and the horrible complicity he'd felt in killing him, all those years ago. It had been so complicated, then. Now, they said it so simply and spoke as if they understood.

"There's rumor of a woman, too. They say he had a lover in Udun."

"If he was a courier, he's likely got a woman in half the cities of the Khaiem. The gods know I would."

"No," the merchant said, shaking his head. He was more than half drunk. "No, they were very clear. All the Siyanti men say he had a lover in Udun and never took another. Loved her like the world, they said. But she left him for another man. I say it's that turned him evil. Love turns on you like . . . like milk."

"Gentlemen," the keep's wife said, her voice powerful enough to cut through any conversation. "It's late, and I'm not sleeping until these rooms are cleaned, so get you all to bed. I'll have bread and honey for you at sunrise."

The guests slurped down the last of the wine, ate the last mouthfuls of dried cherries and fresh cheese, and made their various ways toward their various beds. Otah walked down the inner stairs to the stables and the goat yard, then out through a side door and into the darkness. His body felt like he'd just run a race, or else like he was about to.

Kiyan. Kiyan and the wayhouse her father had run. Old Mani. He had set the dogs on them, and that he hadn't intended to would count for nothing if his brothers found her. Whatever happened, whatever they did, it would be his fault.

He found a tall tree and sat with his back against it, looking out at the stars nearest the horizon. The air had the bite of cold in it. Winter never left this place. It made a little room for summer, but it never left. He thought of writing her a letter, of warning her. It would never reach her in time. It was ten days walk back to Machi, six days forward to Cetani, and his brothers' forces would already be on the road south. He could send to Amiit Foss, beg his old overseer to take Kiyan in, to protect her. But there too, word would reach him too late.

Despair settled into his belly, too deep for tears. He was destroying the woman he loved most in the world simply by being who he was, by doing what he'd done. He thought of the boy he had been, marching away from the school across the western snows. He remembered his fear and the warmth of his rage at the poets and his parents and all in the world that treated boys so unfairly. What a pompous little ass he'd been, young and certain and alone. He should have taken the Dai-kvo's offer and become a poet. He might have tried to bind an andat, and maybe failed and paid the price, dying in the attempt. And then Kiyan would never have met him. She would be safe.

There's still a price, he thought, as clear as a voice speaking in his head. You could still pay it.

Machi was ten days' walk, perhaps as little as four and a half days' ride. If he could turn all eyes back to Machi, Kiyan might have at least the chance to escape his idiocy. And what would she matter, if no one need search for him. He could take a horse from the stables now. After all, if he was an upstart and a poisoner and a man turned evil by love, it hardly mattered being a horse thief as well. He closed his eyes, an angry bark of a laugh forcing its way from his throat.

Everything you have won, you've won by leaving, he thought, remembering a woman whom he had known almost well enough to join his life with though he had never loved her, nor she him. Well, Maj, perhaps this time I'll lose.

THE NIGHT CANDLE WAS PAST ITS MIDDLE MARK; THE AIR WAS FILLED WITH the songs of crickets. Somewhere in the course of things, the pale mist of netting had been pulled from the bed, and the room looked exposed without it. Cehmai could feel Stone-Made-Soft in the back of his mind, but the effort of being truly aware of the andat was too much; his body was thick and heavy and content. Focus and rigor would have their place another time.

Idaan traced her fingertips across his chest, raising gooseflesh. He shivered, took her hand and folded it in his own. She sighed and lay against him. Her hair smelled of roses.

"Why do they call you poets?" she asked.

"It's an old Empire term," Cehmai said. "It's from the binding."

"The andat are poems?" she said. She had the darkest eyes. Like an animal's. He looked at her mouth. The lips were too full to be fashionable. With the paint worn off, he could see how she narrowed them. He raised his head and kissed them again, gently this time. His own mouth felt bruised from their coupling. And then his head grew too heavy, and he let it rest again.

"They're . . . like that. Binding one is like describing something perfectly. Understanding it, and expanding it . . . I'm not saying this well. Have you ever translated a letter? Taken something in the Khaiate tongues and tried to say the same thing in Westland or an east island tongue?"

"No," she said. "I had to take something from the Empire and rewrite it for a tutor once."

Cehmai closed his eyes. He could feel sleep pulling at him, but he fought against it a bit. He wasn't ready to let the moment pass.

"That's near enough. You had to make choices when you did that. *Tilfa* could mean take or it could mean give or it could mean exchange— it's yours to choose, depending on how it's used in the original document. And so a letter or a poem doesn't have a set translation. You could have any number of ways that you say the same thing. Binding the andat means describing them—what the thought of them is—so well that you can translate it perfectly into a form that includes will and volition. Like translating a Galtic contract so that all the nuances of the trade are preserved perfectly."

"But there's any number of ways to do that," she said.

"There are very few ways to do it perfectly. And if a binding goes wrong . . . Existing isn't normal for them. If you leave an imprecision or an inaccuracy, they escape through it, and the poet pays a price for that.

Usually it comes as some particularly gruesome death. And knowing what an andat is can be subtle. Stone-Made-Soft. What do you mean by stone? Iron comes from stone, so is it stone? Sand is made of tiny stones. Is it stone? Bones are like stone. But are they like enough to be called the same name? All those nuances have to be balanced or the binding fails. Happily, the Empire produced some formal grammars that were very precise."

"And you describe this thing. . . ."

"And then you hold that in your mind until you die. Only it's the kind of thought that can think back, so it's wearing sometimes."

"Do you resent it?" Idaan asked, and something in her voice had changed. Cehmai opened his eyes. Idaan was looking past him. Her expression was unfathomable.

"I don't know what you mean," he said.

"You have to carry this thing all your life. Do you ever wish that you hadn't been called to do it?"

"No," he said. "Not really. It's work, but it's work that I like. And I get to meet the most interesting women."

Her gaze cooled, flickered over him, and then away.

"Lucky to be you," she said as she sat up. He watched her as she pulled her robes from the puddle of cloth on the floor. Cehmai sat up. "I have meetings in the morning. I'll need to be in my own rooms to be ready anyway. I might as well go now."

"I might say fewer things that angered you if you talked to me," Cehmai said, gently.

Idaan's head snapped around to him like a hunting cat's, but then her expression softened to chagrin, and she took an apologetic pose.

"I'm overtired," she said. "There are things that I'm carrying, and I don't do it as gracefully as you. I don't mean to take them out on you."

"Why do you do this, Idaan-kya? Why do you come here? I don't think it's that you love me."

"Do you want me to stop?"

"No," Cehmai said. "I don't. But if you choose to, that will be fine as well."

"That's flattering," she said, sarcasm thick in her voice.

"Are you doing this to be flattered?"

He was awake again now. He could see something in her expression—

pain, anger, something else. She didn't answer him now, only knelt by the bed and felt beneath it for her boots. He put his hand on her arm and drew her up. He could sense that she was close to speaking, that the words were already there, just below the surface.

"I don't mind only being your bed mate," he said. "I've known from the start that Adrah is the man you plan to be with, and that I couldn't be that for you even if you wanted it. I assume that's part of why you've chosen me. But I am fond of you, and I would like to be your friend."

"You'd be my friend?" she said. "That's nice to hear. You've bedded me and now you'll condescend to be a friend?"

"I think it's more accurate to say you bedded me," Cehmai said. "And it seems to me that people do what we've done quite often without caring about the other person. Or even while wishing them ill. I'll grant that we haven't followed the usual order—I understand people usually know each other first and then fall into bed afterwards—but in a way that means you should take me more seriously."

She pulled back and took a pose of query.

"You know I'm not just saying it to get your robes open," he said. "When I say I want to be someone you can speak with, it's truth. I've nothing to gain by it but the thing itself."

She sighed and sat on the bed. The light of the single candle painted her in shades of orange.

"Do you love me, Cehmai-kya?" she asked.

Cehmai took a deep breath and then slowly let it out. He had reached the gate. Her thoughts, her fears. Everything that had driven this girl into his bed was waiting to be loosed. All he would have to do was tell one, simple, banal lie. A lie thousands of men had told for less reason. He was badly tempted.

"Idaan-kya," he said, "I don't know you."

To his surprise, she smiled. She pulled on her boots, not bothering to lace the bindings, leaned over and kissed him again. Her hand caressed his cheeks.

"Lucky to be you," she said softly.

Neither spoke as they walked down the corridor to the main rooms. The shutters were closed against the night, and the air felt stuffy and thick. He walked with her to the door, then through it, and sat on the steps, watching her vanish among the trees. The crickets still sang. The moon still hung overhead, bathing the night in blue. He heard the high squeak of bats as they skimmed the ponds and pools, the flutter of an owl's wings.

"You should be sleeping," the low, gravel voice said from behind him.

"Yes, I imagine so."

"First light, there's a meeting with the stone potters."

"Yes, there is."

Stone-Made-Soft stepped forward and lowered itself to sit on the step beside him. The familiar bulk of its body rose and fell in a sigh that could only be a comment.

"She's up to something," Cehmai said.

"She might only find herself drawn to two different men," the andat said. "It happens. And you're the one she couldn't build a life with. The other boy . . ."

"No," Cehmai said, speaking slowly, letting the thoughts form as he gave them voice. "She isn't drawn to me. Not *me*."

"She could be flattered that you want her. I've heard that's endearing."

"She's drawn to you."

The andat shifted to look at him. Its wide mouth was smiling.

"That would be a first," it said. "I'd never thought of taking a lover. I don't think I'd know what to do with her."

"Not like that," Cehmai said. "She wants me because of you. Because I'm a poet. If I weren't, she wouldn't be here."

"Does that offend you?"

A gnat landed on the back of Cehmai's hand. The tiny wings tickled, but he looked at it carefully. A small gray insect unaware of its danger. With a puff of breath, he blew it into the darkness. The andat waited silently for an answer.

"It should," Cehmai said at last.

"Perhaps you can work on that."

"Being offended?"

"If you think you should be."

The storm in the back of him mind shifted. The constant thought that was this thing at his side moved, kicking like a babe in the womb or a prisoner testing the walls of its cell. Cehmai chuckled.

"You aren't trying to help," he said.

"No," the andat agreed. "Not particularly."

"Did the others understand their lovers? The poets before me?"

"How can I say? They loved women, and were loved by them. They used women and were used by them. You may have found a way to put me on a leash, but you're only men."

THE IRONY WAS THAT, HIS WOUND NOT FULLY HEALED, MAATI SPENT MORE time in the library than he had when he had been playing at scholarship. Only now, instead of spending his mornings there, he found it a calm place to retire when the day's work had exhausted him; when the hunt had worn him thin. It had been fifteen days now since Itani Noygu had walked away from the palaces and vanished. Fourteen days since the assassin had put a dagger in Maati's own guts. Thirteen days since the fire in the cages.

He knew now as much as he was likely to know of Itani Noygu, the courier for House Siyanti, and almost nothing of Otah-kvo. Itani had worked in the gentleman's trade for nearly eight years. He had lived in the eastern islands; he was a charming man, decent at his craft if not expert. He'd had lovers in Tan-Sadar and Utani, but had broken things off with both after he started keeping company with a wayhouse keeper in Udun. His fellows were frankly disbelieving that this could be the rogue Otah Machi, night-gaunt that haunted the dreams of Machi. But where he probed and demanded, where he dug and pried, pleaded and coddled and threatened, there was no sign of Otah-kvo. Where there should have been secrecy, there was nothing. Where there should have been meetings with high men in his house, or another house, or *somebody*, there was nothing. There should have been conspiracy against his father, his brothers, the city of his birth. There was nothing.

All of which went to confirm the conclusion that Maati had reached, bleeding on the paving stones. Otah was not scheming for his father's chair, had not killed Biitrah, had not hired the assassin to attack him.

And yet Otah was here, or had been. Maati had written to the Dai-kvo, outlining what he knew and guessed and only wondered, but he had received no word back as yet and might not for several weeks. By which time, he suspected, the old Khai would be dead. That thought alone tired him, and it was the library that he turned to for distraction.

He sat back now on one of the thick chairs, slowly unfurling a scroll with his left hand and furling it again with his right. In the space between, ancient words stirred. The pale ink formed the letters of the Empire, and the scroll purported to be an essay by Jaiet Khai—a man named the Servant of Memory from the great years when the word Khai had still meant servant. The grammar was formal and antiquated, the tongue was nothing spoken now. It was unlikely than anyone but a poet would be able to make sense of it.

There are two types of impossibility in the andat, the man long since dust had written. The first of these are those thoughts which cannot be understood. Time and Mind are examples of this type; mysteries so profound that even the wise cannot do more than guess at their deepest structure. These bindings may someday become possible with greater understanding of the world and our place within it. For this reason they are of no interest to me. The second type is made up of those thoughts by their nature impossible to bind, and no greater knowledge shall ever permit them. Examples of this are Imprecision and Freedom-From-Bondage. Holding Time or Mind would be like holding a mountain in your hands. Holding Imprecision would be like holding the backs of your hands in your palms. One of these images may inspire awe, it is true, but the other is *interesting*.

"Is there anything I can do for you, Maati-cha?" the librarian asked again.

"Thank you, Baarath-cha, but no. I'm quite well."

The librarian took a step forward all the same. His hands seemed to twitch towards the books and scrolls that Maati had gathered to look over. The man's smile was fixed, his eyes glassy. In his worst moments, Maati had considered pretending to catch one of the ancient scrolls on fire, if only to see whether Baarath's knees would buckle.

"Because, if there was anything . . ."

"Maati-cha?" The familiar voice of the young poet rang from the front of the library. Maati turned to see Cehmai stride into the chamber with a casual pose of welcome to Baarath. He dropped into a chair across from Maati's own. The librarian was trapped for a moment between the careful formality he had with Maati and the easy companionship he appeared to enjoy with Cehmai. He hesitated for a moment, then, frowning, retreated.

"I'm sorry about him," Cehmai said. "He's an ass sometimes, but he is good at heart."

"If you say so. And what brings you? I thought there was another celebration of the Khai's daughter making a match."

"A messenger's come from the Dai-kvo," Cehmai said, lowering his voice so that Baarath, no doubt just behind the corner and listening, might not make out the words. "He says it's important."

Maati sat up, his belly twingeing a bit. His messages couldn't have reached the Dai-kvo's village and returned so soon. This had to be something that had been sent before word of his injury had gone out, which meant the Dai-kvo had found something, or wished something done, or . . . He noticed Cehmai's expression and paused.

"Is the seal not right?"

"There is no seal," Cehmai said. "There is no letter. The messenger says he was instructed to only speak the message to you, in private. It was too important, he said, to be written."

"That seems unlikely," Maati said.

"Doesn't it?"

"Where is he now?"

"They brought him to the poet's house when they heard who had sent him. I've had him put in a courtyard in the Fourth Palace. A walled one, with armsmen to keep him there. If this is a fresh assassin . . ."

"Then he'll answer more questions than the last one can," Maati said. "Take me there."

As they left, Maati saw Baarath swoop down on the books and scrolls like a mother reunited with her babe. Maati knew that they would all be hidden in obscure drawers and shelves by the time he came back. Some, he would likely never see again.

The sun was moving toward the mountain peaks in the west, early evening descending on the valley. They walked together down the white gravel path that led to the Fourth Palace, looking, Maati was sure, like nothing so much as a teacher and his student in their matching brown poet's robes. Except that Cehmai was the man who held the andat, and Maati was only a scholar. They didn't speak, but Maati felt a knot of excitement and apprehension tightening in him.

At the palace's great hall, a servant met them with a pose of formal welcome that couldn't hide the brightness in her eyes. At a gesture, she led them down a wide corridor and then up a flight of stairs to a gallery that looked down into the courtyard. Maati forced himself to breathe deeply as he stepped to the edge and looked down, Cehmai at his side.

The space was modest, but lush. Thin vines rose along one wall and part of another. Two small, sculpted maple trees stood, one at either end of a long, low stone bench. It looked like a painting—the perfectly balanced garden, with the laborer in his ill-cut robes the only thing out of place. A breeze stirred the branches of the trees with a sound equal parts flowing water and dry pages turning. Maati stepped back. His throat was tight, but his head felt perfectly clear. So this was how it would happen. Very well.

Cehmai was frowning down warily at Otah-kvo. Maati put his hand on the young man's shoulder.

"I have to speak with him," Maati said. "Alone."

"You don't think he's a threat?"

"It doesn't matter. I still need to speak with him."

"Maati-kvo, please take one of the armsmen. Even if you keep him at the far end of the yard, you can . . ."

Maati took a pose that refused this, and saw something shift in the young man's eyes. Respect, Maati thought. He thinks I'm being brave. How odd that I was that young once.

"Take me there," Maati said.

OTAH SAT IN THE GARDEN, HIS BACK AND NECK TIGHT FROM RIDING AND from fear, and remembered being young in the summer cities. In one of the low towns outside Saraykeht, there had been a rock at the edge of a cliff that jutted out over the water so that, when the tide was just right, a boy of thirteen summers might step out to its edge and peer past his toes at the ocean below him and feel like a bird. There had been a band of them—the homeless young scraping by on pity and small labor—who had dared each other to dive from that cliff. The first time he had made the leap himself, he had been sure the moment his feet left the rough, hot stone that he would die. That pause, divorced from earth and water, willing himself back up, trying to force himself to fly and take back that one irrevocable moment, had felt very much like sitting quiet and alone in this garden. The trees shifted like slow dancers, the flowers trembled, the stone glowed where the sun struck it and faded to gray where it did not. He rubbed his fingers against the gritty bench to remind himself where he was, and to keep the panic in his breast from possessing him.

He heard the door slide open with a whisper, and then shut again. He rose, forcing his body to move deliberately and took a pose of greeting even before he looked up. Maati Vaupathai. Time had thickened him, and there was a sorrow in the lines of his face that hadn't been there even in the weary days when he had stood between his master Heshai-kvo and the death that had eventually come. Otah wondered whether that change had sprung from Heshai's murder, and whether Maati had ever guessed that Otah had been the one who drew the cord across the old poet's throat.

Maati took a pose of welcome appropriate for a student to a teacher.

"It wasn't me," Otah said. "My brother. You. I had nothing to do with any of it."

"I had guessed that." Maati said. He did not come nearer.

"Are you going to call the armsmen? There must be half a dozen out there. Your student could have been more subtle in calling them."

"There's more than that, and he isn't my student. I don't have any students. I don't have anything." A strange smile twitched at the corner of his mouth. "I have been something of a disappointment to the Dai-kvo. Why are you here?"

"Because I need help," Otah said, "and I hoped we might not be enemies."

Maati seemed to weigh the words. He walked to the bench, sat, and leaned forward on clasped hands. Otah sat beside him, and they were silent. A sparrow landed on the ground before them, cocked its head, and fluttered madly away again.

"I came back because it was controlling me," Otah said. "This place. These people. I've spent a lifetime leaving them, and they keep coming back and destroying everything I build. I wanted to see it. I wanted to look at the city and my brothers and my father."

He looked at his hands.

"I don't know what I wanted," Otah said.

"Yes," Maati said, and then, awkwardly, "It was foolish, though. And there will be consequences."

"There have been already."

"There'll be more."

Again, the silence loomed. There was too much to say, and no order for it. Otah frowned hard, opened his mouth to speak, and closed it again.

"I have a son," Maati said. "Liat and I have a son. His name's Nayiit. He's probably just old enough now that he's started to notice that girls aren't always repulsive. I haven't seen them in years."

"I didn't know," Otah said.

"How would you? The Dai-kvo said that I was a fool to keep a family. I am a poet, and my duty is to the world. And when I wouldn't renounce them, I fell from favor. I was given duties that might as well have been done by an educated slave. And you know, there was an odd kind of pride about it for a while. I was given clothing, shelter, food for myself. Only for myself. I thought of leaving. Of folding my robes on the bed and running away as you did. I thought of you, the way you had chosen your own shape for your life instead of the shapes that were offered you. I thought I was doing the same. Gods, Otah-kvo, I wish you had been here. All these years, I wish I had been able to talk to you. To someone."

"I'm sorry. . . ."

Maati raised a hand to stop him.

"My son," Maati said, then his voice thickened, and he coughed and began again. "Liat and I parted ways. My low status among the poets didn't have the air of romance for her that I saw in it. And . . . there were other things. Raising my son called for money and time and I had little to spare of either. My son is thirteen summers. Thirteen. She was carrying him before we left Saraykeht."

Otah felt the words as if he'd been struck an unexpected blow—a sensation of shock without source or location, and then the flood. Maati glanced over at him and read his thoughts from his face, and he nodded.

"I know," Maati said. "She told me about bedding you that one time after you came back, before you left again. Before Heshai-kvo died and Seedless vanished. I suppose she was afraid that if I discovered it someday and she hadn't said anything it would make things worse. She told me the truth. And she swore that my son was mine. And I believe her."

"Do you?"

"Of course not. I mean, some days I did. When he was young and I could hold him in one arm, I was sure that he was mine. And then some nights I would wonder. And even in those times when I was sure that he was yours, I still loved him. That was the worst of it. The nights I lay awake in a village where women and children aren't allowed, in a tiny cell that stank of the disapproval of everyone I had ever hoped to please. I knew that I loved him, and that he wasn't mine. No, don't. Let me finish. I couldn't be a father to him. And if I hadn't fathered him either, what was there left but watching from a distance while this little creature grew up and away from me without even knowing my heart was tucked in his sleeve."

Maati wiped at his eyes with the back of one hand.

"Liat said she was tired of my always mourning, that the boy deserved some joy; that she did too. So after that I didn't have them, and I didn't have the respect of the people I saw and worked beside. I was eaten by guilt over losing them, and having taken her from you. I thought that she would have been happy with you. That you would have been happy with her. If only I hadn't broken faith with you, the world might have been right after all. And you might have stayed.

"And that has been my life until the day they called on me to hunt you."

"I see," Otah said.

"I have missed your company so badly, Otah-kya, and I have never hated anyone more. I have been waiting for years to say that. So. Now I have, what was it you wanted from me?"

Otah caught his breath.

"I wanted your help," he said. "There's a woman. She was my lover once. When I told her . . . when I told her about my family, my past, she turned me out. She was afraid that knowing me would put her and the people she was responsible for in danger."

"She's wise, then," Maati said.

"I hoped you would help me protect her," Otah said. His heart was a lump of cold lead. "Perhaps that was optimistic."

Maati laughed. The sound was hollow.

"And how would I do that?" Maati asked. "Kill your brothers for you? Tell the Khai that the Dai-kvo had decreed that she was not to be harmed? I don't have that power. I don't have any power at all. This was my chance at redemption. They called upon me to hunt you because I knew your face, and I failed at that until you walked into the palaces and asked to speak with me."

"Go to my father with me. I refused the brand, but I won't now. I'll renounce my claim to the chair in front of anyone he wants, only don't let him kill me before I do it."

Maati looked across at him. The sparrow returned for a moment to perch between them.

"It won't work," he said. "Renunciation isn't a simple thing, and once you've stepped outside of form, stepping back in . . ."

"But . . ."

"They won't believe you. And even if they did, they'd still fear you enough to see you dead."

Otah took a deep breath, and then slowly let it out, letting his head sink into his hands. The air itself seemed to have grown heavier, thicker. It had been a mad hope, and even in its failure, at least Kiyan would be safe. It was past time, perhaps, that people stopped paying prices for knowing him.

He could feel himself shaking. When he sat, his hands were perfectly still, though he could still feel the trembling in them.

"So what are you going to do?" Otah asked.

"In a moment, I'm going to call in the armsmen that are waiting outside that door," Maati said, his voice deceptively calm. He was trembling as well. "I am going to bring you before the Khai, who will at some point decide either that you are a murderer who has killed his son Biitrah and put you to the sword, or else a legitimate child of Machi who should be set loose for one of your older brothers to kill. I will speak on your behalf, and any evidence I can find that suggests Biitrah's murder wasn't your work, I will present."

"Well, thank you for that, at least."

"Don't," Maati said. "I'm doing it because it's true. If I thought you'd arranged it, I'd have said that."

"Loyalty to the truth isn't something to throw out either."

Maati took a pose that accepted the gratitude, and then dropped his hands to his sides.

"There's something you should know," Otah said. "It might . . . it seems to be your business. When I was in the islands, after Saraykeht, there was a woman. Not Maj. Another woman. I shared a bed with her for two, almost three years."

"Otah-kvo, I admire your conquests, but . . ."

"She wanted a child. From me. But it never took. Almost three years, and she bled with the moon the whole time. I heard that after I left, she took up with a fisherman from a tribe to the north and had a baby girl."

"I see," Maati said, and there was something in his voice. A brightness. "Thank you, Otah-kvo."

"I missed you as well. I wish we had had more time. Or other circumstances."

"As do I. But it isn't ours to choose. Shall we do this thing?"

"I don't suppose I could shave first?" Otah asked, touching his chin.

"I don't see how," Maati said, rising. "But perhaps we can get you some better robes."

Otah didn't mean to laugh; it simply came out of him. And then Maati was laughing as well, and the birds startled around them, lifting up into the sky. Otah rose and took a pose of respect appropriate to the closing of a meeting. Maati responded in kind, and they walked together to the door. Maati slid it open, and Otah looked to see whether there was a gap in the men, a chance to dodge them and sprint out to the streets. He might as well have looked for a stone cloud. The armsmen seemed to have doubled in number, and two already had bare blades at the ready. The young poet—the one Maati said wasn't his student—was there among them, his expression serious and concerned. Maati spoke as if the bulky men and their weapons weren't there.

"Cehmai-cha," he said. "Good that you're here. I would like to introduce you to my old friend, Otah, the sixth son of the Khai Machi. Otah-kvo, this is Cehmai Tyan and that small mountain in the back is the andat Stone-Made-Soft which he controls. Cehmai assumed you were an assassin come to finish me off."

"I'm not," Otah said with a levity that seemed at odds with his situation, but which felt perfectly natural. "But I understand the misconception. It's the beard. I'm usually better shaved."

Cehmai opened his mouth, closed it, and then took a formal pose of welcome. Maati turned to the armsmen.

"Chain him," he said.

EVEN AT THE HEIGHT OF MORNING, THE WIVES' QUARTERS OF THE HIGH palace were filled with the small somber activity of a street market starting to close at twilight. In the course of his life, the Khai Machi had taken eleven women as wives. Some had become friends, lovers, companions. Others had been little more than permanent guests in his house, sent as a means of assuring favor as one might send a good hunting dog or a talented slave. Idaan had heard that there were several of them with whom he had never shared a bed. It had been Biitrah's wife, Hiami, who'd told her that, trying to explain to a young girl that the Khaiem had a different relationship to their women than other men had, that it was traditional. It hadn't worked. Even the words the older woman had used—*your father chooses not to*—had proven her point that this was a comfort house with high ceilings, grand halls, and only a single client.

But now that was changing, not in character, but in the particulars. The succession would have the same effect on the eight wives who remained, whoever took the seat. It would be time for them to leave—make the journey back to whatever city or family had sent them forth in the first place. The oldest of them, a sharp-tongued woman named Carai, would be returning to a high family in Yalakeht where the man who would choose her disposition had been a delighted toddler grinning and filling his pants the last time she'd seen him. Another woman—one of the recent ones hardly older than Idaan herself—had taken a lover in the court. She was being sent back to Chaburi-Tan, likely to be turned around and shipped off to another of the Khaiem or traded between the houses of the utkhaiem as a token of political alliance. Many of the wives had known each other for decades and would now scatter and lose the friends and companions they had known best. And on and on, every one of them a life shaped by a man's will, constrained by tradition.

Idaan walked through the wide, bright corridors, listened to these women preparing to depart when the inevitable news came, anticipating the grief in a way that was as hard as the grief itself. Perhaps harder. She accepted their congratulations on her marriage. She would be able to remain in the city, and should her man die before her, her family would be there to support her. She, at least, would never be uprooted. Hiami had never understood why Idaan had objected to this way of living. Idaan had never understood why these women hadn't set the palaces on fire.

Her own rooms were set in the back; small apartments with rich tapestries of white and gold on the walls. They might almost have been mistaken for the home of some merchant leader—the overseer of a great trading house, or a trade master who spoke with the voice of a city's craftsmen. If only she had been born one of those. As she entered, one of her servants met her with an expression that suggested news. Idaan took a pose of query.

"Adrah Vaunyogi is waiting to see you, Idaan-cha," the servant girl said. "It was approaching midday, so I've put him in the dining hall. There is food waiting. I hope I haven't . . ."

"No," Idaan said, "you did well. Please see that we're left alone."

He sat at the long, wooden table, and he did not look up when she came in. Idaan was willing to ignore him as well as to be ignored, so she gathered a bowl of food from the platters—early grapes from the south, sticky with their own blood; hard, crumbling cheese with a ripe scent that was both appetizing and not; twice-baked flatbread that cracked sharply when she broke off a piece—and retired to a couch. She forced herself to forget that he was here, to look forward at the bare fire grate. Anger buoyed her up, and she clung to it.

She heard it when he stood, heard his footsteps approaching. It was a little victory, but it pleased her. As he sat cross-legged on the floor before her, she raised an eyebrow and sketched a pose of welcome before choosing another grape.

"I came last night," he said. "I was looking for you."

"I wasn't here," she said.

The pause was meant to injure her. *Look how sad you've made me, Idaan.* It was a child's tactic, and that it partially worked infuriated her.

"I've had trouble sleeping," she said. "I walk. Otherwise, I'd spend the whole night staring at netting and watching the candle burn down. No call for that."

Adrah sighed and nodded his head.

"I've been troubled too," he said. "My father can't reach the Galts. With Oshai . . . with what happened to him, he's afraid they may withdraw their support."

"Your father is an old woman frightened there's a snake in the night bucket," Idaan said, breaking a corner of her bread. "They may lie low now, but once it's clear that you're in position to become Khai, they'll do what they promised. They've nothing to gain by not."

"Once I'm Khai, they'll still own me," Adrah said. "They'll know how I came there. They'll be able to hold it over me. If they tell what they know, the gods only know what would happen."

Idaan took a bite of grape and cheese both—the sweet and the salt mingling pleasantly. When she spoke, she spoke around it.

"They won't. They won't dare, Adrah. Give the worst: we're exposed by the Galts. We're deposed and killed horribly in the streets. Fine. Lift your gaze up from your own corpse for a moment and tell me what happens next?"

"There's a struggle. Some other family takes the chair."

"Yes. And what will the new Khai do?"

"He'll slaughter my family," Adrah said, his voice hollow and ghostly. Idaan leaned forward and slapped him.

"He'll have Stone-Made-Soft level a few Galtic mountain ranges and sink some islands. Do you think there's a Khai in any city that would sit still at the word of the Galtic Council arranging the death of one of their own? The Galts won't own you because your exposure would mean the destruction of their nation and the wholesale slaughter of their people. So worry a little less. You're supposed to be overwhelmed with the delight of marrying me."

"Shouldn't you be delighted too, then?"

"I'm busy mourning my father," she said dryly. "Do we have any wine?"

"How is he? Your father?"

"I don't know," Idaan said. "I try not to see him these days. He makes me . . . feel weak. I can't afford that just now."

"I heard he's failing."

"Men can fail for a long time," she said, and stood. She left the bowl on the floor and walked back to her bedroom, holding her hands out before her, sticky with juice. Adrah followed along behind her and lay on her bed. She poured water into her stone basin and watched him as she washed her hands. He was a boy, lost in the world. Perhaps now was as good a time as any. She took a deep breath.

"I've been thinking, Adrah-kya," she said. "About when you become Khai."

He turned his head to look at her, but did not rise or speak.

"It's going to be important, especially at the first, to gather allies. Founding a line is a delicate thing. I know we agreed that it would always be only the two of us, but perhaps we were wrong in that. If you take other wives, you'll have more the appearance of tradition and the support of the families who bind themselves to us."

"My father said the same," he said.

Oh did he? Idaan thought, but she held her face still and calm. She dried her hands on the basin cloth and came to sit on the bed beside him. To her surprise, he was weeping; small tears coming from the outer corners of his eyes, thin tracks shining on his skin. Without willing it, her hand went to his cheek, caressing him. He shifted to look at her.

"I love you, Idaan. I love you more than anything in the world. You are the only person I've ever felt this way about."

His lips trembled and she pressed a finger against them to quiet him. These weren't things she wanted to hear, but he would not be stopped.

"Let's end this," he said. "Let's just be together, here. I'll find another way to move ahead in the court, and your brother . . . you'll still be his blood, and we'll still be well kept. Can't we . . . can't we, please?"

"All this because you don't want to take another woman?" she said softly, teasing him. "I find that hard to believe."

He took her hand in his. He had soft hands. She remembered thinking that the first time they'd fallen into her bed together. Strong, soft, wide hands. She felt tears forming in her own eyes.

"My father said that I should take other wives," he said. "My mother said that, knowing you, you'd only agree to it if you could take lovers of your own too. And then you weren't here last night, and I waited until it was almost dawn. And you . . . you want to . . ."

"You think I've taken another man?" she asked.

His lips pressed thin and bloodless, and he nodded. His hand squeezed hers as if she might save his life, if only he held onto her. A hundred things came to her mind all at once. *Yes, of course I have. How dare you accuse me? Cehmai is the only clean thing left in my world, and you cannot have him.* She smiled as if Adrah were a boy being silly, as if he were wrong.

"That would be the stupidest thing I could possibly do just now," she said, neither lying nor speaking the truth of it. She leaned forward to kiss him, but before their mouths touched, a voice wild with excitement called out from the atrium.

"Idaan-cha! Idaan-cha! Come quickly!"

Idaan leapt up as if she'd been caught doing something she ought not, then gathered herself, straightened her robes. The mirror showed that the paint on her mouth and eyes was smudged from eating and weeping, but there wasn't time to reapply it. She pushed back a stray lock of hair and stormed out.

The servant girl took a pose of apology as Idaan approached her. She wore the colors of her father's personal retinue, and Idaan's heart sank to her belly. He had died. It had happened. But the girl was smiling, her eyes bright.

"What's happened?" Idaan demanded.

"Everything," the girl said. "You're summoned to the court. The Khai is calling everyone."

"Why? What's happened?"

"I'm not to say, Idaan-cha," the girl said.

Idaan felt the rage-blood in her face as if she were standing near a fire. She didn't think, didn't plan. Her body seemed to move of its own accord as she slid forward and clapped her hand on the servant girl's throat and pressed her to the wall. There was shock in the girl's expression, and Idaan sneered at it. Adrah fluttered like a bird in the corner of her vision.

"Say," Idaan said. "Because I asked you twice, tell me what's happened. And do it now."

"The upstart," the girl said. "They've caught him."

Idaan stepped back, dropping her hand. The girl's eyes were wide. The air of excitement and pleasure were gone. Adrah put a hand on Idaan's shoulder, and she pushed it away.

"He was here," the girl said. "In the palaces. The visiting poet caught him, and they're bringing him before the Khai."

Idaan licked her lips. Otah Machi was here. He had been here for the gods only knew how long. She looked at Adrah, but his expression spoke of an uncertainty and surprise as deep as her own. And a fear that wasn't entirely about their conspiracy.

"What's your name?" she asked.

"Choya," the girl said.

Idaan took a pose of abject apology. It was more than a member of the utkhaiem would have normally presented to a servant, but Idaan felt her guilt welling up like blood from a cut.

"I am very sorry, Choya-cha. I was wrong to—"

"But that isn't all," the servant girl said. "A courier came this morning from Tan-Sadar. He'd been riding for three weeks. Kaiin Machi is dead. Your brother Danat killed him, and he's coming back. The courier guessed he might be a week behind him. Danat Machi's going to be the new Khai Machi. And Idaan-cha, he'll be back in the city in time for your wedding!"

7

>+< On one end, the chain ended at a cube of polished granite the color of soot that stood as high as a man's waist. On the other, it linked to a rough iron collar around Otah's neck. Sitting with his back to the stone—the chain was not so long that he could stand—Otah remembered seeing a brown bear tied to a pole in the main square of a low town outside Tan-Sadar. Dogs had been set upon it three at a time, and with each new wave, the men had wagered on which animal would survive.

Armsmen stood around him with blades drawn and leather armor, stationed widely enough apart to allow anyone who wished it a good view of the captive. Beyond them, the representatives of the utkhaiem in fine robes and ornate jewelry crowded the floor and two tiers of the balconies that rose up to the base of the domed ceiling far above him. The dais before him was empty. Otah wondered what would happen if he should need to empty his bladder. It seemed unlikely that they would let him piss on the fine parquet floor, but neither could he imagine being led away decorously. He tried to picture what they saw, this mob of nobility, when they looked at him. He didn't try to charm them or play on their sympathies. He was the upstart, and there wasn't a man or woman in the hall who wasn't delighted to see him debased and humiliated.

The first of the servants appeared, filing out from a hidden door and spacing themselves around the chair. Otah picked out the brown poet's robe, but it was Cehmai with the bulk of his andat moving behind him. Maati wasn't with him; Cehmai was speaking with a woman in the robes of the Khaiem—Otah's sister, she would be. He wondered what her name was.

The last of the servants and counselors took their places, and the crowd fell silent. The Khai Machi walked out, as graceful as a dying man could be. His robes were lush and full, and served to do little more than show how wasted his frame had become. Otah could see the rouge on his sunken cheeks, trying to give the appearance of vigor long since gone. Whisperers fanned out from the dais and into the crowd. The Khai took a pose of welcome appropriate to the opening of a ritual judgment. Otah rose to his knees.

"I am told that you are my son, Otah Machi, whom I gave over to the poets' school."

The whisperers echoed it through the hall. It was his moment to speak now, and he found his heart was so full of humiliation and fear and anger that he had nothing to say. He raised his hands and took a pose of greeting—a casual one that would have been appropriate for a peasant son to his father. There was a murmur among the utkhaiem.

"I am further told that you were once offered the poet's robes, and you refused that honor."

Otah tried to rise, but the most the chain allowed was a low stoop. He cleared his throat and spoke, pushing the words out clear enough to be heard in the farthest gallery.

"That is true. I was a child, most high. And I was angry."

"And I hear that you have come to my city and killed my eldest child. Biitrah Machi is dead by your hand."

"That is *not* true, father," Otah said. "I won't say that no man has ever died by my hand, but I didn't kill Biitrah. I have no wish or intention to become the Khai Machi."

"Then why have you come here?" the Khai shouted, rising to his feet. His face was twisted in rage, his fists trembled. In all his travels, Otah had never seen the Khai of any city look more like a man. Otah felt something like pity through his humiliation and rage, and it let him speak more softly when he spoke again.

"I heard that my father was dying."

It seemed that the murmur of the crowds would never end. It rolled like waves against the seashore. Otah knelt again; the awkward stooping hurt his neck and back, and there was no point trying to maintain dignity here. They waited, he and his father, staring at each other across the space. Otah tried to feel some bond, some kinship that would bridge this gap, but there was nothing. The Khai Machi was his father by an accident of birth, and nothing more.

He saw the old man's eyes flicker, as if unsure of himself. He couldn't have always been this way—the Khaiem were inhumanly studied in ritual and grace. It was the mark of their calling. Otah wondered what his father had been when he was young and strong. He wondered what he would have been like as a man among his children.

The Khai raised a hand, and the crowd's susurrus tapered down to silence. Otah did not move.

"You have stepped outside tradition," he said. "Whether you took a hand against my son is a question that has already gathered an array of opinion. It is something I must think on.

"I have had other news this day. Danat Machi has won the right of succession. He is returning to the city even now. I will consult with him on your fate. Until then, you shall be confined in the highest room in the great tower. I do not care to have your accomplices taking your death in their own hands this time. Danat and I—the Khai Machi and the Khai yet to come—shall decide together what kind of beast you are."

Otah took a pose of supplication. That he was on his knees only made the gesture clearer. He was dead, whatever happened. He could see that now. If there had been a chance of mercy—and likely there hadn't—having father and son converse would remove it. But in the black dread, there was this one chance to speak as himself—not as Itani Noygu or some other mask. And if it offended the court, there was little worse they could do to him than he faced now. His father hesitated, and Otah spoke.

"I have seen many of the cities of the Khaiem, most high. I have been born into the highest of families, and I have been offered the greatest of honors. And if I am here to meet my death at the hands of those who should by all rights love me, at least hear me out. Our cities are not well, father. Our traditions are not well. You stand there on that dais now because you killed your own. You are celebrating the return of Danat, who killed his brother, and at the same time preparing to condemn me on the suspicion that I did the same. A tradition that calls men to kill their brothers and discard their sons cannot be—"

"Enough!" the Khai roared, and his voice carried. The whisperers were silent and unneeded. "I have not carried this city on my back for all these years to be lectured now by a rebel and a traitor and a poisoner. You are not my son! You lost that right! You squandered it! Tell me that this . . ." The Khai raised his hands in a gesture that seemed to encompass every man and woman of the court, the palaces, the city, the valley, the mountains, the world. ". . . this is evil? Because our traditions are what hold all this from chaos. We are the Khaiem! We rule with the power of the andat, and we do not accept instruction from couriers and laborers who . . . who killed . . ."

The Khai closed his eyes and seemed to sway for a moment. The woman to whom Cehmai had been speaking leapt up, her hand on the old man's elbow. Otah could see them murmuring to each other, but he had no idea what they were saying. The woman walked with him back to the chair and helped him to sit. His face seemed sunken in pain. The woman was crying—streaks of kohl black on her cheeks—but her bearing was more regal and sure than their father's had been. She stepped forward and spoke.

"The Khai is weary," she said, as if daring anyone present to say anything else. "He has given his command. The audience is finished!"

The voices rose almost as high and ran almost as loud as they had at anything that had gone before. A woman—even if she was his daughter—taking the initiative to speak for the Khai? The court would be scandalized. Otah already imagined them placing bets as to whether the man would live the night, and if he died now, whether it would be this woman's fault for shaming him so deeply when he was already weak. And Otah could see that she knew this. The contempt in her expression was eloquent as any oratory. He caught her eye and took a pose of approval. She looked at him as if he were a stranger who had spoken her name, then turned away to help their father walk back to his rooms.

The march up to his cage led through a spiral stone stair so small that his shoulders touched each wall, and his head stayed bent. The chain stayed on his neck, his hands now bound behind him. He watched the armsman before him half walking, half climbing the steep blocks of stone. When Otah slowed, the man behind him struck with the butt of a spear and laughed. Otah, his hands bound, sprawled against the steps, ripping the flesh of his knees and chin. After that, he made a point to slow as little as possible.

His thighs burned with each step and the constant turning to the right left him nauseated. He thought of stopping, of refusing to move. They were taking him up to wait for death anyway. There was nothing to be gained by collaborating with them. But he went on, cursing under his breath.

When the stairs ended, he found himself in a wide hall. The sky doors in the north wall were open, and a platform hung level with them and shifting slightly in the breeze, the great chains taut. Another four armsmen stood waiting.

"Relief?" the man who had pushed him asked.

The tallest of the new armsmen took a pose of affirmation and spoke. "We'll take the second half. You four head up and we'll all go down together." The new armsmen led Otah to a fresh stairway, and the ordeal began again. He had begun almost to dream in his pain by the time they stopped. Thick, powerful hands pushed him into a room, and the door closed behind him with a sound like a capstone being shoved over an open tomb. The armsman said something through a slit in the door, but Otah couldn't make sense of it and didn't have the will to try. He lay on the floor until he realized that his arms had been freed and the iron collar taken from around his neck. The skin where it had rested was chafed raw.

The voices of men seeped through the door, and then the sound of a winch creaking as it lowered the platform and its cargo of men. Then there were only two voices speaking in light, conversational tones. He couldn't make out a word they said.

He forced himself to sit up and take stock. The room was larger than he'd expected, and bare. It could have been used as a storage room or set with table and chairs for a small meeting. There was a bowl of water in one corner, but no food, no candles, nothing but the stone to sleep on. The light came from a barred window. His hip and knees ached as Otah pulled himself up and stumbled over to it. He was facing south, and the view was like he'd become a bird. He leaned out—the bars were not so narrowly spaced that he couldn't climb out and fall to his death if he chose. Below him, the carts in the streets were like ants shuffling along in their lines. A crow launched itself from a crack or beam and circled below him, the sun shining on its black back. Trembling, he pulled himself back in. There were no shutters to close off the sky.

He tried the door's latch, but it had been barred from without, and the hinges were leather and worked iron. Not the sort of thing a man could take apart with teeth. Otah knelt by the bowl of water and drank from his cupped hand. He washed out the worst of his wounds, and left a third in the bowl. There was no knowing how long it might be before they saw fit to give him more. He wondered if there were birds that came up this high to rest, and whether he would be able to trap one. Not that he would have the chance to cook it—there was nothing to burn here, and no grate to burn it in. Otah ran his hands over his face, and despite himself, laughed. It seemed unlikely they would allow him anything sharp enough to shave with. He would die with this sad little beard.

Otah stretched out in a corner, his arm thrown over his eyes, and tried to sleep, wondering as he did whether the sense of movement came from his own abused and exhausted body, or if it were true that so far up even stone swayed.

MAATI LOOKED AT THE FLOOR. HIS FACE WAS HARD WITH FRUSTRATION AND anger.

"If you want him dead, most high," he said, his voice measured and careful, "you might at least have the courtesy to kill him."

The Khai Machi raised the clay pipe to his lips. He seemed less to breathe the smoke in than to drink it. The sweet resin from it had turned every surface in the room slightly tacky to the touch. The servant in the blue and gold robes of a physician sat discreetly in a dim corner, pretending not to hear the business of the city. The rosewood door was closed behind them. Lanterns of sanded glass filled the room with soft light, rendering them all shadowless.

"I've listened to you, Maati-cha. I didn't end him there in the audience chamber. I am giving you the time you asked," the old man said. "Why do you keep pressing me?"

"He has no blankets or fire. The guards have given him three meals in the last four days. And Danat will return before I've had word back from the Dai-kvo. If this is all you can offer, most high—"

"You can state your case to Danat-cha as eloquently as you could to me," the Khai said.

"There'll be no point if Otah dies of cold or throws himself out the tower window before then," Maati said. "Let me take him food and a thick robe. Let me talk with him."

"It's hopeless," the Khai said.

"Then there's nothing lost but my effort, and it will keep me from troubling you further."

"Your work here is complete, isn't it? Why are you bothering me, Maati-cha? You were sent to find Otah. He's found."

"I was sent to find if he was behind the death of Biitrah, and if he was not, to discover who was. I have not carried out that task. I won't leave until I have."

The Khai's expression soured, and he shook his head. His skin had grown thinner, the veins at his temples showing dark. When he leaned forward, tapping the bowl of his pipe against the side of the iron brazier with a sound like pebbles falling on stone, his grace could not hide his discomfort.

"I begin to wonder, Maati-cha, whether you have been entirely honest with me. You say that there is no great love between you and my upstart son. You bring him to me, and for that reason alone, I believe you. Everything else you have done suggests the other. You argue that it was not he who arranged Biitrah's death, though you have no suggestion who else might have. You ask for indulgences for the prisoner, you appeal to the Dai-kvo in hopes . . ."

A sudden pain seemed to touch the old man's features and one near-skeletal hand moved toward his belly.

"There is a shadow in your city," Maati said. "You've called it by Otah's name, but none of it shows any connection with Otah: not Biitrah, not the attack on me, not the murder of the assassin. None of the other couriers of any house report anything that would suggest he was more than he appeared. By his own word, he'd fled the city before the attack on me, and didn't return before the assassin was killed. How is it that he arranged all these things with no one seeing him? No one knowing his name? How is it that, now he's trapped, no one has offered to sell him in trade for their own lives?"

"Who then?"

"I don't . . ."

"Who else gained from these things?"

"Your son, Danat," Maati said. "He broke the pact. If all this talk of Otah was a ploy to distract Kaiin from the real danger, then it worked, most high. Danat will be the new Khai Machi."

"Ask him when he comes. He will be the Khai Machi, and if he has done as you said, then there's no crime in it and no reason that he should hide it."

"A poet was attacked—"

"And did you die? Are you dying? No? Then don't ask sympathy from me. Go, Maati-cha. Take the prisoner anything you like. Take him a pony and let him ride it around his cell, if that pleases you. Only don't return to me. Any business you have with me now, you have with my son."

The Khai took a pose of command that ended the audience, and Maati stood, took a pose of gratitude that he barely felt, and withdrew from the meeting room. He stalked along the corridors of the palace seething.

Back in his apartments, he took stock. He had gathered together his bundle even before he'd gone to the audience. A good wool robe, a rough cloth bag filled with nut breads and dry cheeses, and a flask of fresh water. Everything that he thought the Khai's men would permit. He folded it all together and tied it with twine.

At the base of the great tower, armsmen stood guard at the platform—a metalwork that ran on tracks set into the stone of the tower, large enough to carry twelve men. The chains that held it seemed entirely too thin. Maati identified himself, thinking his poet's robe, reputation, and haughty demeanor might suffice to make the men do as he instructed. Instead, a runner was sent to the Khai's palace to confirm that Maati was indeed permitted to see the prisoner and to give him the little gifts that he carried. Once word was brought back, Maati climbed on the platform, and the signalman on the ground blew a call on a great trumpet. The chains went taut, and the platform rose. Maati held onto the rail, his knuckles growing whiter as the ground receded. Wind plucked at his sleeves as the roofs of even the greatest palaces fell away below him. The only things so high as he was were the towers, the birds, and the mountains. It was beautiful and exhilarating, and all he could think the whole time was what would happen if a single link in any of the four chains gave way. When he reached the open sky doors at the top, the captain of the armsmen took him solidly by his arm and helped him step in.

"First time, eh?" the captain said, and his men chuckled, but not cruelly. It was a journey each of them risked, Maati realized, every day. These men were more likely to die for the vanity of Machi than he. He smiled and nodded, stepping away from the open space of the sky door.

"I've come to see the prisoner," he said.

"I know," the captain said. "The trumpet said as much, if you knew to listen for it. But understand, if he attacks you—if he tries to bargain your life for his freedom—I'll send your body down. You make your choice when you go in there. I can't be responsible for it."

The captain's expression was stern. Maati saw that he thought this possible, the danger real. Maati took a pose of thanks, hampered somewhat by the bundle under his arm. The captain only nodded and led him to a huge wooden door. Four of his men drew their blades as he unbarred it and let it swing in. Maati took a deep breath and stepped through.

Otah was huddled in a corner, his arms wrapped around his knees. He looked up and then back down. Maati heard the door close behind him, heard the bar slide home. All those men to protect him from this half-dead rag.

"I've brought food," Maati said. "I considered wine, but it seemed too much like a celebration."

Otah chuckled, a thick phlegmy sound.

"It would have gone to my head too quickly anyway," he said, his voice weak. "I'm too old to go drinking without a good meal first."

Maati knelt and unfolded the robe and arranged the food he'd brought. It seemed too little now, but when he broke off a corner of nut bread and held it out, Otah nodded his gratitude and took it. Maati opened the flask of water, put it beside Otah's feet, and sat back.

"What news?" Otah asked. "I don't hear much gossip up here."

"It's all as straightforward as a maze," Maati said. "House Siyanti is calling in every favor it has not to be banned from the city. Your old overseer has been going to each guild chapter house individually. There's even rumor he's been negotiating with hired armsmen."

"He must be frightened for his life," Otah said and shook his head wearily. "I'm sorry to have done that to him. But I suppose there's little enough I can do about it now. There does always seem to be a price people pay for knowing me."

Maati looked at his hands. For a moment he considered holding his tongue. It would be worse, he thought, holding out hope if there was none. But it was all that he had left to offer.

"I've sent to the Dai-kvo. I may have a way that you can survive this," he said. "There's no precedent for someone refusing the offer to become a poet. It's possible that . . ."

Otah sipped the water and put down the flask. His brow was furrowed.

"You've asked him to make me a poet?" Otah asked.

"I didn't say it would work," Maati said. "Only that I'd done it."

"Well, thank you for that much."

Otah reached out, took another bit of bread, and leaned back. The effort seemed to exhaust him. Maati rose and paced the room. The view from the window was lovely and inhuman. No one had ever been meant to see so far at once. A thought occurred, and he looked in the corners of the room.

"Have they . . . there's no night bucket," he said.

Otah raised one arm in a wide gesture toward the world outside.

"I've been using the window," he said. Maati smiled, and Otah smiled with him. Then for a moment they were laughing together.

"Well, that must confuse people in the streets," Maati said.

"Very large pigeons," Otah said. "They blame very large pigeons."

Maati grinned, and then felt the smile fade.

"They're going to kill, you Otah-kvo. The Khai and Danat. They can't let you live. You're too well known, and they think you'll act against them."

"They won't make do with blinding me and casting me into the wilderness, eh?"

"I'll make the suggestion, if you like."

Otah's laugh was thinner now. He took up the cheese, digging into its pale flesh with his fingers. He held a sliver out to Maati, offering to share it. Maati hesitated, and then accepted it. It was smooth as cream and salty. It would go well with the nut bread, he guessed.

"I knew this was likely to happen when I chose to come back," Otah said. "I'm not pleased by it, but it will spare Kiyan, won't it? They won't keep pressing her?"

"I can't see why they would," Maati said.

"Dying isn't so bad, then," Otah said. "At least it does something for her."

"Do you mean that?"

"I might as well, Maati-kya. Unless you plan to sneak me out in your sleeve, I think I'm going to be spared the rigors of a northern winter. I don't see there's anything to be done about that."

Maati sighed and nodded. He rose and took a pose of farewell. Even just the little food and the short time seemed to have made Otah stronger. He didn't rise, but he took a pose that answered the farewell.

Maati walked to the door and pounded to be let out. He heard the scrape of the bar being raised. Otah spoke.

"Thank you for all this. It's kind."

"I'm not doing it for you, Otah-kvo."

"All the same. Thank you."

Maati didn't reply. The door opened, and he stepped out. The captain of the armsmen started to speak, but something in Maati's expression stopped him. Maati strode to the sky doors and out to the platform as if he were walking into a hallway and not an abyss of air. He clasped his hands behind him and looked out over the roofs of Machi. What had been vertiginous only recently failed to move him now. His mind and heart were too full. When he reached the ground again, he walked briskly to his apartments. The wound in his belly itched badly, but he kept himself from worrying it. He only gathered his papers, sat on a deck of oiled wood that looked out over gardens of summer trees and ornate flowers a brighter red than blood, and planned out the remainder of his day.

There were still two armsmen from the cages with whom he hadn't spoken. If he knew who had killed the assassin, it would likely lead him nearer the truth. And the slaves and servants of the Third Palace might be persuaded to speak more of Danat Machi, now that he was coming back covered in the glory of his brother's blood. If he had used the story of Otah the Upstart to distract his remaining brother from his schemes . . .

A servant boy interrupted, announcing Cehmai. Maati took a pose of acknowledgment and had the young poet brought to him. He looked unwell, Maati thought. His skin was too pale, his eyes troubled. He couldn't think that Otah-kvo was bothering Cehmai badly, but surely something was.

Still, the boy managed a grin and when he sat, he moved with more energy than Maati himself felt.

"You sent for me, Maati-kvo?"

"I have work," he said. "You offered to help me with this project once. And I could do with your aid, if you still wish to lend it."

"You aren't stopping?"

Maati considered. He could say again that the Dai-kvo had told him to discover the murderer of Biitrah Machi and whether Otah-kvo had

had a hand in it, and that until he'd done so, he would keep to his task. It had been a strong enough argument for the utkhaiem, even for the Khai. But Cehmai had known the Dai-kvo as well as he had, and more recently. He would see how shallow the excuse was. In the end he only shook his head.

"I am not stopping," he said.

"May I ask why not?"

"They are going to kill Otah-kvo."

"Yes," Cehmai agreed, his voice calm and equable. Maati might as well have said that winter would be cold.

"And I have a few days to find whose crimes he's carrying."

Cehmai frowned and took a pose of query.

"They'll kill him anyway," Cehmai said. "If he killed Biitrah, they'll execute him for that. If he didn't, Danat will do the thing to keep his claim to be the Khai. Either way he's a dead man."

"That's likely true," Maati said. "But I've done everything else I can think to do, and this is still left, so I'll do this. If there is anything at all I can do, I have to do it."

"In order to save your teacher," Cehmai said, as if he understood.

"To sleep better twenty years from now," Maati said, correcting him. "If anyone asks, I want to be able to say that I did what could be done. And I want to be able to mean it. That's more important to me than saving him."

Cehmai seemed puzzled, but Maati found no better way to express it without mentioning his son's name, and that would open more than it would close. Instead he waited, letting the silence argue for him. Cehmai took a pose of acceptance at last, and then tilted his head.

"Maati-kvo . . . I'm sorry, but when was the last time you slept?"

Maati smiled and ignored the question.

"I'm going to meet with one of the armsmen who saw my assassin killed," he said. "I was wondering if I could impose on you to find some servant from Danat's household with whom I might speak later this evening. I have a few questions about him . . ."

DANAT MACHI ARRIVED LIKE A HERO. THE STREETS WERE FILLED WITH people cheering and singing. Festivals filled the squares. Young girls danced through the streets in lines, garlands of summer blossoms in their hair. And from his litter strewn with woven gold and silver, Danat Machi looked out like a protective father indulging a well-loved child. Idaan had been present when the word came that Danat Machi waited at the bridge for his father's permission to enter the city. She had gone down behind the runner to watch the doors fly open and the celebration that had been building spill out into the dark stone streets. They would have sung as loud for Kaiin, if Danat had been dead.

While Danat's caravan slogged its way through the crowds, Idaan retreated to the palaces. The panoply of the utkhaiem was hardly more restrained than the common folk. Members of all the high families appeared as if by chance outside the Third Palace's great hall. Musicians and singers entertained with beautiful ballads of great warriors returning home from the field, of time and life renewed in a new generation. They were songs of the proper function of the world. It was as if no one had known Biitrah or Kaiin, as if the wheel of the world were not greased with her family's blood. Idaan watched with a calm, pleasant expression while her soul twisted with disgust.

When Danat reached the long, broad yard and stepped down from his litter, a cheer went up from all those present; even from her. Danat raised his arms and smiled to them all, beaming like a child on Candles Night. His gaze found her, and he strode through the crowd to her side. Idaan raised her chin and took a pose of greeting. It was what she was expected to do. He ignored it and picked her up in a great hug, swinging her around as if she weighed nothing, and then placed her back on her own feet.

"Sister," he said, smiling into her eyes. "I can't say how glad I am to see you."

"Danat-kya," she said, and then failed.

"How are things with our father?"

The sorrow that was called for here was at least easier than the feigned delight. She saw it echoed in Danat's eyes. So close to him, she could see the angry red in the whites of his eyes, the pallor in his skin. He was wearing paint, she realized. Rouge on his cheeks and lips and some warm-toned powder to lend his skin the glow of health. Beneath it, he was sallow. She wondered if he'd grown sick, and whether there was some slow poison that might be blamed for his death.

"He has been looking forward to seeing you," she said.

"Yes. Yes, of course. And I hear that you're to become a Vaunyogi. I'm pleased for you. Adrah's a good man."

"I love him," she said, surprised to find that in some dim way it was still truth. "But how are you, brother? Are you . . . are things well with you?"

For a moment, Danat seemed about to answer. She thought she saw something weaken in him, his mouth losing its smile, his eyes looking into a darkness like the one she carried. In the end, he shook himself and kissed her forehead, then turned again to the crowd and made his way to the Khai's palace, greeting and rejoicing with everyone who crossed his path. And it was only the beginning. Danat and their father would be closeted away for a time, then the ritual welcome from the heads of the families of the utkhaiem. And then festivities and celebrations, feasts and dances and revelry in the streets and palaces and teahouses.

Idaan made her way to the compound of the Vaunyogi, and to Adrah and his father. The house servants greeted her with smiles and poses of welcome. The chief overseer led her to a small meeting room in the back. If it seemed odd that this room—windowless and dark—was used now in the summer when most gatherings were in gardens or open pavilions, the overseer made no note of it. Nothing could have been more different from the mood in the city than the one here; like a winter night that had crept into summer.

"Has House Vaunyogi forgotten where it put its candles?" she asked, and turned to the overseer. "Find a lantern or two. These fine men may be suffering from their drink, but I've hardly begun to celebrate."

The overseer took a pose that acknowledged the command and scampered off, returning immediately with his gathered light. Adrah and his father sat at a long stone table. Dark tapestries hung from the wall, red and orange and gold. When the doors were safely closed behind them, Idaan pulled out one of the stools and sat on it. Her gaze moved from the father's face to the son's. She took a pose of query.

"You seem distressed," she said. "The whole city is loud with my brother's glory, and you two are skulking in here like criminals."

"We have reason to be distressed," Daaya Vaunyogi said. She wondered whether Adrah would age into the same loose jowls and watery eyes. "I've finally reached the Galts. They've cooled. Killing Oshai's made them nervous, and now with Danat back . . . we expected to have the fighting between your brothers to cover our . . . our work. There's no hope of that now. And that poet hasn't stopped hunting around, even with the holes Oshai poked in him."

"The more reason you have to be distressed," Idaan said, "the more important that you should not seem it. Besides, I still have two living brothers."

"Ah, and you have some way to make Danat die at Otah's hand?" the old man said. There was mockery in his voice, but there was also hope. And fear. He had seen what she had done, and perhaps now he thought her capable of anything. She supposed that would be something worthy of his hope and fear.

"I don't have the details. But, yes. The longer we wait, the more suspicious it will look when Danat and the poet die."

"You still want Maati Vaupathai dead?" Daaya asked.

"Otah is locked away, and the poet's digging. Maati Vaupathai isn't satisfied to blame the upstart for everything, even if the whole city besides him is. There are three breathing men between Adrah and my father's chair. Danat, Otah, and the poet. I'll need armsmen, though, to do what I intend. How many could you put together? They would have to be men you trust."

Daaya looked at his son, as if expecting to find some answer there, but Adrah neither spoke nor moved. He might very nearly not have been there at all. Idaan swallowed her impatience and leaned forward, her palms spread on the cool stone of the table. One of the candles sputtered and spat.

"I know a man. A mercenary lord. He's done work for me before and kept quiet," Daaya said at last. He didn't seem certain.

"We'll free the upstart and slit the poet's throat," Idaan said. "There won't be any question who's actually done the thing. No sane person would doubt that it was Otah's hand. And when Danat rides out to find him, our men will be ready to ride with him. That will be the dangerous part. You'll have to find a way to get him apart from anyone else who goes."

"And the upstart?" Daaya asked.

"He'll go where we tell him to go. We'll just have saved him, after all. There will be no reason to think we mean him harm. They'll all be dead in time for the wedding, and if we do it well, the joy that is our bonding will put us as the clear favorites to take the chair. That should be enough to push the Galts into action. Adrah will be Khai before the harvest."

Idaan leaned back, smiling in grim satisfaction. It was Adrah who broke the silence, his voice calm and sure and unlike him.

"It won't work."

Idaan began to take a pose of challenge, but she hesitated when she saw his eyes. Adrah had gone cold as winter. It wasn't fear that drove him, whatever his father's weakness. There was something else in him, and Idaan felt a stirring of unease.

"I can't see why not," Idaan said, her voice still strong and sure.

"Killing the poet and freeing Otah would be simple enough to manage. But the other. No. It supposes that Danat would lead the hunt himself. He wouldn't. And if he doesn't, the whole thing falls apart. It won't work."

"I say that he would," Idaan said.

"And I say that your history planning these schemes isn't one that inspires confidence," Adrah said and stood. The candlelight caught his face at an angle, casting shadows across his eyes. Idaan rose, feeling the blood rushing into her face.

"I was the one who saved us when Oshai fell," she said. "You two were mewling like kittens, and crying despair—"

"That's enough," Adrah said.

"I don't recall you being in a position to order me when to speak and when to be silent."

Daaya coughed, looking from one to the other of them like a lamb caught between wolf and lion. The smile that touched Adrah's mouth was thin and unamused.

"Idaan-kya," Adrah said, "I am to be your husband and the Khai of this city. Sit with that. Your plan to free Oshai failed. Do you understand that? It *failed*. It lost us the support of our backers, it killed the man most effective in carrying out these unfortunate duties we've taken on, and it exposed me and my father to risk. You failed before, and this scheme you've put before us now would also fail if we did as you propose."

Adrah began to pace slowly, one hand brushing the hanging tapestries. Idaan shook her head, remembering some epic she'd seen when she was young. A performer in the role of Black Chaos had moved as Adrah moved now. Idaan felt her heart grow tight.

"It isn't that it's without merit—the shape of it generally is useful, but the specifics are wrong. If Danat is to grab what men he can find and rush out into the night, it can't be because he's off to avenge a poet. He would have to be possessed by some greater passion. And it would help if he were drunk, but I don't know that we can arrange that."

"So if not the Maati Vaupathai...," she began, and her throat closed.

Cehmai, she thought. He means to kill Cehmai and free the andat. Her hands balled into fists, her heart thudded as if she'd been sprinting. Adrah turned to face her, his arms folded, his expression calm as a butcher in the slaughterhouse.

"You said there were three breaths blocking us. There's a fourth. Your father."

No one spoke. When Idaan laughed, it sounded shrill and panicked in her own ears. She took a pose that rejected the suggestion.

"You've gone mad, Adrah-kya. You've lost all sense. My father is dying. He's dying, there's no call to . . ."

"What else would enrage Danat enough to let his caution slip? The upstart escapes. Your father is murdered. In the confusion, we come to him, a hunting party in hand, ready to ride with him. We can put it out today that we're planning to ride out before the end of the week. Fresh meat for the wedding feast, we'll say."

"It won't work," Idaan said, raising her chin.

"And why not?" Adrah replied.

"Because I won't let you!"

She spun and grabbed for the door. As she hauled it open, Adrah was around her, his arms pressing it shut again. Daaya was there too, his wide hands patting at her in placating gestures that filled her with rage. Her mind left her, and she shrieked and howled and wept. She clawed at them both and kicked and tried to bite her way free, but Adrah's arms locked around her, lifted her, tightened until she lost her breath and the room spun and grew darker.

She found herself sitting again without knowing when she'd been set down. Adrah was raising a cup to her lips. Strong, unwatered wine. She sipped it, then pushed it away.

"Have you calmed yourself yet?" Adrah asked. There was warmth in his voice again, as if she'd been sick and was only just recovering.

"You can't do it, Adrah-kya. He's an old man, and . . ."

Adrah let the silence stretch before he leaned toward her and wiped her lips with a soft cloth. She was trembling, and it annoyed her. Her body was supposed to be stronger than that.

"It will cost him a few days," Adrah said. "A few weeks at most. Idaan-kya, his murder is the thing that will draw your brother out if anything will. You said it to me, love. If we falter, we fail."

He smiled and caressed her cheek with back of his hand. Daaya was at the table, drinking wine of his own. Idaan looked into Adrah's dark eyes, and despite the smiles, despite the caresses, she saw the hardness there. I should have said no, she thought. When he asked if I had taken another lover, I shouldn't have danced around it. I should have said no.

She nodded.

"We can make it quick. Painless," Adrah said. "It will be a mercy, really. His life as it is now can hardly be worth living. Sick, weak. That's no way for a proud man to live."

She nodded again. Her father. The simple pleasure in his eyes.

"He wanted so much to see us wed," she murmured. "He wanted so much for me to be happy."

Adrah took a pose that offered sympathy, but she wasn't such a fool as to believe it. She rose shakily to her feet. They did not stop her.

"I should go," she said. "I'll be expected at the palaces. I expect there will be food and song until the sun comes up."

Daaya looked up. His smile was sickly, but Adrah took a pose of reassurance and the old man looked away again.

"I'm trusting you, Idaan-kya," Adrah said. "To let you go. It's because I trust you."

"It's because you can't lock me away without attracting attention. If I vanish, people will wonder why, and my brother not the least. We can't have that, can we? Everything must seem perfectly normal."

"It still might be wise, locking you away," Adrah said. He pretended to be joking, but she could see the debate going on behind his eyes. For a moment, her life spread out before her. The first wife of the Khai Machi, looking into these eyes. She had loved him once. She had to remember that. Idaan smiled, leaned forward, kissed his lips.

"I'm only sad," she said. "It will pass. I'll come and meet you tomorrow. We can plan what needs to be done."

Outside, the revelry had spread. Garlands arched above the streets. Choirs had assembled and their voices made the city chime like a struck bell. Joy and relief were everywhere, except in her. For most of the afternoon, she moved from feast to feast, celebration to celebration—always careful not to be touched or bumped, afraid she might break like a girl made from spun sugar. As the sun hovered three hands' widths above the mountains to the west, she found the face she had been longing for.

Cehmai and Stone-Made-Soft were in a glade, sitting with a dozen children of the utkhaiem. The little boys and girls were sitting on the grass, grinding green into their silk robes with knees and elbows, while three slaves performed with puppets and dolls. The players squealed and whistled and sang, the puppets hopped and tumbled, beat one another, and fled. The children laughed. Cehmai himself was stretched out like a child, and two adventurous girls were sitting in Stone-Made-Soft's wide lap, their arms around each other. The andat seemed mildly amused.

When Cehmai caught sight of her, he came over immediately. She smiled as she had been doing all day, took a greeting pose that her hands had shaped a hundred times since morning. He was the first one, she thought, to see through pose and smile both.

"What's happened?" he asked, stepping close. His eyes were as dark as Adrah's, but they were soft. They were young. There wasn't any hatred there yet, or any pain. Or perhaps she only wished that was true. Her smile faltered.

"Nothing," she said, and he took her hand. Here where they might be seen—where the children at least were sure to see them—he took her hand and she let him.

"What's happened?" he repeated, his voice lower and closer. She shook her head.

"My father is going to die," she said, her voice breaking on the words, her lips growing weak. "My father's going to die, and there's nothing I can do to help it. No way for me to stop it. And the only time crying makes me feel better is when I can do it with you. Isn't that strange?"

8

>+< Cehmai rode up the wide track, switchbacking up the side of the mountain. The ore chute ran straight from the mine halfway up the mountain's face to the carter's base at its foot. When the path turned toward it, Cehmai considered the broad beams and pillars that held the chute smooth and even down the rough mountainside. When they turned away, he looked south to where the towers of Machi stood like reeds in the noonday sun. His head ached.

"We do appreciate your coming, Cehmai-cha," the mine's engineer said again. "With the new Khai come home, we thought everyone would put business off for a few days."

Cehmai didn't bother taking a pose accepting the thanks as he had the first few times. Repetition had made it clear that the gratitude was less than wholly sincere. He only nodded and angled his horse around the next bend, swinging around to a view of the ore chute.

There were six of them; Cehmai and Stone-Made-Soft, the mine's engineer, the overseer with the diagrams and contracts in a leather satchel on his hip, and two servants to carry the water and food. Normally there would have been twice as many people. Cehmai wondered how many miners would be in the tunnels, then found he didn't particularly care, and returned to contemplating the ore chute and his headache.

They had left before dawn, trekking to the Raadani mines. It had been arranged weeks before, and business and money carried a momentum that even stone didn't. A landslide might overrun a city, but it only went down. Something had to have tremendous power to propel something as tired and heavy as he felt *up* the mountainside. Something in the back of his mind twitched at the thought—attention shifting of its own accord like an extra limb moving without his willing it.

"Stop," Cehmai snapped.

The overseer and engineer hesitated for a moment before Cehmai understood their confusion.

"Not you," he said and gestured to Stone-Made-Soft. "Him. He was judging what it would take to start a landslide."

"Only as an exercise," the andat said, its low voice sounding both hurt and insincere. "I wasn't going to do it."

The engineer looked up the slope with an expression that suggested Cehmai might not hear any more false thanks. Cehmai felt a spark of vindictive pleasure at the man's unease and saw Stone-Made-Soft's lips thin so slightly that no other man alive would have recognized the smile.

Idaan had spent the first night of the festival with him, weeping and laughing, taking comfort and coupling until they had both fallen asleep in the middle of their pillow talk. The night candle had hardly burned down a full quarter mark when the servant had come, tapping on his door to wake him. He'd risen for the trek to the mines, and Idaan—alone in his bed—had turned, wrapping his bedclothes about her naked body, and watched him as if afraid he would tell her to leave. By the time he had found fresh robes, her eyelids had closed again and her breath was deep and slow. He'd paused for a moment, considering her sleeping face. With the paint worn off and the calm of sleep, she looked younger. Her lips, barely parted, looked too soft to bruise his own, and her skin glowed like honey in sunlight.

But instead of slipping back into bed and sending out a servant for new apples, old cheese, and sugared almonds, he'd strapped on his boots and gone out to meet his obligations. His horse plodded along, flies buzzed about his face, and the path turned away from the ore chute and looked back toward the city.

There would be celebrations from now until Idaan's wedding to Adrah Vaunyogi. Between those two joys—the finished succession and the marriage of the high families—there would also be the preparations for the Khai Machi's final ceremony. And, despite everything Maati-kvo had done, likely the execution of Otah Machi in there as well. With as many rituals and ceremonies as the city faced, they'd be lucky to get any real work done before winter.

The yipping of the mine dogs brought him back to himself, and he realized he'd been half-dozing for the last few switchbacks. He rubbed

his eyes with the heel of his palm. He would have to pull himself together when they began working in earnest. It would help, he told himself, to have some particular problem to set his mind to instead of the
tedium of travel. Thankfully, Stone-Made-Soft wasn't resisting him today. The effort it would have taken to force the unwilling andat to do as
it was told could have pushed the day from merely unpleasant to awful.

They reached the mouth of the mine and were greeted by several
workers and minor functionaries. Cehmai dismounted and walked un-
steadily to the wide table that had been set up for their consultations.
His legs and back and head ached. When the drawings and notes were
laid out before him, it took effort to turn his attention to them. His
mind wandered off to Idaan or his own discomfort or the mental windstorm that was the andat.

"We would like to join these two passages," the overseer was saying,
his fingers tracing lines on the maps. Cehmai had seen hundreds of sets
of plans like this, and his mind picked up the markings and translated
them into holes dug through the living rock of the mountain only
slightly less easily than usual. "The vein seems richest here and then
here. Our concern is—"

"My concern," the engineer broke in, "is not bringing half the mountain down on us while we do it."

The structure of tunnels that honeycombed the mountain wasn't the
most complicated Cehmai had ever seen, but neither was it simple.
The mines around Machi were capable of a complexity difficult in the
rest of the world, mostly because he himself was not in the rest of the
world, and mines in the Westlands and Galt weren't interested in paying the Khai Machi for his services. The engineer made his case—
where the stone would support the tunnels and where it would not.
The overseer made his counter-case—pointing out where the ores
seemed richest. The decision was left to him.

The servants gave them bowls of honeyed beef and sausages that
tasted of smoke and black pepper; a tart, sweet paste made from last
year's berries; and salted flatbread. Cehmai ate and drank and looked at
the maps and drawings. He kept remembering the curve of Idaan's
mouth, the feeling of her hips against his own. He remembered her
tears, her reticence. He would have sacrificed a good deal to better understand her sorrow.

It was more, he thought, than the struggle to face her father's mortality. Perhaps he should talk to Maati about it. He was older and had greater experience with women. Cehmai shook his head and forced himself to concentrate. It was half a hand before he saw a path through the stone that would yield a fair return and not collapse the works. Stone-Made-Soft neither approved nor dissented. It never did.

The overseer took a pose of gratitude and approval, then folded up the maps. The engineer sucked his teeth, craning his neck as the diagrams and notes vanished into the overseer's satchel, as if hoping to see one last objection, but then he too took an approving pose. They lit the lanterns and turned to the wide, black wound in the mountain's side.

The tunnels were cool, and darker than night. The smell of rock dust made the air thick. As he'd guessed, there were few men working, and the sounds of their songs and the barking of their dogs only made the darkness seem more isolating. They talked very little as they wound their way through the maze. Usually Cehmai made a practice of keeping a mental map, tracking their progress through the dark passages. After the second unexpected intersection, he gave up and was content to let the overseer lead them.

Unlike the mines on the plain, even the deepest tunnels here were dry. When they reached the point Cehmai had chosen, they took out the maps one last time, consulting them in the narrow section of the passageway that the lanterns lit. Above them, the mountain felt bigger than the sky.

"Don't make it too soft," the engineer said.

"It doesn't bear any load," the overseer said. "Gods! Who's been telling you ghost stories? You're nervous as a puppy first time down the hole."

Cehmai ignored them, looked up, considering the stone above him as if he could see through it. He wanted a path wide as two men walking with their arms outstretched. And it would need to go forward from here and then tilt to the left and then up. Cehmai pictured the distances as if he would walk them. It was about as far from where he was now to the turning point as from the rose pavilion to the library. And then, the shorter leg would be no longer than the walk from the library to Maati's apartments. He turned his mind to it, pressed the whirlwind, applied it to the stone before him, slowly, carefully loosening the stone in the path he had imagined. Stone-Made-Soft resisted—not in the body that scowled now looking at the tunnel's blank side, but in their shared mind. The andat shifted and writhed and pushed, though not so badly as it might have. Cehmai reached the turning point, shifted his attention and began the shorter, upward movement.

The storm's energy turned and leapt ahead, spreading like spilled water, pushing its influence out of the channel Cehmai's intention had prepared. Cehmai gritted his teeth with the effort of pulling it back in before the structure above them weakened and failed. The andat pressed again, trying to pull the mountain down on top of them. Cehmai felt a rivulet of sweat run down past his ear. The overseer and the engineer were speaking someplace a long way off, but he couldn't be bothered by them. They were idiots to distract him. He paused and gathered the storm, concentrated on the ideas and grammars that had tied the andat to him in the first place, that had held it for generations. And when it had been brought to heel, he took it the rest of the way through his pathway and then slowly, carefully, brought his mind, and its, back to where they stood.

"Cehmai-cha?" the overseer asked again. The engineer was eyeing the walls as if they might start speaking with him.

"I'm done," he said. "It's fine. I only have a headache."

Stone-Made-Soft smiled placidly. Neither of them would tell the men how near they had all just come to dying: Cehmai, because he wished to keep it from them, Stone-Made-Soft, because it would never occur to it to care.

The overseer took a hand pick from his satchel and struck the wall. The metal head chimed and a white mark appeared on the stone. Cehmai waved his hand.

"To your left," he said. "There."

The overseer struck again, and the pick sank deep into the stone with a sound like a footstep on gravel.

"Excellent," the overseer said. "Perfect."

Even the engineer seemed grudgingly pleased. Cehmai only wanted to get out, into the light and back to the city and his own bed. Even if they left now, they wouldn't reach Machi before nightfall. Probably not before the night candle hit its half mark.

On the way back up, the engineer started telling jokes. Cehmai allowed himself to smile. There was no call to make things unpleasant even if the pain in his head and spine were echoing his heartbeats.

When they reached the light and fresh air, the servants had laid out a more satisfying meal—rice, fresh chickens killed here at the mine, roasted nuts with lemon, cheeses melted until they could be spread over their bread with a blade. Cehmai lowered himself into a chair of strung cloth and sighed with relief. To the south, they could see the smoke of the forges rising from Machi and blowing off to the east. A city perpetually afire.

"When we get there," Cehmai said to the andat, "we'll be playing several games of stones. You'll be the one losing."

The andat shrugged almost imperceptibly.

"It's what I am," it said. "You may as well blame water for being wet."

"And when it soaks my robes, I do," Cehmai said. The andat chuckled and then was silent. Its wide face turned to him with something like concern. Its brow was furrowed.

"The girl," it said.

"What about her?"

"It seems to me the next time she asks if you love her, you could say yes."

Cehmai felt his heart jump in his chest, startled as a bird. The andat's expression didn't change; it might have been carved from stone. Idaan wept in his memory, and she laughed, and she curled herself in his bed-clothes and asked silently not to be sent away. Love, he discovered, could feel very much like sorrow.

"I suppose you're right," he said, and the andat smiled in what looked like sympathy.

MAATI LAID HIS NOTES OUT ON THE WIDE TABLE AT THE BACK OF THE LI-brary's main chamber. The distant throbbing of trumpet and drum wasn't so distracting here as in his rooms. Three times on the walk here, his sleeves heavy with paper and books, he'd been grabbed by some masked reveler and kissed. Twice, bowls of sweet wine had been forced into his hand. The palaces were a riot of dancing and song, and despite his best intentions, the memory of those three kisses drew his attention. It would be sweet to go out, to lose himself in that crowd, to find some woman willing to dance with him, and to take comfort in her body and her breath. It had been years since he had let himself be so young as that.

He turned himself to his puzzle. Danat, the man destined to be Khai

Machi, had seemed the most likely to have engineered the rumors of Otah's return. Certainly he had gained the most. Kaiin Machi, whose death had already given Maati three kisses, was the other possibility. Until he dug in. He had asked the servants and the slaves of each household every question he could think of. No, none of them recalled any consultations with a man who matched the assassin's description. No, neither man had sent word or instruction since Maati's own arrival. He'd asked their social enemies what they knew or guessed or speculated on.

Kaiin Machi had been a weak-lunged man, pale of face and watery of eye. He'd had a penchant for sleeping with servant girls, but hadn't even gotten a child on one—likely because he was infertile. Danat was a bully and a sneak, a man whose oaths meant nothing to him—and the killing of noble, scholarly Kaiin showed that. Danat's triumph was the best of all possible outcomes or else the worst.

Searching for conspiracy in court gossip was like looking for raindrops in a thunderstorm. Everyone he spoke to seemed to have four or five suggestions of what might have happened, and of those, each half contradicted the other. By far, the most common assumption was that Otah had been the essential villain in all of it.

Maati had diagrammed the relationships of Danat and Kaiin with each of the high families—Kamau, Daikani, Radaani and a dozen more. Then with the great trading houses, with mistresses and rumored mistresses and the teahouses they liked best. At one point he'd even listed which horses each preferred to ride. The sad truth was that despite all these facts, all these words scribbled onto papers, referenced and checked, nothing pointed to either man as the author of Biitrah's death, the attempt on Maati's own life, or the slaughter of the assassin. He was either too dimwitted to see the pattern before him, it was too well hidden, or he was looking in the wrong place. Clearly neither man had been present in the city to direct the last two attacks, and there seemed to be no supporters in Machi who had managed the plans for them.

Nor was there any reason to attack *him*. Maati had been on the verge of exposing Otah-kvo. That was in everyone's best interest, barring Otah's. Maati closed his eyes, sighed, then opened them again, gathered up the pages of his notes and laid them out again, as if seeing them in a different pattern might spark something.

Drunken song burst from the side room to his left, and Baarath, librarian of Machi, stumbled in, grinning. His face was flushed, and he smelled of wine and something stronger. He threw open his arms and strode unevenly to Maati, embracing him like a brother.

"No one has ever loved these books as you and I have, Maati-kya," Baarath said. "The most glorious party of a generation. Wine flowing in the gutters, and food and dancing, and I'll jump off a tower if we don't see a crop of babes next spring that look nothing like their fathers. And where do we go, you and I? Here."

Baarath turned and made a sweeping gesture that took in the books and scrolls and codices, the shelves and alcoves and chests. He shook his head and seemed for a moment on the verge of tears. Maati patted him on the back and led him to a wooden bench at the side of the room. Baarath sat back, his head against the stone, and smiled like a baby.

"I'm not as drunk as I look," Baarath said.

"I'm sure you aren't," Maati agreed.

Baarath pounded the board beside him and gestured for Maati to sit. There was no graceful way to refuse, and at the moment, he could think of no reason. Going back to stand, frustrated, over the table had no appeal. He sat.

"What is bothering you, Maati-kya? You're still searching for some way to keep the upstart alive?"

"Is that an option? I don't see Danat-cha letting him walk free. No, I suppose I'm just hoping to see him killed for the right reasons. Except . . . I don't know. I can't find anyone else with reason to do the things that have been done."

"Perhaps there's more than one thing going on then?" Baarath suggested.

Maati took a pose of surrender.

"I can't comprehend one. The gods will have to lead me by the hand if there's two. Can you think of any other reason to kill Biitrah? The man seems to have moved through the world without making an enemy."

"He was the best of us," Baarath agreed and wiped his eyes with the end of his sleeve. "He was a good man."

"So it had to be one of his brothers. Gods, I wish the assassin hadn't been killed. He could have told us if there was a connection between Biitrah and what happened to me. Then at least I'd know if I were solving one puzzle or two."

"Doesn't have to," Baarath said.

Maati took a pose that asked for clarification. Baarath rolled his eyes and took on an expression of superiority that Maati had seen beneath his politeness for weeks now.

"It doesn't *have* to be one of his brothers," Baarath said. "You say it's not the upstart. Fine, that's what you choose. But then you say you can't find anything that Danat or Kaiin's done that makes you think they've done it. And why would they hide it, anyway? It's not shameful for them to kill their brother."

"But no one else has a reason," Maati said.

"No one? Or only no one you've found?"

"If it isn't about the succession, I can't find any call to kill Biitrah. If it isn't about my search for Otah, I can't think of any reason to want me dead. The only killing that makes sense at all was poking the assassin full of holes, and that only because he might have answered my questions."

"Why couldn't it have been the succession?"

Maati snorted. It was difficult being friendly with Baarath when he was sober. Now, with him half-maudlin, half-contemptuous, and reeking of wine, it was worse. Maati's frustration peaked, and his voice, when he spoke, was louder and angrier than he'd intended.

"Because Otah *didn't*, and Kaiin *didn't*, and Danat *didn't*, and there's no one else who's looking to sit on the chair. Is there some fifth brother I haven't been told about?"

Baarath raised his hands in a pose of a tutor posing an instructive question to a pupil. The effect was undercut by the slight weaving of his hands.

"What would happen if all three brothers died?"

"Otah would be Khai."

"Four. I meant four. What if they all die? What if none of them takes the chair?"

"The utkhaiem would fight over it like very polite pit dogs, and whichever one ended with the most blood on its muzzle would be elevated as the new Khai."

"So someone else might benefit from this yet, you see? They would have to hide it because having slaughtered the whole family of the previous Khai wouldn't help their family prestige, seeing as all their heads would be hanging from poles. But it would be about your precious succession, and there would be someone besides the three . . . four brothers with reason to do the thing."

"Except that Danat's alive and about to be named Khai Machi, it's a pretty story."

Baarath sneered and made a grand gesture at the world in general.

"What is there but pretty stories? What is history but the accumulation of plausible speculation and successful lies? You're a scholar, Maati-kya, you should enjoy them more."

Baarath chuckled drunkenly, and Maati rose to his feet. Outside, something cracked with a report like a stone slab broken or a roof tile dropped from a great height. A moment later, laughter followed it. Maati leaned against the table, his arms folded and each hand tucked into the opposite sleeve. Baarath shifted, lay back on the bench, and sighed.

"You don't think it's true," Maati said. "You don't think it's one of the high families plotting to be Khai."

"Of course not," Baarath said. "It's an idiot plan. If you were to start something like that, you'd need to be certain you'd win it, and that would take more money and influence than any one family could gather. Even the Radaani don't have that much gold, and they've got more than the Khai."

"Then you think I'm chasing mist," Maati said.

"I think the upstart is behind all of it, and that you're too much in awe of him to see it. Everyone knows he was your teacher when you were a boy. You still think he's twice what you are. Who knows, maybe he is."

His anger gave Maati the illusion of calm, and a steadiness to his voice. He took a pose of correction.

"That was rude, Baarath-cha. I'd thank you not to say it again."

"Oh, don't be ashamed of it," Baarath said. "There are any number of boys who have those sorts of little infatuations with—"

Maati's body lifted itself, sliding with an elegance and grace he didn't know he posessed. His palm moved out by its own accord and slapped Baarath's jaw hard enough to snap the man's head to the side. He put a hand on Baarath's chest, pinning him firmly to the bench. Baarath yelped in surprise and Maati saw the shock and fear in his face. Maati kept his voice calm.

"We aren't friends. Let's not be enemies. It would distract me, and you may have perfect faith that it would destroy you. I am here on the Dai-kvo's work, and no matter who becomes Khai Machi, he'll have need of the poets. Standing beside that, one too-clever librarian can't count for much."

Outrage shone in Baarath's eyes as he pushed Maati's hand away. Maati stepped back, allowing him to rise. The librarian pulled his disarrayed robes back into place, his features darkening. Maati's rage began to falter, but he kept his chin held high.

"You're a bully, Maati-cha," Baarath said, then he took a pose of farewell and marched proudly out of the library. His library. Maati heard the door slam closed and felt himself deflate.

It galled him, but he knew he would have to apologize later. He should never have struck the man. If he had borne the insults and insinuations, he could have forced contrition from Baarath, but he hadn't.

He looked at his scattered notes. Perhaps he was a bully. Perhaps there was nothing to be found in all this. After all, Otah would die regardless. Danat would take his father's place, and Maati would go back to the Dai-kvo. He would even be able to claim a measure of success. Otah was starving to death in the high air above Machi thanks to him, after all. And what was that if not victory? One small mystery left unsolved could hardly matter in the end.

He pulled his papers together, stacking them, folding them, tucking the packet away into his sleeve. There was nothing to be done here. He was tired and frustrated, ashamed of himself and in despair. There was a city of wine and distraction that would welcome him with open arms and delighted smiles.

He remembered Heshai-kvo—the poet of Saraykeht, the controller of Removing-the-Part-That-Continues who they'd called Seedless. He remembered his teacher's pilgrimages to the soft quarter with its drugs and gambling, its wine and whores. Heshai had felt this, or something like it; Maati knew he had.

He pulled the brown leather-bound book from his sleeve, where it always waited. He opened it and read Heshai's careful, beautiful handwriting. The chronicle and examination of his errors in binding the andat. He recalled Seedless' last words. *He's forgiven you.*

Maati turned back, his limbs heavy with exhaustion and dread. He put the book back into his sleeve and pulled out his notes. He rearranged them on the table. He began again, and the night stretched out endlessly before him.

THE PALACES WERE DRUNKEN AND DIZZY AND LOST IN THE RELIEF THAT comes when a people believe that the worst is over. It was a celebration of fratricide, but of all the dancers, the drinkers, the declaimers of small verse, only Idaan seemed to remember that fact. She played her part, of course. She appeared in all the circles of which she had been part back before she'd entered this darkness. She drank wine and tea, she accepted the congratulations of the high families on her joining with the house of Vaunyogi. She blushed at the ribald comments made about her and Adrah, or else replied with lewder quips.

She played the part. The only sign was that she was more elaborate when she painted her face. Even if people noticed, what would they think but that the colors on her eyelids and the plum-dark rouge on her lips were a part of her celebration. Only she knew how badly she needed the mask.

The night candle was just past its middle mark when they broke away, she and Adrah with their arms around each other as if they were lovers. No one they saw had any question what they were planning, and no one would object. Half of the city had paired off already and slunk away to find an empty bed. It was the night for it. They laughed and stumbled toward the high palaces—her father's.

Once, when they were hidden behind a high row of hedges and it wasn't a performance for anyone, Adrah kissed her. He smelled of wine and the warm, musky scent of a young man's skin. Idaan kissed him back, and for that moment—that long silent, sensual moment—she meant it. Then he pulled away and smiled, and she hated him again.

The celebrations in the halls and galleries of the Khai's palace were the nearest to exhaustion—everyone from the highest family of the utkhaiem to the lowest firekeeper had dressed in their finest robes and set out to stain them with something. The days of revelry had taken their toll, and with the night half-passed, the wildest celebrations were over. Music and song still played, people still danced and talked, drew one another away into alcoves and corners. Old men talked gravely of who would benefit from Danat's survival and promotion. But the sense was growing that the time was drawing near when the city would catch its breath and rest a while.

She and Adrah made their way through to the private wings of the palace, where only servants and slaves and the wives of the Khai moved freely. They made no secret of their presence. There was no need.

Idaan led the way up a series of wide, sweeping staircases to apartments on the south side of the palace. A servant—an old man with gray hair, a limp, and a rosy smile—greeted them, and Idaan instructed him that they were not to be disturbed for any reason. The old man took a solemn expression and a pose of acknowledgment, but there was merriment in his eyes. Idaan let him believe what she, after all, intended him to. Adrah opened the great wooden doors, and he also closed them behind her.

"They aren't the best rooms, are they?" Adrah said.

"They'll do," Idaan said, and went to the windows. She pulled open the shutters. The great tower, Otah Machi's prison, stood like a dark line inked in the air. Adrah moved to stand beside her.

"One of us should have gone with them," she said. "If the upstart's found safely in his cell come morning . . ."

"He won't be," Adrah said. "Father's mercenaries are competent men. He wouldn't have hired them for this if he hadn't been sure of them."

"I don't like using hired men," Idaan said. "If we can buy them, so can anyone."

"They're armsmen, not whores," Adrah said. "They've taken a contract, and they'll see it through. It's how they survive."

There were five lanterns, from small glass candleboxes to an oil lamp with a wick as wide as her thumb and heavy enough to require both of them to move it. They pulled them all as near the open window as they could, and Adrah lit them while Idaan pulled the thin silks from under her robes. The richest dyes in the world had given these their color— one blue, the other red. Idaan hung the blue over the window's frame, and then peered out, squinting into the night for the signal. And there, perhaps half a hand from the top of the tower, shone the answering light. Idaan turned away.

With all the light gathered at the window, the rooms were cast into darkness. Adrah had pulled a hooded cloak over his robes. Idaan remembered again the feeling of hanging over the void, feeling the wind tugging at her. This wasn't so different, except that the prospect of her own death had seemed somehow cleaner.

"He would want it," Idaan said. "If he knew that we'd planned this, he would allow it. You know that."

"Yes, Idaan-kya. I know."

"To live so weak. It disgraces him. It makes him seem less before the court. It's not a fit ending for a Khai."

Adrah drew a thin, blackened blade. It looked no wider than a finger, and not much longer. Adrah sighed and squared his shoulders. Idaan felt her stomach rise to her throat.

"I want to go with you," she said.

"We discussed this, Idaan-kya. You stay in case someone comes. You have to convince them that I'm still in here with you."

"They won't come. They've no reason to. And he's my father."

"More reason that you should stay."

Idaan moved to him, touching his arm like a beggar asking alms. She felt herself shaking and loathed the weakness, but she could not stop it. Adrah's eyes were as still and empty as pebbles. She remembered Danat, how he had looked when he arrived from the south. She had thought he was ill, but it had been this. He had become a killer, a murderer of the people he had once respected and loved. That he still respected and loved. Adrah had those eyes now, the look of near-nausea. He smiled, and she saw the determination. There were no words that would stop him now. The stone had been dropped, and not all the wishing in the world could call it back into her hand.

"I love you, Idaan-kya," Adrah said, his voice as cool as a gravestone. "I have always loved you. From the first time I kissed you. Even when you have hurt me, and you have hurt me worse than anyone alive, I have only ever loved you."

He was lying. He was saying it as she'd said that her father would welcome death, because he needed it to be true. And she found that she needed that as well. She stepped back and took a pose of gratitude. Adrah walked to the door, turned, nodded to her, and was gone. Idaan sat in the darkness and looked at nothing, her arms wrapped around herself. The night seemed unreal: absurd and undeniable at the same time, a terrible dream from which she might wake to find herself whole again. The weight of it was like a hand pressing down on her head.

There was time. She could call for armsmen. She could call for Danat. She could go and stop the blade with her own body. She sat silent, trying not to breathe. She remembered the ceremony of her tenth summer, the year after her mother's death. Her father had taken her to sit at his side during all that day's ritual. She had hated it, bored by the petitions and formality until tears ran down her cheeks. She remembered a meal with a representative from some Westlands warden where her father had forced her to sit on a hard wooden chair and swallow a cold bean soup that made her gag rather than seem ungracious to the Westlander for his food.

She fought to remember a smile, an embrace. She wanted a moment in the long years of her childhood to which she could point and say *here is how I know he loved me.* The blue silk stirred in the breeze. The lantern flames flickered, dimmed, and rose again. It must have happened. For him to be so desperate for her happiness now, there must have been some sign, some indication.

She found herself rocking rapidly back and forth. When a sound came from the door, she jumped up, panicked, looking around for some excuse to explain Adrah's absence. When he himself came in, she could see in his eyes that it was over.

Adrah pulled off the cloak, letting it pool around his ankles. His bright robes seemed incongruous as a butterfly in a butcher's shop. His face was stone.

"You've done it," Idaan said, and two full breaths later, he nodded. Something as much release as despair sank into her. She could feel her body made heavy by it.

She walked to him, pulled the blade and its soft black leather sheath from his belt, and let them drop to the floor. Adrah didn't try to stop her.

"Nothing we ever do will be so bad as this," she said. "This now is the worst it will ever be. Everything will be better than this."

"He never woke," Adrah said. "The drugs that let him sleep . . . He never woke."

"That's good."

A slow, mad grin bloomed on his face, stretching until the blood left his lips. There was a hardness in his eyes and a heat. It looked like fury or possession. He took her shoulders in his hands and pulled her near him. Their kiss was a gentle violence. For a moment, she thought he meant to open her robes, to drag her back to the bed in a sad parody of what they were expected to be doing. She pressed a palm to his sex and was surprised to find that he was not aroused. Slowly, with perfect control and a grip that bruised her, Adrah brought her away from him.

"I did this thing for you," he said. "I did this for *you*. Do you understand that?"

"I do."

"Never ask me for anything again," he said and released her, turning away. "From now until you die, you are in debt to me, and I owe you nothing."

"For the favor of killing my father?" she asked, unable to keep the edge from her voice.

"For what I have sacrificed to you," he said without looking back. Idaan felt her face flush, her hands ball into fists. She heard him groan from the next room, heard his robes shushing against the stone floor. The bed creaked.

A lifetime, married to him. There wouldn't be a moment in the years that followed that would not be poisoned. He would never forgive her, and she would never fail to hate him. They would go to their graves, each with teeth sunk in the other's neck.

They were perfect for each other.

Idaan walked silently to the window, took down the blue silk and put up the red.

THE ARMSMEN GAVE HIM ENOUGH WATER TO LIVE, THOUGH NOT SO MUCH AS to slake his thirst. Almost enough food to live as well, though not quite. He had no clothing but the rags he'd worn when he'd come back to Machi and the cloak that Maati had brought. When dawn was coming near and the previous day's heat had gone from the tower, he would be huddling in that cloth. Through the day, sun heated the great tower, and that heat rose. And as it rose, it grew. In his stone cage, Otah lay sweating as if he'd been working at hard labor, his throat dry and his head pounding.

The towers of Machi, Otah had decided, were the stupidest buildings in the world. Too cold in winter, too hot in summer, unpleasant to use, exhausting to climb. They existed only to show that they could exist.

More and more of the time, his mind was in disarray; hunger and boredom, the stifling heat and the growing presentiment of his own death conspired to change the nature of time. Otah felt outside it all, apart from the world and adrift. He had always been in this room; the memories from before were like stories he'd heard told. He would always be in this room unless he wriggled out the window and into the cool, open air. Twice already he had dreamed that he'd leapt from the tower. Both times, he woke in a panic. It was that as much as anything that kept him from taking the one control left to him. When despair washed through him, he remembered the dream of falling, with its shrill regret. He didn't want to die. His ribs were showing, he was almost nauseated with thirst, his mind would not slow down or be quiet. He was going to be put to death, and he did not want to die.

The thought that his suffering saved Kiyan had ceased to comfort him. Part of him was glad that he had not known how wretched his father's treatment of him would be. He might have faltered. At least now he could not run. He would lose—he had lost, and badly—but he could not run. Maj sat on her chair—the tall, thin one with legs of woven cane that she'd had in their island hut. When she spoke, it was in the soft liquid sounds of her native language and too fast for Otah to follow. He struggled, but when he croaked out that he couldn't understand her, his own voice woke him until he drifted away again into nothing, troubled only by the conviction that he could hear rats chewing through the stone.

The shriek woke him completely. He sat upright, his arms trembling. The room was real again, unoccupied by visions. Outside the great door, he heard someone shout, and then something heavy pounded once against the door, shaking it visibly. Otah rose. There were voices—new ones. After so many days, he knew the armsmen by their rhythms and the timbre of their murmurs. The throats that made the sounds he heard now were unfamiliar. He walked to the door and leaned against it, pressing his ear to the hairline crack between the wood and its stone frame. One voice rose above the others, its tone commanding. Otah made out the word "chains."

The voices went away again for so long Otah began to suspect he'd imagined it all. The scrape of the bar being lifted from the door startled him. He stepped back, fear and relief coming together in his heart. This might be the end. He knew his brother had returned; this could be his death come for him. But at least it was an end to his time in this cell. He tried to hold himself with some dignity as the door swung open. The torches were so bright that Otah could hardly see.

"Good evening, Otah-cha," a man's voice said. "I hope you're well enough to move. I'm afraid we're in a bit of a hurry."

"Who are you?" Otah asked. His own voice sounded rough. Squinting, he could make out perhaps ten men in black leather armor. They had blades drawn. The armsmen lay in a pile against the far wall, stacked like goods in a warehouse, a black pool of blood surrounding them. The smell of them wasn't rotten, not yet, but it was disturbing—coppery and intimate. They had only been dead for minutes. If all of them were dead.

"We're the men who've come to take you out of here," the commander said. He was the one actually standing in the doorway. He had the long face of a man of the winter cities, but a westlander's flowing hair. Otah moved forward and took a pose of gratitude that seemed to amuse him.

"Can you walk?" he asked as Otah came out into the larger room. The signs of struggle were everywhere—spilled wine, overturned chairs, blood on the walls. The armsmen had been taken by surprise. Otah put a hand against the wall to steady himself. The stone felt warm as flesh.

"I'll do what I have to," Otah said.

"That's admirable," the commander said, "but I'm more curious about what you *can* do. I've suffered long confinement myself a time or two, and I know what it does. We can't take the easy way down. We've got to walk. If you can do this, that's all to the good. If you can't, we're prepared to carry you, but I need to have you out of the city quickly."

"I don't understand. Did Maati send you?"

"There's better places to discuss this, Otah-cha. We can't go down by the chains. Even if there weren't more armsmen waiting there, we've just broken them. Can you walk down the tower?"

A memory of the endlessly turning stairs and the ghost of pain in his knees and legs. Otah felt a stab of shame, but pulled himself up and shook his head.

"I don't believe I can," he said. The commander nodded and two of his men pulled lengths of wood from their backs and fitted them together in a cripple's litter. There was a small seat for Otah, canted against the slope of the stairway, and the poles were set one longer than the other to fit the tight curve. It would have been useless in any other situation, but for this task it was perfect. As one of the men helped Otah take his place on it, he wondered if the device had been built for this moment, or if things like it existed in service of these towers. The largest of the men spat on his hands and gripped the carrying poles that would start down the stairs and bear most of Otah's weight. One of his fellows took the other end, and Otah lurched up.

They began their descent, Otah with his back to the center of the spiral staircase. He watched the stone of the wall curl up from below. The men grunted and cursed, but they moved quickly. The man on the higher poles stumbled once, and the one below shouted angrily back at him.

The journey seemed to last forever—stone and darkness, the smell of sweat and lantern oil. Otah's knees bumped against the wall before him, his head against the wall behind. When they reached the halfway point, another huge man was waiting to take over the worst of the carrying. Otah felt his shame return. He tried to protest, but the commander put a strong, hard hand on his shoulder and kept him in the chair.

"You chose right the first time," the commander said.

The second half of the journey down was less terrible. Otah's mind was beginning to clear, and a savage hope was lifting him. He was being saved. He couldn't think who or why, but he was delivered from his cell. He thought of the armsmen new-slaughtered at the tower's height, and recalled Kiyan's words. *How do you expect to protect me and my house?* They could all be killed, his jailers and his rescuers alike. All in the name of tradition.

He could tell when they reached the level of the street—the walls had grown so thick there was almost no room for them to walk, but thin windows showed glimmers of light, and drunken, disjointed music filled the air. At the base of the stair, his carriers lowered Otah to the ground and took his arms over their shoulders as if he were drunk or sick. The commander squeezed to the front of the party. Despite his frown, Otah sensed the man was enjoying himself immensely.

They moved quickly and quietly through maze-like passages and out at last into an alley at the foot of the tower. A covered cart was waiting, two horses whickering restlessly. The commander made a sign, and the two bearers lifted Otah into the back of the cart. The commander and two of the men climbed in after, and the driver started the horses. Shod hooves rapped the stone, and the cart lurched and bumped. The commander pulled the back cloth closed and tied it, but loose enough he could peer out the seam. The lantern was extinguished, and the scent of its dying smoke filled the cart for a moment and was gone.

"What's happening out there?" Otah asked.

"Nothing," the commander said. "And best we keep it that way. No talking."

In silence and darkness, they continued. Otah felt lightheaded. The cart turned twice to the left and then again to the right. The driver was hailed and replied, but they never stopped. A breeze fluttered the thick cloth of the cover, and when it paused, Otah heard the sound of water; they were on the bridge heading south. He was free. He grinned, and then as the implications of his freedom unfolded themselves in his mind, his relief faltered.

"Forgive me. I don't know your name. I'm sorry. I can't do this."

The commander shifted. It was nearly black in the cart, so Otah couldn't see the man's face, but he imagined incredulity on the long features.

"I went to Machi to protect someone—a woman. If I vanish, they'll still have reason to suspect her. My brother might kill her on the chance that she's involved with this. I can't let that happen. I'm sorry, but we have to turn back."

"You love her that much?" the commander asked.

"This isn't her fault. It's mine."

"All this is your fault, eh? You have a lot to answer for." There was amusement in the man's voice. Otah felt himself smile.

"Well, perhaps not all my fault. But I can't let her be hurt. This is the price of it, and I'll pay it if I have to."

They were all silent for a long moment, then the commander sighed.

"You're an honorable man, Otah Machi. I want you to know I respect that. Boys. Chain him and gag him. I don't want him calling out."

They were on him in an instant, pushing him hard onto the rough wood of the cart. Someone's knee drove in between his shoulder blades; invisible hands bent his arms backwards. When he opened his mouth to scream, a wad of heavy cloth was shoved in so deeply he gagged. A leather strap followed, keeping it in place. He didn't know when his legs were bound, but in fewer than twenty breaths, he was immobile—his arms chained painfully behind him at his wrists and elbows, his mouth stuffed until it was hard to breathe. The knee moved to the small of his back, digging into his spine with every shift of the cart. He tried once to move, and the pressure from above increased. He tried again, and the man cursed him and rapped his head with something hard.

"I said no talking," the commander murmured, and returned to peering out the opening in the back cloth. Otah shifted, snarling in impotent rage that none of these men seemed to see or recognize. The cart moved off through the night. He could feel it when they moved from the paving of the main road to a dirt track; he could hear the high grass hushing against the wheels. They were taking him nowhere, and he couldn't think why.

He guessed it was almost three hands before the first light started to come. Dawn was still nothing more than a lighter kind of darkness, the commander's feet—the only part of the man Otah could see without lifting his head—were a dim form of shadow within shadow. It was something. Otah heard the trill of a daymartin, and then a rough rattling and the sound of water. A bridge over some small river. When the cart lurched back to ground, the commander turned.

"Have him stop," he said, and then a moment later, "I said stop the cart. Do it."

One of the other two—the one who wasn't kneeling on Otah—shifted and spoke to the driver. The jouncing slowed and stopped.

"I thought I heard something out there. In the trees on the left. Baat. Go check. If you see anything at all get back fast."

The pressure on Otah's back eased and one of the men clambered out. Otah turned over and no one tried to stop him. There was more light now. He could make out the grim set of the commander's features, the unease in the one remaining armsman.

"Well, this is interesting," the commander said.

"What's out there," the other man asked, his blade drawn. The commander looked out the slit of cloth and motioned for the armsman to pass over his sword. He did, and the commander took it, holding it with the ease of long familiarity.

"It may be nothing," he said. "Were you with me when I was working for the Warden of Elleais?"

"I'd just signed on then," the armsman said.

"You've always been a good fighter, Lachmi. I want you to know I respect that."

With the speed of a snake, the commander's wrist flickered, and the armsman fell back in the cart, blood flowing from his opened neck. Otah tried to push himself away as the commander turned and drove the sword into the armsman's chest. He dropped the blade then, letting it fall to the cart's floor, and took a pose of regret to the dying man.

"But," the commander said, "you should never have cheated me at tiles. *That* was stupid."

The commander stepped over the body and spoke to the driver. He spoke clearly enough for Otah to hear.

"Is it done?"

The driver said something.

"Good," the commander replied, and came back. He flipped Otah onto his belly with casual disregard, and Otah felt his bonds begin to loosen.

"All apologies, Otah-cha," the commander said. "But there's a lesson you can take from all this: just because someone's bought a mercenary captain, it doesn't mean his commanders aren't still for sale. Now I will need your robes, such as they are."

Otah pulled the leather strap from around his head and spat out the cloth, retching as he did so. Before he could speak, the commander had climbed out of the cart, and Otah was left to follow.

They had stopped at a clearing by a river, surrounded by white oaks. The bridge was old wood and looked almost too decrepit to cross. Six men with gray robes and hunting bows were walking toward them from the trees, two of them dragging the arrow-riddled body of the armsman the commander had sent out. Two others carried a litter with what was clearly another dead man—thin and naked. The commander took a pose of welcome, and the first archer returned it. Otah stumbled forward, rubbing his wrists. The archers were all smiling, pleased with themselves. When he came close enough, Otah saw the second corpse was on its back, and a wide swath of intricate black ink stained its breast. The first half of an east island marriage mark. A tattoo like his own.

"That's why we'll need your robes, Otah-cha," the commander said. "This poor bastard will have been in the water for a while before he reaches the main channel of the river. But the closer he seems to you, the less people will bother looking at him. I'll see whether I can find something for you to wear after, but you might consider sponging off in the brook there first. No offense, but you've been a while without a bath."

"Who is he?" Otah asked.

The commander shrugged.

"Nobody, now."

He clapped Otah on the shoulder and turned back toward the cart. The archers were pitching the corpses of the two armsmen into the water. Otah saw arrows rising from the river like reeds. The driver was coming forward now, his thumbs stuck in his belt. He was a hairy man, his full beard streaked with gray. He smiled at Otah and took a pose of welcome.

"I don't understand," Otah said. "What's happening?"

"We don't understand either, Itani-cha. Not precisely. We're only sure that it's something terrible," the carter said, and Otah's mouth dropped open. He spoke with the voice of Amiit Foss, his overseer in House Siyanti. Amiit grinned beneath his beard. "And we're sure that it isn't happening to you."

9

>+< The first few breaths after she woke were like rising new born. She didn't know who or where she was, she had no thought of the night before or the day ahead. There was only sensation—the warmth of the body beside her, the crisp softness of the bedclothes, the netting above the bed glowing in the captured light of dawn, the scent of black tea brought in by a servant with cat-quiet footsteps. She sat up, almost smiling until memory rushed in on her like a flood of black water. Idaan rose and pulled on her robes. Adrah stirred and moaned.

"You should go," she said, lifting the black iron teapot. "You're expected to go on a hunt today."

Adrah sat up, scratching his back and yawning. His hair stuck out in all directions. He looked older than he had the day before, or perhaps it was only how she felt. She poured a bowl of tea for him as well.

"Have they found him?" Adrah asked.

"I haven't heard the screams or lamentations yet, so I'd assume not."

She held out the porcelain bowl. It was thin enough to see through and hot enough to burn her fingertips, but Idaan didn't try to reduce the pain. When Adrah took it from her, he drank from it straight, though she knew it must have scalded. Perhaps what they'd done had numbed them.

"And you, Idaan-kya?"

"I'm going to the baths. I'll join you after."

Adrah drank the last of the tea, grimaced as if it was distilled wine, and took a pose of leave-taking which Idaan returned. When he was gone, she took herself to the women's quarters and the baths. She hardly had time to wash her hair before the cry went up. The Khai Machi was dead. Killed horribly in his chambers. Idaan dried herself with a cloth and strode out to meet her brother. She was halfway there before she realized her face was bare; she hadn't put on her paints. She was surprised that she felt no need for them now.

Danat was pacing the great hall. The high marble archways echoed with the sound of his boots. There was blood on his sleeve, and his face was empty. When Idaan caught sight of him, she raised her chin but took no formal pose. Danat stopped. The room was silent.

"You've heard," he said. There was no question to it.

"Tell me anyway."

"Otah has killed our father," Danat said.

"Then yes. I've heard."

Danat resumed his pacing. His hands worried each other, as if he were trying to pluck honey off them. Idaan didn't move.

"I don't know how he did it, sister. There must be people backing him within the palaces. The armsmen in the tower were slaughtered."

"How did he find our father?" Idaan asked, uninterested in the answer. "He must have found a secret way into the palaces. Someone would have seen him."

Danat shook his head. There was rage in him, and pain. She could see them, could feel them resonate in her own breast. But more than that, there was an almost superstitious fear in him. The upstart had slipped his bonds, had struck in the very heart of the city, and her brother feared him like Black Chaos.

"We have to secure the city," he said. "I've called for more guards. You should stay here. We can't know how far he will take his vendetta."

"You're going to let him escape?" Idaan demanded. "You aren't going to hunt him down?"

"He has resources I can't guess at. Look! Look what he's done. Until I know what I'm walking towards, I don't dare follow."

The plan was failing. Danat was staying safe in his walls with his armsmen around him like a blanket. Idaan sighed. It was up to her, of course, to save it.

"Adrah Vaunyogi has a hunt prepared. It was to be for fresh meat for my wedding feast. You stay here, Danat-kya. I'll bring you Otah's head."

She turned and walked away. She couldn't hesitate, couldn't invite him to follow her. He would see it in her gait if she were anything less than totally committed. For a moment, she even believed herself that she was going out to find her father's killer and bring him down—riding with her hunt into the low towns and the fields to track down the evil Otah Machi, her fallen brother. Danat's voice stopped her.

"I forbid you, Idaan. You can't do this."

She paused and looked back at him. He was thicker than her father had been. Already his jaw line ran toward jowls. She took a pose that disagreed.

"I'm actually quite good with a bow," she said. "I'll find him. And I will see him dead."

"You're my child sister," Danat said. "You can't do this."

Something flared in her, dark and hot. She stepped back toward Danat, feeling the rage lift her up like a leaf in the wind.

"Ah, and if I do this thing, you'll be shamed. Because I have breasts and you've a prick, I'm supposed to muzzle myself and be glad. Is that it? Well I won't. You hear me? I will not be controlled, I will not be owned, and I will not step back from anything to protect your petty pride. It's gone too far for that, brother. If a woman shrinks meekly back into the shadows, then you be the woman. See how it feels to you!"

By the end she was shrieking. Her fists were balled so tight they hurt. Danat's expression was hard as stone and as gray.

"You shame me," he said.

"Live with it," she said and spat.

"Send my body servant," he said. "I'll want my own bow. And then go to Adrah. The hunt won't leave without me."

She was on the edge of refusing, of telling him that this wasn't courage. He was only more afraid of losing the respect of the utkhaiem than of dying, and that made him not only a coward but a stupid one. *She* was the one with courage. *She* was the one who had the will to act. What was he after all but a mewling kitten lost in the world, while she . . . she was Otah Machi. She was the upstart who had earned the Khai's chair. She had killed her father for it; it was more than Danat would have done.

But, of course, truth would destroy everything. That was its nature. So she swallowed it down deep where it could go on destroying her and took an acquiescing pose. She'd won. He'd know that soon enough.

Once Danat's body servant had been sent scampering for his bow, Idaan returned to her apartments, shrugged out of her robes and put on the wide, loose trousers and red leather shirt of a hunter. She paused by her table of paints, her mirror. She sat for a moment and looked at her bare face. Her eyes seemed small and flat without the kohl. Her lips seemed pale and wide as a fish's, her cheeks pallid and low. She could be a peasant girl, plowing fields outside some low town. Her beauty had been in paint. Perhaps it would be again, someday. This was a poor day for beauty.

The huntsmen were waiting impatiently outside the palaces of the Vaunyogi, their mounts' hooves clattering against the dark stones of the courtyard. Adrah took a pose of query when he saw her clothes. Idaan didn't answer it, but went to one of the horsemen, ordered him down, took his blade and his bow and mounted in his place. Adrah cantered over to her side. His mount was the larger, and he looked down at her as if he were standing on a step.

"My brother is coming," she said. "I'll ride with him."

"You think that wise?" he asked coolly.

"I have asked too much of you already, Adrah-kya."

His expression was cold, but he didn't object further. Danat Machi rode in wearing pale robes of mourning and seated on a great hunting stallion, the very picture of vigor and manly prowess. Five riders were with him: his friends, members of the utkhaiem unfortunate enough to have heard of this hunt and marry themselves to the effort. They would have to be dealt with. Adrah took a pose of obeisance before Danat.

"We've had word that a cart left by the south gate last night," Adrah said. "It was seen coming from an alley beside the tower."

"Then let us follow it," Danat said. He turned and rode. Idaan followed, the wind whipping her hair, the smell of the beast under her rich and sweet. There was no keeping up the gallop, of course. But this was theater—the last remaining sons of the Khai Machi, one the assassin and servant of chaos slipping away in darkness, one the righteous avenger riding forth in the name of justice. Danat knew the part he was to act, and Idaan gave him credit for playing it, now that she had goaded him into action. Those who saw them in the streets would tell others, and the word would spread. It was a sight songs were made from.

Once they had crossed the bridge over the Tidat, they slowed, looking for people who had heard or seen the cart go by. Idaan knew where it had really gone—the ruins of an old stone wayhouse a half-hand's walk from the nearest low town west of the city. The morning hadn't half passed before the hunt had taken a wrong scent, turned north and headed into the foothills. The false trail took them to a crossroad—a mining track led east and west, the thin road from the city winding north up the side of a mountain. Danat looked frustrated and tired. When Adrah spoke—his voice loud enough for everyone in the party to hear—Idaan's belly tightened.

"We should fan out, Danat-cha. Eight east, eight west, eight north, and two to stay here. If one group finds sign of the upstart, they can send back a runner, and the two waiting here will retrieve the rest."

Danat weighed the thought, then agreed. Danat claimed the north road for himself, and the members of the utkhaiem, smelling the chance of glory, divided themselves among the bands heading east and west.

Adrah took the east, his eyes locked on hers as he turned to go. She saw the meaning in his expression, daring her to do this thing. Idaan made no reply to him at all. She, six huntsmen of the Vaunyogi loyal to their house and master, and Danat rode into the mountains.

When the sun had reached the highest point in the day's arc, they stopped at small lake. The huntsmen rode out in their wide-ranging search as they had done at every pause before this. Danat dismounted, stretched, and paced. His eyes were dark. Idaan waited until the others disappeared into the trees, unslung her bow, and went to stand near her brother. He looked at her, then away.

"He didn't come this way," Danat said. "He's tricked us again."

"Perhaps. But he won't survive. Even if he killed you, he could never become Khai Machi. The utkhaiem and the poets wouldn't support him."

"It's hatred now," Danat said. "He's doing it from hatred."

"Perhaps," Idaan said. Out on the lake, a bird skimmed the shining surface of the water, then shrieked and plunged in, rising moments later with a flash of living silver in its claws. A quarter moon was in the sky—white crescent showing through the blue. The lake smelled colder than it was, and the wind tugged at her hair and the reeds alike. Danat sighed.

"Was it hard killing Kaiin?" Idaan asked.

Danat looked at her, as if shocked that she had asked. She met his gaze, her eyes fixed on his until he turned away.

"Yes," he said. "Yes it was. I loved him. I miss them both."

"But you did the thing anyway."

He nodded. Idaan stepped forward and kissed him on the cheek. His stubble tickled her lips, and she wiped her mouth with the back of her hand as she walked away, trying to stop the sensation. At ten paces she put an arrow to her bow, drew back the string. Danat was still looking out over the water. Passionlessly, she judged the wind, the distance.

The arrow struck the back of his head with a sound like an axe splitting wood. Danat seemed at first not to notice, and then slowly sank to the ground. Blood soaked the collar of his robes, the pale cloth looking like cut meat by the time she walked back to him. She knelt by him, took his hand in her own, and looked out over the lake.

She was singing before she knew she intended to sing. In her imagination, she had screamed and shrieked, her cries calling the hunters back to her, but instead she sang. It was an old song, a lamentation she'd heard in the darkness of the tunnels and the cold of winter. The words were from the Empire, and she hardly knew what they all meant. The rising and falling melody, aching and sorrowful, seemed to fill her and the world.

Two hunters approached her at last, unsure of themselves. She had not seen them emerge from the trees, and she didn't look at them now as she spoke.

"My brother has been murdered by Otah or one of his agents," she said. "While we were waiting for you."

The hunters looked at one another. For a long, sick moment, she thought they might not believe her. She wondered if they would be loyal enough to the Vaunyogi to overlook the crime. And then the elder of them spoke.

"We will find him, Idaan-cha," the man said, his voice trembling with rage. "We'll send for the others and turn every stone on this mountain until we find him."

"It won't bring back my father. Or Danat. There won't be anyone to stand at my wedding."

She broke off, half surprised to find her sobs unfeigned. Gently, she cradled the corpse of her brother to her, feeling the blood soak her robes.

"I'll gather his horse," another of the hunters said. "We can strap him to it—"

"No," Idaan said. "You can give him to me. I'll carry him home."

"It's a long ride back to the city. Are you sure that—"

"I'll carry him home. He'd have done the same if our places were re-versed," she said. "It is the way of our family."

In the end, they draped him over her mount's haunches. The scent of the blood made him skittish, but Idaan held control firmly, cooing in the animal's ears, coaxing and demanding. When she could think of nothing else, she sang to the beast, and the dirges possessed her. She felt no sorrow, no regret. She felt no triumph. It was as if she was in the moment of grace between the blow and the pain. In her mind were only the sounds of the songs and of an arrow splitting bone.

THE FARMSTEAD WAS SET BACK A SHORT WALK FROM THE ROAD. A CREEK RAN beside it, feeding, no doubt, into the river that was even now carrying dead men down to the main channel. The walls were as thick as a man's outstretched arm with a set of doors on both the inside and outside faces. On the second story, snow doors had been opened, letting in the summer air. Trees stood in close, making the house seem a part of the landscape. The horses were kept in the stables on the ground floor, hidden from casual observers.

Amiit led Otah up the stairs and into a bright, simple room with a table, a few rough wooden chairs, an unlit lantern and a wide, low cabinet. Roast chicken, fresh cheese, and apples just on the edge of ripeness had been laid out for them. Sharpened by Otah's hunger and relief and wonder, the smell of them was wonderful. Amiit gestured toward the table, then opened the cabinet and took out two earthenware mugs and flasks of wine and water. Otah took a leg from the chicken and bit into it—the flesh tasted of tarragon and black pepper. He closed his eyes and grinned. Nothing had ever in his life tasted so good.

Amiit chuckled.

"You've grown thinner, old friend," Amiit said as he poured himself wine and Otah a mixture of wine and water. "You'd think accommodations in Machi would be better."

"What's going on, Amiit-cha?" Otah asked, taking the proffered drink. "Last I heard, I was going to be either executed as a criminal or honorably killed in the succession. This . . . ," he gestured at the room with his mug. "This wasn't suggested as an option."

"It wasn't approved by the Khaiem, that's truth," Amiit said. He sat across from Otah and picked up one of the apples, turning it over slowly as he spoke, inspecting it for worm holes. "The fact is, I only know half of what's going on in Machi, if that. After our last talk—when you were first coming up here—I thought it might be best to put some plans in motion. In case an opportunity arose, you understand. It would be very convenient for House Siyanti if one of their junior couriers became the Khai Machi. It didn't seem likely at the time. But . . ."

He shrugged and bit into the apple. Otah finished the chicken and took one of the fruits himself. Even watered, the wine was nearly too strong to drink.

"We put out men and women to listen," Amiit went on. "To gather what information we could find. We weren't looking for anything in particular, you understand. Just an opportunity."

"You were looking to sell information of me to the Khai in return for a foothold in Machi," Otah said.

"Only as a last resort," Amiit agreed. "It's business. You understand."

"But they found me instead," Otah said. The apple was sweet and chalky and just slightly bitter. Amiit pushed a platter of cheese toward him.

"That looked bleak. It's truth. And that you'd been in our pay seemed to seal it. House Siyanti wasn't going to be welcome, whichever of your brothers took the title."

"And taking me out of their tower was intended to win back their favor?"

Amiit's expression clouded. He shook his head.

"That wasn't our plan. Someone hired a mercenary company to take you from the city to a low town and hold you there. We don't know who it was; they only met with the captain, and he's not on our side. But I'm fairly certain it wasn't your brother or your father."

"But you got word of it?"

"I had word of it. Mercenaries . . . well, they aren't always the most reliable of companions. Sinja-cha knew I was in the city, and would be interested in your situation. He was ready to make a break with his old cohort for other reasons, and offered me the opportunity to . . . what? Outbid his captain for his services in the matter?"

"Sinja-cha is the commander?"

"Yes. Or, was. He's in my employ now. With luck, his old captain thinks him dead along with you and the other armsmen involved."

"And what will you do now? Ransom me back to the Khai?"

"No," Amiit said. "I've already made a bargain that won't allow that.

Besides, I really did enjoy working with you. And . . . and you may yet be in a position to help me more as an ally than a commodity, ne?"

"It's a bad bet," Otah said and smiled.

Amiit grinned again.

"Ah, but the stakes are high. Would you rather just have water? I wasn't thinking."

"No, I'll keep this."

"Whatever you like. So. Yes, something's happening in Machi. I expect they're out scouring the world for you even now. And in a day, perhaps two, they'll find you floating down the river or caught on a sandbar."

"And then?"

"I don't know," Amiit said. "And then we'll know what's happened in the meantime. Things are moving quickly, and there's more going on than I can fathom. For instance, I don't know what the Galts have to do with it."

Otah put down his cup. Even under the blanket of whiskers, he could see the half-smile twitch at Amiit's mouth. The overseer's eyes sparkled.

"But perhaps you do?" Amiit suggested.

"No, but . . . no. I've dealt with something else once. Something happened. The Galts were behind it. What are they doing here? How do they figure in?"

"They're making contracts with half the houses in Machi. Large contracts at disadvantageous terms. They've been running roughshod over the Westlands so long they're sure to be good for it—they have almost as much money as the Khaiem. It may just be they've a new man acting as the overseer for the Machi contracts, and he's no good. But I doubt it. I think they're buying influence."

"Influence to do what?"

"I haven't the first clue," Amiit said. "I was hoping you might know."

Otah shook his head. He took another piece of chicken, but his mind was elsewhere. The Galts in Machi. He tried to make Biitrah's death, the attack on Maati, and his own improbable freedom into some pattern, but no two things seemed to fit. He drank his wine, feeling the warmth spread through his throat and belly.

"I need your word on something, Amiit-cha. That if I tell you what I know, you won't act on it lightly. There are lives at stake."

"Galtic lives?"

"Innocent ones."

Amiit considered silently. His face was closed. Otah poured more water into his cup. Amiit silently took a pose that accepted the offered terms. Otah looked at his hands, searching for the words he needed to say.

"Saraykeht. When Seedless acted against Heshai-kvo there, the Galts were involved. They were allied with the andat. I believe they hoped to find the andat willing allies in their own freedom, only Seedless was . . . unreliable. They hurt Heshai badly, even though their plan failed. They aren't the ones who murdered him, but Heshai-kvo let himself be killed rather than expose them."

"Why would he do an idiot thing like that?"

"He knew what would happen. He knew what the Khai Saraykeht would do."

Otah felt himself on the edge of confession, but he stopped before admitting that the poet had died at his hands. There was no need, and that, at least, was one secret that he chose to keep to himself. Instead, he looked up and met Amiit's gaze. When the overseer spoke, his voice was calm, measured, careful.

"He would have slaughtered Galt," Amiit said.

"Innocent lives."

"And some guilty ones."

"A few."

Amiit leaned back in his chair, his fingers steepled before his lips. Otah could almost see the calculations taking place behind those calm, dark eyes.

"So you think this is about the poets?"

"It was last time," Otah said. "Let me send a letter to Maati. Let me warn him—"

"We can't. You're dead, and half the safety we can give you depends on your staying dead until we know more than this. But . . . but I can tell a few well-placed people to be on alert. And give them some idea what to be alert for. Another Saraykeht would be devastating." Amiit sighed deeply. "And here I thought only the succession, your life, and my house were in play. Poets now, too."

Amiit's smile was thoughtful.

"I'll give you this. You make the world more interesting, Itani-cha. Or . . . ?"

He took a pose that asked for correction.

"Otah. Much as I've fought against it, my name is Otah Machi. We might as well both get used to saying it."

"Otah-cha, then," Amiit said. He seemed pleased, as if he'd won some small victory.

Voices came up through the window. The commander's was already familiar even after so short a time. Otah couldn't make out the words, but he sounded pleased. Another voice answered him that Otah didn't know, but the woman's laughter that pealed out after it was familiar as water.

Otah felt the air go thin. He stood and walked slowly to the open shutters. There in the yard behind the farmhouse Sinja and one of the archers were standing beside a lovely woman in loose cotton robes the blue of the sky at twilight. Her fox-thin face was smiling, one eyebrow arched as she said something to the commander, who chuckled in his turn. Her hair was dark and shot with individual strands of white that she had had since birth.

He saw the change in Kiyan's stance when she noticed him—a release and relaxation. She walked away from the two men and toward the open window. Otah's heart beat fast as if he'd been running. She stopped and put out her hands, palms up and open. It wasn't a formal pose, and seemed to mean *here I am* and *here you are* and *who would have guessed this* all at once.

"She came to me not long after you left," Amiit said from where he sat. "I'm half-partner in her wayhouse down in Udun. We've been keeping it a quiet arrangement, though. There's something to be said for having a whole wayhouse of one's own without the couriers of other houses knowing it's yours."

Otah wanted to look back at the man, but his gaze seemed fastened on Kiyan. He thought he caught a faint blush rising in her cheeks. She shook her head as if clearing away some unwanted thought and walked in toward the house and out of his view. She was smiling, though. Sinja had also caught sight of Otah in the window and took a pose of congratulation.

"She's changed her mind, then. About me?"

"Apparently."

Otah turned back and leaned against the wall. Its coolness surprised him. After so many days in the cell at the tower's height, he'd come to think of stone as warm. Amiit poured himself another cup of wine. Otah swallowed to loosen his throat. The question didn't want to be asked.

"Why? What changed it?"

"I have known Kiyan-cha well for almost a quarter of this year. Not even that. You've been her lover for what? Three summers? And you want me to explain her mind to you? You've become an optimist."

Otah sat because his knees felt too weak to hold him. Amiit chuckled again and rose.

"You'll need rest for a few days. And some food and space enough to move again. We'll have you strong enough to do whatever it is needs doing, I hope. This place is better watched than it looks. We'll have warning if anyone comes near. Don't let any of this trouble you for now; you can trust us to watch over things."

"I want to see her," Otah said.

"I know," Amiit said, clapping him on the shoulder. "And she wants to see you. It's why I'm leaving. Just remember you haven't eaten to speak of in days, you're weak from the cell, you've hardly slept, and you were abducted last night. Don't expect too much from yourself. There really is no hurry."

Otah blushed now, and Amiit grabbed one last apple and made for the door. Kiyan reached it just as he did, and he stepped back to let her through. He closed the door gently behind him. Otah rose to his feet, suddenly tongue-tied. Kiyan also didn't speak, but her gaze traveled over him. He could see the distress in it even though she tried to keep it hidden.

"'Tani," she said, "you . . . you look terrible."

"It's the beard," Otah said. "I'll shave it."

She didn't take up the humor, only walked across the room and folded him into her arms. The scent of her skin flooded him with a hundred jumbled memories of her. He put his arm around her, embarrassed to notice that his hand was unsteady.

"I didn't think I'd be seeing you again," he murmured. "I never meant to put you at risk."

"What did they do to you? Gods, what have they done?"

"Not so much. They only didn't feed me well for a time and locked me away. It wasn't so bad."

She kissed his cheek and pulled back from him until each could see the other's face. There were tears in her eyes, but she was angry.

"They were going to kill you," she said.

"Well, yes. I mean, I thought that was assumed."

"I'll kill them all with my bare hands if you'd like," she said with a smile that meant she was only half joking.

"That might be more than the situation calls for. But . . . why are you here? I thought . . . I thought I was too much a risk to you."

"That didn't change. Other things . . . other things did. Come. Sit with me."

Kiyan took a bite of the cheese and poured herself water. Her hands were thin and strong and as lovely as a sculpture. Otah rubbed his temples with the palms of his hands, hoping that this was all as real as it seemed, that he wouldn't wake again in the cell above the city.

"Sinja-cha told me you wanted to turn back. He said it was because of me. That your being there kept them from searching me out."

"Knowing me shouldn't have that kind of price on it," Otah said. "It was . . . it was what I could do. That's all."

"Thank you," she said, her voice solemn.

Kiyan looked out the window. There was a dread in the lines of her mouth, a fear that confused him. He reached out, thinking to take her hand in his own, but the movement brought her back and a smile flitted over her and was gone.

"I don't know if you want to hear this. But I've been waiting to say it for longer than I can stand, and so I'm going to be selfish. And I don't know how to. Not well."

"Is it something I'll want to hear?"

"I don't know. I hope . . . I . . . Gods. Here. When you left, I missed you worse than I'd expected. I was sick with it. Physically ill. I thought I should be patient. I thought it would pass. And then I noticed that I seemed to miss you most in the early mornings. You understand?"

She looked Otah deep in the eye, and he frowned, trying to find some deeper significance in the words. And then he did, and he felt the world drop away from under him. He took a pose of query, and she replied with a confirmation.

"Ah," he said and then sat, utterly at a loss. After ten or twenty breaths, Kiyan spoke again.

"The midwife thinks sometime around Candles Night. Maybe a little after. So you see, I knew there was no avoiding the issue, not as long as I was carrying a baby with your blood in it. I went to Amiit-cha and we . . . he, really . . . put things in motion."

"There are blood teas," Otah said.

"I know. The midwife offered them to me. Would you . . . I mean, is that what you would have wanted?"

"No! Only I . . . I'd thought you wouldn't give up what you had. Your father's wayhouse. I don't know that I have much of a life to give you. I was a dead man until a little before dawn today. But if you want . . ."

"I wouldn't have left the wayhouse for you, 'Tani. It's where I grew up. It's my home, and I wouldn't give it up for a man. Not even a good man. I made that decision the night you told me who your father was. But for the both of you. Or really, even just for her. That's a harder question."

"Her?"

"Or him," Kiyan said. "Whichever. But I suppose that puts the decision in your hands now. The last time I saw you, I turned you out of my house. I won't use this as a means of forcing you into something you'd rather not. I've made my choice, not yours."

Perhaps it was the fatigue or the wine, but it took Otah the space of two or three breaths to understand what she was saying. He felt the grin draw back the corners of his mouth until they nearly ached.

"I want you to be with me, Kiyan-kya. I want you to always be with me. And the baby too. If I have to flee to the Westlands and herd sheep, I want you both with me."

Kiyan breathed in deeply, and let the breath out with a rough stutter. He hadn't seen how unsure she'd been until now, when the relief relaxed her face. She took his hand and squeezed it until he thought both of their bones were creaking.

"That's good. That's very good. I would have been . . ." laughter entered her voice ". . . very disappointed."

A knock at the door startled them both. The commander opened the door and then glanced from one of the laughing pair to the other. His face took a stern expression.

"You told him," Sinja said. "You should at least let the man rest before you tell him things like that. He's had a hard day."

"He's been up to the task," Kiyan said.

"Well, I've come to make things worse. We've just had a runner from the city, Otah-cha. It appears you've murdered your father in his sleep. Your brother Danat led a hunting party bent on bringing back your head on a stick, but apparently you've killed him too. You're running out of family, Otah-cha."

"Ah," Otah said, and then a moment later. "I think perhaps I should lie down now."

10

They burned the Khai Machi and his son together in the yard outside the temple. The head priest wore his pale robes, the hood pulled low over his eyes in respect, and tended the flames. Thick, black smoke rose from the pyre and vanished into the air high above the city. Machi had woken from its revels to find the world worse than when they'd begun, and Cehmai saw it in every face he passed. A thousand of them at least stood in the afternoon sun. Shock and sorrow, confusion and fear.

And excitement. In a few eyes among the utkhaiem, he saw the bright eyes and sharp ears of men who smelled opportunity. He walked among them, Stone-Made-Soft at his side, peering through the funereal throng for the one familiar face. Idaan had to be there, but he could not find her.

The lower priests also passed through the crowds, singing dirges and beating the dry notes of drums. Slaves in ceremonially torn robes passed out tin cups of bittered water. Cehmai ignored them. The burning would go on through the night until the ashes of the men and the ashes of the coal were indistinguishable. And then a week's mourning. And then these men weeping or staring, grim or secretly pleased, would meet and decide which of their number would have the honor of sitting on the dead family's chair and leading the hunt for the man who had murdered his own father. Cehmai found himself unable to care particularly who won or lost, whether the upstart was caught or escaped. Somewhere among all these mourners was the woman he'd come to love, in more pain than she had ever been in since he'd known her. And he—he who could topple towers at a whim and make mountains flow like floodwater—couldn't find her.

Instead, he found Maati in brown poet's robes standing on a raised walkway that overlooked the mourning throng. Though they were on the edge of the ceremony, Cehmai saw the pyre light reflecting in Maati's fixed eyes. Cehmai almost didn't approach him, almost didn't speak. There was a darkness wrapped around the poet. But it was possible he had been there from the ceremony's beginning. He might know where Idaan was. Cehmai took a pose of greeting which Maati did not return.

"Maati-kvo?"

Maati looked over first at Cehmai, then Stone-Made-Soft, and then back again at the fire. After a moment's pause, his face twisted in disgust.

"Not *kvo*. Never *kvo*. I haven't taught you anything, so don't address me as a teacher. I was wrong. From the beginning, I was wrong."

"Otah was very convincing," Cehmai said. "No one thought he would—"

"Not about that. He didn't do this. Baarath . . . Gods, why did it have to be Baarath that saw it? Prancing, self-important, smug . . ."

Maati fumbled with a sewn-leather wineskin and took a long deep, joyless drink from it. He wiped his mouth with the back of a hand, then held the skin out in offering. Cehmai declined. Maati offered it to the andat, but Stone-Made-Soft only smiled as if amused.

"I thought it was someone in the family. One of his brothers. It had to be. Who else would benefit? I was stupid."

"Forgive me, Maati-kvo. But no one did benefit."

"One of *them* did," he said, gesturing out at the mourners. "One of them is going to be the new Khai. He'll tell you what to do, and you'll do it. He'll live in the high palaces, and everyone else in the city will lick his ass if he tells them to. That's what it's all about. Who has to lick whose ass. And there's blood enough to fill a river answering that." He took another long pull from the wineskin, then dropped it idly to the ground at his feet. "I hate all of them."

"So do I," Stone-Made-Soft said, his tone light and conversational.

"You're drunk, Maati-kvo."

"Not half enough. Here, look at this. You know what this is?"

Cehmai glanced at the object Maati had pulled from his sleeve.

"A book."

"This is my teacher's masterwork. Heshai-kvo, poet of Saraykeht. The Dai-kvo sent me to him when I was hardly younger than you are now. I was going to study under him, take control of Seedless. Removing-the-Part-That-Continues. We called him Seedless. This is Heshai-kvo's examination of everything he'd done wrong. Every improvement he could have made to his binding, if he'd had it to do over again. It's brilliant."

"But it can't work, can it?" Cehmai said. "It would be too close. . . ."

"Of course not, it's a refinement of his work, not how to bind Seedless again. It's a record of his failure. Do you understand what I'm saying?"

Cehmai grasped for a right answer to the question and ended with honesty.

"No," he said.

"Heshai-kvo was a drunkard. He was a failure. He was haunted his whole life by the woman he loved and the child he lost, and every measure of the hatred he had for himself was in his binding. He imagined the andat as the perfect man and implicit in that was the disdain he imagined such a man would feel looking at him. But Heshai was strong enough to look his mistake in the face. He was strong enough to sit with it and catalog it and *understand*. And the Dai-kvo sent me to him. Because he thought we could be the same. He thought I would understand him well enough to stand in his place."

"Maati-kvo, I'm sorry. Have you seen Idaan?"

"Well," Maati said, ignoring the question as he swayed slightly and frowned at the crowd. "I can face my stupidities just as well as he did. The Dai-kvo wants to know who killed Biitrah? I'll find out. He can tell me it's too late and he can tell me to come home, but he can't make me stop looking. Whoever gets that chair . . . whoever gets it . . ."

Maati frowned, confused for a moment, and a sudden racking sob shook him. He leaned forward. Cehmai moved to him, certain for a moment that Maati was about to pitch off the walkway and down to the distant ground, but instead the older poet gathered himself and took a pose of apology.

"I'm . . . making an ass of myself," he said. "You were saying something."

Cehmai was torn for a moment. He could see the red that lined Maati's eyes, could smell the sick reek of distilled wine on his breath and something deeper—some drug mixed with the wine. Someone needed to see Maati back to his apartments, needed to see that he was cared for. On another night, Cehmai would have done it.

"Idaan," he said. "She must have been here. They're burning her brother and her father. She had to attend the ceremony."

"She did." Maati agreed. "I saw her."

"Where's she gone?"

"With her man, I think. He was there beside her," Maati said. "I don't know where they went."

"Are you going to be all right, Maati-kvo?"

Maati seemed to think about this, then nodded once and turned back to watch the pyre burning. The brown leather book had fallen to the ground by the wineskin, and the andat retrieved it and put it back in Maati's sleeve. As they walked away, Cehmai took a pose of query.

"I didn't think he'd want to lose it," the andat said.

"So that was a favor to him?" Cehmai said. Stone-Made-Soft didn't reply. They walked toward the women's quarters and Idaan's apartments. If she was not there, he would go to the Vaunyogi's palace. He would say he was there to offer condolences to Idaan-cha. That it was his duty as poet and representative of the Dai-kvo to offer condolences to Idaan Machi on this most sorrowful of days. It was his duty. Gods. And the Vaunyogi would be chewing their own livers out. They'd contracted to marry their son to the Khai Machi's sister. Now she was no one's family.

"Maybe they'll cancel the arrangement," Stone-Made-Soft said. "It isn't as if anyone would blame them. She could come live with us."

"You can be quiet now," Cehmai said.

At Idaan's quarters, the servant boy reported that Idaan-cha had been there, but had gone. Yes, Adrah-cha had been there as well, but he had also gone. The unease in the boy's manner made Cehmai wonder. Part of him hoped that they had been fighting, those two. It was despicable, but it was there: the desire that he and not Adrah Vaunyogi be the one to comfort her.

He stopped next at the palace of the Vaunyogi. A servant led him to a waiting chamber that had been dressed in pale mourning cloth fragrant from the cedar chests in which it had been stored. The chairs and statuary, windows and floors were all swathed in white rags that candlelight made gold. The andat stood at the window, peering out at the courtyard while Cehmai sat on the front handspan of a seat. Every breath he took here made him wonder if coming had been a mistake.

The door to the main hall swung open. Adrah Vaunyogi stepped in. His shoulders rode high and tight, his lips thin as a line drawn on paper. Cehmai stood and took a pose of greeting which Adrah mirrored before he closed the door.

"I'm surprised to see you, Cehmai-cha," Adrah said, walking forward slowly, as if unsure what precisely he was approaching. Cehmai smiled to keep his unease from showing. "My father is occupied. But perhaps I might be able to help you?"

"You're most kind. I came to offer my sympathies to Idaan-cha. I had heard she was with you, and so . . ."

"No. She was, but she's left. Perhaps she went back to the ceremony." Adrah's voice was distant, as if only half his attention was on the conversation. His eyes, however, were fixed on Cehmai like a snake on a mouse, only Cehmai wasn't sure which of them would be the mouse, which the serpent.

"I will look there," Cehmai said. "I didn't mean to disturb you."

"We are always pleased by an audience with the poet of Machi. Wait. Don't . . . don't go. Sit with me a moment."

Stone-Made-Soft didn't shift, but Cehmai could feel its interest and amusement in the back of his mind. Cehmai sat in a rag-covered chair. Adrah pulled a stool near to him, nearer than custom required. It was as if Adrah wanted to make him feel they were in a smaller room together. Cehmai kept his face as placid as the andat's.

"The city is in terrible trouble, Cehmai-cha. You know how bad these things can get. When it's only the three sons of the Khai, it's bad enough. But with all the utkhaiem scheming and fighting and betraying one another, the damage to the city . . ."

"I'd thought about that," Cehmai said, though in truth he cared more about Idaan than the political struggles that the coming weeks would bring. "And there's still the problem of Otah. He has a claim . . ."

"He's murdered his own father."

"Have we proven that?"

"You doubt that he did the thing?"

"No," Cehmai said after a moment's pause. "No, I don't." *But Maati-kvo still does.*

"It would be best to end this quickly. To name the new Khai before things can get out of control. You are a man of tremendous power. I know the Dai-kvo takes no sides in matters of succession. But if you were to let it be known that you favored some particular house, without taking any formal position, it would make things easier."

"Only if I backed a house that was prepared to win," Cehmai said. "If I chose poorly, I'd throw some poor unprepared family in with the pit hounds."

"My family is ready. We are well respected, we have partners in all the great trading houses, and the silversmiths and ironworkers are closer to us than to any other family. Idaan is the only blood of the old Khai remaining in the city. Her brothers will never be Khai Machi, but someday, her son might."

Cehmai considered. Here was a man asking his help, asking for political backing, unaware that Cehmai knew the shape and taste of his lover's body as well as he did. It likely was in his power to elevate Adrah Vaunyogi to the ranks of the Khaiem. He wondered if it was what Idaan would want.

"That may be wise," Cehmai said. "I would need to think about it, of course, before I could act."

Adrah put his hand on Cehmai's knee, familiar as if they were brothers. The andat moved first, ambling toward the door, and then Cehmai stood and adopted a pose appropriate to parting. The amusement coming from Stone-Made-Soft was like constant laughter that only Cehmai could hear.

When they had made their farewells, Cehmai started east again, toward the burning bodies and the priests. His mind was a jumble— concern for Idaan, frustration at not finding her, unease with Adrah's proposal, and at the back, stirring like something half asleep, a dread that seemed wrapped up with Maati Vaupathai staring drunk into the fire.

One of *them*, Maati had said, meaning the high families of the utkhaiem. One of them would benefit. Unless Cehmai took a hand and put his own lover's husband in the chair. That wasn't the sort of thing that could have been planned for. No scheme for power could include the supposition that Cehmai would fall in love with Idaan, or that her husband would ask his aid, or that his guilt and affection would drive him to give it. It was the kind of thing that could come from nowhere and upset the perfect plan.

If it wasn't Otah Machi who had engineered all this bloodletting, then some other viper was in the city, and the prospect of Adrah Vaunyogi taking the prize away by marrying Idaan and wooing the poets would drive the killer mad. And even if it *was* Otah Machi, he might still hope to take his father's place. Adrah's rise would threaten *that* claim as well.

"You're thinking too hard," the andat said.

"Thinking never hurt anyone."

"So you've all said," the andat sighed.

She wasn't at the ceremony. She wasn't at her quarters. Cehmai and Stone-Made-Soft walked together through the gardens and pavilions, the courtyards and halls and passages. Mourning didn't fill the streets and towers the way celebration had. The dry music of the funeral drums wasn't taken up in the teahouses or gardens. Only the pillar of smoke blotting out the stars stood testament to the ceremony. Twice, Cehmai took them past his own quarters, hoping that Idaan might be there waiting for him, but without effect. She had vanished from the city like a bird flying up into darkness.

HIS OLD NOTES WERE GONE, LEFT IN A PACKET IN HIS ROOMS. KAIIN AND Danat were forgotten, and instead, Maati had fresh papers spread over the library table. Lists of the houses of the utkhaiem that might possibly succeed in a bid to become the next Khai. Beside them, a fresh ink brick, a pen with a new bronze nib, and a pot of tea that smelled rich, fresh cut, and green. Summer tea in the winter cities. Maati poured himself a bowl, then blew across the pale surface, his eyes going over the names again.

According to Baarath, who had accepted his second apology with a grace that had surprised him, the most likely was Kamau—a family that traced its bloodline back to the Second Empire. They had the wealth and the prestige. And, most important, an unmarried son in his twenties who was well-respected and active in the court. Then the Vaunani, less wealthy, less prestigious, but more ruthless. Or possibly the Radaani, who had spent generations putting their hands into the import and export trade until almost every transaction in the city fed their coffers. They were the richest of the utkhaiem, but apparently unable to father males. There were seventeen daughters, and the only candidates for the Khai's chair were the head of the house, his son presently overseeing a trading venture in Yalakeht, and a six-year-old grandson.

And then there were the Vaunyogi. Adrah Vaunyogi was a decent candidate, largely because he was young and virile, and about to be married to Idaan Machi. But the rumors held that the family was underfunded and not as well connected in court. Maati sipped his tea and considered whether to leave them on his list. One of these houses—most likely one of these, though there were certainly other possibilities—had engineered the murder of the Khai Machi. They had placed the blame on Otah. They had spirited him away, and once the mourning was finished with . . .

Once the mourning was finished, the city would attend the wedding of Adrah Vaunyogi to Idaan. No, no, he would keep the Vaunyogi on his list. It was such a convenient match, and the timing so apt.

Others, of course, put the crimes down to Otah-kvo. A dozen hunting packs had gone out in the four days since the bloody morning that killed the Khai and Danat both. The utkhaiem were searching the low towns for Otah and those who had aided his escape, but so far no one had succeeded. It was Maati's task now to solve the puzzle before they found him. He wondered how many of them had guessed that he alone in the city was working to destroy all their chances. If someone else had done these things . . . if he could show it . . . Otah would still be able to take his father's place. He would become Khai Machi.

And what, Maati wondered, would Liat think of that, once she heard of it? He imagined her cursing her ill judgment in losing the ruler of a city and gaining half a poet who hadn't proved worth keeping.

"Maati," Baarath said.

Maati jumped, startled, and spilled a few drops of tea over his papers. Ink swirled into the pale green as he blotted them with a cloth. Baarath clicked his teeth and hurried over to help.

"My fault," the librarian said. "I thought you had noticed me. You were scowling, after all."

Maati didn't know whether to laugh at that, so he only took a pose of gratitude as Baarath blew across the still damp pages. The damage was minor. Even where the ink had smudged, he knew what he had meant. Baarath fumbled in his sleeve and drew out a letter, its edges sewn in green silk.

"It's just come for you," he said. "The Dai-kvo, I think?"

Maati took it. The last he had reported, Otah had been found and turned over to the Khai Machi. It was a faster response than he had expected. He turned the letter over, looking at the familiar handwriting that formed his name. Baarath sat across the table from him, smiling as if he were, of course, welcome, and waiting to see what the message said. It was one of the little rudenesses to which the librarian seemed to feel himself entitled since Maati's apology. Maati had the uncomfortable feeling Baarath thought they were becoming friends.

He tore the paper at the sewn seams, pulled the thread free, and unfolded it. The chop was clearly the Dai-kvo's own. It began with the traditional forms and etiquette. Only at the end of the first page did the matter become specific to the situation at hand.

With Otah discovered and given over to the Khai, your work in Machi is completed. Your suggestion that he be accepted again as a poet is, of course, impossible but the sentiment is commendable. I am quite pleased with you, and trust that this will mark a change in your work. There are many tasks that a man in your position might take on to the benefit of all—we shall discuss these opportunities upon your return.

The critical issue now is that you withdraw from Machi. We have performed our service to the Khai, and your continued presence would only serve to draw attention to the fact that he and whichever of his sons eventually takes his place were unable to discover the plot without aid. It is dangerous for the poets to involve themselves with the politics of the courts.

For this reason, I now recall you to my side. You are to announce that you have found the citations in the library that I had desired, and must now return them to me. I will expect you within five weeks. . . .

It continued, though Maati did not. Baarath smiled and leaned forward in obvious interest as Maati tucked the letter into his own sleeve. After a moment's silence, Baarath frowned.

"Fine," he said. "If it's the sort of thing you have to keep to yourself, I can certainly respect that."

"I knew you could, Baarath-cha. You're a man of great discretion."

"You needn't flatter me. I know my proper place. I only thought you might want someone to speak with. In case there were questions that someone with my knowledge of the court could answer for you."

"No," Maati said, taking a pose that offered thanks. "It's on another matter entirely."

Maati sat with a pleasant, empty expression until Baarath huffed, stood, took a pose of leave-taking, and walked deeper into the galleries of the library. Maati turned back to his notes, but his mind would not stay focused on them. After half a hand of frustration and distress, he packed them quietly into his sleeve and took himself away.

The sun shone bright and clear, but to the west, huge clouds rose white and proud into the highest reaches of the sky. There would be storms later—if not today, in the summer weeks to come. Maati imagined he could smell the rain in the air. He walked toward his rooms, and then past them and into a walled garden. The cherry trees had lost their flowers, the fruits forming and swelling toward ripeness. Netting covered the wide branches like a bed, keeping the birds from stealing the harvest. Maati walked in the dappled shade. The pangs from his belly were fewer now and farther between. The wounds were nearly healed.

It would be easiest, of course, to do as he was told. The Dai-kvo had taken him back into his good graces, and the fact that things had gone awry since his last report could in no way be considered his responsibility. He had discovered Otah, and if it was through no skill of his own, that didn't change the result. He had given Otah over to the Khai. Everything past that was court politics; even the murder of the Khai was nothing the Dai-kvo would want to become involved with.

Maati could leave now with honor and let the utkhaiem follow his investigations or ignore them. The worst that would happen was that Otah would be found and slaughtered for something he had not done and an evil man would become the Khai Machi. It wouldn't be the first time in the world that an innocent had suffered or that murder had been rewarded. The sun would still rise, winter would still become spring. And Maati would be restored to something like his right place among the poets. He might even be set over the school, set to teach boys like himself the lessons that he and Otah-kvo and Heshai-kvo and Cehmai had all learned. It would be something worth taking pride in.

So why was it, he wondered, that he would not do as he was told? Why was the prospect of leaving and accepting the rewards he had dreamed of less appealing than staying, risking the Dai-kvo's displeasure, and discovering what had truly happened to the Khai Machi? It wasn't love of justice. It was more personal than that.

Maati paused, closed his eyes, and considered the roiling anger in his breast. It was a familiar feeling, like an old companion or an illness so protracted it has become indistinguishable from health. He couldn't say

who he was angry with or why the banked rage demanded that he follow his own judgment over anyone else's. He couldn't even say what he
hoped he would find.

He plucked the Dai-kvo's letter from his sleeve, read it again slowly
from start to finish, and began to mentally compose his reply.

Most high Dai-kvo, I hope you will forgive me, but the situation in
Machi is such that . . .

Most high Dai-kvo, I am sure that, had you known the turns of event
since my last report . . .

Most high, I must respectfully . . .

Most high Dai-kvo, what have you ever done for me that I should do
anything you say? Why do I agree to be your creature when that agreement has only ever caused me pain and loss, and you still instruct me to
turn my back on the people I care for most?

Most high Dai-kvo, I have fed your last letter to pigs. . . .

"Maati-kvo!"

Maati opened his eyes and turned. Cehmai, who had been running
toward him, stopped short. Maati thought he saw fear in the boy's expression and wondered for a moment what Cehmai had seen in his face
to inspire it. Maati took a pose that invited him to speak.

"Otah," Cehmai said. "They've found him."

Too late, then, Maati thought. I've been too slow and come too late.

"Where?" he asked.

"In the river. There's a bend down near one of the low towns. They
found his body, and a man in leather armor. One of the men who helped
him escape, or that's what they've guessed. The Master of Tides is having them brought to the Khai's physicians. I told him that you had seen
Otah most recently. You would be able to confirm it's really him."

Maati sighed and watched a sparrow try to land on the branch of a
cherry tree. The netting confused it, and the bird pecked at the lines that
barred it from the fruit just growing sweet. Maati smiled in sympathy.

"Let's go, then," he said.

There was a crowd in the courtyard outside the physician's apartments. Armsmen wearing mourning robes barred most of the onlookers
but parted when Maati and Cehmai arrived. The physician's workroom
was wide as a kitchen, huge slate tables in the center of the room and
thick incense billowing from a copper brazier. The bodies were laid out
naked on their bellies—one thick and well-muscled with a heaped pile

of black leather on the table beside it, the other thinner with what might have been the robes of a prisoner or cleaning rags clinging to its back. The Master of Tides—a thin man named Saani Vaanga—and the Khai's chief physician were talking passionately, but stopped when they saw the poets.

The Master of Tides took a pose that offered service.

"I have come on behalf of the Dai-kvo," Maati said. "I wished to confirm the reports that Otah Machi is dead."

"Well, he isn't going dancing," the physician said, pointing to the thinner corpse with his chin.

"We're pleased by the Dai-kvo's interest," the Master of Tides said, ignoring the comment. "Cehmai-cha suggested that you might be able to confirm for us that this is indeed the upstart."

Maati took a pose of compliance and stepped forward. The reek was terrible—rotting flesh and something deeper, more disturbing. Cehmai hung back as Maati circled the table.

Maati gestured at the body, his hand moving in a circle to suggest turning it over that he might better see the dead man's face. The physician sighed, came to Maati's side, and took a long iron hook. He slid the hook under the body's shoulder and heaved. There was a wet sound as it lifted and fell. The physician put away the hook and arranged the limbs as Maati considered the bare flesh before him. Clearly the body had spent its journey face down. The features were bloated and fish-eaten—it might have been Otah-kvo. It might have been anyone.

On the pale, water-swollen flesh of the corpse's breast, the dark ink was still visible. The tattoo. Maati had his hand halfway out to touch it before he realized what he was doing and pulled his fingers back. The ink was so dark, though, the line where the tattoo began and ended so sharp. A stirring of the air brought the scent fully to his nose, and Maati gagged, but didn't look away.

"Will this satisfy the Dai-kvo?" the Master of Tides asked.

Maati nodded and took a pose of thanks, then turned and gestured to Cehmai that he should follow. The younger poet was stone-faced. Maati wondered if he had seen many dead men before, much less smelled them. Out in the fresh air again, they navigated the crowd, ignoring the questions asked them. Cehmai was silent until they were well away from any curious ear.

"I'm sorry, Maati-kvo. I know you and he were—"

"It's not him," Maati said.

Cehmai paused, his hands moved up into a pose that spoke of his confusion. Maati stopped, looking around.

"It isn't him," Maati said. "It's close enough to be mistaken, but it isn't him. Someone wants us to think him dead—someone willing to go to elaborate lengths. But that's no more Otah Machi than I am."

"I don't understand," Cehmai said.

"Neither do I. But I can say this, someone wants the rumor of his death but not the actual thing. They're buying time. Possibly time they can use to find who's really done these things, then—"

"We have to go back! You have to tell the Master of Tides!"

Maati blinked. Cehmai's face had gone red and he was pointing back toward the physician's apartments. The boy was outraged.

"If we do that," Maati said, "we spoil all the advantage. It can't get out that—"

"Are you blind? Gods! It *is* him. All the time it's *been* him. This as much as proves it! Otah Machi came here to slaughter his family. To slaughter you. He has backers who could free him from the tower, and he has done everything that he's been accused of. Buying time? He's buying safety! Once everyone thinks him dead, they'll stop looking. He'll be free. You have to tell them the truth!"

"Otah didn't kill his father. Or his brothers. It's someone else."

Cehmai was breathing hard and fast as a runner at the race's end, but his voice was lower now, more controlled.

"How do you know that?" he asked.

"I know Otah-kvo. I know what he would do, and—"

"Is he innocent because he's innocent, or because you love him?" Cehmai demanded.

"This isn't the place to—"

"Tell me! Say you have proof and not just that you wish the sky was red instead of blue, because otherwise you're blinded and you're letting him escape because of it. There were times I more than half believed you, Maati-kvo. But when I look at this I see nothing to suggest any conspiracy but his."

Maati rubbed the point between his eyes with his thumb, pressing hard to keep his annoyance at bay. He shouldn't have spoken to the boy, but now that he had, there was nothing for it.

"Your anger—" he began, but Cehmai cut him off.

"You're risking people's lives, Maati-kvo. You're hanging them on the thought that you can't be wrong about the upstart."

"Whose lives?"

"The lives of people he would kill."

"There is no risk from Otah-kvo. You don't understand."

"Then teach me." It was as much an insult as a challenge. Maati felt the blood rising to his cheeks even as his mind dissected Cehmai's reaction. There was something to it, some reason for the violence and frustration of it, that didn't make sense. The boy was reacting to something more than Maati knew. Maati swallowed his rage.

"I'll ask five days. Trust me for five days, and I will show you proof. Will that do?"

He saw the struggle in Cehmai's face. The impulse to refuse, to fight, to spread the news across the city that Otah Machi lived. And then the respect for his elders that had been ground into him from his first day in the school and for all the years since he'd taken the brown robes they shared. Maati waited, forcing himself to patience. And in the end, Cehmai nodded once, turned, and stalked away.

Five days, Maati thought, shaking his head. I wonder what I thought to manage in that time. I should have asked for ten.

THE RAINS CAME IN THE EARLY EVENING: LIGHTNING AND THE BLUE-GRAY bellies of cloudbank. The first few drops sounded like stones, and then the clouds broke with a sudden pounding—thousands of small drums rolling. Otah sat in the window and looked out at the courtyard as puddles appeared and danced white and clear. The trees twisted and shifted under gusts of wind and the weight of water. The little storms rarely lasted more than a hand and a half, but in that time, they seemed like doomsday, and they reminded Otah of being young, when everything had been full and torrential and brief. He wished now that he had the skill to draw this brief landscape before the clouds passed and it was gone. There was something beautiful in it, something worth preserving.

"You're looking better."

Otah shifted, glancing back into the room. Sinja was there, his long hair slicked down by the rain, his robes sodden. Otah took a welcoming pose as the commander strode across the room toward him, dripping as he came.

"Brighter about the eyes, blood in your skin again. One would think you'd been eating, perhaps even walking around a bit."

"I feel better," Otah said. "That's truth."

"I didn't doubt you would. I've seen men far worse off than you pull through just fine. They've found your corpse, by the way. Identified it as you, just as we'd hoped. There are already half a hundred stories about how that came to be, and none of them near the truth. Amiit-cha is quite pleased, I think."

"I suppose it's worth being pleased over," Otah said.

"You don't seem overjoyed."

"Someone killed my father and my brothers and placed the blame on me. It just seems an odd time to celebrate."

Sinja didn't answer this, and for a moment, the two men sat in silence broken only by the rain. Then Otah spoke again. "Who was he? The man with my tattoo? Where did you find him?"

"He wasn't the sort of man the world will miss," Sinja said. "Amiit found him in a low town, and we arranged to purchase his indenture from the low magistrate before they hung him."

"What had he done?"

"I don't know. Killed someone. Raped a puppy. Whatever soothes your conscience, he did that."

"You really don't care."

"No," Sinja agreed. "And perhaps that makes me a bad person, but since I don't care about that, either . . ."

He took a pose of completion, as if he had finished a demonstration. Otah nodded, then looked away.

"Too many people die over this," Otah said. "Too many lives wasted. It's an idiot system."

"This is nothing. You should see a real war. There is no bigger waste than that."

"You have? Seen war, I mean?"

"Yes. I fought in the Westlands. Sometimes when the Wardens took issue with each other. Sometimes against the nomad bands when they got big enough to pose a real threat. And then when the Galts decide to come take another bite out of them. There's more than enough opportunity there."

A distant flash of lightning lit the trees, and then a breath later, a growl of thunder. Otah reached his hand out, letting the cool drops wet his palm.

"What's it like?" he asked.

"War? Violent. Brutish, stupid. Unnecessary, as often as not. But I like the part where we win."

Otah chuckled.

"You seem . . . don't mind my prying at you, but for a man pulled from certain death, you don't seem to be as happy as I'd expected," Sinja said. "Something weighing on you?"

"Have you even been to Yalakeht?"

"No, too far east for me."

"They have tall gates on the mouths of their side streets that they close and lock every night. And there's a tower in the harbor with a permanent fire that guides ships in the darkness. In Chaburi-Tan, the street children play a game I've never seen anywhere else. They get just within shouting distance, strung out all through the streets, and then one will start singing, and the next will call the song on to the next after him, until it loops around to the first singer with all the mistakes and misunderstandings that make it something new. They can go on for hours. I stayed in a low town halfway between Lachi and Shosheyn-Tan where they served a stew of smoked sausage and pepper rice that was the best meal I've ever had. And the eastern islands.

"I was a fisherman out there for a few years. A very bad one, but . . . but I spent my time out on the water, listening to the waves against my little boat. I saw the way the water changed color with the day and the weather. The salt cracked my palms, and the woman I was with made me sleep with greased cloth on my hands. I think I'll miss that the most."

"Cracked palms?"

"The sea. I think that will be the worst of it."

Sinja shifted. The rain intensified and then slackened as suddenly as it had come. The trees stood straighter. The pools of water danced less.

"The sea hasn't gone anywhere," Sinja said.

"No, but I have. I've gone to the mountains. And I don't expect I'll ever leave them again. I knew it was the danger when I became a courier. I was warned. But I hadn't understood it until now. It's the problem in seeing too much of the world. In loving too much of it. You can only live in one place at a time. And eventually, you pick your spot, and the memories of all the others just become ghosts."

Sinja nodded, taking a pose that expressed his understanding. Otah smiled, and wondered what memories the commander carried with him. From the distance in his eyes, it couldn't all have been blood and terror. Something of it must have been worth keeping.

"You've decided, then," Sinja said. "Amiit-cha was thinking he'd need to speak with you about the issue soon. Things will be moving in Machi as soon as the mourning's done."

"I know. And yes, I've decided."

"Would you mind if I asked why you chose to stay?"

Otah turned and let himself down into the room. He took two bowls from the cabinet and poured the deep red wine into both before he answered. Sinja took the one he was offered and drank half at a swig. Otah sat on the table, his feet on the seat of the bench and swirled the red of the wine against the bone white of the bowl.

"Someone killed my father and my brothers."

"You didn't know them," Sinja said. "Don't tell me this is love."

"They killed my old family. Do you think they'd hesitate to kill my new one?"

"Spoken like a man," Sinja said, raising his bowl in salute. "The gods all know it won't be easy. As long as the utkhaiem think you've done everything you're accused of, they'll kill you first and crown you after. You'll have to find who did the thing and feed them to the crowds, and even then half of them will think you're guilty and clever. But if you don't do the thing . . . No, I think you're right. The options are live in fear or take the world by the balls. You can be the Khai Machi, or you can be the Khai Machi's victim. I don't see a third way."

"I'll take the first. And I'll be glad about it. It's only . . ."

"You mourn that other life, I know. It comes with leaving your boyhood behind."

"I wouldn't have thought I was still just a boy."

"It doesn't matter what you've done or seen. Every man's a child until he's a father. It's the way the world's made."

Otah raised his brows and took a pose of query only slightly hampered by the bowl of wine.

"Oh yes, several," Sinja said. "So far the mothers haven't met one another, so that's all for the best. But your woman? Kiyan-cha?"

Otah nodded.

"I traveled with her for a time," Sinja said. "I've never met another like her, and I've known more than my share of women. You're lucky to have her, even if it means freezing your prick off for half the year up here in the north."

"Are you telling me you're in love with my lover?" Otah asked, half joking, half serious.

"I'm saying she's worth giving up the sea for," Sinja said. He finished the last of his wine, spun the bowl on the table, and then clapped Otah's shoulder. Otah met his gaze for a moment before Sinja turned and strode out. Otah looked into the wine bowl again, smelled the memory of grapes hot from the sun, and drank it down. Outside, the sun broke through, and the green of the trees and blue of the sky where it peeked past the gray and white and yellow clouds showed vibrant as something newly washed.

Their quarters were down a short corridor, and then through a thin wooden door on leather hinges halfway to wearing through. Kiyan lay on the cot, the netting pulled around her to keep the gnats and mosquitoes off. Otah slipped through and lay gently beside her, watching her eyes flutter and her lips take up a smile as she recognized him.

"I heard you talking," she said, sleep slurring the words.

"Sinja-cha came up."

"What was the matter?"

"Nothing," he said, and kissed her temple. "We were only talking about the sea."

CEHMAI CLOSED THE DOOR OF THE POET'S HOUSE AGAIN AND STARTED PACing the length of the room. The storm in the back of his mind was hardly a match for the one at the front. Stone-Made-Soft, sitting at the empty, cold brazier, looked up. Its face showed a mild interest.

"Trees still there?" the andat asked.

"Yes."

"And the sky?"

"And the sky."

"But still no girl."

Cehmai dropped onto the couch, his hands worrying each other, restless. The andat sighed and went back to its contemplation of the ashes and fire-black metal. Cehmai smelled smoke in the air. It was likely just the forges, but his mind made the scent into Idaan's father and brother burning. He stood up again, walked to the door, turned back and sat down again.

"You could go out and look for her," the andat said.

"And why should I find her now? The mourning week's almost done. You think if she wanted me, there wouldn't have been word? I just . . . I don't understand it."

"She's a woman. You're a man."

"Your point being?"

The andat didn't reply. It might as well have been a statue. Cehmai probed at the connection between them, at the part of him that was the binding of the andat, but Stone-Made-Soft was in retreat. It had never been so passive in all the years Cehmai had held it. The quiet was a blessing, though he didn't understand it. He had enough to work through, and he was glad not to have his burden made any heavier.

"I shouldn't have been angry with Maati-kvo," Cehmai said. "I shouldn't have confronted him like that."

"No?"

"No. I should have gone back to the Master of Tides and told him what Maati-kvo had said. Instead, I promised him five days, and now three of them have passed and I can't do anything but chew at the grass."

"You can break promises," the andat said. "It's the definition, really. A promise is something that can be broken. If it can't, it's something else."

"You're singularly unhelpful," Cehmai said. The andat nodded as if remembering something, and then was still again. Cehmai stood, went to the shutters, and opened them. The trees were still lush with summer—the green so deep and rich he could almost see the autumn starting to creep in at the edge. In winter, he could see the towers rising up to the sky through the bare branches. Now he only knew they were there. He turned to look at the path that led back to the palaces, then went to the door, opened it, and looked down it, willing someone to be there. Willing Idaan's dark eyes to greet his own.

"I don't know what to do about Adrah Vaunyogi. I don't know if I should back him or not."

"For something you consider singularly unhelpful, I seem to receive more than my share of your troubles."

"You aren't real," Cehmai said. "You're like talking to myself."

The andat seemed to weigh that for a moment, then took a pose that conceded the point. Cehmai looked out again, then closed the door.

"I'm going to lose my mind if I stay here. I have to do something," he said. Stone-Made-Soft didn't respond, so Cehmai tightened the straps of his boots, stood, and pulled his robes into place. "Stay here."

"All right."

Cehmai paused at the door, one foot already outside, and turned back.

"Does nothing bother you?" he asked the andat.

"Being," Stone-Made-Soft suggested.

The palaces were still draped with rags of mourning cloth, the dry, steady beat of the funeral drum and the low wailing dirges still the only music. Cehmai took poses of greeting to the utkhaiem whom he passed. At the burning, they had all worn pale mourning cloth. Now, as the week wore on, there were more colors in the robes—here a mix of pale cloth and yellow or blue, there a delicate red robe with a wide sash of mourning cloth. No one went without, but few followed the full custom. It reminded Cehmai of a snow lily, green under the white and budding, swelling, preparing to burst out into new life and growth, new conflict and struggle. The sense of sorrow was slipping from Machi, and the sense of opportunity was coming forth.

He found he could not say whether that reassured or disgusted him. Perhaps both.

Idaan was, of course, not at her chambers. The servants assured him that she had been by—she was in the city, she hadn't truly vanished. Cehmai thanked them and continued on his way to the palace of the Vaunyogi. He didn't allow himself to think too deeply about what he was going to do or say. It would happen soon enough anyway.

A servant brought him to one of the inner courtyards to wait. An apple tree stood open to the air, its fruits unpecked by birds. Still unripe. Cehmai sat on a low stone bench and watched the branches bob as sparrows landed and took wing. His mind was deeply unquiet. On the one hand, he had to see Idaan, had to speak with her at least if not hold her against him. On the other, he could not bring himself to love Adrah Vaunyogi only because she loved him. And the secret he held twisted in his breast. Otah Machi lived. . . .

"Cehmai-cha."

Adrah was dressed in full mourning robes. His eyes were sunken and bloodshot, his movements sluggish. He looked like a man haunted. Cehmai wondered how much sleep Adrah had managed in these last days. He wondered how many of those late hours had been spent comforting Idaan. The image of Idaan, her body entwined with Adrah's, flashed in his mind and was pressed away. Cehmai took a pose of greeting.

"I'm pleased you've come," Adrah said. "You've considered what I said?"

"Yes, Adrah-cha. I have. But I'm concerned for Idaan-cha. I'm told she's been by her apartments, but I haven't been able to find her. And now, with the mourning week almost gone . . ."

"You've been looking for her, then?"

"I wished to offer my condolences. And then, after our conversation, I thought it would be wise to consult her on the matter as well. If it were not her will to go on living in the palaces after all that's happened, I would feel uncomfortable lending my support to a cause that would require it."

Adrah's eyes narrowed, and Cehmai felt a touch of heat in his cheeks. He coughed, looked down, and then, composed once again, raised his eyes to Adrah. He half expected to see rage there, but Adrah seemed pleased. Perhaps he was not so obvious as he felt. Adrah sat on the bench beside him, leaning in toward him as if they were intimate friends.

"But if you could satisfy yourself that this is what she would wish, you're willing? You would back me for her sake?"

"It's what would be best for the city," Cehmai said, trying to make it sound more like agreement than denial. "The sooner the question is resolved, the better we all are. And Idaan-cha would provide a sense of continuity, don't you think?"

"Yes," Adrah said. "I think she would."

They sat silent for a moment. The sense that Adrah knew or suspected something crept into Cehmai's throat, drawing it tight. He tried to calm himself; there was ultimately nothing Adrah could do to him. He was the poet of Machi, and the city itself rode on his shoulders and on Stone-Made-Soft. But Adrah was about to marry Idaan, and she loved him. There was quite a bit Adrah might yet do to hurt her.

"We're allies, then," Adrah said at last. "You and I. We've become allies."

"I suppose we have. Provided Idaan-cha . . ."

"She's here," Adrah said. "I'll take you to her. She's been here since her brother died. We thought it would be best if she were able to grieve in private. But if we need to break into her solitude now in order to assure her future for the rest of her life, I don't think there's any question what the right thing is to do."

"I don't . . . I don't mean to intrude."

Adrah grinned and slapped him on the back. He rose as he spoke.

"Never concern yourself with that, Cehmai-kya. You've come to our aid on an uncertain day. Think of us as your family now."

"That's very kind," Cehmai said, but Adrah was already striding away, and he had to hurry to keep pace.

He had never been so far into the halls and chambers that belonged to the Vaunyogi before. The dark stone passageways down which Cehmai was led seemed simpler than he had expected. The halls, more sparely furnished. Only the statuary—bronze likenesses of emperors and of the heads of the Vaunyogi—spoke of the wealth of a high family of the utkhaiem, and these were displayed in the halls and courtyards with such pride that they seemed more to point out the relative spareness of their surroundings than to distract from it. Diamonds set in brass.

Adrah spoke little, but when he did, his voice and demeanor were pleasant enough. Cehmai felt himself watched, evaluated. There was some reason that Adrah was showing him these signs of a struggling family—the worn tapestry, the great ironwork candleholders filled with half a hundred candles of tallow instead of wax, the empty incense burners, the long stairway leading up to the higher floors that still showed the marks where cloth runners had once softened the stone corners and no longer did—but Cehmai couldn't quite fathom it. In another man, at another time, it would have been a humbling thing to show a poet through a compound like this, but Adrah seemed anything but humble. It might have been a challenge or a play for Cehmai's sympathy. Or it might have been a boast. *My house has little, and still Idaan chose me.*

They stopped at last at a wide door—dark wood inlaid with bone and black stone. Adrah knocked, and when a servant girl opened the door a fraction, he pressed his way in, gesturing Cehmai to follow. They were summer quarters with wide arched windows, the shutters open to the air. Silk banners with the yellow and gray of the Vaunyogi bellied and fluttered in the breeze, as graceful as dancers. A desk stood at one wall, a brick of ink and a metal pen sitting on it, ready should anyone wish to use them. This room smelled of cedar and sandalwood. And sitting in one of the sills, her feet out over the void, Idaan. Cehmai breathed in deep, and let the air slide out slowly, taking with it a tension he'd only half known he carried. She turned, looking at them over her shoulder. Her face was unpainted, but she was just as lovely as she had ever been. The bare, unadorned skin reminded Cehmai of the soft curve of her mouth when she slept and the slow, languorous way she stretched when she was on the verge of waking.

He took a pose of formal greeting. There was perhaps a moment's surprise, and then she pulled her legs back into the room. Her expression asked the question.

"Cehmai-kya wished to speak with you, love," Adrah said.

"I am always pleased to meet with the servant of the Dai-kvo," Idaan said. Her smile was formal and calm, and gave away nothing. Cehmai hoped that he had not been wrong to come, but feared that her pleasant words might cover anger.

"Forgive me," he said. "I hadn't meant to intrude. Only I had hoped to find you at your own quarters, and these last few days . . ."

Something in her demeanor softened slightly, as if she had heard the deeper layer of his apology—*I had to see you, and there was no other way*—and accepted it. Idaan returned his formal greeting, then sauntered to the desk and sat, her hands folded on her knees, her gaze cast down in what would have been proper form for a girl of the utkhaiem before a poet. From her, it was a bitter joke. Adrah coughed. Cehmai glanced at him and realized the man thought she was being rude.

"I had hoped to offer my sympathies before this, Idaan-cha," Cehmai said.

"Your congratulations, too, I hope," Idaan said. "I am to be married once the mourning week has passed."

Cehmai felt his heart go tighter, but only smiled and nodded.

"Congratulations as well," he said.

"Cehmai-kya and I have been talking," Adrah said. "About the city and the succession."

Idaan seemed almost to wake at the words. Her body didn't move, but her attention sharpened. When she spoke, her voice had lost a slowness Cehmai had hardly known was there.

"Is that so? And what conclusions have you fine gentlemen reached?"

"Cehmai-kya agrees with me that the longer the struggle among the utkhaiem, the worse for the city. It would be better if it were done quickly. That's the most important thing."

"I see," Idaan said. Her gaze, dark as skies at midnight, shifted to Cehmai. She moved to brush her hair back from her brow, though Cehmai saw no stray lock there. "Then I suppose he would be wise to back whichever house has the strongest claim. If he has decided to back anyone. The Dai-kvo has been scrupulous about removing himself from these things."

"A man may voice an opinion," Adrah said, an edge in his voice, "without shouting on street corners."

"And what opinion would you voice, Cehmai-cha?"

Cehmai stood silent, his breath deep and fast. With every impotent thread of his will, he wished Adrah away. His hands were drawn toward Idaan, and he felt himself lean toward her like a reed in the wind. And yet her lover's eyes were on him, holding him back as effectively as chains.

"Whatever opinion you should choose," he said.

Idaan smiled, but there was more in her face than pleasure. Her jaw shifted forward, her eyes brightened. There was rage beneath her calm, and Cehmai felt it in his belly like an illness. The silence stretched out for three long breaths, four, five. . . .

"Love," Adrah said in a voice without affection. "I know our good fortune at this unexpected ally is overwhelming, but—"

"I didn't want to take any action until I spoke to you," Cehmai said. "That's why I had Adrah-cha bring me here. I hope I haven't given offense."

"Of course not, Cehmai-cha," she said. "But if you can't take my husband's word for my mind, whose could you trust? Who could know me better than he?"

"I would still prefer to discuss it with you," Cehmai said, packing as much meaning into the words as he could without sounding forced. "It will have some influence over the shape your life takes, and I wouldn't wish to guess wrong."

A spark of amusement flashed in her eyes, and she took a pose of gratitude before turning to Adrah.

"Leave us, then."

"Leave you . . ."

"Certainly he can't expect a woman to speak her mind openly with her husband floating above her like a hunting hawk. If Cehmai-cha is to trust what I say, he must see that I'm free to do my own will, ne?"

"It might be best," Cehmai agreed, trying to make his voice conciliatory. "If it wouldn't disturb you, Adrah-kya?"

Adrah smiled without even the echo of pleasure.

"Of course," he said. "I've arrangements to see to. The wedding is almost upon us, you know. There's so much to do, and with the mourning week . . . I do regret that the Khai did not live long enough to see this day come."

Adrah shook his head, then took a pose of farewell and retreated, closing the door behind him. When they were alone, Idaan's face shifted, naked venom in her stare.

"I'm sorry," Cehmai began, but Idaan cut him off.

"Not here. Gods only know how many servants he's set to listening. Come with me."

Idaan took him by the arm and led him through the door Adrah had used, then down a long corridor, and up a flight of winding stairs. Cehmai felt the warmth of her hand on his arm, and it felt like relief. She was here, she was well, she was with him. The world could be falling to pieces, and her presence would make it bearable.

She led him through a high hall and out to an open garden that looked down over the city. There were six or seven floors between them and the streets below. Idaan leaned against the rail and looked down, then back at him.

"So he's gotten to you, has he?" she asked, her voice gray as ashes.

"No one's gotten to me. If Adrah had wanted me to bray like a mule and paint my face like a whore's before he'd take me to you, I'd have been a stranger sight than this."

And, almost as if it was against her will, Idaan laughed. Not long, and not deep, hardly more than a faint smile and a fast exhalation, but it was there. Cehmai stepped in and pulled her body to his. He felt her start to push him back, hesitate, and then her cheek was pressed to his, her hair filling his breath with its scent. He couldn't say if the tears between them were hers or his or both.

"Why?" he whispered. "Why did you go? Why didn't you come to me?"

"I couldn't," she said. "There was . . . there's too much."

"I love you, Idaan. I didn't say it before because it wasn't true, but it is now. I love you. Please let me help."

Now she did push him away, holding one arm out before her to keep him at a distance and wiping her eyes with the sleeve of the other.

"Don't," she said. "Don't say that. You . . . you don't love me, Cehmai. You don't love me, and I do not love you."

"Then why are we weeping?" he asked, not moving to dry his own cheek.

"Because we're young and stupid," she said, her voice catching. "Because we think we can forget what happens to things that I care for."

"And what's that?"

"I kill them," she said, her voice soft and choking. "I cut them or I poison them or I turn them into something wrong. I won't do that to you. You can't be part of this, because I won't do that to you."

Cehmai didn't step toward her. Instead, he pulled back, walked to the edge of the garden and looked out over the city. The scent of flowers and forge-smoke mixed. "You're right, Idaan-kya. You won't do that. Not to me. You couldn't if you tried."

"Please," she said, and her voice was near him. She had followed. "You have to forget me. Forget what happened. It was . . ."

"Wrong?"

For a breath, he waited.

"No," she said. "Not wrong. But it was dangerous. I'm being married in a few days time. Because I choose to be. And it won't be you on the other end of the cord."

"Do you want me to support Adrah for the Khai's chair?"

"No. I want you to have nothing to do with any of this. Go home. Find someone else. Find someone better."

"I can love you from whatever distance you wish—"

"Oh shut up," Idaan snapped. "Just stop. Stop being the noble little boy who's going to suffer in silence. Stop pretending that your love of me started in anything more gallant than opening my robes. I don't need you. And if I want you . . . well, there are a hundred other things I want and I can't have them either. So just go."

He turned, surprised, but her face was stony, the tears and tenderness gone as if they'd never been.

"What are you trying to protect me from?" he asked.

"The answer to that question, among other things," she said. "I want you away from me, Cehmai. I want you elsewhere. If you love me as much as you claim, you'll respect that."

"But—"

"You'll respect it."

Cehmai had to think, had to pick the words as if they were stuck in mud. The confusion and distress rang in his mind, but he could see what any protests would bring. He had walked away from her, and she had followed. Perhaps she would again. That was the only comfort here.

"I'll leave you," he said. "If it's what you want."

"It is. And remember this: Adrah Vaunyogi isn't your friend. Whatever he says, whatever he does, you watch him. He will destroy you if he can."

"He can't," Cehmai said. "I'm the poet of Machi. The worst he can do to me is take you, and that's already done."

That seemed to stop her. She softened again, but didn't move to him, or away.

"Just be careful, Cehmai-kya. And *go*."

Cehmai's leaden hands took a pose of acceptance, but he did not move. Idaan crossed her arms.

"You also have to be careful. Especially if Adrah wants to become Khai Machi," Cehmai said. "It's the other thing I came for. The body they found was false. Your brother Otah is alive."

He might have told her that the plague had come. Her face went pale and empty. It was a moment before she seemed able to draw a breath.

"What . . . ?" she said, then coughed and began again. "How do you know that?"

"If I tell you, will you still send me away?"

Something washed through Idaan's expression—disappointment or depair or sorrow. She took a pose that accepted a contract.

"Tell me everything," Idaan said.

Cehmai did.

11

>+<   Idaan walked through the halls, her hands clenched in fists. Her body felt as if a storm were running through it, as if flood waters were washing out her veins. She trembled with the need to do something, but there was nothing to be done. She remembered seeing the superstitious dread with which others had treated the name Otah Machi. She had found it amusing, but she no longer knew why.

She had made Cehmai repeat himself until she was certain that she'd understood what he was saying. It had taken all the pain and sorrow of seeing him again and put it aside. Cehmai had meant to save her by it.

Adrah was in the kitchens, talking with his father's house master. She took a pose of apology and extracted him, leading him to a private chamber, pulling closed the shutters, and sliding home the door before she spoke. Adrah sat in a low chair of pale wood and red velvet as she paced. The words spilled out of her, one upon another as she repeated the story Cehmai had told her. Even she could hear the tones of panic in her voice.

"Tell me," she said as the news came to its end. "Tell me it's not true. Tell me you're sure he's dead."

"He's dead. It's a mistake. It has to be. No one knew when he'd be leaving the city. No one could have rescued him."

"Tell me that you *know*!"

Adrah scowled.

"How would I do that? We hired men to free him, take him away, and kill him. They took him away, and his body floated back down the river. But I wasn't there, I didn't strangle him myself. I can't keep these men from knowing who's paid their fee and also be there to hold their hands, Idaan. You know that."

Idaan put her hands to her mouth. Her fingers were shaking. It was a dream. It was a sick dream, and she would wake from it. She would wake up, and none of it would have been true.

"He's used us," she said. "Otah's used us to do his work."

"What?"

"Look at it! We've done everything for him. We've killed them all. Even . . . even my father. We've done everything he would have needed to do. He *knew*. He knew from the start. He's planned for everything we've done."

Adrah made an impatient sound at the back of his throat.

"You're imagining things," he said. "He can't have known what we were doing, or how we would do it. He isn't a god, and he isn't a ghost."

"You're sure of that, are you? We've fallen into his trap, Adrah! It's a trap!"

"It is a rumor started by Cehmai Tyan. Or maybe it's Maati Vaupathai who's set you a trap. He could suspect us and say these things to make us panic. Or Cehmai could."

"He wouldn't do that," Idaan said. "Cehmai wouldn't do that to—to us."

"To you, you mean," Adrah said, pulling the words out slow and bitter.

Idaan stopped her pacing and took a pose of query, her gaze locked on Adrah's. As much challenge as question. Adrah leaned back in his chair, the wood creaking under his weight.

"He's your lover, isn't he?" Adrah said. "This limp story about wanting to offer condolences and being willing to back my claim only if he could see you, could speak with you. And you sending me away like I was a puppy you'd finished playing with. Do you think I'm dim, Idaan?"

Her throat closed, and she coughed to loosen it, only the cough didn't end. It became laughter, and it shook her the way a dog might shake a rat. It was nothing about mirth, everything about violence. Adrah's face went red, and then white.

"This?" Idaan finally managed to stammer. "This is what we're going to argue about?"

"Is there something else you'd prefer?"

"You're about to live a life filled with women who aren't me. You and your father must have a list drawn up of allies we can make by taking their daughters for wives. You have no right to accuse me of anything."

"That was your choice," he said. "We agreed when we started this . . . this landslide. It would be the two of us, together, no matter if we won this or lost."

"And how long would that have lasted after you took my father's place?" she asked. "Who would I appeal to when you broke your word?"

Adrah rose to his feet, stepping toward her. His hand open flat, pointed toward her like a knife.

"That isn't fair to me. You never gave me the chance to fail you. You assumed it and went on to punish me as though it had happened."

"I'm not wrong, Adrah. You know I'm not wrong."

"There's a price for doing what you say, do you know that? I loved you more than I loved anything. My father, my mother, my sisters, anything or anyone. I did all of this because it was what you wanted."

"And not for any gain of your own? How selfless. Becoming Khai Machi must be such a chore for you."

"You wouldn't have *had* me if my ambition didn't match yours," Adrah said. "What I've become, I've become for you."

"That isn't fair," Idaan said.

Adrah whooped and turned in a wide circle, like a child playing before an invisible audience.

"Fair! When did this become about fair? When someone finally asked you to take some responsibility? You made the plans, love. This is yours, Idaan! All of it's yours, and you won't blame me that you've got to live with it!"

He was breathing fast now, as if he'd been running, but she could see in his shoulders and the corners of his mouth that the rage was failing. He dropped his arms and looked at her. His breath slowed. His face relaxed. They stood in silence, considering each other for what felt like half a hand. There was no anger now and no sorrow. He only looked tired and lost, very young and very old at once. He looked the way she felt. It was as if the air they both breathed had changed. He was the one to look away and break the silence.

"You know, love, you never said Cehmai wasn't your lover."

"He is," Idaan said, then shrugged. The battle was over. They were both too thin now for any more damage to matter. "He has been for a few weeks."

"Why?"

"I don't know. Because he wasn't part of all this. Because he was clean."

"Because he is power, and you're drawn to that more than anything?"

Idaan bit back her first response and let the accusation sit. Then she nodded.

"Perhaps a bit of that, yes," she said.

Adrah sighed and leaned against the wall. Slowly, he slid down until he was sitting on the floor, his arms resting on his knees.

"There is a list of houses and their women," he said. "There was before you and Cehmai took up with each other. I argued against it, but my father said it was just as an exercise. Just in case it was needed later. Only tell me . . . today, when he came . . . you didn't . . . the two of you didn't . . ."

Idaan laughed again, but this was a lower sound, gentler.

"No, I haven't lain down for another man in your house, Adrah-kya. I can't say why I think that would be worse than what I have done, but I do."

Adrah nodded. She could see another question in the way he shifted his eyes, the way he moved his hands. They had been lovers and conspirators for years. She knew him as if he were her family, or a distant part of herself. It didn't make her love him, but she remembered when she had.

"The first time I kissed you, you looked so frightened," she said. "Do you remember that? It was the middle of winter, and we'd all gone skating. There must have been twenty of us. We all raced, and you won."

"And you kissed me for the prize," he said. "Noichi Vausadar was chewing his own tongue, he was so jealous of me."

"Poor Noichi. I half did it to annoy him, you know."

"And the other half?"

"Because I wanted to," she said. "And then it was weeks before you came back for another."

"I was afraid you'd laugh at me. I went to sleep every night thinking about you, and woke up every morning just as possessed. Can you imagine only being afraid that someone would laugh at you?"

"Now? No."

"Do you remember the night we both went to the inn. With the little dog out front?"

"The one that danced when the keep played flute? Yes."

Idaan smiled. It had been a tiny animal with gray hair and soft, dark eyes. It had seemed so delighted, rearing up on its hind legs and capering, small paws waving for balance. It had seemed happy. She wiped away the tear before it could mar her kohl, then remembered that her eyes were only her eyes now. In her mind, the tiny dog leapt and looked at her. It had been so happy and so innocent. She pushed her own heart out toward that memory, pleading with the cold world that the pup was somewhere out there, still safe and well, trusting and loved as it had been that day. She didn't bother wiping the tears away now.

"We were other people then," she said.

They were silent again. After a moment, Idaan went to sit on the floor beside Adrah. He put his arm across her shoulder, and she leaned into him, weeping silently for too many things for one mind to hold. He didn't speak until the worst of the tears had passed.

"Do they bother you?" he asked at last, his voice low and hoarse.

"Who?"

"Them," he said, and she knew. She heard the sound of the arrow again, and shivered.

"Yes," she said.

"Do you know what's funny? It isn't your father who haunts me. It should be, I know. He was helpless, and I went there knowing what I was going to do. But he isn't the one."

Idaan frowned, trying to think who else there had been. Adrah saw her confusion and smiled, as if confirming something for himself. Perhaps only that she hadn't known some part of him, that his life was something different from her own.

"When we went in for the assassin, Oshai. There was a guard. I hit him. With a blade. It split his jaw. I can still see it. Have you ever swung a thin bar of iron into hard snow? It felt just like that. A hard, fast arc and then something that both gave way and didn't. I remember how it sounded. And afterward, you wouldn't touch me."

"Adrah . . ."

He raised his hands, stopping anything that might have been sympathy. Idaan swallowed it. She had no right to pardon him.

"Men do this," Adrah said. "All over the world, in every land, men do this. They slaughter each other over money or sex or power. The Khaiem do it to their own families. I never wondered how. Even now, I can't imagine it. I can't imagine doing the things I've done, even after I've done them. Can you?"

"There's a price they pay," Idaan said. "The soldiers and the arms-men. Even the thugs and drunkards who carve each other up outside comfort houses. They pay a price, and we're paying it too. That's all."

She felt him sigh.

"I suppose you're right," he said.

"So what do we do from here? What about Otah?"

Adrah shrugged, as if the answer were obvious.

"If Maati Vaupathai's set himself to be Otah's champion, Otah will eventually come to him. And Cehmai's already shown that there's one person in the world he'll break his silence for."

"I want Cehmai kept out of this."

"It's too late for that," Adrah said. His voice should have been cold or angry or cruel, and perhaps those were in him. Mostly, he sounded ex-hausted. "He's the only one who can lead us to Otah Machi. And you're the only one he'll tell."

PORSHA RADAANI GESTURED TOWARD MAATI'S BOWL, AND A SERVANT BOY moved forward, graceful as a dancer, to refill it. Maati took a pose of gratitude toward the man. There were times and places that he would have thanked the servant, but this was not one of them. Maati lifted the bowl and blew across the surface. The pale green-yellow tea smelled richly of rice and fresh, unsmoked leaves. Radaani laced thick fingers over his wide belly and smiled. His eyes, sunk deep in their sockets and padded by generous fat, glittered like wet stones in a brook.

"I confess, Maati-cha, that I hadn't expected a visit from the Dai-kvo's envoy. I've had men from every major house in the city here to talk with me these last few days, but the most high Dai-kvo usually keeps clear of these messy little affairs."

Maati sipped his tea though it was still too hot. He had to be careful how he answered this. It was a fine line between letting it be assumed that he had the Dai-kvo's backing and actually saying as much, but that difference was critical. He had so far kept away from anything that might reach back to the Dai-kvo's village, but Radaani was an older man than Ghiah Vaunani or Adaut Kamau. And he seemed more at home with the bullying attitude of wealth than the subtleties of court. Maati put down his bowl.

"The Dai-kvo isn't taking a hand in it," Maati said, "but that hardly means he should embrace ignorance. The better he knows the world, the better he can direct the poets to everyone's benefit, ne?"

"Spoken like a man of the court," Radaani said, and despite the smile in his voice, Maati didn't think it had been a compliment.

"I have heard that the Radaani might have designs on the Khai's chair," Maati said, dropping the oblique path he had intended. It would have done no good here. "Is that the case?"

Radaani smiled and pointed for the servant boy to go. The boy dropped into a formal pose and retreated, sliding the door closed behind him. Maati sat, smiling pleasantly, but not filling the silence. It was a small room, richly appointed—wood varnished until it seemed to glow and ornaments of worked gold and carved stone. The windows were adorned with shutters of carved cedar so fine that they let the breeze in and kept the birds and insects out even as they scented the air. Radaani tilted his head, distant eyes narrowing. Maati felt like a gem being valued by a merchant.

"I have one son in Yalakeht, overseeing our business interests. I have a grandson who has recently learned how to sing and jump sticks at the same time. I can't see that either of them would be well suited to the Khai's chair. I would have to either abandon my family's business or put a child in power over the city."

"Certainly there must be some financial advantages to being the Khai Machi," Maati said. "I can't think it would hurt your family to exchange your work in Yalakeht to join the Khaiem."

"Then you haven't spoken to my overseers," Radaani laughed. "We are pulling in more gold from the ships in Yalakeht and Chaburi-Tan than the Khai Machi can pull out of the ground, even with the andat. No. If I want power, I can purchase it and not have to compromise anything. Besides, I have six or eight daughters I'd be happy for the new Khai to marry. He could have one for every day of the week."

"You could take the chair for yourself," Maati said. "You're not so old. . . ."

"And I'm not so young as to be that stupid. Here, Vaupathai, let me lay this out for you. I am old, gouty as often as not, and rich. I have what

I want from life, and being the Khai Machi would mean that if I were lucky, my grandsons would be slitting each other's throats. I don't want that for them, and I don't want the trouble of running a city for myself. Other men want it, and they can have it. None of them will cross me, and I will support whoever takes the name."

"So you have no preference," Maati said.

"Now I didn't go so far as to say that, did I? Why does the Dai-kvo care which of us becomes the Khai?"

"He doesn't. But that doesn't mean he's uninterested."

"Then let him wait two weeks, and he can have the name. It doesn't figure. Either he has a favorite or . . . or is this about your belly getting opened for you?" Radaani pursed his lips, his eyes darting back and forth over Maati's face. "The upstart's dead, so it isn't that. You think someone was working with Otah Machi? That one of the houses was backing him?"

"I didn't go so far as to say that, did I? And even if they were, it's no concern of the Dai-kvo's," Maati said.

"True, but no one tried to fish-gut the Dai-kvo. Could it be, Maati-cha, that you're here on your own interest?"

"You give me too much credit," Maati said. "I'm only a simple man trying to make sense of complex times."

"Yes, aren't we all," Radaani said with an expression of distaste.

Maati kept the rest of the interview to empty niceties and social forms, and left with the distinct feeling that he'd given out more information than he'd gathered. Chewing absently at his inner lip, he turned west, away from the palaces and out into the streets of the city. The pale mourning cloth was coming down already, and the festival colors were going back up for the marriage of Adrah Vaunyogi and Idaan Machi. Maati watched as a young boy, skin brown as a nut, sat atop a lantern pole with pale mourning rags in one hand and a garland of flowers in the other. Maati wondered if a city had ever gone from celebration to sorrow and back again so quickly.

Tomorrow ended the mourning week, marked the wedding of the dead Khai's last daughter, and began the open struggle to find the city's new master. The quiet struggle had, of course, been going on for the week. Adaut Kamau had denied any interest in the Khai's chair, but had spent enough time intimating that support from the Dai-kvo might sway his opinion that Maati felt sure the Kamau hadn't abandoned their ambitions. Ghiah Vaunani had been perfectly pleasant, friendly, open, and had managed in the course of their conversation to say nothing at all. Even now, Maati saw messengers moving through the streets and alleyways. The grand conversation of power might put on the clothes of sorrow, but the chatter only changed form.

Maati walked more often these days. The wound in his belly was still pink, but the twinges of pain were few and widely spaced. While he walked the streets, his robes marked him as a man of importance, and not someone to interrupt. He was less likely to be disturbed here than in the library or his own rooms. And moving seemed to help him think.

He had to speak to Daaya Vaunyogi, the soon-to-be father of Idaan Machi. He'd been putting off that moment, dreading the awkwardness of condolence and congratulations mixed. He wasn't sure whether to be long-faced and formal or jolly and pleasant, and he felt a deep certainty that whatever he chose would be the wrong thing. But it had to be done, and it wasn't the worst of the errands he'd set himself for the day.

There wasn't a soft quarter set aside for the comfort houses in Machi as there had been in Saraykeht. Here the whores and gambling, drug-laced wine and private rooms were distributed throughout the city. Maati was sorry for that. For all its subterranean entertainments, the soft quarter of Saraykeht had been safe—protected by an armed watch paid by all the houses. He'd never heard of another place like it. In most cities of the Khaiem, a particular house might guard the street outside its own door, but little more than that. In low towns, it was often wise to travel in groups or with a guard after dark.

Maati paused at a waterseller's cart and paid a length of copper for a cup of cool water with a hint of peach to it. As he drank, he looked up at the sun. He'd spent almost a full hand's time reminiscing about Saraykeht and avoiding any real consideration of the Vaunyogi. He should have been thinking his way through the puzzles of who had killed the Khai and his son, who had spirited Otah-kvo away, and then falsified his death, and why.

The sad truth was, he didn't know and wasn't sure that anything he'd done since he'd come had brought him much closer. He understood more of the court politics, he knew the names of the great houses and trivia about them: Kamau was supported by the breeders who raised mine dogs and the copper workers, the Vaunani by the goldsmiths, tanners and leatherworkers, Vaunyogi had business ties to Eddensea, Galt and the Westlands and little money to show for it when compared to the Radaani. But none of that brought him close to understanding the simple facts as he knew them. Someone had killed these men and meant the world to put the blame on Otah-kvo. And Otah-kvo had not done the thing.

Still, there had to be someone backing Otah-kvo. Someone who had freed him and staged his false death. He ran through his conversation with Radaani again, seeing if perhaps the man's lack of ambition masked support for Otah-kvo, but there was nothing.

He gave back the waterseller's cup and let his steps wander through the streets, his hands tucked inside his sleeves, until his hip and knee started to complain. The sun was shifting down toward the western mountains. Winter days here would be brief and bitter, the swift winter sun ducking behind stone before it even reached the horizon. It hardly seemed fair.

By the time he regained the palaces, the prospect of walking all the way to the Vaunyogi failed to appeal. They would be busy with preparations for the wedding anyway. There was no point intruding now. Better to speak to Daaya Vaunyogi afterwards, when things had calmed. Though, of course, by then the utkhaiem would be in council, and the gods only knew whether he'd be able to get through then, or if he'd be in time.

He might only find who'd done the thing by seeing who became the next Khai.

There was still the one other thing to do. He wasn't sure how he would accomplish it either, but it had to be tried. And at least the poet's house was nearer than the Vaunyogi. He angled down the path through the oaks, the gravel of the pathway scraping under his weight. The mourning cloth had already been taken from the tree branches and the lamp posts and benches, but no bright banners or flowers had taken their places.

When he stepped out from the trees, he saw Stone-Made-Soft sitting on the steps before the open doorway, its wide face considering him with a calm half-smile. Maati had the impression that had he been a sparrow or an assassin with a flaming sword, the andat's reaction would have been the same. He saw the large form lean back, turning to face into the house, and heard the deep, rough voice if not the words themselves. Cehmai was at the door in an instant, his eyes wide and bright, and then bleak with disappointment before becoming merely polite.

With an almost physical sensation, it fit together—Cehmai's rage at holding back news of Otah's survival, the lack of wedding decoration, and the disappointment that Maati was only himself and not some other, more desired guest. The poor bastard was in love with Idaan Machi.

Well, that was one secret discovered. It wasn't much, but the gods all knew he'd take anything these days. He took a pose of greeting and Cehmai returned it.

"I was wondering if you had a moment," Maati said.

"Of course, Maati-kvo. Come in."

The house was in a neat sort of disarray. Tables hadn't been over-turned or scrolls set in the brazier, but things were out of place, and the air seemed close and stifling. Memories rose in his mind. He recalled the moments in his own life when a woman had left him. The scent was very much the same. He suppressed the impulse to put his hand on the boy's shoulder and say something comforting. Better to pretend he hadn't guessed. At least he could spare Cehmai that indignity. He lowered himself into a chair, groaning with relief as the weight left his legs and feet.

"I've gotten old. When I was your age I could walk all day and never feel it."

"Perhaps if you made it more a habit," Cehmai said. "I have some tea. It's a little tepid now, but if you'd like . . ."

Maati raised a hand, refusing politely. Cehmai, seeming to notice the state of the house now there were someone else's eyes on it, opened the shutters wide before he came to sit at Maati's side.

"I've come to ask for more time," Maati said. "I can make excuses first if you like, or tell you that as your elder and an envoy of the Dai-kvo it's something you owe me. Any of that theater you'd like. But it comes to this: I don't know yet what's happening, and it's important to me that if something does go wrong for Otah-kvo it not have been my doing."

Cehmai seemed to weigh this.

"Baarath tells me you had a message from the Dai-kvo," Cehmai said.

"Yes. After he heard I'd turned Otah-kvo over to his father, he called me back."

"And you're disobeying that call."

"I'm exercising my own judgment."

"Will the Dai-kvo make that distinction?"

"I don't know," Maati said. "If he agrees with me, I suppose he'll agree with me. If not, then not. I can only guess what he would have said if he'd known everything I know, and move from there."

"And you think he'd want Otah's secret kept?"

Maati laughed and rubbed his hands together. His legs were twitching pleasantly, relaxing from their work. He stretched and his shoulder cracked.

"Probably not," he said. "He'd more likely say that it isn't our place to take an active role in the succession. That he'd sent me here with that story about rooting through the library so that it wouldn't be clear to everyone over three summers old what I was really here for. He might also mention that the questions I've been asking have been bad enough without lying to the utkhaiem while I'm at it."

"You haven't lied," Cehmai said, and then a moment later. "Well, actually, I suppose you have. You aren't really doing what you believe the Dai-kvo would want."

"No."

"And you want my complicity?"

"Yes. Or, that is, I have to ask it of you. And I have to persuade you if I can, though in truth I'd be as happy if you could talk me out of it."

"I don't understand. Why *are* you doing this? And don't only say that you want to sleep well after you've seen another twenty summers. You've done more than anyone could have asked of you. What is it about Otah Machi that's driving you to this?"

Oh, Maati thought, you shouldn't have asked that question, my boy. Because *that* one I know how to answer, and it'll sting you as much as me.

He steepled his fingers and spoke.

"He and I loved the same woman once, when we were younger men. If I do him harm or let him come to harm that I could have avoided, I couldn't look at her again and say it wasn't my anger that drove me. My anger at her love for him. I haven't seen her in years, but I will someday. And when I do, I need it to be with a clear conscience. The Dai-kvo may not need it. The poets may not. But despite our reputations, we're men under these robes, and as a man . . . As a man to a man, it's something I would ask of you. Another week. Just until we can see who's likely to be the new Khai."

There was a shifting sound behind him. The andat had come in silently at some point and was standing at the doorway with the same simple, placid smile. Cehmai leaned forward and ran his hands through his hair three times in fast succession, as if he were washing himself without water.

"Another week," Cehmai said. "I'll keep quiet another week."

Maati blinked. He had expected at least an appeal to the danger he was putting Idaan in by keeping silent. Some form of *at least let me warn her* . . . Maati frowned, and then understood.

He'd already done it. Cehmai had already told Idaan Machi that Otah was alive. Annoyance and anger flared brief as a firefly, and then faded, replaced by something deeper and more humane. Amusement, pleasure, and even a kind of pride in the young poet. We are men beneath these robes, he thought, and we do what we must.

SINJA SPUN, THE THICK WOODEN CUDGEL HISSING THROUGH THE AIR. OTAH stepped inside the blow, striking at the man's wrist. He missed, his own rough wooden stick hitting Sinja's with a clack and a shock that ran up his arm. Sinja snarled, pushed him back, and then ruefully considered his weapon.

"That was decent," Sinja said. "Amateur, granted, but not hopeless."

Otah set his stick down, then sat—head between his knees—as he fought to get his breath back. His ribs felt as though he'd rolled down a rocky hill, and his fingers were half numb from the shocks they'd absorbed. And he felt good—exhausted, bruised, dirty, and profoundly back in control of his own body again, free in the open air. His eyes stung with sweat, his spit tasted of blood, and when he looked up at Sinja, they were both grinning. Otah held out his hand and Sinja hefted him to his feet.

"Again?" Sinja said.

"I wouldn't . . . want to . . . take advantage . . . when you're . . . so tired."

Sinja's face folded into a caricature of helplessness as he took a pose of gratitude. They turned back toward the farmhouse. The high summer afternoon was thick with gnats and the scent of pine resin. The thick gray walls of the farmhouse, the wide low trees around it, looked like a painting of modest tranquility. Nothing about it suggested court intrigue or violence or death. That, Otah supposed, was why Amiit had chosen it.

They had gone out after a late breakfast. Otah had felt well enough, he thought, to spar a bit. And there was the chance that this would all come to blades before it was over, whether he chose it or not. He'd never been trained as a fighter, and Sinja was happy to offer a day's instruction. There was an easy camaraderie that Otah had enjoyed on the way out. The work itself reminded him that Sinja had slaughtered his last comrades, and the walk back was somehow much longer than the one out had been.

"A little practice, and you'd be a decent soldier," Sinja said as they walked. "You're too cautious. You'll lose a good strike in order to protect yourself, and that's a vice. You'll need to be careful of it."

"I'm actually hoping for a life that doesn't require much blade work of me."

"I wasn't only talking about fighting."

When they reached the farmhouse, the stables had four unfamiliar horses in them, hot from the road. An armsman of House Siyanti—one Otah recognized, but whose name he'd never learned—was caring for them. Sinja traded a knowing look with the man, then strode up the stairs to the main rooms. Otah followed, his aches half-forgotten in the mingled curiosity and dread.

Amiit Foss and Kiyan were sitting at the main table with two other men. One—an older man with heavy, beetled brows and a hooked nose—wore robes embroidered with the sun and stars of House Siyanti. The other, a young man with round cheeks and a generous belly, wore a simple blue robe of inexpensive cloth, but enough rings on his fingers to pay for a small house. Their conversation stopped as Otah and Sinja entered the room. Amiit smiled and gestured toward the benches.

"Well timed," Amiit said. "We've just been discussing the next step in our little dance."

"What's the issue?" Sinja asked.

"The mourning's ending. Tomorrow, the heads of all the houses of the utkhaiem meet. I expect it will take them a few days before the assassinations start, but within the month it'll be decided who the new Khai is to be."

"We'll have to act before that," Otah said.

"True enough, but that doesn't mean we'd be wise to act now," Amiit said. "We know, or guess well enough, what power is behind all this—the Galts. But we don't know the mechanism. Who are they backing? Why? I don't like the idea of moving forward without that in hand. And yet, time's short."

Amiit held out his open hands, and Otah understood this choice was being laid at his door. It was his life most at risk, and Amiit wasn't going to demand anything of Otah that he wasn't prepared to do. Otah sat, laced his fingers together, and frowned. It was Kiyan's voice that interrupted his uncertainty.

"Either we stay here or we go to Machi. If we stay here, we're unlikely to be discovered, but it takes half a day for us to get news, and half a day at least to respond to it. Amiit-cha thinks the safety might be worth it, but Lamara-cha," she gestured to the hook-nosed man, "has been arguing that we'll want the speed we can only have by being present. He's arranged a place for us to stay—in the tunnels below the palaces."

"I have an armsman of the Saya family in my employ," the hook-nosed Lamara said. His voice was a rough whisper, and Otah noticed for the first time a long, deep, old scar across the man's throat. "The Saya are a minor family, but they will be at the council. We can keep clear on what's said and by whom."

"And if you're discovered, we'll all be killed," Sinja said. "As far as the world's concerned, you've murdered a Khai. It's not a precedent anyone wants set. Especially not the other Khaiem. Bad enough they have to watch their brothers. If it's their sons, too. . . ."

"I understand that," Otah said. Then, to Amiit, "Are we any closer to knowing who the Galts are backing?"

"We don't know for certain that they're backing anyone," Amiit said. "That's an assumption we've made. We can make some educated guesses, but that's all. It may be that their schemes are about the poets, the way you suggested, and not the succession at all."

"But you don't believe that," Otah said.

"And the poets don't either," the round-cheeked man said. "At least not the new one."

"Shojen-cha is the man we set to follow Maati Vaupathai," Amiit said.

"He's been digging at all the major houses of the utkhaiem," Shojen said, leaning forward, his rings glittering in the light. "In the last week, he's had audiences with all the highest families and half the low ones. And he's been asking questions about court politics and money and power. He hasn't been looking to the Galts in particular, but it's clear enough he thinks some family or families of the utkhaiem are involved in the killings."

"What's he found out?" Otah asked,

"We don't know. I can't say what he's looking for or what he's found, but there's no question he's conducting an investigation."

"He's the one who gave you over to the Khai in the first place, isn't he, Otah-cha?" Lamara said in his ruined voice.

"He's also the one who took a knife in the gut," Sinja said.

"Can we say why he's looking?" Otah asked. "What would he do if he discovered the truth? Report it to the utkhaiem? Or only the Dai-kvo?"

"I can't say," Shojen said. "I know what he's doing, not what he's thinking."

"We *can* say this," Amiit said, his expression dour and serious. "As it stands, there's no one in the city who'll think you innocent, Otah-cha. If you're found in Machi, you'll be killed. And whoever sticks the first knife in will use it as grounds that he should be Khai. The only protection you'll have is obscurity."

"No armsmen?" Otah asked.

"Not enough," Amiit said. "First, they'd only draw attention to you, and second, there aren't enough guards in the city to protect you if the utkhaiem get your scent in their noses."

"But that's true wherever he is," Lamara said. "If they find out he's alive on a desolate rock in the middle of the sea, they'll send men to kill him. He's murdered the Khai!"

"Then best to keep him where he won't be found," Amiit said. There was an impatience in his tone that told Otah this debate had been going on long before he'd come in the room. Tempers were fraying, and even Amiit Foss's deep patience was wearing thin. He felt Kiyan's eyes on him, and looked up to meet her gaze. Her half-smile carried more meaning than half a hand's debate. *They will never agree* and *you may as well practice giving orders now—if it goes well, you'll be doing it for the rest of your life* and *I'm sorry, love.*

Otah felt a warmth in his chest, felt the panic and distress relax like a stiff muscle rubbed in hot oils. Lamara and Amiit were talking over each other, each making points and suggestions it was clear they'd made before. Otah coughed, but they paid him no attention. He looked from one, flushed, grim face to the other, sighed, and slapped his palm on the table hard enough to make the wine bowls rattle. The room went silent, surprised eyes turning to him.

"I believe, gentlemen, that I understand the issues at hand," Otah said. "I appreciate Amiit-cha's concern for my safety, but the time for caution has passed."

"It's a vice," Sinja agreed, grinning.

"Next time, you can give me your advice without cracking my ribs," Otah said. "Lamara-cha, I thank you for the offer of the tunnels to work from, and I accept it. We'll leave tonight."

"Otah-cha, I don't think you've . . . ," Amiit began, his hands held out in an appeal, but Otah only shook his head. Amiit frowned deeply, and then, to Otah's surprise, smiled and took a pose of acceptance.

"Shojen-cha," Otah said. "I need to know what Maati is thinking. What he's found, what he intends, whether he's hoping to save me or destroy me. Both are possible, and everything we do will be different depending on his stance."

"I appreciate that," Shojen said, "but I don't know how I'd discover it. It isn't as though he confides in me. Or in anyone else that I can tell."

Otah rubbed his fingertips across the rough wood of the table, considering that. He felt their eyes on him, pressing him for a decision. This one, at least, was simple enough. He knew what had to be done.

"Bring him to me," he said. "Once we've set ourselves up and we're sure of the place, bring him there. I'll speak with him."

"That's a mistake," Sinja said.

"Then it's the mistake I'm making," Otah said. "How long before we can be ready to leave?"

"We can have all the things we need on a cart by sundown," Amiit said. "That would put us in Machi just after the half-candle. We could be in the tunnels and tucked as safely away as we're likely to manage by dawn. But there are going to be some people in the streets, even then."

"Get flowers. Decorate the cart as if we're preparing for the wedding," Otah said. "Then even if they think it odd to see us, they'll have a story to tell themselves."

"I'll collect the poet whenever you like," Shojen said, his confident voice undermined by the nervous way he fingered his rings.

"Also tomorrow. And Lamara-cha, I'll want reports from your man at the council as soon as there's word to be had."

"As you say," Lamara said.

Otah moved his hands into a pose of thanks, then stood.

"Unless there's more to be said, I'm going to sleep now. I'm not sure when I'll have the chance again. Any of you who aren't involved in preparations for the move might consider doing the same."

They murmured their agreement, and the meeting ended, but when later Otah lay in the cot, one arm thrown over his eyes to blot out the light, he was certain he could no more sleep than fly. He was wrong. Sleep came easily, and he didn't hear the old leather hinges creak when Kiyan entered the room. It was her voice that pulled him into awareness.

"*It's a mistake I'm making?* That's quite the way to lead men."

He stretched. His ribs still hurt, and worse, they'd stiffened.

"Was it too harsh, do you think?"

Kiyan pushed the netting aside and sat next to him, her hand seeking his.

"If Sinja-cha's that delicate, he's in the wrong line of work," she said. "He may think you're wrong, but if you'd turned back because he told you to, you'd have lost part of his respect. You did fine, love. Better than fine. I think you've made Amiit a very happy man."

"How so?"

"You've become the Khai Machi. Oh, I know, it's not done yet, but out there just then? You weren't speaking like a junior courier or an east islands fisherman."

Otah sighed. Her face was calm and smooth. He brought her hand to his lips and kissed her wrist.

"I suppose not," he said. "I didn't want this, you know. The wayhouse would have been enough."

"I'm sure the gods will take that into consideration," she said. "They're usually so good about giving us the lives we expect."

Otah chuckled. Kiyan let herself be pulled down slowly, until she lay beside him, her body against his own. Otah's hand strayed to her belly, caressing the tiny life growing inside her. Kiyan raised her eyebrows and tilted her head.

"You look sad," she said. "Are you sad, 'Tani?"

"No, love," Otah said. "Not sad. Only frightened."

"About going back to the city?"

"About being discovered," he said. And a moment later, "About what I'm going to have to say to Maati."

12

>+< Cehmai sat back on a cushion, his back aching and his mind askew. Stone-Made-Soft sat beside him, its stillness unbroken even by breath. At the front of the temple, on a dais where the witnesses could see her, sat Idaan. Her eyes were cast down, her robe the vibrant rose and blue of a new bride. The distance between them seemed longer than the space within the walls, as if a year's journey had been fit into the empty air.

The crowd was not as great as the occasion deserved: women and the second sons of the utkhaiem. Elsewhere, the council was meeting, and those who had a place in it were there. Given the choice of spectacle, many others would choose the men, their speeches and arguments, the debates and politics and subtle drama, to the simple marrying off of an orphan girl of the best lineage and the least influence to the son of a good, solid family.

Cehmai stared at her, willing the kohl-dark eyes to look up, the painted lips to smile at him. Cymbals chimed, and the priests dressed in gold and silver robes with the symbols of order and chaos embroidered in black began their chanting procession. Their voices blended and rose until the temple walls themselves seemed to ring with the melody. Cehmai plucked at the cushion. He couldn't watch, and he couldn't look away. One priest—an old man with a bare head and a thin white beard—stopped behind Idaan in the place that her father or brother should have taken. The high priest stood at the back of the dais, lifted his hands slowly, palms out to the temple, and, with an embracing gesture, seemed to encompass them all. When he spoke, it was in the language of the Old Empire, syllables known to no one on the cushions besides himself.

Eyan ta nyot baa, dan salaa khai dan umsalaa.

The will of the gods has always been that woman shall act as servant to man.

An old tongue for an old thought. Cehmai let the words that followed it—the ancient ritual known more by its rhythm than its significance—wash over him. He closed his eyes and told himself he was not drowning. He focused on his breath, smoothing its ragged edges until he regained the appearance of calm. He watched the sorrow and the anger and the jealousy writhe inside him as if they were afflicting someone else.

When he opened his eyes, the andat had shifted, its gaze on him and expressionless. Cehmai felt the storm on the back of his mind shift, as if taking stock of the confusion in his heart, testing him for weakness. Cehmai waited, prepared for Stone-Made-Soft to press, for the struggle to engulf him. He almost longed for it.

But the andat seemed to feel that anticipation, because it pulled back. The pressure lessened, and Stone-Made-Soft smiled its idiot, empty smile, and turned back to the ceremony. Adrah was standing now, a long cord looped in his hand. The priest asked him the ritual questions, and Adrah spoke the ritual answers. His face seemed drawn, his shoulders too square, his movements too careful. Cehmai thought he seemed exhausted.

The priest who stood behind Idaan spoke for her family in their absence, and the end of the cord, cut and knotted, passed from Adrah to the priest and then to Idaan's hand. The rituals would continue for some time, Cehmai knew, but as soon as the cord was accepted, the binding was done. Idaan Machi had entered the house of the Vaunyogi and only Adrah's death would cast her back into the ghost arms of her dead family. Those two were wed, and he had no right to the pain the thought caused him. He had no right to it.

He rose and walked silently to the wide stone archway and out of the temple. If Idaan looked up at his departure, he didn't notice.

The sun wasn't halfway through its arc, and a fresh wind from the north was blowing the forge smoke away. High, thin clouds scudded past, giving the illusion that the great stone towers were slowly, endlessly toppling. Cehmai walked the temple grounds, Stone-Made-Soft a pace behind him. There were few others there—a woman in rich robes sitting alone by a fountain, her face a mask of grief; a round-faced man with rings glittering on his fingers reading a scroll; an apprentice priest

raking the gravel paths smooth with a long metal rake. And at the edge
of the grounds, where temple became palace, a familiar shape in brown
poet's robes. Cehmai hesitated, then slowly walked to him, the andat
close by and trailing him like a shadow.

"I hadn't expected to see you here, Maati-kvo."

"No, but I expected you," the older poet said. "I've been at the
council all morning. I needed some time away. May I walk with you?"

"If you like. I don't know that I'm going anywhere in particular."

"Not marching with the wedding party? I thought it was traditional
for the celebrants to make an appearance in the city with the new couple.
Let the city look over the pair and see who's allied themselves with the
families. I assume that's what all the flowers and decorations out there
are for."

"There will be enough without me."

Cehmai turned north, the wind blowing gently into his face, drawing
his robes out behind him as if he were walking through water. A slave
girl was standing beside the path singing an old love song, her high,
sweet voice carrying like a flute's. Cehmai felt Maati-kvo's attention,
but wasn't sure what to make of it. He felt as examined as the corpse on
the physician's table. At length, he spoke to break the silence.

"How is it?"

"The council? Like a very long, very awkward dinner party. I imagine it will deteriorate. The only interesting thing is that a number of
houses are calling for Vaunyogi to take the chair."

"Interesting," Cehmai said. "I knew Adrah-cha was thinking of it,
but I wouldn't have thought his father had the money to sway many
people."

"I wouldn't have either. But there are powers besides money."

The comment seemed to hang in the air.

"I'm not sure what you mean, Maati-kvo."

"Symbols have weight. The wedding coming as it does might sway
the sentimental. Or perhaps Vaunyogi has advocates we aren't aware of."

"Such as?"

Maati stopped. They had reached a wide courtyard, rich with the
scent of cropped summer grass. The andat halted as well, its broad head
tilted in an attitude of polite interest. Cehmai felt a brief flare of hatred
toward it, and saw its lips twitch slightly toward a smile.

"If you've spoken for the Vaunyogi, I need to know it," Matti said.

"We're not to take sides in these things. Not without direction from the Dai-kvo."

"I'm aware of that, and I don't mean to accuse you or pry into what's not mine, but on this one thing, I have to know. They did ask you to speak for them, didn't they?"

"I suppose," Cehmai said.

"And did you speak for them?"

"No. Why should I?"

"Because Idaan Machi is your lover," Maati said, his voice soft and full of pity.

Cehmai felt the blood come into his face, his neck. The anger at everything that he had seen and heard pressed at him, and he let himself borrow certainty from the rage.

"Idaan Machi is Adrah's wife. No, I did not speak for Vaunyogi. Despite your experience, not everyone falls in love with the man who's taken his lover."

Maati leaned back. The words had struck home, and Cehmai pressed on, following the one attack with another.

"And, forgive me, Maati-cha, but you seem in an odd position to take me to task for following my private affairs where they don't have a place. You are still doing all this without the Dai-kvo's knowledge?"

"He might have a few of my letters," Maati-kvo said. "If not yet, then soon."

"But since you're a man under those robes, on you go. I am doing as the Dai-kvo set me to do. I am carrying this great bastard around; I am keeping myself apart from the politics of the court; I'm not willing to stand accused of lighting candles while you're busy burning the city down!"

"Calling me a bastard seems harsh," Stone-Made-Soft said. "*I* haven't told you how to behave."

"Be quiet!"

"If you think it will help," the andat said, its voice amused, and Cehmai turned the fury inward, pressing at the space where he and Stone-Made-Soft were one thing, pushing the storm into a smaller and smaller thing. He felt his hands in fists, felt his teeth ache with the pressure of his clenched jaw. And the andat, shifted, bent to his fire-bright will, knelt and cast down its gaze. He forced its hands into a pose of apology.

"Cehmai-cha."

He turned on Maati. The wind was picking up, whipping their robes. The fluttering of cloth sounded like a sail.

"I'm sorry," Maati-kvo said. "I truly am very sorry. I know what it must mean to have these things questioned, but I have to know."

"Why? Why is my heart suddenly your business?"

"Let me ask this another way," Maati said. "If you aren't backing Vaunyogi, who is?"

Cehmai blinked. His rage whirled, lost its coherence, and left him feeling weaker and confused. On the ground beside them, Stone-Made-Soft sighed and rose to its feet. Shaking its great head, it gestured to the green streaks on its robe.

"The launderers won't be pleased by that," it said.

"What do you mean?" Cehmai said, not to the andat, but to Maati-kvo. And yet, it was Stone-Made-Soft's deep rough voice that answered him.

"He's asking you how badly Adrah Vaunyogi wants that chair. And he's suggesting that Idaan-cha may have just married her father's killer, all unaware. It seems a simple enough proposition to me. They aren't going to blame *you* for these stains, you know. They never do."

Maati stood silently, peering at him, waiting. Cehmai held his hands together to stop their shaking.

"You think that?" he asked. "You think that Adrah might have arranged the wedding because he knew what was going to happen? You think *Adrah* killed them?"

"I think it worth considering," Maati said.

Cehmai looked down and pressed his lips together until they ached. If he didn't—if he looked up, if he relaxed—he knew that he would smile. He knew what that would say about himself and his small, petty soul, so he swallowed and kept his head low until he could speak. Unbidden, he imagined himself exposing Adrah's crime, rejoining Idaan with her sole remaining family. He imagined her eyes looking into his as he told her what Maati knew.

"Tell me how I can help," he said.

MAATI SAT IN THE FIRST GALLERY, LOOKING DOWN INTO THE GREAT HALL and waiting for the council to go on. It was a rare event, all the houses of the utkhaiem meeting without a Khai to whom they all answered, and they seemed both uncertain what the proper rituals were and unwilling to let the thing move quickly. It was nearly dark now, and candles were being set out on the dozen long tables below him and the speaker's pulpit beyond them. The small flames were reflected in the parquet floor and the silvered glass on the walls below him. A second gallery rose above him, where women and children of the lower families and representatives of the trading houses could sit and observe. The architect had been brilliant—a man standing as speaker need hardly raise his voice and the stone walls would carry his words through the air without need of whisperers. Even over the murmurs of the tables below and the galleries above, the prepared, elaborate, ornate, deathly dull speeches of the utkhaiem reached every ear. The morning session had been interesting at least—the novelty of the situation had held his attention. But apart from his conversation with Cehmai, Maati had filled the hours of his day with little more than the voices of men practiced at saying little with many words. Praise of the utkhaiem generally and of their own families in particular, horror at the crimes and misfortunes that had brought them here, and the best wishes of the speaker and his father or his son or his cousin for the city as a whole, and on and on and on.

Maati had pictured the struggle for power as a thing of blood and fire, betrayal and intrigue and danger. And, when he listened for the matter beneath the droning words, yes, all that was there. That even this could be made dull impressed him.

The talk with Cehmai had gone better than he had hoped. He felt guilty using Idaan Machi against him that way, but perhaps the boy had been ready to be used. And there was very little time.

He was relying now on the competence of his enemies. There would be only a brief window between the time when it became clear who would take the prize and the actual naming of the Khai Machi. In that moment, Maati would know who had engineered all this, who had used Otah-kvo as a cover, who had attempted his own slaughter. And if he were wise and lucky and well-positioned, he might be able to take action. Enlisting Cehmai in his service was only a way to improve the chances of setting a lever in the right place.

"The concern our kind brother of Saya brings up is a wise one to consider," a sallow-faced scion of the Daikani said. "The days are indeed growing shorter, and the time for preparation is well upon us. There are roofs that must be made ready to hold their burden of snow. There are granaries to be filled and stocks to be prepared. There are crops to be harvested, for men and beasts both."

"I didn't know the Khai did all that," a familiar voice whispered. "He must have been a very busy man. I don't suppose there's anyone could take up the slack for him?"

Baarath shifted down and sat beside Maati. He smelled of wine, his cheeks were rosy, his eyes too bright. But he had an oilcloth cone filled with strips of fried trout that he offered to Maati, and the distraction was almost welcome. Maati took a bit of the fish.

"What have I missed?" Baarath said,

"The Vaunyogi appear to be a surprise contender," Maati said. "They've been mentioned by four families, and praised in particular by two others. I think the Vaunani and Kamau are feeling upset by it, but they seem to hate each other too much to do anything about it."

"That's truth," Baraath said. "Ijan Vaunani came to blows with old Kamau's grandson this afternoon at a teahouse in the jeweler's quarter. Broke his nose for him, I heard."

"Really?"

Baarath nodded. The sallow man droned on half forgotten now as Baarath spoke close to Maati's ear.

"There are rumors of reprisal, but old Kamau's made it clear that anyone doing anything will be sent to tar ships in the Westlands. They say he doesn't want people thinking ill of the house, but I think it's his last effort to keep an alliance open against Adrah Vaunyogi. It's clear enough that someone's bought little Adrah a great deal more influence than just sleeping with a dead man's daughter would earn."

Baarath grinned, then coughed and looked concerned.

"Don't repeat that to anyone, though," he said. "Or if you do, don't say it was me. It's terribly rude, and I'm rather drunk. I only came up here to sober up a bit."

"Yes, well, I came up to keep an eye on the process, and I think it's more likely to put your head on a pillow than clear it."

Baarath chuckled.

"You're an idiot if you came here to see what's happening. It's all out in the piss troughs where a man can actually speak. Didn't you know that? Honestly, Maati-kya, if you went to a comfort house, you'd spend all your time watching the girls in the front dance and wondering when the fucking was supposed to start."

Maati's jaw went tight. When Baarath offered the fish again, Maati refused it. The sallow man finished, and an old, thick-faced man rose, took the pulpit, announced himself to be Cielah Pahdri, and began listing the various achievements of his house dating back to the fall of the Empire. Maati listened to the recitation and Baraath's overloud chewing with equal displeasure.

He was right before, Maati told himself. Baarath was the worst kind of ass, but he wasn't wrong.

"I assume," Maati said, "that 'piss troughs' is a euphemism."

"Only half. Most of the interesting news comes to a few teahouses at the south edge of the palaces. They're near the moneylenders, and that always leads to lively conversations. Going to try your luck there?"

"I thought I might," Maati said as he rose.

"Look for the places with too many rich people yelling at each other. You'll be fine," Baarath said and went back to chewing his trout.

Maati took the steps two at a time, and slipped out the rear of the gallery into a long, dark corridor. Lanterns were lit at each end, and Maati strode through the darkness with the slow burning runout of annoyance that the librarian always seemed to inspire. He didn't see the woman at the hallway's end until he had almost reached her. She was thin, fox-faced, and dressed in a simple green robe. She smiled when she caught his eye and took a pose of greeting.

"Maati-cha?"

Maati hesitated, then answered her greeting.

"I'm sorry," he said. "I seem to have forgotten your name."

"We haven't met. My name is Kiyan. Itani's told me all about you."

It took the space of a breath for him to truly understand what she'd said and all it meant. The woman nodded confirmation, and Maati stepped close to her, looking back over his shoulder and then down the corridor behind her to be sure they were alone.

"We were going to send you an escort," the woman said, "but no one could think of how to approach you without seeming like we were assassins. I thought an unarmed woman coming to you alone might suffice."

"You were right," he said, and then a moment later, "That's likely naïve of me, isn't it?"

"A bit."

"Please. Take me to him."

Twilight had soaked the sky in indigo. In the east, stars were peeking over the mountain tops, and the towers rose up into the air as if they led up to the clouds themselves. Maati and the woman walked quickly; she didn't speak, and he didn't press her to. His mind was busy enough already. They walked side by side along darkening paths. Kiyan smiled and nodded to those who took notice of them. Maati wondered how many people would be reporting that he had left the council with a woman. He looked back often for pursuers. No one *seemed* to be tracking them, but even at the edge of the palaces, there were enough people to prevent him from being sure.

They reached a teahouse, its windows blazing with light and its air rich with the scent of lemon candles to keep off the insects. The woman strode up the wide steps and into the warmth and light. The keep seemed to expect her, because they were led without a word into a back room where red wine was waiting along with a plate of rich cheese, black bread, and the first of the summer grapes. Kiyan sat at the table and gestured to the bench across from her. Maati sat as she plucked two of the small bright green grapes, bit into them and made a face.

"Too early?" he asked.

"Another week and they'll be decent. Here, pass me the cheese and bread."

Kiyan chewed these and Maati poured himself a bowl of wine. It was good—rich and deep and clean. He lifted the bottle but she shook her head.

"He'll be joining us, then?"

"No. We're just waiting a moment to be sure we're not leading anyone to him."

"Very professional," he said.

"Actually I'm new to all this. But I take advice well."

She had a good smile. Maati felt sure that this was the woman Otah had told him about that day in the gardens when Otah had left in chains. The woman he loved and whom he'd asked Maati to help protect. He tried to see Liat in her—the shape of her eyes, the curve of her cheek. There was nothing. Or perhaps there was something the two women shared that was simply beyond his ability to see.

As if feeling the weight of his attention, Kiyan took a querying pose. Maati shook his head.

"Reflecting on ages past," he said. "That's all."

She seemed about to ask something when a soft knock came at the door and the keep appeared, carrying a bundle of cloth. Kiyan stood, accepted the bundle, and took a pose that expressed her gratitude only slightly hampered by her burden. The keep left without speaking, and Kiyan pulled the cloth apart—two thin gray hooded cloaks that would cover their robes and hide their faces. She handed one to Maati and pulled the other on.

When they were both ready, Kiyan dug awkwardly in her doubled sleeve for a moment before coming out with four lengths of silver that she left on the table. Seeing Maati's surprise, she smiled.

"We didn't ask for the food and wine," she said. "It's rude to underpay."

"The grapes were sour," Maati said.

Kiyan considered this for a moment and scooped one silver length back into her sleeve. They didn't leave through the front door or out to the alley, but descended a narrow stairway into the tunnels beneath the city. Someone—the keep or one of Kiyan's conspirators—had left a lit lantern for them. Kiyan took it in hand and strode into the black tunnels as assured as a woman who had walked this maze her whole life. Maati kept close to her, dread pricking at him for the first time.

The descent seemed as deep as the mines in the plain. The stairs were worn smooth by generations of footsteps, the path they traveled inhabited by the memory of men and women long dead. At length the stairs gave way to a wide, tiled hallway shrouded in darkness. Kiyan's small lantern lit only part way up the deep blue and worked gold of the walls, the darkness above them more profound than a moonless sky.

The mouths of galleries and halls seemed to gape and close as they passed. Maati could see the scorch marks rising up the walls where torches had been set during some past winter, the smoke staining the tiles. A breath seemed to move through the dim air, like the earth exhaling.

The tunnels seemed empty except for them. No glimmer of light came from the doors and passages they passed, no voices however distant competed with the rustle of their robes. At a branching of the great hallway, Kiyan hesitated, then bore left. A pair of great brass gates opened onto a space like a garden, the plants all designed from silk, the birds perched on the branches dead and dust-covered.

"Unreal, isn't it?" Kiyan said as she picked her way across the sterile terrain. "I think they must go a little mad in the winters down here. All those months without seeing the sunlight."

"I suppose," Maati said.

After the garden, they went down a series of corridors so narrow that Maati could place his palms on both walls without stretching. She came to a high wooden doorway with brass fittings that was barred from within. Kiyan passed the lantern to Maati and knocked a complex pattern. A scraping sound spoke of the bar being lifted, and then the door swung in. Three men with blades in their hands stood. The center one smiled, stepped back and silently gestured them through.

Lanterns filled the stone-walled passage with warm, buttery light and the scent of burnt oil. There was no door at the end, only an archway that opened out into a wide, tall space that smelled of sweat and damp wool and torch smoke. A storehouse, then, with the door frames stuffed with rope to keep out even a glimmer of light.

Half a dozen men stopped their conversations as Kiyan led him across the empty space to the overseer's office—a shack within the structure that glowed from within.

Kiyan opened the office door and stood aside, smiling encouragement to Maati as he stepped past her and into the small room. A desk. Four chairs. A stand for scrolls. A map of the winter cities nailed to the wall. Three lanterns. And Otah-kvo rising now from his seat.

He was still thin, but there was an energy about him—in the way he held his shoulders and his hands. In the way he moved.

"You're looking well for a dead man," Maati said.

"Feeling better than expected, too," Otah said, and a smile spread across his long, northern face. "Thank you for coming."

"How could I not?" Maati drew one of the chairs close to him and sat, his fingers laced around one knee. "So you've chosen to take the city after all?"

Otah hesitated a moment, then sat. He rubbed the desktop with his open palm—a dry sound—and his brow furrowed.

"I don't see my option," he said at last. "That sounds convenient, I know. But . . . you said before that you'd realized I had nothing to do with Biitrah's death and your assault. I didn't have a part in Danat's murder either. Or my father's. Or even my own rescue from the tower, come to that. It's all simply *happened* up to now. And I didn't know whether you still believed me innocent."

Maati smiled ruefully. There was something in Otah's voice that sounded like hope. Maati didn't know his own heart—the resentment,

the anger, the love of Otah-kvo and of Liat and the child she'd borne.
He couldn't say even what they all had to do with this man sitting across
his appropriated desk.

"I do," Maati said at last. "I've been looking into the matter, but I
suppose you know that if you've had me watched."

"Yes. That's one reason I wanted to speak to you."

"There are others?"

"I have a confession to make. I'd likely be wiser to keep quiet until
this whole round is finished, but . . . I've lied to you, Maati. I told you
that I'd been with a woman in the east islands and failed to father a
child on her. She . . . she wasn't real. That never happened."

Maati considered this, waiting for his heart to rise in anger or shrivel,
but it only beat in its customary rhythm. He wondered when it had
stopped mattering to him, the father of the boy he'd lost. Since the last
time he had spoken with Otah in the high stone cell, certainly, but looking back, he couldn't put a moment to it. If the boy was his get or
Otah's, neither would bring him back. Neither would undo the years
gone by. And there were other things that he had that he might still
lose, or else save.

"I thought I was going to die," Otah said. "I thought it wouldn't matter to me, and if it gave you some comfort, then . . ."

"Let it go," Maati said. "If there's anything to be said about it, we
can say it later. There are other matters at hand."

"Have you found something, then?"

"I have a family name, I think. Certainly there's someone putting
money and influence behind the Vaunyogi."

"Likely the Galts," Otah said. "They've been making contracts bad
enough to look like bribes. We didn't know what influence they were
buying."

"It could be this," Maati said. "Do you know why they'd do it?"

"No," Otah said. "But if you've proof that the Vaunyogi are behind
the murderers—"

"I don't," Maati said. "I have a suspicion, but nothing more than
that. Not yet. And if we don't uncover them quickly, they'll likely have
Adrah named Khai Machi and have the resources of the whole city to
find you and kill you for crimes that everyone outside this warehouse
assumes you guilty of."

They sat in silence for the space of three breaths.

"Well," Otah-kvo said, "it appears we have some work to do then. But at least we've an idea where to look."

IN HER DREAM, IDAAN WAS AT A CELEBRATION. FIRE BURNED IN A RING ALL around the pavilion, and she knew with the logic of dreams that the flames were going to close, that the circle was growing smaller. They were all going to burn. She tried to shout, tried to warn the dancers, but she could only croak; no one heard her. There was someone there who could stop the thing from happening—a single man who was Cehmai and Otah and her father all at once. She beat her way through the bodies, trying to find him, but there were dogs in with the people. The flames were too close already, and to keep themselves alive, the women were throwing the animals into the fire. She woke to the screams and howls in her mind and the silence in her chamber.

The night candle had failed. The chamber was dim, silvered by moonlight beyond the dark web of the netting. The shutters along the wall were all open, but no breath of air stirred. Idaan swallowed and shook her head, willing the last wisps of nightmare into forgetfulness. She waited, listening to her breath, until her mind was her own again. Even then she was reluctant to sleep for fear of falling into the same dream. She turned to Adrah, but the bed at her side was empty. He was gone.

"Adrah?"

There was no answer.

Idaan wrapped herself with a thin blanket, pushed aside the netting and stepped out of her bed—her new bed. Her marriage bed. The smooth stone of the floor was cool against her bare feet. She walked through the chambers of their apartments—hers and her husband's— silently. She found him sitting on a low couch, a bottle beside him. A thick earthenware bowl on the floor stank of distilled wine. Or perhaps it was his breath.

"You aren't sleeping?" she asked.

"Neither are you," he said. The slurred words were half accusation.

"I had a dream," she said. "It woke me."

Adrah lifted the bottle, drinking from its neck. She watched the delicate shifting mechanism of his throat, the planes of his cheeks, his eyes closed and as smooth as a man asleep. Her fingers twitched toward him, moving to caress that familiar skin without consulting him on her wishes.

Coughing, he put down the wine, and the eyes opened. Whatever beauty had been in him, however briefly, was gone now.

"You should go to him," Adrah said. Perversely, he sounded less drunk now. Idaan took a pose of query. Adrah waved it away with the sloshing bottle. "The poet boy. Cehmai. You should go to him. See if you can get more information."

"You don't want me here?"

"No," Adrah said, pressing the bottle into her hand. As he rose and staggered past her, Idaan felt the insult and the rejection and a certain relief that she hadn't had to find an excuse to slip away.

The palaces were deserted, the empty paths dreamlike in their own way. Idaan let herself imagine that she had woken into a new, different world. As she slept, everyone had vanished, and she was walking now alone through an empty city. Or she had died in her sleep and the gods had put her here, into a world with nothing but herself and darkness. If they had meant it for punishment, they had misjudged.

The bottle was below a quarter when she stepped under the canopy of sculpted oaks. She had expected the poet's house to be dark as well, but as she advanced, she caught glimpses of candle glow, more light than a single night candle could account for. Something like hope surged in her, and she slowly walked forward. The shutters and door were open, the lanterns within all lit. But the wide, still figure on the steps wasn't him. Idaan hesitated. The andat raised its hand in greeting and motioned her closer.

"I was starting to think you wouldn't come," Stone-Made-Soft said in its distant, rumbling voice.

"I hadn't intended to," Idaan said. "You had no call to expect me."

"If you say so," it agreed, amiably. "Come inside. He's been waiting to see you for days."

Going up the steps felt like walking downhill, the pull to be there and see him was more powerful than weight. The andat stood and followed her in, closing the door behind her and then proceeding around the room, fastening the shutters and snuffing the flames. Idaan looked around the room, but there were only the two of them.

"It's late. He's in the back," the andat said and pinched out another small light. "You should go to him."

"I don't want to disturb him."

"He'd want you to."

She didn't move. The spirit tilted its broad head and smiled.

"He said he loves me," Idaan said. "When I saw him last, he said that he loved me."

"I know."

"Is it true?"

The smile broadened. Its teeth were white as marble and perfectly regular. She noticed for the first time that it had no canines—every tooth was even and square as the one beside it. For a moment, the inhuman mouth disturbed her.

"Why are you asking me?"

"You know him," she said. "You are him."

"True on both counts," Stone-Made-Soft said. "But I'm not credited as being the most honest source. I'm his creature, after all. And all dogs hate the leash, however well they pretend otherwise."

"You've never lied to me."

The andat looked startled, then chuckled with a sound like a boulder rolling downhill.

"No," it said. "I haven't, have I? And I won't start now. Yes, Cehmai-kya has fallen in love with you. He's young. His passions are still a large part of what he is. In forty years, he won't burn so hot. It's the way it's been with all of them."

"I don't want him hurt," she said.

"Then stay."

"I'm not sure that would save him pain. Not in the long term."

The andat went still a moment, then shrugged.

"Then go," it said. "But when he finds you've gone, he'll chew his own guts out over it. There's been nothing he's wanted more than for you to come here, to him. Coming this close, talking to me, and leaving? It'd hardly make him feel better about things."

Idaan looked at her feet. The sandals weren't laced well. She'd done the thing in darkness, and the wine had, perhaps, had more effect on her than she'd thought. She shook her head as she had when shaking off the dreams.

"He doesn't have to know I came."

"Late for that," the andat said and put out another candle. "He woke up as soon as we started talking."

"Idaan-kya?" his voice came from behind her.

Cehmai stood in the corridor that led back to his bedchamber. His hair was tousled by sleep. His feet were bare. Idaan caught her breath, seeing him here in the dim light of candles. He was beautiful. He was innocent and powerful, and she loved him more than anyone in the world.

"Cehmai."

"Only Cehmai?" he asked, stepping into the room. He looked hurt and hopeful both. She had no right to feel this young. She had no right to feel afraid or thrilled.

"Cehmai-kya," she whispered. "I had to see you."

"I'm glad of it. But . . . but you aren't, are you? Glad to see me, I mean."

"It wasn't supposed to be like this," she said, and the sorrow rose up in her like a flood. "It's my wedding night, Cehmai-kya. I was married today, and I couldn't go a whole night in that bed."

Her voice broke. She closed her eyes against the tears, but they simply came, rolling down her cheeks as fast as raindrops. She heard him move toward her, and between wanting to step into his arms and wanting to run, she stood unmoving, feeling herself tremble.

He didn't speak. She was standing alone and apart, the sorrow and guilt beating her like storm waves, and then his arms folded her into him. His skin smelled dark and musky and male. He didn't kiss her, he didn't try to open her robes. He only held her there as if he had never wanted anything more. She put her arms around him and held on as though he was a branch hanging over a precipice. She heard herself sob, and it sounded like violence.

"I'm sorry," she said. "I'm so sorry. I'm so sorry. I want it back. I want it all back. I'm so sorry."

"What, love? What do you want back?"

"All of it," she wailed, and the blackness and despair and rage and sorrow rose up, taking her in its teeth and shaking her. Cehmai held her close, murmured soft words to her, stroked her hair and her face. When she sank to the ground, he sank with her.

She couldn't say how long it was before the crying passed. She only knew that the night around them was perfectly dark, that she was curled in on herself with her head in his lap, and that her body was tired to the bone. She felt as if she'd swum for a day. She found Cehmai's hand and laced her fingers with his, wondering where dawn was. It seemed the night had already lasted for years. Surely there would be light soon.

"You feel better?" he asked, and she nodded her reply, trusting him to feel the movement against his flesh.

"Do you want to tell me what it is?" he asked.

Idaan felt her throat go tighter for a moment. He must have felt some change in her body, because he raised her hand to his lips. His mouth was so soft and so warm.

"I do," she said. "I want to. But I'm afraid."

"Of me?"

"Of what I would say."

There was something in his expression. Not a hardening, not a pulling away, but a change. It was as if she'd confirmed something.

"There's nothing you can say that will hurt me," Cehmai said. "Not if it's true. It's the Vaunyogi, isn't it? It's Adrah."

"I can't, love. Please don't talk about it."

But he only ran his free hand over her arm, the sound of skin against skin loud in the night's silence. When he spoke again, Cehmai's voice was gentle, but urgent.

"It's about your father and your brothers, isn't it?"

Idaan swallowed, trying to loosen her throat. She didn't answer, not even with a movement, but Cehmai's soft, beautiful voice pressed on.

"Otah Machi didn't kill them, did he?"

The air went thin as a mountaintop's. Idaan couldn't catch her breath. Cehmai's fingers pressed hers gently. He leaned forward and kissed her temple.

"It's all right," he said. "Tell me."

"I can't," she said.

"I love you, Idaan-kya. And I will protect you, whatever happens."

Idaan closed her eyes, even in the darkness. Her heart seemed on the edge of bursting she wanted it so badly to be true. She wanted so badly to lay her sins before him and be forgiven. And he knew already. He knew the truth or else guessed it, and he hadn't denounced her.

"I love you," he repeated, his voice softer than the sound of his hand stroking her skin. "How did it start?"

"I don't know," she said. And then, a moment later, "When I was young, I think."

Quietly, she told him everything, even the things she had never told Adrah. Seeing her brothers sent to the school and being told that she could not go herself because of her sex. Watching her mother brood and suffer and know that one day she would be sent away or else die there, in the women's quarters and be remembered only as something that had borne a Khai's babies.

She told him about listening to songs about the sons of the Khaiem battling for the succession and how, as a girl, she'd pretend to be one of them and force her playmates to take on the roles of her rivals. And the sense of injustice that her older brothers would pick their own wives and command their own fates, while she would be sold at convenience.

At some point, Cehmai stopped stroking her, and only listened, but that open, receptive silence was all she needed of him. She poured out everything. The wild, impossible plans she'd woven with Adrah. The intimation, one night when a Galtic dignitary had come to Machi, that the schemes might not be impossible after all. The bargain they had struck—access to a library's depth of old books and scrolls traded for power and freedom. And from there, the progression, inevitable as water flowing toward the sea, that led Adrah to her father's sleeping chambers and her to the still moment by the lake, the terrible sound of the arrow striking home.

With every phrase, she felt the horror of it ease. It lost none of the sorrow, none of the regret, but the bleak, soul-eating despair began to fade from black to merely the darkest gray. By the time she came to the end of one sentence and found nothing following it, the birds outside had begun to trill and sing. It would be light soon. Dawn would come after all. She sighed.

"That was a longer answer than you hoped for, maybe," she said.

"It was enough," he said.

Idaan shifted and sat up, pulling her hair back from her face. Cehmai didn't move.

"Hiami told me once," she said, "just before she left, that to become Khai you had to forget how to love. I see why she believed that. But it isn't what's happened. Not to me. Thank you, Cehmai-kya."

"For what?"

"For loving me. For protecting me," she said. "I didn't guess how much I needed to tell you all that. It was . . . it was too much. You see that."

"I do," Cehmai said.

"Are you angry with me now?"

"Of course not," he said.

"Are you horrified by me?"

She heard him shift his weight. The pause stretched, her heart sickening with every beat.

"I love you, Idaan," he said at last, and she felt the tears come again, but this time with a very different pressure behind them. It wasn't joy, but it was perhaps relief.

She shifted forward in the darkness, found his body there waiting, and held him for a time. She was the one who kissed him this time. She was the one who moved their conversation from the intimacy of confession to the intimacy of sex. Cehmai seemed almost reluctant, as if afraid that taking her body now would betray some deeper moment that they had shared. But Idaan led him to his bed in the darkness, opened her own robes and his, and coaxed his flesh until whatever objection he'd fostered was forgotten. She found herself at ease, lighter, almost as if she was half in dream.

Afterwards, she lay nestled in his arms, warm, safe, and calm as she had never been in years. Sunlight pressed at the closed shutters as she drifted down to sleep.

13

>+< The tunnels beneath Machi were a city unto themselves. Otah found himself drawn out into them more and more often as the days crept forward. Sinja and Amiit had tried to keep him from leaving the storehouse beneath the underground palaces of the Saya, but Otah had overruled them. The risk of a few quiet hours walking abandoned corridors was less, he judged, than the risk of going quietly mad waiting in the same sunless room day after day. Sinja had convinced him to take an armsman as guard when he went.

Otah had expected the darkness and the quiet—wide halls empty, water troughs dry—but the beauty he stumbled on took him by surprise. Here a wide square of stone smooth as beach sand, delicate pillars spiraling up from it like bolts of twisting silk made from stone. And down another corridor, a bathhouse left dry for the winter but rich with the scent of cedar and pine resin.

Even when he returned to the storehouse and the voices and faces he knew, he found his mind lingering in the dark corridors and galleries, unsure whether the images of the spaces lit with the white shadowless light of a thousand candles were imagination or memory.

A sharp rapping brought him back to himself, and the door of his private office swung open. Amiit and Sinja walked in, already half into a conversation. Sinja's expression was mildly annoyed. Amiit, Otah thought, seemed worried.

"It would only make things worse," Amiit said.

"We'd earn more time. And it isn't as if they'd accuse Otah-cha here of it. They think he's dead."

"Then they'll accuse him of it once they find he's alive," Amiit said and turned to Otah. "Sinja wants to assassinate the head of a high family in order to slow the work of the council."

"We won't do that," Otah said. "My hands aren't particularly blood-ied yet, and I'd like to keep it that way—"

"It isn't as though people are going to believe it," Sinja said. "If you're going to carry the blame you may as well get the advantages from doing the thing."

"It'll be easier to convince them of my innocence later if I'm actually innocent of something," Otah said, "but there may be other roads that come to the same place. Is there something else that would slow the council and doesn't involve putting holes in someone?"

Sinja frowned, his eyes shifting as if he were reading text written in the air. He half-smiled.

"Perhaps. Let me look into that."

With a pose that ended his conversation, Sinja left. Amiit sighed and lowered himself into one of the chairs.

"What news?" Amiit asked.

"Kamau and Vaunani are talking about merging their forces," Otah said. "Most of the talks seem to involve someone hitting someone or throwing a knife. The Loiya, Bentani, and Coirah have all been quietly, and so far as I can tell, independently, backing the Vaunyogi."

"And they all have contracts with Galt," Amiit said. "What about the others?"

"Of the families we know? None have come out against them. And none for, or at least not openly."

"There should be more fighting," Amiit said. "There should be struggles and coalitions. Alliances should be forming and breaking by the moment. It's too steady."

"Only if there was a real struggle going on. If the decision was al-ready made, it would look exactly like this."

"Yes. There are times I hate being right. Any word from the poet?"

Otah shook his head and sat, then stood again. Maati had gone from their first meeting, and he'd seemed convinced. Otah had been sure at the time that he wouldn't betray them. He was sure in his bones. He only wished he'd had his thoughts more in order at the time. He'd been swept up in the moment, more concerned with his lies about Liat's son than anything else. He'd had time since to reflect, and the other worries had swarmed out. Otah had sat up until the night candle was at its halfway mark, listing the things he needed to consider. It hadn't lent him peace.

"It's hard, waiting," Amiit said. "You must feel like you're back up in that tower."

"That was easier. Then at least I knew what was going to happen. I wish I could go *out*. If I could be up there listening to the people themselves . . . If I spent half an evening in the right teahouse, I'd know more than I'll learn skulking down here for days. Yes, I know. You've the best minds of the house out watching for us. But listening to reports isn't the same as putting my hands to something."

"I know it. More than half my work has been trying to guess the truth out of a dozen different reports of a thing. There's a knack to it. You'll have your practice with it."

"If this ends well," Otah said.

"Yes," Amiit agreed. "If that."

Otah filled a tin cup with water from a stone jar and sat back down. It was warm, and a thin grit swam at the cup's bottom. He wished it were wine and pushed the thought away. If there was any time in his life to be sober as stone, this was it, but his unease shifted and tightened. He looked up from his water to see Amiit's gaze on him, his expression quizzical.

"We have to make a plan for if we lose," Otah said. "If the Vaunyogi are to blame and the council gives them power, they'll be able to wash away any number of crimes. And all those families that supported them will be invested in keeping things quiet. If it comes out that Daaya Vaunyogi killed the Khai in order to raise up his son and half the families of the utkhaiem took money to support it, they'll all share in the guilt. Being in the right won't mean much then."

"There's time yet," Amiit said, but he was looking away when he said it.

"And what happens if we fail?"

"That all depends on how we fail. If we're discovered before we're ready to move, we'll all be killed. If Adrah is named Khai, we'll at least have a chance to slip away quietly."

"You'll take care of Kiyan?"

Amiit smiled. "I hope to see to it that you can perform that duty."

"But if not?"

"Then of course," Amiit said. "Provided I live."

The rapping came again, and the door opened on a young man. Otah

recognized him from the meetings in House Siyanti, but he couldn't recall his name.

"The poet's come," the young man said.

Amiit rose, took a pose appropriate to the parting of friends, and left.
The young man went with him, and for a moment the door swung free,
half closing. Otah drank the last of his water, the grit rough in his throat.
Maati came in slowly, a diffidence in his body and his face, like a man
called in to hear news that might bring him good or ill or some unimag-
ined change that folded both inextricably together. Otah gestured to
the door, and Maati closed it.

"You sent for me?" Maati asked. "That's a dangerous habit, Otah-kvo."

"I know it, but . . . Please. Sit. I've been thinking. About what we do
if things go poorly."

"If we fail?"

"I want to be ready for it, and when Kiyan and I were talking last
night, something occurred to me. Nayiit? That's his name, isn't it? The
child that you and Liat had?"

Maati's expression was cool and distant and misleading. Otah could
see the pain in it, however still the eyes.

"What of him?"

"He mustn't be my son. Whatever happens, he has to be yours."

"If you fail, you don't take your father's title—"

"If I don't take his title, and someone besides you decides he's mine,
they'll kill him to remove all doubt of the succession. And if I succeed,
Kiyan may have a son," Otah said. "And then they would someday have
to kill each other. Nayiit is *your* son. He has to be."

"I see," Maati said.

"I've written a letter. It looks like something I'd have sent Kiyan before, when I was in Chaburi-Tan. It talks about the night I left
Saraykeht. It says that on the night I came back to the city, I found the
two of you together. That I walked into her cell, and you and she were
in her cot. It makes it clear that I didn't touch her, that I couldn't have
fathered a child on her. Kiyan's put it in her things. If we have to flee,
we'll take it with us and find a way for it to come to light—we can hide
it at her wayhouse, perhaps. If we're found and killed here, it will be
found with us. You have to back that story."

Maati steepled his fingers and leaned back in the chair.

"You've put it with Kiyan-cha's things to be found in case she's slaughtered?" he asked.

"Yes," Otah said. "I don't think about it when I can help it, but I know she could die here. There's no reason that your son should die with us."

Maati nodded slowly. He was struggling with something, Otah could see that much, but whether it was sorrow or anger or joy, he had no way to know. When the question came, though, it was the one he had been dreading for years.

"What did happen?" Maati asked at last, his voice low and hushed. "The night Heshai-kvo died. What happened? Did you just leave? Did you take Maj with you? Did . . . did you kill him?"

Otah remembered the cord cutting into his hands, remembered the way Maj had balked and he had taken the task himself. For years, those few minutes had haunted him.

"He knew what was coming," Otah said. "He knew it was necessary. The consequences if he had lived would have been worse. Heshai was right when he warned you to let the thing drop. The Khai Saraykeht would have turned the andat against Galt. There would have been thousands of innocent lives ruined. And when it was over, you would still have been yoked to Seedless. Trapped in the torture box just the way Heshai had been all those years. Heshai knew that, and he waited for me to do the thing."

"And you did it."

"I did."

Maati was silent. Otah sat. His knees seemed less solid than he would have liked, but he didn't let the weakness stop him.

"It was the worst thing I have ever done," Otah said. "I never stopped dreaming about it. Even now, I see it sometimes. Heshai was a good man, but what he'd created in Seedless. . . ."

"Seedless was only part of him. They all are. They couldn't be anything else. Heshai-kvo hated himself, and Seedless was that."

"Everyone hates themselves sometimes. There isn't often a price in blood," Otah said. "You know what would happen if that were proven. Killing a Khai would pale beside murdering a poet."

Maati nodded slowly, and still nodding, spoke.

"I didn't ask on the Dai-kvo's behalf. I asked for myself. When

Heshai-kvo died, Seedless . . . vanished. I was with him. I was there. He was asking me whether I would have forgiven you. If you'd committed some terrible crime, like what he had done to Maj, if I would forgive you. And I told him I would. I would forgive you, and not him. Because . . ."

They were silent. Maati's eyes were dark as coal.

"Because?" Otah asked.

"Because I loved you, and I didn't love him. He said it was a pity to think that love and justice weren't the same. The last thing he said was that you had forgiven me."

"Forgiven you?"

"For Liat. For taking your lover."

"I suppose it's true," Otah said. "I was angry with you. But there was a part of me that was . . . relieved, I suppose."

"Why?"

"Because I didn't love her. I thought I did. I wanted to, and I enjoyed her company and her bed. I liked her and respected her. Sometimes, I wanted her as badly as I've ever wanted anyone. And that was enough to let me mistake it for love. But I don't remember it hurting that deeply or for that long. Sometimes I was even glad. You had each other to take care of, and so it wasn't mine to do."

"You said, that last time we spoke before you left . . . before Heshai-kvo died, that you didn't trust me."

"That's true," Otah said. "I do remember that."

"But you've come to me now, and you've told me this. You've told me all of it. Even after I gave you over to the Khai. You've brought me in here, shown me where you've hidden. You know there are half a hundred people I could say a word to, and you and all these other people would be dead before the sun set. So it seems you trust me now."

"I do," Otah said without hesitating.

"Why?"

Otah sat with the question. His mind had been consumed for days with a thousand different things that all nipped and shrieked and robbed him of his rest. To reach out to Maati had seemed natural and obvious, and even though when he looked at it coldly it was true that each had in some way betrayed the other, his heart had never been in doubt. He could feel the heaviness in the air, and he knew that *I don't know* wouldn't be answer enough. He looked for words to give his feelings shape.

"Because," he said at last, "in all the time I knew you, you never once did the wrong thing. Even when what you did hurt me, it was never wrong."

To his surprise, there were tears on Maati's cheeks.

"Thank you, Otah-kvo," he said.

A shout went up in the tunnels outside the storehouse and the sound of running feet. Maati wiped his eyes with the sleeve of his robes, and Otah stood, his heart beating fast. The murmur of voices grew, but there were no sounds of blade against blade. It sounded like a busy corner more than a battle. Otah walked to the door and, Maati close behind him, stepped out into the main space. A knot of men were talking and gesturing one to the other by the mouth of the stairs. Otah caught a glimpse of Kiyan in their midst, frowning deeply and speaking fast. Amiit detached himself from the throng and strode to Otah.

"What's happened?"

"Bad news, Otah-cha. Daaya Vaunyogi has called for a decision, and enough of the families have backed the call to push it through."

Otah felt his heart sink.

"They're bound to decide by morning," Amiit went on, "and if all the houses that backed him for the call side with him in the decision, Adrah Vaunyogi will be the Khai Machi by the time the sun comes up."

"And then what?" Maati asked.

"And then we run," Otah said, "as far and fast and quiet as we can, and we hope he never finds us."

THE SUN HAD PASSED ITS HIGHEST POINT AND STARTED THE LONG, SLOW slide toward darkness. Idaan had chosen robes the blue-gray of twilight and bound her hair back with clasps of silver and moonstone. Around her, the gallery was nearly full, the air thick with heat and the mingled scents of bodies and perfumes. She stood at the rail, looking down into the press of bodies below her. The parquet of the floor was scuffed with the marks of boots. There were no empty places at the tables or against the stone walls, no quiet negotiations going on in hallways or teahouses. That time had passed, and in its wake, they were all brought here. Voices washed together like the hushing of wind, and she could feel the weight of the eyes upon her—the men below her sneaking glances up, the representatives of the merchant houses at her side considering her, and the lower orders in the gallery above staring down at her and the men over whom she loomed. She was a woman, and not welcome to speak or sit at the tables below. But still, she would make her presence felt.

"How is it that we accept the word of these men that they are the wisest?" Ghiah Vaunani pounded the speaker's pulpit before him with each word, a dry, shallow sound. Idaan almost thought she could see flecks of foam at the corners of his mouth. "How is it that the houses of the utkhaiem are so much like sheep that they would consent to be led by this shepherd boy of Vaunyogi?"

It was meant, Idaan knew, to be a speech to sway the others from their confidence, but all she heard in the words was the confusion and pain of a boy whose plans have fallen through. He could pound and rail and screech his questions as long as his voice held out. Idaan, standing above the proceedings like a protective ghost, knew the answers to every one, and she would never tell them to him.

Below her, Adrah Vaunyogi looked up, his expression calm and certain. It had been late in the morning that she'd woken in the poet's house, later still when she'd returned to the rooms she shared now with her husband. He had been there, waiting for her. The night's excesses had weighed heavy on him. They hadn't spoken—she had only called for a bath and clean robes. When she'd cleaned herself and washed her hair, she sat at her mirror and painted her face with all her old skill and delicacy. The woman who looked out at her when she put down her brushes might have been the loveliest in Machi.

Adrah had left without a word. It had been almost half a hand before she learned that her new father, Daaya Vaunyogi, had called for the decision, and that the houses had agreed. No one had told her to come here, no one had asked her to lend the sight of her silent presence to the cause. She had done it, perhaps, *because* Adrah had not demanded it of her.

"We must not hurry! We must not allow sentiment to push us into a decision that will change our city forever!"

Idaan allowed herself a smile. It would seem to most people that the force of the story had won the day. The last daughter of the old line would be the first mother of the new, and if a quiet structure of money and obligation supported it, if she were really the lover of the poet a hundred times more than the Khai, it hardly mattered. It was what the city would see, and that was enough.

Ghiah's energy was beginning to flag. She heard his words lose their crispness and the pounding on his table fall out of rhythm. The anger in his voice became merely petulance, and the objections to Adrah in particular and the Vaunyogi in general lost their force. It would have been better, she thought, if he'd ended half a hand earlier. Still insufficient, but less so.

The Master of Tides stood when Ghiah at last surrendered the floor. He was an old man with a long, northern face and a deep, sonorous voice. Idaan saw his eyes flicker up to her and then away.

"Adaut Kamau has also asked to address the council," he said, "before the houses speak on the decision to accept Adrah Vaunyogi as the Khai Machi. . . ."

A chorus of jeers rose from the galleries and even the council tables. Idaan held herself still and quiet. Her feet were starting to ache, but she didn't shift her weight. The effect she desired wouldn't be served by showing her pleasure. Adaut Kamau rose, his face gray and pinched. He opened his arms, but before he could speak, a bundle of rough cloth arced from the highest gallery. A long tail of brown fluttered behind it like a banner as it fell, and in the instant that it struck the floor, the screaming began.

Idaan's composure broke, and she leaned forward. The men at the tables nearest the thing waved their arms and fled, shrieking and pounding at the air. Voices buzzed and a cloud of pale, moving smoke rose toward the galleries.

No. The buzzing was not voices, the cloud was not smoke. These were wasps. The bundle on the council floor had been a nest wrapped in cloth and wax. The first of the insects buzzed past her, a glimpse of black and yellow. She turned and ran.

Bodies filled the corridors, panic pressing them together until there was no air, no space. People screamed and cursed—men, women, children. Their shrill voices mixed with the angry buzz. She was pushed from all sides. An elbow dug into her back. The surge of the crowd pressed the breath from her. She was suffocating, and insects filled the air above her. Idaan felt something bite the flesh at the back of her neck like a hot iron burning her. She screamed and tried to reach back to bat the thing away, but there was no room to move her arm, no air. She lashed out at whoever, whatever was near. The crowd was a single, huge, biting beast and Idaan flailed and shrieked, her mind lost to fear and pain and confusion.

Stepping into the open air of the street was like waking from a nightmare. The bodies around her thinned, becoming only themselves again. The fierce buzz of tiny wings was gone, the cries of pain and terror replaced by the groans of the stung. People were still streaming out of the palace, arms flapping, but others were sitting on benches or else the ground. Servants and slaves were rushing about, tending to the hurt and the humiliated. Idaan felt the back of her neck—three angry bumps were already forming.

"It's a poor omen," a man in the red robes of the needle wrights said. "Something more's going on than meets the eye if someone's willing to attack the council to keep old Kamau from talking."

"What could he have said?" the man's companion asked.

"I don't know, but you can be sure whatever it was, he'll be saying something else tomorrow. Someone wanted him stopped. Unless this is about Adrah Vaunyogi. It could be that someone wants him closed down."

"Then why loose the things when his critics were about to speak?"

"Good point. Perhaps . . ."

Idaan moved on down the street. It was like the aftermath of some gentle, bloodless battle. People bound bruised limbs. Slaves brought plasters to suck out the wasps' venom. But already, all down the wide street, the talk had turned back to the business of the council.

Her neck was burning now, but she pushed the pain aside. There would be no decision made today. That was clear. Kamau or Vaunani had disrupted the proceedings to get more time. It had to be that. It couldn't be more, except that of course it could. The fear was different now, deeper and more complex. Almost like nausea.

Adrah was leaning against the wall at the mouth of an alleyway. His father was sitting beside him, a serving girl dabbing white paste on the angry welts that covered his arms and face. Idaan went to her husband. His eyes were hard and shallow as stones.

"May I speak with you, Adrah-kya?" she said softly.

Adrah looked at her as if seeing her for the first time, then at his father. He nodded toward the shadows of the alley behind him, and Idaan followed him until the noises of the street were vague and distant.

"It was Otah," she said. "He did this. He knows."

"Are you about to tell me that he's planned it all from the start again? It was a cheap, desperate trick. It won't matter, except that anyone who doesn't like us will say we did it, and anyone who has a grudge against our enemies will put it to them. Nothing changes."

"Who would do it?"

Adrah shook his head, impatient, and turned to walk back out into the street and noise and light. "Anyone might have. There's no point trying to solve every puzzle in the world."

"Don't be stupid, Adrah. Someone's acted against—"

The violence and suddenness of his movement was shocking. He was walking away, his back to her, and then a heartbeat later, there was no more room between them than the width of a leaf. His face was twisted, flushed, possessed by anger.

"Don't be *stupid*? Is that what you said?"

Idaan took a step back, her feet unsteady beneath her.

"How do you mean, stupid, Idaan? Stupid like calling out my lover's name in a crowd?"

"What?"

"Cehmai. The poet boy. When you were running, you called his name."

"I did?"

"Everyone heard it," Adrah said. "Everybody knows. At least you could keep it between us and not parade it all over the city!"

"I didn't mean to," she said. "I swear it, Adrah. I didn't know I had."

He stepped back and spat, the spittle striking the wall beside him and dripping down toward the ground. His gaze locked on her, daring her to push him, to meet his anger with defiance or submission. Either would be devastating. Idaan felt herself go hard. It wasn't unlike the feeling of seeing her father dying breath by breath, his belly rotting out and taking him with it.

"It won't get better, will it?" she asked. "It will go on. It will change. But it will never get better than it is right now."

The dread in Adrah's eyes told her she'd struck home. When he turned and stalked away, she didn't try to stop him.

TELL ME, HE'D SAID.

I can't, she'd replied.

And now Cehmai sat on a chair, staring at the bare wall and wished that he'd left it there. The hours since morning had been filled with a kind of anguish he'd never known. He'd told her he loved her. He did love her. But . . . Gods! She'd murdered her own family. She'd engineered her own father's death and as much as sold the Khai's library to the Galts. And the only thing that had saved her was that she loved him and he'd sworn he'd protect her. He'd sworn it.

"What did you expect?" Stone-Made-Soft asked.

"That it was Adrah. That I'd be protecting her from the Vaunyogi," Cehmai said.

"Well. Perhaps you should have been more specific."

The sun had passed behind the mountains, but the daylight hadn't yet taken on the ruddy hues of sunset. This was not night but shadow. The andat stood at the window, looking out. A servant had come from the palaces earlier bearing a meal of roast chicken and rich, dark bread. The smell of it filled the house, though the platter had been set outside to be taken away. He hadn't been able to eat.

Cehmai could barely feel where the struggle in the back of his mind met the confusion at the front. Idaan. It had been Idaan all along.

"You couldn't have known," the andat said, its tone conciliatory. "And it isn't as if she asked you to be part of the thing."

"You think she was using me."

"Yes. But since I'm a creature of your mind, it seems to follow that you'd think the same. She did extract a promise from you. You're sworn to protect her."

"I love her."

"You'd better. If you don't, then she told you all that under a false impression that you led her to believe. If she hadn't truly thought she could trust you, she'd have kept her secrets to herself."

"I do love her."

"And that's good," Stone-Made-Soft said. "Since all that blood she spilled is part yours now."

Cehmai leaned forward. His foot knocked over the thin porcelain bowl at his feet. The last dregs of the wine spilled to the floor, but he didn't bother with it. Stained carpet was beneath his notice now. His head was stuffed with wool, and none of his thoughts seemed to connect. He thought of Idaan's smile and the way she turned toward him, nestling into him as she slept. Her voice had been so soft, so quiet. And then, when she had asked him if he was horrified by her, there had been so much fear in her.

He hadn't been able to say yes. It had been there, waiting in his throat, and he'd swallowed it. He'd told her he loved her, and he hadn't lied. But he hadn't slept either. The andat's wide hand turned the bowl upright and pressed a cloth onto the spill. Cehmai watched the red wick up into the white cloth.

"Thank you," he said.

Stone-Made-Soft took a brief, dismissive pose and lumbered away. Cehmai heard it pouring water into a basin to rinse the cloth, and felt a pang of shame. He was falling apart. The andat itself was taking care of him now. He was pathetic. Cehmai rose and stalked to the window. He felt as much as heard the andat come up behind him.

"So," the andat said. "What are you going to do?"

"I don't know."

"Do you think she's got her legs around him now? Just at the moment, I mean," the andat said, its voice as calm and placid and distantly amused as always. "He is her husband. He must get her knees apart now and again. And she must enjoy him on some level. She did slaughter her family to elevate Adrah. It's not something most girls would do."

"You're not helping," Cehmai said.

"It could be you're just a part of her plan. She did fall into your bed awfully easily. Do you think they talk about it, the two of them? About what she can do to you or for you to win your support? Having the poet's oath protecting you would be a powerful thing. And if you protect her, you protect them. You can't suggest anything evil of the Vaunyogi now without drawing her into it."

"She isn't like that!"

Cehmai gathered his will, but before he could turn it on the andat, before he pushed the rage and the anger and the hurt into a force that would make the beast be quiet, Stone-Made-Soft smiled, leaned forward, and gently kissed Cehmai's forehead. In all the years he'd held it, Cehmai had never seen the andat do anything of the sort.

"No," it said. "She isn't. She's in terrible trouble, and she needs you to save her if you can. If she can be saved. And she trusts you. Standing with her is the only thing you could do and still be a decent man."

Cehmai glared at the wide face, the slow, calm eyes, searching for a shred of sarcasm. There was none.

"Why are you trying to confuse me?" he asked.

The andat turned to look out the window and stood as still as a statue. Cehmai waited, but it didn't shift, even to look at him. The rooms darkened and Cehmai lit lemon candles to keep the insects away. His mind was divided into a hundred different thoughts, each of them powerful and convincing and no two fitting together.

When at last he went up to his bed, he couldn't sleep. The blankets still smelled of her, of the two of them. Of love and sleep. Cehmai wrapped the sheets around himself and willed his mind to quiet, but the whirl of thoughts didn't allow rest. Idaan loved him. She had had her own father killed. Maati had been right, all this time. It was his duty to tell what he knew, but he couldn't. It was possible—she might have tricked him all along. He felt as cracked as river ice when a stone had been dropped through it, jagged fissures cut through him in all directions. There was no center of peace within him.

And yet he must have drifted off, because the storm pulled him awake. Cehmai stumbled out of bed, pulling down half his netting with a soft ripping sound. He crawled to the corridor almost before he understood that the pitching and moaning, the shrieking and the nausea were all in the private space behind his eyes. It had never been so powerful.

He fell as he went to the front of the house, barking his knee against the wall. The thick carpets were sickening to touch, the fibers seeming to writhe under his fingers like dry worms. Stone-Made-Soft sat at the gaming table. The white marble, the black basalt. A single white stone was shifted out of its beginning line.

"Not now," Cehmai croaked.

"Now," the andat said, its voice loud and low and undeniable.

The room pitched and spun. Cehmai dragged himself to the table and tried to focus on the pieces. The game was simple enough. He'd played it a thousand times. He shifted a black stone forward. He felt he was still half dreaming. The stone he'd moved was Idaan. Stone-Made-Soft's reply moved a token that was both its fourth column and also Otah Machi. Groggy with sleep and distress and annoyance and the angry pressure of the andat struggling against him, he didn't understand how far things had gone until twelve moves later when he shifted a black stone one place to the left, and Stone-Made-Soft smiled.

"Maybe she'll still love you afterwards," the andat said. "Do you think she'll care as much about your love when you're just a man in a brown robe?"

Cehmai looked at the stones, the shifting line of them, flowing and sinuous as a river, and he saw his mistake. Stone-Made-Soft pushed a white stone forward and the storm in Cehmai's mind redoubled. He could hear his own breath rattling. He was sticky with the rancid sweat of effort and fear. He was losing. He couldn't make himself think, controlling his own mind was like wrestling a beast—something large and angry and stronger than he was. In his confusion, Idaan and Adrah and the death of the Khai all seemed connected to the tokens glowing on the board. Each was enmeshed with the others, and all of them were lost. He could feel the andat pressing toward freedom and oblivion. All the generations of carrying it, gone because of him.

"It's your move," the andat said.

"I can't," Cehmai said. His own voice sounded distant.

"I can wait as long as you care to," it said. "Just tell me when you think it'll get easier."

"You knew this would happen," Cehmai said. "You knew."

"Chaos has a smell to it," the andat agreed. "Move."

Cehmai tried to study the board, but every line he could see led to failure. He closed his eyes and rubbed them until ghosts bloomed in the darkness, but when he reopened them, it was no better. The sickness grew in his belly. He felt he was falling. The knock on the door behind him was something of a different world, a memory from some other life, until the voice came.

"I know you're in there! You won't believe what's happened. Half the utkhaiem are spotty with welts. Open the door!"

"Baarath!"

Cehmai didn't know how loud he'd called—it might have been a whisper or a scream. But it was enough. The librarian appeared beside him. The stout man's eyes were wide, his lips thin.

"What's wrong?" Baarath asked. "Are you sick? Gods, Cehmai. . . . Stay here. Don't move. I'll have a physician—"

"Paper. Bring me paper. And ink."

"It's your *move*!" the andat shouted, and Baarath seemed about to bolt.

"Hurry," Cehmai said.

It was a week, a month, a year of struggle before the paper and ink brick appeared at his side. He could no longer tell whether the andat was shouting to him in the real world or only within their shared mind. The game pulled at him, sucking like a whirlpool. The stones shifted with significance beyond their own, and confusion built on confusion in waves so that Cehmai grasped his one thought until it was a certainty.

There was too much. There was more than he could survive. The only choice was to simplify the panoply of conflicts warring within him; there wasn't room for them all. He had to fix things, and if he couldn't make them right, he could at least make them end.

He didn't let himself feel the sorrow or the horror or the guilt as he scratched out a note—brief and clear as he could manage. The letters were shaky, the grammar poor. Idaan and the Vaunyogi and the Galts. Everything he knew written in short, unadorned phrases. He dropped the pen to the floor and pressed the paper into Baarath's hand.

"Maati," Cehmai said. "Take it to Maati. Now."

Baarath read the letter, and whatever blood had remained in his face drained from it now.

"This . . . this isn't . . ."

"Run!" Cehmai screamed, and Baarath was off, faster than Cehmai could have gone if he'd tried, Idaan's doom in his hands. Cehmai closed his eyes. That was over, then. That was decided, and for good or ill, he was committed. The stones now could be only stones.

He pulled himself back to the game board. Stone-Made-Soft had gone silent again. The storm was as fierce as it had ever been, but Cehmai found he also had some greater degree of strength against it. He forced himself along every line he could imagine, shifting the stones in his mind until at last he pushed one black token forward. Stone-Made-Soft didn't pause. It shifted a white stone behind the black that had just moved, trapping it. Cehmai took a long deep breath and shifted a black stone on the far end of the board back one space.

The andat stretched out its wide fingers, then paused. The storm shifted, lessened. Stone-Made-Soft smiled ruefully and pulled back its hand. The wide brow furrowed.

"Good sacrifice," it said.

Cehmai leaned back. His body was shuddering with exhaustion and effort and perhaps something else more to do with Baarath running through the night. The andat moved a piece forward. It was the obvious move, but it was doomed. They had to play it out, but the game was as good as finished. Cehmai moved a black token.

"I think she does love you," the andat said. "And you did swear you'd protect her."

"She killed two men and plotted her own father's slaughter," Cehmai said.

"You love her. I know you do."

"I know it too," Cehmai said, and then a long moment later. "It's your move."

14

>+< Rain came in from the south. By midmorning tall clouds of bil-
lowing white and yellow and gray had filled the wide sky of the
valley. When the sun, had it been visible, would have reached the top of
its arc, the rain poured down on the city like an upended bucket. The
black cobbled streets were brooks, every slant roof a little waterfall.
Maati sat in the side room of the teahouse and watched. The water
seemed lighter than the sky or the stone—alive and hopeful. It chilled
the air, making the warmth of the earthenware bowl in his hands more
present. Across the smooth wooden table, Otah-kvo's chief armsman
scratched at the angry red weals on his wrists.

"If you keep doing that, they'll never heal," Maati said.

"Thank you, grandmother," Sinja said. "I had an arrow through my
arm once that hurt less than this."

"It's no worse than what half the people in that hall suffered," Maati
said.

"It's a thousand times worse. Those stings are on them. These are on
me. I'd have thought the difference obvious."

Maati smiled. It had taken three days to get all the insects out of the
great hall, and the argument about whether to simply choose a new
venue or wait for the last nervous slave to find and crush the last dying
wasp would easily have gone on longer than the problem itself. The
time had been precious. Sinja scratched again, winced, and pressed his
hands flat against the table, as if he could pin them there and not rely on
his own will to control himself.

"I hear you've had another letter from the Dai-kvo," Sinja said.

Maati pursed his lips. The pages were in his sleeve even now.
They'd arrived in the night by a special courier who was waiting in
apartments Maati had bullied out of the servants of the dead Khai. The

message included an order to respond at once and commit his reply to the courier. He hadn't picked up a pen yet. He wasn't sure what he wanted to say.

"He ordered you back?" Sinja asked.

"Among other things," Maati agreed. "Apparently he's been getting information from someone in the city besides myself."

"The other one? The boy?"

"Cehmai you mean? No. One of the houses that the Galts bought, I'd guess. But I don't know which. It doesn't matter. He'll know the truth soon enough."

"If you say so."

A bolt of lightning flashed and a half breath later, thunder rolled through the thick air. Maati raised the bowl to his lips. The tea was smoky and sweet, and it did nothing to unknot his guts. Sinja leaned toward the window, his eyes suddenly bright. Maati followed his gaze. Three figures leaned into the slanting rain—one a thick man with a slight limp, the others clearly servants holding a canopy over the first in a vain attempt to keep their master from being soaked to the skin. All wore cloaks with deep hoods that hid their faces.

"Is that him?" Sinja asked.

"I think so," Maati said. "Go. Get ready."

Sinja vanished and Maati refilled his bowl of tea. It was only moments before the door to the private room opened again and Porsha Radaani came into the room. His hair was plastered back against his skull, and his rich, ornately embroidered robes were dark and heavy with water. Maati rose and took a pose of welcome. Radaani ignored it, pulled out the chair Sinja had only recently left, and sat in it with a grunt.

"I'm sorry for the foul weather," Maati said. "I'd thought you'd take the tunnels."

Radaani made an impatient sound.

"They're half flooded. The city was designed with snow in mind, not water. The first thaw's always like a little slice of hell in the spring. But tell me you didn't bring me here to talk about rain, Maati-cha. I'm a busy man. The council's just about pulled itself back together, and I'd like to see an end to this nonsense."

"That's what I wanted to speak to you about, Porsha-cha. I'd like you to call for the council to disband. You're well respected. If you were to adopt the position, the lower families would take interest. And the Vau-nani and Kamau can both work with you without having to work with each other."

"I'm a powerful enough man to do that," Radaani agreed, his tone matter-of-fact. "But I can't think why I would."

"There's no reason for the council to be called."

"No reason? We're short a Khai, Maati-cha."

"The last one left a son to take his place," Maati said. "No one in that hall has a legitimate claim to the name Khai Machi."

Radaani laced his thick fingers over his belly and narrowed his eyes. A smile touched his lips that might have meant anything.

"I think you have some things to tell me," he said.

Maati began not with his own investigation, but with the story as it had unfolded. Idaan Machi and Adrah Vaunyogi, the backing of the Galts, the murder of Biitrah Machi. He told it like a tale, and found it was easier than he'd expected. Radaani chuckled when he reached the night of Otah's escape and grew somber when he drew the connection between the murder of Danat Machi and the hunting party that had gone with him. It was all true, but it was not all of the truth. In the long conversations that had followed Baarath's delivery of Cehmai's letter, Otah and Maati, Kiyan and Amiit had all agreed that the Galts' interest in the library was something that could be safely neglected. It added nothing to their story, and knowing more than they seemed to might yet prove an advantage. Watching Porsha Radaani's eyes, Maati thought it had been the right decision.

He outlined what he wanted of the Radaani—the timing of the pro-posal to disband, the manner in which it would be best approached, the support they would need on the council. Radaani listened like a cat watching a pigeon until the whole proposal was laid out before him. He coughed and loosened the belt of his robe.

"It's a pretty story," Radaani said. "It'll play well to a crowd. But you'll need more than this to convince the utkhaiem that your friend's hem isn't red. We're all quite pleased to have a Khai who's walked through his brothers' blood, but fathers are a different thing."

"I'm not the only one to tell it," Maati said. "I have one of the hunt-ing party who watched Danat die to swear there was no sign of an am-bush. I have the commander who collected Otah from the tower to say what he was bought to do and by whom. I have Cehmai Tyan and

Stone-Made-Soft. And I have them in the next room if you'd like to speak with them."

"Really?" Radaani leaned forward. The chair groaned under his weight.

"And if it's needed, I have a list of all the houses and families who've supported Vaunyogi. If it's a question what their relationships are with Galt, all we have to do is open those contracts and judge the terms. Though there may be some of them who would rather that didn't happen. So perhaps it won't be necessary."

Radaani chuckled again, a deep, wet sound. He rubbed his fingers against his thumbs, pinching the air.

"You've been busy since last we spoke," he said.

"It isn't hard finding confirmation once you know what the truth is. Would you like to speak to the men? You can ask them whatever you like. They'll back what I've said."

"Is he here himself?"

"Otah thought it might be better not to attend. Until he knew whether you intended to help him or have him killed."

"He's wise. Just the poet, then," Radaani said. "The others don't matter."

Maati nodded and left the room. The teahouse proper was a wide, low room with fires burning low in two corners. Radaani's servants were drinking something that Maati doubted was only tea and talking with one of the couriers of House Siyanti. There would be more information from that, he guessed, than from the more formal meeting. At the door to the back room, Sinja leaned back in a chair looking bored but commanding a view of every approach.

"Well?" Sinja asked.

"He'd like to speak with Cehmai-cha."

"But not the others?"

"Apparently not."

"He doesn't care if it's true, then. Just whether the poets are backing our man," Sinja let his chair down and stood, stretching. "The forms of power are fascinating stuff. Reminds me why I started fighting for a living."

Maati opened the door. The back room was quieter, though the rush of rain was everywhere. Cehmai and the andat were sitting by the fire. The huntsman Sinja-cha had tracked down was at a small table, half drunk. It was best, perhaps, that Radaani hadn't wanted him. And three armsmen in the colors of House Siyanti also lounged about. Cehmai looked up, meeting Maati's gaze. Maati nodded.

Radaadni's expression when Cehmai and Stone-Made-Soft entered the room was profoundly satisfied. It was as if the young poet's presence answered all the questions that were important to ask. Still, Maati watched Cehmai take a pose of greeting and Radaani return it.

"You wished to speak with me," Cehmai asked. His voice was low and tired. Maati could see how much this moment was costing him.

"Your fellow poet here's told me quite a tale," Radaani said. "He says that Otah Machi's not dead, and that Idaan Machi's the one who arranged her family's death."

"That's so," Cehmai agreed.

"I see. And you were the one who brought that to light?"

"That's so."

Radaani paused, his lips pursed, his fingers knotted around each other.

"Does the Dai-kvo back the upstart, then?"

"No," Maati said before Cehmai could speak. "We take no side in this. We support the council's decision, but that doesn't mean we withhold the truth from the utkhaiem."

"As Maati-kvo says," Cehmai agreed. "We are servants here."

"Servants with the world by its balls," Radaani said. "It's easy, Cehmai-cha, to support a position in a side room with no one much around to hear you. It's a harder thing to say the same words in front of the gods and the court and the world in general. If I take this to the council and you decide that perhaps it wasn't all quite what you've said it was, it will go badly for me."

"I'll tell what I know," Cehmai said. "Whoever asks."

"Well," Radaani said, then more than half to himself, "Well well well."

In the pause that followed, another roll of thunder rattled the shutters. But Porsha Radaani's smile had faded into something less amused, more serious. We have him, Maati thought. Radaani clapped his hands on his thighs and stood.

"I have some conversations I'll have to conduct, Maati-cha," he said. "You understand that I'm taking a great personal risk doing this? Me and my family both."

"And I know that Otah-kvo will appreciate that," Maati said. "In my experience, he has always been good to his friends."

"That's best," Radaani said. "After this, I expect he'll have about two of them. Just so long as he remembers what he owes me."

"He will. And so will the Kamau and the Vaunani. And I imagine a fair number of your rival families will be getting less favorable terms from the Galts in the future."

"Yes. That had occurred to me too."

Radaani smiled broadly and took a formal pose of leavetaking that included the room and all three of them in it—the two poets, the one spirit. When he was gone, Maati went to the window again. Radaani was walking fast down the street, his servants half-skipping to keep the canopy over him. His limp was almost gone.

Maati closed the shutters.

"He's agreed?" Cehmai asked.

"As near as we can expect. He smells profit in it for himself and disappointment for his rivals. That's the best we can offer, but I think he's pleased enough to do the thing."

"That's good."

Maati sat in the chair Radaani had used, sighing. Cehmai leaned against the table, his arms folded. His mouth was thin, his eyes dark. He looked more than half ill. The andat pulled out the chair beside him and sat with a mild, companionable expression.

"What did the Dai-kvo say?" Cehmai asked. "In the letter?"

"He said I was under no circumstances to take sides in the succession. He repeated that I was to return to his village as soon as possible. He seems to think that by involving myself in all this court intrigue, I may be upsetting the utkhaiem. And then he went into a long commentary about the andat being used in political struggle as the reason that the Empire ate itself."

"He's not wrong," Cehmai said.

"Well, perhaps not. But it's late to undo it."

"You can blame me if you'd like," Cehmai said.

"I think not. I chose what I'd do, and I don't think I chose poorly. If the Dai-kvo disagrees, we can have a conversation about it."

"He'll throw you out," Cehmai said.

Maati thought for a moment of his little cell at the village, of the years spent in minor tasks at the will of the Dai-kvo and the poets senior to himself. Liat had asked him to leave it all a hundred times, and he'd refused. The prospect of failure and disgrace faced him now, and he heard her words, saw her face, and wondered why it had all seemed so wrong when she'd said it and so clear now. Age perhaps. Experience. Some tiny sliver of wisdom that told him that in the balance between the world and a woman, either answer could be right.

"I'm sorry for all this, Cehmai. About Idaan. I know how hard this is for you."

"She picked it. No one made her plot against her family."

"But you love her."

The young poet frowned now, then shrugged.

"Less now than I did two days ago," he said. "Ask again in a month. I'm a poet, after all. There's only so much room in my life. Yes, I loved her. I'll love someone else later. Likely someone that hasn't set herself to kill off her relations."

"It's always like this," Stone-Made-Soft said. "Every one of them. The first love always comes closest. I had hopes for this one. I really did."

"You'll live with the disappointment," Cehmai said.

"Yes," the andat said amiably. "There's always another first girl."

Maati laughed once, amused though it was also unbearably sad. The andat shifted to look at him quizzically. Cehmai's hands took a pose of query. Maati tried to find words to fit his thoughts, surprised by the sense of peace that the prospect of his own failure brought him.

"You're who I was supposed to be, Cehmai-kvo, and you're much better at it. I never did very well."

IDAAN LEANED FORWARD, HER HANDS ON THE RAIL. THE GALLERY BEHIND her was full but restless, the air thick with the scent of their bodies and perfumes. People shifted in their seats and spoke in low tones, prepared for some new attack, and Idaan had noticed a great fashion for veils that covered the heads and necks of men and women alike that tucked into their robes like netting on a bed. The wasps had done their work, and even if they were gone now, the feeling of uncertainty remained. She took another deep breath and tried to play her role. She was the last blood of her murdered father. She was the bride of Adrah Vaunyogi. Looking down over the council, her part was to remind them of how Adrah's marriage connected him to the old line of the Khaiem.

And yet she felt like nothing so much as an actor, put out to sing a part on stage that she didn't have the range to voice. It had been so recently that she'd stood here, inhabiting this space, owning the air and the hall around her. Today, everything was the same—the families of the utkhaiem arrayed at their tables, the leaves-in-wind whispering from the galleries, the feeling of eyes turned toward her. But it wasn't working. The air itself seemed different, and she couldn't begin to say why.

"The attack leveled against this council must not weaken us," Daaya, her father now, half-shouted. His voice was hoarse and scratched. "We will not be bullied! We will not be turned aside! When these vandals tried to make mockery of the powers of the utkhaiem, we were preparing to consider my son, the honorable Adrah Vaunyogi, as the proper man to take the place of our lamented Khai. And to that matter we must return."

Applause filled the air, and Idaan smiled sweetly. She wondered how many of the people now present had heard her cry out Cehmai's name in her panic. Those that hadn't had no doubt heard it from other lips. She had kept clear of the poet's house since then, but there hadn't been a moment her heart hadn't longed toward it. He would understand, she told herself. He would forgive her absence once this was all finished. All would be well.

And yet, when Adrah looked up to her, when their gaze met, it was like looking at a stranger. He was beautiful: his hair fresh cut, his robes of jeweled silk. He was her husband, and she no longer knew him.

Daaya stepped down, glittering, and Adaut Kamau rose. If, as the gossipmongers had told, the wasps had been meant to keep old Kamau silent that day, this would be the moment when something more should follow. The galleries became suddenly quiet as the old man stepped to the stage. Even from across the hall, Idaan could see the red weal on his face where the sting had marked him.

"I had intended," he said, "to speak in support of Ghiah Vaunani in his urging of caution and against hasty decision. Since that time, however, my position has changed, and I would like to invite my old, dear friend Porsha Radaani to address the council."

With nothing more than that, old Kamau stepped down. Idaan leaned forward, looking for the green and gray robes of the Radaani. And there, moving between the tables, was the man striding toward the speaker's dais. Adrah and his father were bent together, speaking swiftly and softly. Idaan strained to hear something of what they said. She didn't notice how tight she was holding the rail until her fingers started to ache with it.

Radaani rose up in the speaker's pulpit, looking over the council and the galleries for the space of a half-dozen breaths. His expression was considering, like a man at a fish market judging the freshest catch. Idaan felt her belly tighten. Below her and across the hall, Radaani lifted his arms to the crowd.

"Brothers, we have come here in these solemn times to take the fate of our city into our hands," he intoned, and his voice was rich as cream. "We have suffered tragedy and in the spirit of our ancestors, we rise to overcome it. No one can doubt the nobility of our intentions. And yet the time has come to dissolve this council. There is no call to choose a new Khai Machi when a man with legitimate claim to the chair still lives."

The noise was like a storm. Voices rose and feet stamped. On the council floor, half the families were on their feet, the others sitting with stunned expressions. And yet it was as if it were happening in some other place. Idaan felt the unreality of the moment wash over her. It was a dream. A nightmare.

"I have not stood down!" Radaani shouted. "I have not finished! Yes, an heir lives! And he has the support of my family and my house! Who among you will refuse the son of the Khai Machi his place? Who will side with the traitors and killers that slaughtered his father?"

"Porsha-cha!" one of the men of the council said, loud enough to carry over the clamor. "Explain yourself or step down! You've lost your mind!"

"I'll better that! Brothers, I give my place before you to the son of the Khai and his one surviving heir!"

Had she thought the hall loud before? It was deafening. No one was left seated. Bodies pressed at her back, jostling her against the railing as they craned and stretched for a glimpse of the man entering the chamber. He stood tall and straight, his dark robes with their high collar looking almost priestly. Otah Machi, the upstart, strode into the hall, with the grace and calm of a man who owned it and every man and woman who breathed air.

He's mad, she thought. He's gone mad to come here. They'll tear him apart with their hands. And then she saw behind him the brown robes of a poet—Maati Vaupathai, the envoy of the Dai-kvo. And be-hind him . . .

Her mouth went dry and her body began to tremble. She shrieked, she screamed, but no one could hear her over the crowd. She couldn't even hear herself. And yet, walking at Maati's side, Cehmai looked up. His face was grim and calm and distant. The poets strode together be-hind the upstart. And then the armsmen of Radaani and Vaunani, Ka-mau and Daikani and Saya. Hardly a tenth of the families of the utkhaiem, but still a show of power. The poets alone would have been enough.

She didn't think, couldn't recall pushing back the people around her, she only knew her own intentions when she was over the rail and falling. It wasn't so far to the ground—no more than the height of two men, and yet in the roar and chaos, the drop seemed to last forever. When she struck the floor at last, it jarred her to the bone. Her ankle bloomed with pain. She put it aside and ran as best she could through the stunned men of the utkhaiem. Men all about her, unable to act, un-able to move. They were like statues, frozen by their uncertainty and confusion. She knew that she was screaming—she could feel it in her throat, could hear it in her ears. She sounded crazed, but that was unim-portant. Her attention was single, focused. The rage that possessed her, that lifted her up and sped her steps by its power alone, was only for the upstart, Otah Machi, who had taken her lover from her.

She saw Adrah and Daaya already on the floor, an armsman kneeling on each back. There was a blade still in Adrah's hand. And then there before her like a fish rising to the surface of a pond was Otah Machi, her brother. She launched herself at him, her hands reaching for him like claws. She didn't see how the andat moved between them; perhaps it had been waiting for her. Its wide, cold body appeared, and she collided with it. Huge hands wrapped her own, and the wide, inhuman face bent close to hers.

"Stop this," it said. "It won't help."

"This isn't right!" she shouted, aware now that the pandemonium had quieted, that her voice could be heard, but she could no more stop herself now than learn to fly. "He swore he'd protect me. He swore it. It's not right!"

"Nothing is," the andat agreed, as it pulled her aside, lifted her as if she was still a child, and pressed her against the wall. She felt herself sinking into it, the stone giving way to her like mud. She fought, but the wide hands were implacable. She shrieked and kicked, sure that the stone would close over her like water, and then she stopped fighting. Let it kill her, let her die.

Let it end.

The hands went away, and Idaan found herself immobile, trapped in stone that had found its solidity again. She could breathe, she could see, she could hear. She opened her mouth to scream, to call for Cehmai. To beg. Stone-Made-Soft put a single finger to her lips.

"It won't help," the andat said again, then turned and lumbered up beside the speaker's pulpit where Cehmai stood waiting for it. She didn't look at her brother as he took the pulpit, only Cehmai. He didn't look back at her. When Otah spoke, his words cut through the air, clean and strong as wine.

"I am Otah Machi, sixth son of the Khai Machi. I have never renounced my claim to this place; I have never killed or plotted to kill my brothers or my father. But I know who has, and I have come here before this council to show you what has been done, and by whom, and to claim what is mine by right."

Idaan closed her eyes and wept, surprised to find her desolation complicated by relief.

"I notice you never mentioned the Galts," Amiit said.

The waiting area to which the protocol servant had led them was open and light, looking out over a garden of flowering vines. A silver bowl with water cooling fresh peaches sat on a low table. Amiit leaned against the railing. He looked calm, but Otah could see the white at the corners of his mouth and the small movements of his hands; Amiit's belly was as much in knots as his own.

"There was no call," Otah said. "The families that were involved know that they were being used, and if they only suspect that I know it, that's almost as good as being sure. How long are we going to have to wait?"

"Until they've finished deciding whether to kill you as a murderer or raise you up as the Khai Machi," Amiit said. "It shouldn't take long. You were very good out there."

"You could sound more sure of all this."

"We'll be fine," Amiit said. "We have backing. We have the poets."

"And yet?"

Amiit forced a chuckle.

"This is why I don't play tiles. Just before the tiles man turns the last chit, I convince myself that there's something I've overlooked."

"I hope you aren't right this time."

"If I am, I won't have to worry about next. They'll kill me as dead as you."

Otah picked up a peach and bit into it. The fuzz made his lips itch, but the taste was sweet and rich and complex. He sighed and looked out. Above the garden wall rose the towers, and beyond them the blue of the sky.

"If we win, you will have to have them killed, you know," Amiit said. "Adrah and his father. Your sister, Idaan."

"Not her."

"Otah-cha, this is going to be hard enough as it stands. The utkhaiem are going to accept you because they have to. But you won't be hailed as a savior. And Kiyan-cha's a common woman from no family. She kept a wayhouse. Showing mercy to the girl who killed your father isn't going to win you anyone's support."

"I am the Khai Machi," Otah said. "I'll make my way."

"You don't understand how complex this is likely to be."

Otah shrugged.

"I trust your advice, Amiit-cha," Otah said. "You'll have to trust my judgment."

The overseer's expression soured for a moment, and then he laughed. They lapsed into silence. It was true. It was early in his career to appear weak, and the Vaunyogi had killed two of his brothers and his father, and had tried to kill Maati as well. And behind them, the Galts. And the library. There had been something in there, some book or scroll or codex worth all those lives, all that money, and the risk. By the time the sun fled behind the mountains in the west, he would know whether he'd have the power to crush their nation, reduce their houses to slag, their cities to ruins. A word to Cehmai would put it in motion. All it would require of him would be to forget that they also had children and lovers, that the people of Galt were as likely as anyone in the cities of the Khaiem to love and betray, lie and dream. And he was having pangs over executing his own father's killer. He took another bite of the peach.

"You've gone quiet," Amiit said softly.

"Thinking about how complex this is likely to be," Otah said.

He finished the last of the peach flesh and threw the stone out into the garden before he washed his hands clean in the water bowl it had come from. A company of armsmen in ceremonial mail appeared at the door with a grim-faced servant in simple black robes.

"Your presence is requested in the council chamber," the servant said.

"I'll see you once it's over," Amiit said.

Otah straightened his robes, took and released a deep breath, and adopted a pose of thanks. The servant turned silently, and Otah followed with armsmen on either side of him and behind. Their pace was solemn.

The halls with their high, arched ceilings and silvered glass, adornments of gold and silver and iron, were empty except for the jingle of mail and the tread of boots. Slowly the murmur of voices and the smells of bodies and lamp oil filled the air. The black-robed servant turned a corner, and a pair of double doors swung open to the council hall. The Master of Tides stood on the speaker's pulpit.

The black lacquer chair reserved for the Khai Machi had been brought, and stood empty on a dais of its own. Otah held himself straight and tall. He strode into the chamber as if his mind were not racing, his heart not conflicted.

He walked to the base of the pulpit and looked up. The Master of Tides was a smaller man than he'd thought, but his voice was strong enough.

"Otah Machi. In recognition of your blood and claim, we of the high families of Machi have chosen to dissolve our council, and cede to you the chair that was your father's."

Otah took a pose of thanks that he realized as he took it was a thousand times too casual for the moment, dropped it, and walked up the dais. Someone in the second gallery high above him began to applaud, and within moments, the air was thick with the sound. Otah sat on the black and uncomfortable chair and looked out. There were thousands of faces, all of them fixed upon him. Old men, young men, children. The highest families of the city and the palace servants. Some were exultant, some stunned. A few, he thought, were dark with anger. He picked out Maati and Cehmai. Even the andat had joined in. The tables at which the Kamau and Vaunani, Radaani and Saya and Daikani all sat were surrounded by cheering men. The table of the Vaunyogi was empty.

They would never all truly believe him innocent. They would never all give him their loyalty. He looked out into their faces and he saw years of his life laid out before him, constrained by necessity and petty expedience. He guessed at the mockery he would endure behind his back while he struggled to learn his new-acquired place. He tried to appear gracious and grave at once, certain he was failing at both.

For this, he thought, I have given up the world.

And then, at the far back of the hall, he caught sight of Kiyan. She, perhaps alone, wasn't applauding him. She only smiled as if amused and perhaps pleased. He felt himself soften. Amid all the meaningless celebration, all the empty delight, she was the single point of stillness. Kiyan was safe, and she was his, and their child would be born into safety and love.

If all the rest was the price for those few things, it was one he would pay.

EPILOG

>+< It was winter when Maati Vaupathai returned to Machi. The days were brief and bitter, the sky often white with a scrim of cloud that faded seamlessly into the horizon. Roads were forgotten; the snow covered road and river and empty field. The sledge dogs ran on the thick glaze of ice wherever the teamsman aimed them. Maati sat on the skidding waxed wood, his arms pulled inside his clothes, the hood of his cloak pulled low and tight to warm the air before he breathed it. He'd been told that he must above all else be careful not to sweat. If his robes got wet, they would freeze, and that would be little better than running naked through the drifts. He had chosen not to make the experiment.

His guide seemed to stop at every wayhouse and low town. Maati learned that the towns had been planned by local farmers and merchants so that no place was more than a day's fast travel from shelter, even on the short days around Candles Night when the darkness was three times as long as the light. When Maati walked up the shallow ramps and through the snow doors, he appreciated their wisdom. A night in the open during a northern winter might not kill someone who had been born and bred there. A northerner would know the secrets of carving snow into shelter and warming the air without drenching himself. He, on the other hand, would simply have died, and so he made certain that his guide and the dogs were well housed and fed. Even so, when the time came to sleep in a bed piled high with blankets and dogs, he often found himself as exhausted from the cold as from a full day's work.

What in summer would have been the journey of weeks took him from just before Candles Night almost halfway to the thaw. The days began to blend together—blazing bright white and then warm, close darkness—until he felt he was traveling through a dream and might wake at any moment.

When at last the dark stone towers of Machi appeared in the distance—lines of ink on a pale parchment—it was difficult to believe. He had lost track of the days. He felt as if he had been traveling forever, or perhaps that he had only just begun. As they drew nearer, he opened his hood despite the stinging air and watched the towers thicken and take form.

He didn't know when they passed over the river. The bridge would have been no more than a rise in the snow, indistinguishable from a random drift. Still, they must have passed it, because they entered into the city itself. The high snow made the houses seemed shorter. Other dog teams yipped and called, pulled wide sledges filled with boxes or ore or the goods of trade; even the teeth of winter would not stop Machi. Maati even saw men with wide, leather-laced nets on their shoes and goods for sale strapped to their backs tramping down worn paths that led from one house to the next. He heard voices lifted in loud conversation and the barking of dogs and the murmur of the platform chains that rose up with the towers and shifted, scraping against the stone.

The city seemed to have nothing in common with the one he had known, and still there was a beauty to it. It was stark and terrible, and the wide sky forgave it nothing, but he could imagine how someone might boast they lived here in the midst of the desolation and carved out a life worth living. Only the verdigris domes over the forges were free from snow, the fires never slackening enough to bow before the winter.

On the way to the palace of the Khai Machi, his guide passed what had once been the palaces of the Vaunyogi. The broken walls jutted from the snow. He thought he could still make out scorch marks on the stones. There were no bodies now. The Vaunyogi were broken, and those who were not dead had scattered into the world where they would be wise never to mention their true names again. The bones of their house made Maati shiver in a way that had little to do with the biting air. Otah-kvo had done this, or ordered it done. It had been necessary, or so Maati told himself. He couldn't think of another path, and still the ruins disturbed him.

He entered the offices of the Master of Tides through the snow door, tramping up the slick painted wood of the ramp and into rooms he'd known in summer. When he had taken off his outer cloaks and let himself be led to the chamber where the servants of the Khai set schedules, Piyun See, the assistant to the Master of Tides, fell at once into a pose of welcome.

"It's a pleasure to have you back," he said. "The Khai mentioned that we should expect you. But he had thought you might be here earlier."

Though the air in the offices felt warm, the man's breath was still visible. Maati's ideas of cold had changed during his journey.

"The way was slower than I'd hoped," Maati said.

"The most high is in meetings and cannot be disturbed, but he has left us with instructions for your accommodation. . . ."

Maati felt a pang of disappointment. It was naïve of him to expect Otah-kvo to be there to greet him, and yet he had to admit that he had harbored hopes.

"Whatever is most convenient will, I'm sure, suffice," Maati said.

"Don't bother yourself Piyun-cha," a woman's voice said from behind them. "I can see to this."

The changes of the previous months had left Kiyan untransformed. Her hair—black with its lacing of white—was tied back in a simple knot that seemed out of place above the ornate robes of a Khai's wife. Her smile didn't have the chill formal distance or false pleasure of a player at court intrigue. When she embraced him, her hair smelled of lavender oil. For all her position and the incarcerating power of being her husband's wife she would, Maati thought, still look at home at a wayhouse watching over guests or haggling with the farmers, bakers and butchers at the at the market.

But perhaps that was only his own wish that things could change and still be the same.

"You look tired," she said, leading him down a long flight of smooth-worn granite stairs. "How long have you been traveling?"

"I left the Dai-kvo before Candles Night," he said.

"You still dress like a poet," she said, gently. So she knew.

"The Dai-kvo agreed to Otah-kvo's proposal. I'm not formally removed so long as I don't appear in public ceremony in my poet's robes. I'm not permitted to live in a poet's house or present myself in any way as carrying the authority of the Dai-kvo."

"And Cehmai?"

"Cehmai's had some admonishing letters, I think. But I took the worst of it. It was easier that way, and I don't mind so much as I might have when I was younger."

The doors at the stairway's end stood open. They had descended below the level of the street, even under its burden of snow, and the candlelit tunnel before them seemed almost hot. His breath had stopped ghosting.

"I'm sorry for that," Kiyan said, leading the way. "It seems wrong that you should suffer for doing the right thing."

"I'm not suffering," Maati said. "Not as badly as I did when I was in the Dai-kvo's good graces, at least. The more I see of the honors I was offered, the better I feel about having lost them."

She chuckled.

The passageway glowed gold. A high, vaulted arch above them was covered with tiles that reflected the light back into the air where it hung like pollen. An echo of song came from a great distance, the words blurred by the tunnels. And then the melody was joined and the whispering voices of the gods seemed to touch the air. Maati's steps faltered, and Kiyan turned to look at him and then followed his gaze into the air.

"The winter choir," she said. Her voice was suddenly smaller, sharing his awe. "There are a lot of idle hands in the colder seasons. Music becomes more important, I think, when things are cold and dark."

"It's beautiful," Maati said. "I knew there were tunnels, but . . ."

"It's another city," Kiyan said. "Think how I feel. I didn't know half the depth of it until I was supposed to help rule it."

They began walking again, their words rising above the song.

"How is he?"

"Not idle," she said with both amusement and melancholy in her tone. "He's been working until he's half exhausted every day and then getting up early. There's a thousand critical things that he's called on to do, and a thousand more that are nothing more than ceremony that only swallow his time. It makes him cranky. He'll be angry that he wasn't free to meet you, but it will help that I could. That's the best I can do these days. Make sure that the things most important to him are seen to while he's off making sure the city doesn't fall into chaos."

"I'd think it would be able to grind on without him for a time just from habit," Maati said.

"Politics takes all the time you can give it," Kiyan said with distaste. They walked through a wide gate and into a great subterranean hall.

A thousand lanterns glowed, their white light filling the air. Men and women and children passed on their various errands, the gabble of voices like a brook over stones. A beggar sang, his lacquered begging box on the stone floor before him. Maati saw a waterseller's cart, and another vendor selling waxpaper cones of rice and fish. It was almost like a street, almost like a wide pavilion with a canopy of stone.

"Your rooms?" Kiyan asked. "Or would you rather have something to eat first? There's not much fresh this deep into winter, but I've found a woman who makes a hot barley soup that's simply lovely."

"Actually . . . could I meet the child?"

Kiyan's smile seemed to have a light of its own.

"Can you imagine a world where I said no?" she asked.

She nodded to a branching in the wide hall, and led him west, deeper into the underground. The change was subtle, moving from the public space of the street to the private tunnels beneath the palaces. There were gates, it was true, but they were open. There were armsmen here and there, but only a few of them. And yet soon all the people they passed wore the robes of servants or slaves of the Khai, and they had entered the Khai's private domain. Kiyan stopped at a thin oak door, pulled it open and gestured him to follow her up the staircase it revealed.

The nursery was high above the tunnel-world. The air was kept warm by a roaring fire in a stone grate, but the light was from the sun. The nurse, a young girl, no more than sixteen summers, sat dozing in her chair while the baby cooed and gurgled to itself. Maati stepped to the edge of the crib, and the child quieted, staring up at him with distrustful eyes, and then breaking into a wide toothless grin.

"She's only just started sleeping through the night," Kiyan said, speaking softly to keep from waking her servant. "And there were two weeks of colic that were close to hell. I don't know what we'd have done with her if it hadn't been for the nurses. She's been doing better now. We've named her Eiah."

She reached down, scooped up her daughter, and settled her in her arms. It was a movement so natural as to seem inevitable. Maati remembered having done it himself, many years ago, in a very different place. Kiyan seemed almost to know his mind.

" 'Tani-kya said that if things went as you'd expected with the Dai-kvo you were thinking of seeking out your son. Nayiit?"

"Nayiit," Maati agreed. "I sent letters to the places I knew to send them, but I haven't heard back yet. I may not. But I'll be here, in one place. If he and his mother want to find me, it won't be difficult."

"I'm sorry," Kiyan said. "Not that it will be easy for them, only that . . ."

Maati only shook his head. In Kiyan's arms, the tiny girl with deep brown eyes grasped at air and gurgled, unaware, he knew, of all the blood and pain and betrayal that had gone into bringing her here.

"She's beautiful," he said.

"Be reasonable!"

Cehmai lay back in his bath. Beside him, Stone-Made-Soft had put its feet into the warm water and was gazing placidly out into the thick salt-scented steam that rose from the water and filled the bathhouse. Against the far wall, a group of young women was rising from the pool and walking back toward the dressing rooms, leaving a servant to fish the floating trays with their teapots and bowls from the small, bobbing waves. Baarath slapped the water impatiently.

"You can look at naked girls later," he said. "This is important. If Maati-cha's come back to help me catalog the library . . ."

"He might quibble on 'help you,'" Cehmai said, and might as well have kept silent.

". . . then it's clearly of critical importance to the Dai-kvo. I've heard the rumors. I know the Vaunyogi were looking to sell the library to some Westlands warden. That's why Maati was sent here in the first place."

Cehmai closed his eyes. Rumors and speculation had run wild, and perhaps it would have been a kindness to correct Baarath. But Otah had asked him to keep silent, and the letters from the Dai-kvo had encouraged this strategy. If it were known what the Galts had done, what they had intended to do, it would mean the destruction of their nation: cities drowned, innocent men and women and children starved when a quiet word heavy with threat might suffice instead. There was always recourse to destruction. So long as one poet held one andat, they could find a path to ruin. So instead of slaughtering countless innocents, Cehmai put up with the excited, inaccurate speculation of his old friend and waited for the days to grow longer and warmer.

"If the collection is split," Baraath went on, his voice dropping to a rough whisper, "we might overlook the very thing that made the library so important. You have to move your collection over to the library, or terrible things might happen."

"Terrible things like what?"

"I don't know," Baraath said, his whisper turning peevish. "That's what Maati-cha and I are trying to find out."

"Well, once you've gone through your collection and found nothing, the two of you can come to the poet's house and look through mine."

"That would take years!"

"I'll make sure they're well kept until then," Cehmai said. "Have you spoken with the Khai about his private collection?"

"Who'd want that? It's all copies of contracts and agreements from five generations ago. Unless it's the most obscure etiquette ever to see sunlight. Anyone who wants that, let them have it. You've got all the *good* books. The philosophy, the grammars, the studies of the andat."

"It's a hard life you lead," Cehmai said. "So close and still, no."

"You are an arrogant prig," Baraath said. "Everyone knows it, but I'm the only man in the city with the courage to say it to your face. Arrogant and selfish and small-souled."

"Well, perhaps it's not too much to go over to the library. It isn't as if it was that long a walk."

Baraath's face brightened for a moment, then, as the insincerity of the comment came clear, squeezed as if he'd taken a bite of fresh lemon. With a sound like an angry duck, he rose up and stalked from the baths and into the fog.

"He's a terrible person," the andat said.

"I know. But he's a friend of mine."

"And terrible people need friends as much as good ones do," the andat said, its tone an agreement. "More, perhaps."

"Which of us are you thinking of?"

Stone-Made-Soft didn't speak. Cehmai let the warmth of the water slip into his flesh for a moment longer. Then he too rose, the water sluicing from him, and walked to the dressing rooms. He dried himself with a fresh cloth and found his robes, newly cleaned and dry. The other men in the room spoke among themselves, joked, laughed. Cehmai was more aware than usual of the formal poses with which they greeted him. In this quiet season, there was little work for him, and the days were filled with music and singing, gatherings organized by the young men and women of the utkhaiem. But all the cakes tasted slightly of ashes, and the brightest songs seemed tinny and false. Somewhere in the city, under her brother's watchful eye, the woman he'd sworn to protect was locked away. He adjusted his robes in the mirror, smiled as if trying the expression like a party mask, and for the thousandth time noticed the weight of his decision.

He left the bathhouse, following a broad, low tunnel to the east where it would join a larger passage, one of the midwinter roads, which in turn ran beneath the trees outside the poet's house before it broke into a thousand maze-like corridors running under the old city. Along the length of the passage, men and women stood or sat, some talking, some singing. An old man, his dog lying at his feet, sold bread and sausages from a hand cart. The girls he'd seen in the bathhouse had been joined by young men, joking and posing in the timeless rituals of courtship. Stone-Made-Soft was kneeling by the wall, looking out over all of it, silently judging what it would take to bring the roof down and bury them all. Cehmai reached out with his will and tugged at the andat. Still smiling, Stone-Made-Soft rose and ambled over.

"I think the one on the far left was hoping to meet you," it said, gesturing to the knot of young men and women as it drew near. "She was watching you all the time we were in the baths."

"Perhaps it was Baraath she was looking at," Cehmai said.

"You think so?" the andat said. "I suppose he's a decent looking man. And many women are overcome by the romance of the librarian. No doubt you're right."

"Don't," Cehmai said. "I don't want to play that game again."

Something like real sympathy showed in the andat's wide face. The struggle at the back of Cehmai's mind neither worsened nor diminished as Stone-Made-Soft's broad hand reached out to rest on his shoulder.

"Enough," it said. "You did what you had to do, and whipping yourself now won't help you or her. Let's go meet that girl. Talk to her. We can find someone selling sweetcakes. Otherwise we'll only go back to the rooms and sulk away another night."

Cehmai looked over, and indeed, the girl farthest to the left—her long, dark hair unbound, her robes well cut and the green of jade—caught his eyes, and blushing, looked away. He had seen her before, he realized. She was beautiful, and he did not know her name.

"Perhaps another day," he said.

"There are only so many other days," the andat said, its voice low and gentle. "I may go on for generations, but you little men rise and fall with the seasons. Stop biting yourself. It's been months."

"One more day. I'll bite myself for one more day at least," Cehmai said. "Come on."

The andat sighed and dropped its hand to its side. Cehmai turned east, walking into the dim tunnels. He felt the temptation to look back, to see whether the girl was watching his departure and if she was, what expression she wore. He kept his eyes on the path before him and the moment passed.

THE KHAI MACHI HAD NO OTHER NAME NOW THAT HE HAD TAKEN HIS FA-ther's office. It had been stripped from him in formal ceremony. He had renounced it and sworn before the gods and the Emperor that he would be nothing beyond this trust with which he had been charged. Otah had forced his way through the ceremony, bristling at both the waste of time and the institutional requirement that he lie in order to preserve eti-quette. Of Itani Noygu, Otah Machi, and the Khai Machi, the last was the one least in his heart. But he was willing to pretend to have no other self and the utkhaiem and the priests and the people of the city were all willing to pretend to believe him. It was all like some incredibly long, awkward, tedious game. And so when the rare occasion arose when he could do something real, something with consequences, he found him-self enjoying it more perhaps than it deserved.

The emissary from Galt looked as if he were trying to convince him-self he'd misunderstood.

"Most high," he said, "I came here as soon as our ambassadors sent word that they'd been expelled. It was a long journey, and winter travel's difficult in the north. I had hoped that we could address your concerns and . . ."

Otah took a pose that commanded silence, then sat back on the black lacquer chair that had grown no more comfortable in the months since he'd first taken it. He switched from speaking in the Khaiate tongue to Galtic. It seemed, if anything, to make the man more uncomfortable.

"I appreciate that the generals and lords of Galt are so interested in . . . what? Addressing my concerns? And I thank you for coming so quickly, even when I'd made it clear that you were not particularly welcome."

"I apologize, most high, if I've given offense."

"Not at all," Otah said, smiling. "Since you've come, you can do me the favor of explaining *again* to the High Council how precarious their position is with me. The Dai-kvo has been alerted to all I've learned, and he shares my opinion and my policy."

"But I—"

"I know the role your people played in the succession. And more than that, I know what happened in Saraykeht. Your nation survives now on my sufferance. If word reaches me of one more intervention in the matters of the cities of the Khaiem or the poets or the andat, I will wipe your people from the memory of the world."

The emissary opened his mouth and closed it again, his eyes darting about as if there was a word written somewhere on the walls that would open the floodgates of his diplomacy. Otah let the silence press at him.

"I don't understand, most high," he managed at last.

"Then go home," Otah said, "and repeat what I've told you to your overseer and then to his, and keep doing so until you find someone who does. If you reach the High Council, you'll have gone far enough."

"I'm sure if you'll just tell me what's happened to upset you, most high, there must be something I can do to make it right."

Otah pressed his steepled fingers to his lips. For a moment, he remembered Saraykeht—the feel of the poet's death struggles under his own hand. He remembered the fires that had consumed the compound of the Vaunyogi and the screams and cries of his sister as her husband and his father met their ends.

"You can't make this right," he said, letting his weariness show in his voice. "I wish that you could."

"But the contracts . . . I can't go back without some agreement made, most high. If you want me to take your message back, you have to leave me enough credibility that anyone will hear it."

"I can't help you," Otah said. "Take the letter I've given you and go home. Now."

As he turned and left the room, the letter in his hand sewn shut and sealed, the Galt moved like a man newly awakened. At Otah's gesture, the servants followed the emissary and pulled the great bronze doors closed behind them, leaving him alone in the audience chamber. The pale silk banners shifted in the slight breath of air. The charcoal in the iron braziers glowed, orange within white. He pressed his hands to his eyes. He was tired, terribly tired. And there was so much more to be done.

He heard the scrape of the servant's door behind him, heard the soft, careful footsteps and the faintest jingling of mail. He rose and turned, his robes shifting with a sound like sand on stone. Sinja took a pose of greeting.

"You sent for me, most high?"

"I've just sent the Galts packing again," Otah said.

"I heard the last of it. Do you think they'll keep sending men to bow and scrape at your feet? I was thinking how gratifying it must be, being able to bully a whole nation of people you've never met."

"Actually, it isn't. I imagine news of it will have spread through the city by nightfall. More stories of the Mad Khai."

"You aren't called that. Upstart's still the most common. After the wedding, there was a week or so of calling you the shopkeeper's wife, but I think it was too long. An insult can only sustain a certain number of syllables."

"Thank you," Otah said. "I feel much better now."

"You are going to have to start caring what they think, you know. These are people you're going to be living with for the rest of your life. Starting off by proving how disrespectful and independent you can be is only going to make things harder. And the Galts carry quite a few contracts," Sinja said. "Are you sure you want me away just now? It's traditional to have a guard close at hand when you're cultivating new enemies."

"Yes, I want you to go. If the utkhaiem are talking about the Galts, they may talk less about Idaan."

"You know they won't forget her. It doesn't matter what other issues you wave at them, they'll come back to her."

"I know. But it's the best I can do for now. Are you ready?"

"I have everything I need prepared. We can do it now if you'd like."

"I would."

THREE ROOMS HAD BEEN HER WORLD. A NARROW BED, A CHEAP IRON BRA-zier, a night pot taken away every second day. The armsmen brought her bits of candle—stubs left over from around the palaces. Once, someone had slipped a book in with her meal—a cheap translation of Westland court poems. Still, she'd read them all and even started composing some of her own. It galled her to be grateful for such small kindnesses, especially when she knew they would not have been extended to her had she been a man.

The only breaks came when she was taken out to walk down empty tunnels, deep under the palaces. Armsmen paced behind her and before her, as if she were dangerous. And her mind slowly folded in on itself, the days passing into weeks, the ankle she'd cracked in her fall mending. Some days she felt lost in dreams, struggling to wake only to wish herself back asleep when her mind came clear. She sang to herself. She spoke to Adrah as if he were still there, still alive. As if he still loved her. She raged at Cehmai or bedded him or begged his forgiveness. All on her narrow bed, by the light of candle stubs.

She woke to the sound of the bolt sliding open. She didn't think it was time to be fed or walked, but time had become a strange thing lately. When the door opened and the man in the black and silver robes of the Khai stepped in she told herself she was dreaming, half fearing he had come to kill her at last, and half hoping for it.

The Khai Machi looked around the cell. His smile seemed forced.

"You might not think it, but I've lived in worse," he said.

"Is that supposed to comfort me?"

"No," he said.

A second man entered the room, a thick bundle under his arm. A soldier, by his stance and by the mail that he wore under his robes. Idaan sat up, gathering herself, preparing for whatever came and desperate that the men not turn and close the door again behind them. The Khai Machi hitched up his robes and squatted, his back against the stone wall as if he was a laborer at rest between tasks. His long face was very much like Biitrah's, she saw. It was in the corners of his eyes and the shape of his jaw.

"Sister," he said.

"Most high," she replied.

He shook his head. The soldier shifted. She had the feeling that the two movements were the continuation of some conversation they had had, a subtle commentary to which she was not privileged.

"This is Sinja-cha," the Khai said. "You'll do as he says. If you fight him, he'll kill you. If you try to leave him before he gives you permission, he'll kill you."

"Are you whoring me to your pet thug then?" she asked, fighting to keep the quaver from her voice.

"What? No. Gods," Otah said. "No, I'm sending you into exile. He's to take you as far as Cetani. He'll leave you there with a good robe and a few lengths of silver. You can write. You have numbers. You'll be able to find some work, I expect."

"I am a daughter of the Khaiem," she said bitterly. "I'm not permitted to work."

"So lie," Otah said. "Pick a new name. Noygu always worked fairly well for me. You could be Sian Noygu. Your mother and father were merchants in . . . well, call it Udun. You don't want people thinking about Machi if you can help it. They died in a plague. Or a fire. Or bandits killed them. It isn't as if you don't know how to lie. Invent something."

Idaan stood, something like hope in her heart. To leave this hole. To leave this city and this life. To become someone else. She hadn't understood how weary and exhausted she had become until this moment. She had thought the cell was her prison.

The soldier looked at her with perfectly empty eyes. She might have been a cow or a large stone he'd been set to move. Otah levered himself back to standing.

"You can't mean this," Idaan said, her voice hardly a whisper. "I killed Danat. I as much as killed our father,"

"I didn't know them," her brother said. "I certainly didn't love them."

"I did."

"All the worse for you, then."

She looked into his eyes for the first time. There was a pain in them that she couldn't fathom.

"I tried to kill you."

"You won't do it again. I've killed and lived with it. I've been given mercy I didn't deserve. Sometimes that I didn't want. So you see, we may not be all that different, sister." He went silent for a moment, then, "Of course if you come back, or I find you conspiring against me—"

"I wouldn't come back here if they begged me," she said. "This city is ashes to me."

Her brother smiled and nodded as much to himself as to her.

"Sinja?" he said.

The soldier tossed the bundle to her. It was a leather traveler's cloak lined with wool and thick silk robes and leggings wrapped around heavy boots. She was appalled at how heavy they were, at how weak she'd become. Her brother ducked out of the room, leaving only the two of them. The soldier nodded to the robes in her arms.

"Best change into those quickly, Idaan-cha," he said. "I've got a sledge and team waiting, but it's an unpleasant winter out there, and I want to make the first low town before dark."

"This is madness," she said.

The soldier took a pose of agreement.

"He's making quite a few bad decisions," he said. "He's new at this, though. He'll get better."

Idaan stripped under the soldier's impassive gaze and pulled on the robes and the leggings, the cloak, the boots. She stepped out of her cell with the feeling of having shed her skin. She didn't understand how much those walls had become everything to her until she stepped out the last door and into the blasting cold and limitless white. For a moment, it was too much. The world was too huge and too open, and she was too small to survive even the sight of it. She wasn't conscious of shrinking back from it until the soldier touched her arm.

"The sledge is this way," he said.

Idaan stumbled, her boots new and awkward, her legs unaccustomed to the slick ice on the snow. But she followed.

THE CHAINS WERE FROZEN TO THE TOWER, THE LIFTING MECHANISM BRITtle with cold. The only way was to walk, but Otah found he was much stronger than he had been when they'd marched him up the tower before, and the effort of it kept him warm. The air was bitterly cold; there weren't enough braziers in the city to keep the towers heated in winter. The floors he passed were filled with crates of food, bins of grains and dried fruits, smoked fish and meats. Supplies for the months until summer came again, and the city could forget for a while what the winter had been.

Back in the palaces, Kiyan was waiting for him. And Maati. They were to meet and talk over the strategies for searching the library. And other things, he supposed. And there was a petition from the silversmiths to reduce the tax paid to the city on work that was sold in the nearby low towns. And the head of the Saya wanted to discuss a proper match for his daughter, with the strong and awkward implication that the Khai Machi might want to consider who his second wife might be. But for now, all the voices were gone, even the ones he loved, and the solitude was sweet.

He stopped a little under two-thirds of the way to the top, his legs aching but his face warm. He wrestled open the inner sky doors and then unlatched and pushed open the outer. The city was splayed out beneath him, dark stone peeking out from under the snow, plumes of smoke rising as always from the forges. To the south, a hundred crows rose from the branches of dead trees, circled briefly, and took their perches again.

And beyond that, to the east, he saw the distant forms he'd come to see: a sledge with a small team and two figures on it, speeding out across the snowfields. He sat, letting his feet dangle out over the rooftops, and watched until they were only a tiny black mark in the distance. And then as they vanished into the white.

ABOUT THE AUTHOR

Daniel Abraham's first published novel, *A Shadow in Summer*, is the first volume of the Long Price Quartet. He has had stories published in the *Vanishing Acts*, *Bones of the World*, and *The Dark* anthologies, and has been included in Gardner Dozois's *Year's Best Science Fiction* anthology as well. His story "Flat Diane" won the International Horror Guild award for mid-length fiction.

He is currently working on the Long Price Quartet, the third volume of which, *An Autumn War*, will be published in 2008. He lives in New Mexico with his wife and daughter.